THE HERON PRINCE

KIM ALEXANDER

Editor: Carly Bornstein
Cover Designer/Interior Formatting: MadHat Books
Publisher: Kim Alexander

ISBN-13: 978-1537283128
ISBN-10: 153728312X

Dedication:

For Dyon—it's adventure day!

Chapter 1

Mistra

RHUUN, THE DEMON prince and heir to the High Seat of Eriis, his world's lone tourist in the human world of Mistra, was having an exceptionally good day. No one had set any part of him on fire for months, and his human companion (Lover? Friend? Yes, he thought she was his friend) Lelet observed that his scars seemed to be fading.

"Doubt it," he replied. "I've had them so long I'd be surprised if they went away in just a few months." But he was happy to have her continue her inspection.

"I can tell," she said. "The, um, handprint? I can barely see it now."

The handprint she referred to had been seared onto his chest by the companion, friend, and lover previous to Lelet. Aelle had been annoyed with him that afternoon, although, as he recalled, that was hardly unusual. And of course she never knew he could feel the fire she carried in her hands, because he never told her. He wondered if they might have walked different paths if he'd been brave enough to let her know about his simple, fundamental failing—that unlike everyone else, unlike she herself, he could feel pain—or if it wouldn't have mattered at all. Either way, she left him with a mark he assumed he'd carry forever.

He rarely thought of Aelle since he'd fallen into Mistra, and he found himself thinking less of his home city, family, and friends as the cool green days went by.

He and Lelet started the morning making more sex, and that was unlike his experiences with Aelle as well (Making? Surely not. Doing the sex? Perhaps that was it). There was nothing to guard against; no pain alongside the pleasure they took in each other. He was slowly coming to trust that it could always be that way. He told himself over and over, he'd have to go home, and soon. Even as he and Lelet wandered through their days, he knew that back on Eriis, Ilaan was working on a charm to open The Door and bring him home. But while he had once hoped his friend would hurry, now he found that 'soon' was turning into 'eventually' and sometimes even 'never.'

For the moment, at least, he was more than content to drift along, and look at the river, and eat apples and bread, and stop (as often as possible) for sex having.

"We are going to have to talk about protection," she told him. The sun was just up and she lay with her head on his shoulder looking up at the bottom of the cart—it had rained the night before and it was his idea to use the cart as a sort of roof. It worked very nicely. But she looked worried and he tried to calm her.

"You know I'll protect you. I've promised you. What are you afraid of?"

She smiled but still looked concerned. "I don't mean like that, I know you will. I mean we've been joining. A lot. And it'll no longer be safe for me soon—probably taking some chances I shouldn't right now."

He loved that she called it joining, as that was what his people called it and it showed she paid attention, but he still had no idea what she meant. "Safe? From me?" Was she worried he might hurt her somehow? She shouldn't be, he'd been nothing but careful of her fragile human body.

"No, not exactly. It's just we don't want something to happen accidentally." She put a peculiar emphasis on the final word.

So she was afraid of having an accident? While they were joining? She'd never been coy or shy before. "A sex-having accident?"

She made a growling noise. "Are you not understanding me on purpose? I mean we can't take the chance of me getting pregnant. Hasn't that crossed your mind?"

"No, of course not." What did she take him for? He found himself becoming offended. "Do you really think I'd do that to you now? With nothing formal between us? Without even asking?"

Now he could see she was becoming offended. "I was thinking we had something between us." She paused and rubbed her forehead, then rolled onto her stomach and propped herself onto her elbows. "Let's make sure we're talking about the same thing. I'm talking about having a baby. About me accidentally getting pregnant. That word means the same thing over on Eriis?" He agreed that it did. "A human woman can get pregnant about three weeks out of the month. Give or take. No contract required. Now you."

"An Eriisai woman, a demon woman, can always catch the spark," he told her. "And she and her partner decide together, and it is considered an important event. So, a couple would make their choice, and he would give her the spark, and she would catch it. It is an occasion to be celebrated."

"Catch the spark," she repeated. "So you decide, whenever you are with a woman, whether or not to give her the spark?"

This was becoming uncomfortable, making the process, which was quite formal, sound base. People didn't talk about things like this. Aelle brought it up every once in a great while when she wanted to provoke him, but never with anything other than the idea it was an event which may or may not happen in some far distant future. And of course, with his deformities and disabilities, he doubted she'd ever agree to it anyway, should he ask. Which of course he never would. "I want to say it's not as simple as that, but I suppose it is. It would be an unforgiveable violation for me to give you the spark without your consent."

"Sweetheart, it's very different here." He liked when she called him that. "Men and women have almost no control over the result of sex. We can do some things afterwards to stop it from progressing, and there are things you can do during, but if two people have sex, well, it can result in a child no matter if they want it to or not."

"Every time? Without knowing?"

"Without knowing, without trying, and definitely without planning. But like I said, we have ways of preventing it from happening also. Just, you and I aren't using any of them. And if you were a different kind of person, a human person—or maybe just a careless one, you could just leave and not have anything to do with a child. In fact, you might never know you'd made one."

He sat up and cracked his head on the wagon's axle. "Ow! *Rushta.* That explains it." He rubbed his head. "I couldn't figure out why my mother would have accepted the spark from a human man. But it sounds like she didn't. My father—the human. He left. Or he was careless. Or he didn't know. Maybe he never knew. And my mother, I imagine she assumed our two races were the same. She probably thinks he did it to her on purpose. What a surprise for her." *No wonder she hates me.* And then, immediately, *She doesn't, don't say that.* If he'd been a completely human person, Lelet could be with child right now and he—and she—wouldn't know it. These people, these humans, he thought, were one step from spinning out of control at all times. He could pretend he belonged here, and look at the river until the moons fell into the sand, but it wouldn't change the fact that this was not his home.

I have to go back soon. Not eventually and not never. Soon.

* * *

Neither one of them wanted to talk about the details of his conception, or about his mother in particular, while unclothed and still flushed from having (having!) sex themselves, so they hastily dressed and got back on the road. She wanted to continue towards the ocean, an entire valley filled with water. He suspected it was her idea of a joke, but she insisted he had to see it since he was new to this world, if he saw nothing else. He corrected her pronunciation of boats (it was bo-hats, he was surprised she'd gotten that wrong) and she nodded and thanked him.

They'd eaten the last of their bread and sausage the night before and she told him she was not only starving, but if she didn't have a cup of coffee she couldn't be responsible for her actions. He was about to say he felt the same way about *sarave*, or wine, or whatever came in a glass, but then realized he didn't actually feel that way.

"Chocolate," he said instead. "You promised."

Chapter 2

Eriis

NIICO HAD ONLY been caught stealing once.

The stall keeper had gripped the boy's skinny upper arm while his father paid for the meat pie he'd lifted; the market crowds either ignored the scene or chose to stand and watch. Most everyone knew the family, and knew it was only by the grace of the old king—Rest him now—that the boy and his father even lived inside the Arch. The boy's mother had caught old Fadeer's eye, and the lot of them had been scooped up out of the Quarter and deposited in a lovely home quite near the Palace, and their home was full of food and drink and nice things. But Niico didn't remember any of that. He was still an infant during the War, and his pretty young mother and the old king were long gone, and so were the nice things. If he wanted nice things, he had to take them for himself.

But he'd only been caught once.

Well, this is nice, thought Niico, looking around the dining table, *compared to being tossed into a firewhirl or eaten by rats.* The Zaal, as if having heard his thoughts, was furtively staring at him, but it was probably only because Niico was lately something of a celebrity. Between his unbroken winning streak in the air and his rising fortunes as the closest companion to the daughter of the Counselor, he drew all eyes. *That must be it,* Niico told himself. Still, he felt a damp film on his flesh where the Mage's eye's touched it. For someone who previously never came above ground, the man was now making himself quite at home at the Counselor's dinner table.

Yuenne poured his dinner guests each a cup of water, and they in turn exchanged it with the seatmate to their left: Yuenne and Siia, Niico and Aelle, and as host, Yuenne doing double duty with the Zaal. That done, the maid brought in platters of meat and greens, a nice light soup, and a decent bottle of *sarave*.

"Aelle will be returning to classes soon, won't you, *Shan*?" Siia said. Aelle gave a vague nod; she hadn't been listening and Niico knew she would have agreed to anything her mother said. "Too much time indoors is bad for the mind," Siia added. Then she blushed and added, "I don't include your brothers in the Raasth, of course, Zaal. Their sacrifice is our continued comfort."

The Zaal shrugged. "Of course. In the Raasth we have a saying, as well. Too much time in the air makes a mind fall open." He was still looking at Niico.

Niico looked at his plate and said, "What a lovely meal. Aelle, I have a match coming up later this week. Think about attending?"

Now she did look up, and her look was icy. "If my schedule permits," she said.

"Speaking of schedules," the Zaal said, "ours is growing more and more overdue. Any news from the quarry?"

Quarry? Niico sipped his drink and wondered why the man was talking about mining rocks. Did he and Yuenne plan a trip to the Edge?

Looking at her daughter, Siia said, "Perhaps this talk can wait for a quieter moment." Aelle was staring at her hands, expressionless.

Yuenne gave his daughter a hard look (which she did not notice) shrugged and said, "We'll continue this after dinner, then?" The Zaal scowled, but nodded assent. The conversation turned to the weather (the dust was rising later in the day, thanks to the work of the Zaal and his tireless Mages), and who was seen at the theater with whom, and what matches Niico was looking forward to. When the last plate had been cleared, Niico thanked Siia for her hospitality, and complimented Yuenne on the vintages in his cellar.

At last he retired with Aelle to her suite of rooms. They threw themselves onto piles of cushions and put their feet on the side table.

"Why must Father invite that man all the time?" Aelle moaned. "He makes me want to change my face ten times every time he looks at me."

"He does give off a certain...stickiness," agreed Niico. He wandered to the corner cabinet and pulled out a bottle of *sarave* and some glasses. He held the bottle up. "Just like old times, almost empty." There were names that weren't spoken, by common agreement. It was too hard.

"Stop it. We all help ourselves to my father's cellar." She stretched out on the cushions and accepted a glass.

"Let's go out and do something. That Night Café of Rhoosa's, when is that?"

"Don't know. I haven't seen her for ages. Maybe she shimmered into a mountainside." Aelle shuddered. "I take that back." She held out her glass. He upended the bottle; empty. She made a face and said, "That didn't take long. Be the rain and go get another? Mother had a delivery from the farms, there're new bottles in the cupboard behind the kitchen door."

"If your father walks in on me raiding his pantry—"

"He's ready to adopt you. You have nice manners and you're popular with the right people. You keep me from being a famous recluse and the talk of the boulevard."

He knew she was already both of those things. But he didn't want to add to her burdens.

"Off I go, then."

Appearing in a smear of pale light in the now-dark kitchen, Niico found the stash of *sarave* and put a bottle under each arm. As he readied himself for the quick return trip to Aelle's room, he heard a voice. Voices. He froze.

Don't get caught.

It was the Zaal and Yuenne, making their way from the walled courtyard back into the house. Niico moved without thinking behind the kitchen door and stood silently. Yuenne was talking.

"Speaking of, any sign of our beloved queen?"

The Zaal cleared his throat. "None. Perhaps she's thrown herself into the Crosswinds as penance for her behavior."

"You are still looking?"

So, thought Niico. That's why Yuenne caters to the Zaal. He employs his services. Still, he thought Yuenne sounded suspicious. Not as close as two mice in a bolthole, then.

The Zaal's voice was bland. "Did I accidentally divulge my inability to do two things at once?"

There was a sigh that was also a snort. "I have no demonstration in either direction."

"If you were so interested in our methods, you should have become a mage. The conclave is always looking for clever boys. Too bad about your son."

Niico gasped. Surely Yuenne would strike the Zaal dead. But he just laughed, although to Niico's ear it sounded a bit forced.

"A job for every hand. Mine has led me to the service of the High Seat. If you find the same occupation too wearisome I can petition what's left of the High Seat to relieve you of the burden."

"You and your little upstart family—" the Zaal hissed.

"So allow me to rephrase. I worry about our queen, yes—what she's done and where she is. I fear she and I parted with harsh words between us. I would repair that." He paused. "But hopefully not at the expense of my cordial fellowship with the conclave."

There was another pause. Niico could just picture them, smiling blandly at the air just past the other's shoulder. Niico hoped they would continue. Gossip this good was almost worth one's life.

Finally the Zaal spoke, conceding this small victory to Yuenne. "Do you...are you afraid she'll find something you missed in the Vastness? I wouldn't have thought there's a hill or dune without your bootprints on it out there."

“There’s nothing,” Yuenne said. “There are no Hidden Kingdoms no matter what the sand trash in town might say. Araan is dead. Her brother, the lot of them, all dead. I would have found them.”

“I’m sure you’re correct. As to the other matter…” the Zaal said, and Niico pressed himself against the back of the door and listened with his heart in his throat.

Chapter 3

Mistra

AROUND MID-DAY MOTH and Lelet came across a real road, a hard packed dirt road wide enough for the cart and horse, leading to a collection of whitewashed buildings. One was two storied and had smoke curling from the chimney. They could smell the aroma of cooking. He was hesitant; there were people walking about, and what if someone saw him?

"So let them," she said. "We're traveling together, what could they say? 'Oh look, that beautiful man has funny colored eyes. That's a lucky girl.'" He still looked nervous. "Honestly, Moth. No one believes demons exist."

"You did," he reminded her.

"Only after I was thoroughly convinced. Once I decided you weren't an actor or a lunatic, it was the only thing left." That made him laugh. "Come on. We should have lunch, at least. No! I know. We should stay. We can get a room and stay the night!"

"I don't think we should be doing this at all," he answered. He pulled fretfully at the end of his long, silky horsetail. "There's too many people. We should keep moving."

"Ugh!" She looked at the sky. "Another night on the open road? With the bears? Honestly, if I don't have a bath the bears will run away from me." She reached for his hand and led him to the doorway, whispering for him to stay put. He did as she asked, and she considered how their roles had changed in the week since they'd met. Being kidnapped and hauled around the countryside by mythological creatures was not how most people found their mates, and if her reading of romance novels was correct, kidnappers usually did not end up taking orders from their victims. But there was nothing about him that was usual.

The inn looked to be one large room which ran the length of the front side of the building, with another visible through a swinging door at the back, and a stair leading to the guest rooms above. There was a small bar with a few day time drinkers, and a number of wooden plank benches, sparsely populated, she was pleased to note. A few smaller tables lined the walls, also unoccupied. There were few windows and a large fireplace that was invitingly warm. The innkeeper appeared to also be the barkeep, and she waved Lelet to the bar.

Lelet handed the woman one of the gold rings, keeping the other safely tucked away for emergencies.

"This real?" the innkeeper asked. She had a lined face and wore a clean smock over a dark dress. Lelet was impressed that she ran a tavern and kept her clothing so neat. "It is, isn't it? Mind, I'm no expert." She might not have been an expert, but she pulled a jewelers loupe out of a pocket like a very serious student, at least. Lelet noted the older woman's ragged cuticles and downgraded her assessment.

"It is real, ma'am," answered Lelet, "and I hate to part with it, but our journey has been more difficult than we planned, and there's still so far to go." She hoped the woman would sympathize and not ask any more questions, like why they had no luggage, or what happened to her shoes.

The woman set the ring on the bar between them. "No one going to come around looking for this thing?"

Lelet drew herself up. "I am relieved that we've chosen an establishment that questions its patrons so thoroughly. If our gold meets with your approval we'll sleep well indeed."

The woman twisted her mouth in a smile that suggested she'd dealt with hard luck stories before. But she nodded. "One night. It's nice enough, but I can't very well sell one earring."

"Fine," Lelet agreed. "With a meal now plus dinner and a hot bath. And breakfast tomorrow. And laundry service."

"It's a deal." She answered so quickly Lelet knew she had been robbed. The ring must be worth a month of luxury service. She slid a key on a wooden fob across the counter, and Lelet slipped it into her pocket. "Top of the stairs, second on the left. Leave your clothes on the floor to the right of the door, the water'll be hot in an hour. Dinner's at second moonrise."

"What's for dinner?" she asked.

"I hope you like lunch," the woman replied. She looked at Moth, hovering in the doorway. "Your friend all right?"

"Oh, my poor husband. After the accident he's just not the same, I'm afraid. He's got a good heart though, and strong as an ox."

"Big as one," the woman noted.

"Yes, well, he's become quite shy. Doesn't like to make eye contact. And he probably won't answer if you speak to him." She sighed mournfully and tapped her forehead. "But I do love him so."

She turned to call to Moth to follow her and sighed again at the sight of him, simply filling the doorway, the sun streaming around him. This was him trying to be inconspicuous. She would have to do something dramatic to settle his nerves or run the risk of having him vanish on her—there were plenty of shadows in the tavern and no way to explain a disappearing dining companion.

They sat at a small table in the farthest, darkest corner, and once the thick-armed young serving girl delivered bread, bowls of stew, and beer, she went to work. Nothing and no one—not even a beautiful, mythological nervous creature—would stand between her and a bath.

"This will be perfect." Lelet looked around the dim, low ceilinged dining hall. A handful of people had come in after them—it appeared to be mostly rural workers and their wives, or sisters, or sweethearts—and had sat at the wooden benches nearby and tried not to stare at the newcomers. "There'll be a bed. A bed, Moth."

"People are looking at us," he said unhappily. "We should eat and be on our way." He poked at the bowl. "This has oil on top of it. Is it supposed to?"

Lelet told him he had the palate of a gourmand, and then she had to explain about what rich people ate and what poor people ate. "And this," she said, holding up a dripping forkful of carrots and stringy hen, "is the latter. But I still think we should stay."

He did not look convinced. "What did you tell that woman?" He took a bite of bread and made a face.

"About what?" she replied. "I told her we were traveling rough and had been for some time, and might I trade this golden ring for a hot meal? And I could. Did you want another beer?" And she waved at the young lady serving the few guests, who was busy talking with an older man sitting at the bar. The man hoisted his heavy leather carrier over his shoulder, and with another sharp look in their direction, he finished his beer and left the inn.

"You said something to that woman, about me. She keeps looking over here." She followed his eye to the table, where his hand rested. For a moment she wondered at the scars on his hand, and how they lined up perfectly with the wood grain. Then she realized it *was* the wood grain.

"Oh, that?" she said quickly, thinking of how to distract him "I told her we were childhood sweethearts, recently betrothed and traveling to your family's farmsteads in the southern provinces. I told her it was a blessing to have such a wonderfully tall and powerful person to protect me. So, can we stay?"

It worked. He'd looked up at her around 'betrothed', and his hand was back. She glanced around. No one seemed to have noticed. "I still don't think—"

"Oh, look!" she said, "Here's more beer." The serving girl backed away from their small table, openly staring at Moth. Lelet could feel his discomfort rising off him like smoke. She could understand the girl's reaction, though. He looked as out of place in the dark, rather dingy room as a ruby set in straw. Yes, he was big, but many of the other men were also big. But all the other men had cropped hair and everyone had the tanned skin that comes from working outside. His hair, even though it was tied back, was as long as a woman's, and his unlined skin was a richer shade by far than the summer sun would allow. And, of course, those eyes. Different, special, beautiful. She leaned on her hand and looked at him, feeling as if it were for the first time. No, she didn't blame anyone for staring.

"What?" he said. He was getting agitated, and drawing more attention to himself. "Why are you looking at me like that?"

"It's just...I've never seen you indoors before. You're so...different." His reaction was to hunch over, and she stomped on his foot. "Don't do that. It makes you look guilty. People are looking at you because you're someone new, that's all."

He shook his head. "Then why aren't they staring at you?"

"I am a reasonably attractive girl in an ugly dress. You're like...a unicorn, or something."

He folded his arms and leaned back. "I don't know what that is."

He was getting a little pissy, she thought. Time to change the tone. "It's like a horse, with a big horn." She smiled. "Sort of appropriate. It's magical and beautiful, and you never get to see one."

"Why not? I'd like to see one. Like a mouse with wings."

"A mouse with...yes, like that. But I'm sorry that you can't see one because unicorns aren't real." She paused and traced a finger across his hand. He relaxed a bit and let her stroke his palm. She lowered her voice. "But then, I thought demons weren't real either. If I was lucky enough to see a unicorn, I'd take really good care of it. Maybe I ought to be taking better care of you. Maybe I ought to be hand feeding you off of a golden plate."

He liked that, and nodded. "That would be appropriate. Seeing as how I am the prince."

Now he was just being smug. “Oh, so now you’re the prince? Not just a...let’s see...kidnapper...”

“We’ve established that wasn’t my fault,” he interjected.

“A kidnapper, a book lover, horse enthusiast...”

“Don’t forget blanket warmer,” he reminded her.

She nodded, smiling. “Ah, of course. Demon, human—excuse me, half a human...you’re lots of things. But a prince? Hmmm.” She pulled his hand to her lips.

“I assure you, madam. You’re licking sauce off the fingers of the heir to the High Seat of Eriis.”

She let go of his hand and tilted her head. “Are you really? How can I be sure? You don’t fuck like a prince.”

“I don’t...I don’t?” He shifted uncomfortably in his chair.

“Nope.”

He took two breaths and a swallow of his beer and said, “You make a habit of *scorping* royalty?”

She smiled serenely. “Princes are my specialty.”

“So in your educated opinion, how do I...”

“Come on, you know this one. Ffff...” she prompted.

“Tell me then, how do I fuck?”

“Like someone who only ever wants to please.”

He dropped the game for a moment and looked at her curiously. “Isn’t that the point?”

“It’s a point, but not the only one. Haven’t you ever wanted to take that beautiful gold plated cock of yours and just...use it for yourself? And not worry about anyone or anything else?” Taking advantage of the dark corner, he’d walked his fingers under her dress and she clamped his hand firmly between her thighs. Then she reached over and helped herself to his last bite of bread. “Haven’t you ever wanted that?”

“Right now. I want that now.”

It had gotten so warm in the room that by this point everyone was watching them, the innkeeper with a deepening frown, but she didn’t notice any of them.

Chapter 4

Mistra

THEIR ROOM AT the top of the stairs was just big enough to hold a bed (it was big enough for both of them, he was happy to see) with a chair under the window and a copper tub in the corner next to a tiny fireplace. It was when they put their travel stained clothes in a basket outside the door that he realized he'd been set up. He wanted to leave, she wanted to stay, and she figured out how to make sure she got her room and her bath. He was disappointed that she'd played a game with him—not because of the game itself, but because it reminded him of everything he'd left behind.

"Don't you need a key? Isn't that how this works?" he asked.

"Sorry." She rubbed her arms, happy to be out of the scratchy dress. "I got the room key in exchange for your ring, along with dinner and all the other stuff. I just really wanted to stay here, so I made sure you'd want to stay also. I was afraid you'd say no."

He didn't think she looked particularly sorry. "I would have let us stay. You didn't have to trick me." He stretched out on the smooth white coverlet, realizing he hadn't slept in a proper bed since he'd left home. It felt so soft, as if he might fall through it. It was also strange to be unclothed in front of her and not under the stars, but he decided he could get used to it. And it was a step up from the ground under the cart, to be sure.

She laid down next to him, skimming her hands along the roadmap of silvery scars along his body. “Are you angry?”

“No. You deserve better than those dirty blankets and the hard ground. I prefer to be convinced than connived, though.”

“Noted.” She kissed him by way of an apology and said, “I’ve been thinking. I want to make sure I don’t hurt you.”

He smiled. “Do you think you’re likely to?”

“Well, you never know. People like different things. Like this.” She flicked his nipple with her fingernail, a little harder than she had before.

“Hey!” He swatted her hand away.

“See? Now, if I do something like that—by accident—then you say, “Ouch, stop.” And I’ll know not to do it again.”

“Ouch, stop. I see.” He pushed her legs apart with his knee and reached for that funny tuft of fur that sat above her *ama.* It was rather like a kitten, now that he thought about it, and he covered it with his palm. “So, your ‘stop’ words work both ways? If I were to do something you don’t like?” He moved his hand and made her gasp. “Would you tell me “ouch stop’?”“

She writhed under his hand. “If you stop I’ll cry.”

He kept his hand where it was (he didn’t want her to cry, after all) and with the other flipped her onto her stomach. Now he could see her beautiful pale bottom, and he touched her there, too. She gave a shuddering moan and leaned hard into his hands. *Just take something for yourself*, well it was her idea, and too late to stop even if he wanted to. “Sorry,” he told her, “can’t wait.” And this time he didn’t need her to guide him, and he didn’t have to stop and put the pain away, because with her, there wasn’t any at all.

Beds, now, human beds were a fine thing, especially pillows. She was making a lot of noise; he’d never heard anything quite like it, but he was pretty sure he wanted to hear a lot more of it. He listened for the “stop” words, but like the flames, they never came. He once again felt the rush of pleasure gathering at the base of his wings, *But I don’t have wings,* until it shot down his spine and set every part of him alight. She grabbed the bed frame and pushed backwards against him; he saw white and took her by her hips. The room could have been on fire and he'd have never known it.

When his vision cleared he rolled onto his back and pulled her on top of him. But within three heartbeats she'd leapt up and jumped off the bed in a panic.

The room was on fire.

No, one of the towels, the towel that hung over the edge of the tub was on fire. She tossed it into the tub and turned the tap. It was out in a moment, but blackened along one side. She held it up for him to see.

He gaped at her. "Did you do that?"

She laughed in amazement, tossed the ruined towel in the tub and sat next to him. "Do you *think* I did that?"

"But, I can't. I don't have fire." He was still feeling fairly dazed, but he held his hand out to check. *Did I do that?*

"Sweetheart, I think you'd better revisit what you can and cannot do." She shook her head in wonderment. "Won't they be surprised when you get back home?"

He wiggled his fingers and tried finding the white light he'd seen behind his eyes. "If I only have fire when you and I are joining, that'll be an unusual battlefield tactic." He looked up at her. "I did it, I must have, but it has something to do with you." She'd given him the best hours of his life, why not fire as well? "I suppose there's only one thing to do."

She laughed again. "Let me guess. Practice?"

"Precisely." He reached for her.

"Again? Already? That is...impressive. But absolutely not until I've had a bath," she said. "I feel like I've been rolled in dirt. I *have* been. It won't kill you to wait an hour."

He knew what an hour was from listening to the servants plan their schedules at her home, it was roughly the space between first and second moonrise. Unlike his own people, the humans struggled to stay inside the lines they drew through their days. An 'hour' was a line.

The copper tub, big enough for one person to sit with their knees drawn up, sat in the corner, and she set to playing with the knobs. He watched her wash her hands, did the same, and then she made him smell the different colored soaps.

"No, none of them," he said through a sneeze. "I like the way you smell by yourself." He had an idea. "Go ahead and fill the tub. I know it's cold. Just fill it now."

When it was nearly full, he pulled up a little three legged stool from the corner. He thought it must look comical, it was barely tall enough to keep him off the ground.

"Want to see something?" he asked. She readily agreed. He had already decided there was never going to be a time she would answer that question with a "no." It made him worry for her, and at the same time he wanted to show her everything, or at least be with her when she saw it. "Then come over here and sit."

Muttering something about a one track mind, she bent down and put her arms around his neck. He pulled her onto his lap. She licked his lower lip.

"You taste good," she told him, and kissed him. He held her close, and she was such a lovely warm weight in his arms that he got distracted. But he had to admit that despite what he'd told her, a bath was probably a good idea. She couldn't simply burn off the top layer as he could. He leaned over her and plunged his arm into the cold water. It only took a few moments for steam to rise from the tub.

He sat back and flicked water from his hands. "Now I don't have to wait an hour."

She kissed him again. "You are magical."

He thought he could watch the look on her face as she lowered herself into the hot water for an hour. But she put him to work washing her hair. "No, it doesn't get clean with just water, just use a little of the soap—the green one—that's it." She slapped his hand. "That is not my hair! Focus."

"Lelet," he said, pouring clean water over her head, "There's something wrong with your hair."

She looked up at him. "Is it falling out or something?"

"No, it's a different color where it's growing. It's changing color." He had a horrible thought. "It's not going to be pink again, is it?"

She laughed. "I am the only one who liked the pink. No, it's going to be dark, not as dark as yours, though. But I'll probably make it white again when I have the chance. I don't know anyone who has naturally white hair."

He marveled. "Humans. So many colors, and you use them all."

She stood up, water streaming from her hair and down her slender form, and reached for a fresh towel. "If you want a turn..."

"Maybe another time. But I do need the tub when it's empty." The thought of sitting in a pot of water did not appeal, it was a little too much like making soup. As far as he was concerned, if there was water, it was going to be his river. Or maybe her ocean, if it really existed. He took a breath and said, "I want to change my form, and I don't want to set anything else on fire or scorch the floorboards." He busied himself drying her back.

She looked over her shoulder at him. "Are you sure about that? You know I'll be able to see you. I can close my eyes, I guess. If you don't want me to watch."

He shrugged. "You keep telling me you like how I look. This is part of how I look. Just don't come too close." He wasn't sure at all, but he wanted to give her something, and he had nothing else.

She sat on the bed with her knees tucked under her, and as he stepped into the empty copper tub her eyes never left his face. He took a deep breath. She nodded. He wanted to close his eyes or look away, but she didn't, so he didn't either. It only took to the count of ten, and he was himself again. A scattering of ash lay at the bottom of the tub.

Since she hadn't leapt to her feet or run for the door, he lay down beside her. Instead of the disgust he was used to feeling upon showing his true face, right now he felt only calm.

"I have to tell you," she said, "I was expecting something...else. I didn't really see you, that other time. It was dark and I was so tired. But now? You looked sort of like a statue of yourself, made out of ash and smoke. You looked soft. I wanted to touch you. It wasn't ugly, although if I didn't understand what you were doing I might have been afraid. But ugly? No." She watched his face. "Do you believe me?"

"You don't have to keep asking me that. I believe you." And, he realized, he nearly did.

Once she had finished toweling off her hair she went around the room and showed him how to light the gas lamps, as they had left the afternoon behind. He knew, of course, as he'd watched the maids light the lamps at her own home every evening for weeks. It was usually his signal to visit the kitchen and see what he could steal away with for his own dinner.

"I can't believe I'm saying this, but I'm hungry again," he said.

"I believe it. Setting things on fire takes a lot out of you." She brushed his long hair out of his eyes. "You stay here. I'll go down there and see what's for dinner." She smiled. "Probably something with chicken in it."

They could hear the chatter and bustle from the people at their evening meal downstairs. He tried to hide the panic rising in his throat, and then felt ashamed. They were just humans. He wanted to argue, but found he couldn't.

She was already poking around the little room. "I need something to wear."

They ended up wrapping her in the bed sheet with the bedspread as sort of a shawl, and she set off in her bare feet to collect their dinner.

He pulled the chair to the door and waited. How had she convinced him this was clever? What was there to be afraid of? He knew he was in no real danger from the humans, but as they had found in the forest, she certainly was. All eyes would be on her, and though she was modestly wrapped from chin to ankle that was no guarantee of safety.

He got up and paced, an unsatisfactory three or four of his long strides took him from door to window. This was ridiculous. He should have gone himself. While the Duke had been less of a role model than he'd hoped, in this case he was certain his fictional hero wouldn't have let his lady fetch and carry. No. It wasn't too late. He would act.

He had the remaining dry towel wrapped around his waist in a sort of skirt and had a hand on the doorknob, when she pushed it open and thrust the heavy tray into his hands. She looked pale and leaned against the door, she made certain it was locked, and then took the chair he'd sat in and wedged it under the handle.

"Are you going to tell me?" he asked.

"Hmm? Oh, nothing. That serving girl gave me a nasty eye, and there were a few men at the bar...this may not have been my finest idea."

"I should not have let you go."

"Well, done is done," she replied. She gave herself a shake, and added, "Just because I say something doesn't mean you have to agree with me, you know."

That, he thought, was as close as she would get to admitting she'd made a mistake. He wanted to tell her how grateful he was, but again found he could not. The Duke would disapprove of this entire venture.

"I'm afraid I forgot knives and forks. Or cups." She smiled at him. "I like your outfit. Very *soigne*."

They ate the platter of roast chicken with their fingers and passed the bottle back and forth cross-legged on the floor in front of the tiny fireplace. While they ate, she suggested he concentrate on lighting the fireplace, but the dark, smoky wine went to his head and made that sort of focus impossible. They finally gave up and used matches.

Once the bird was gone and the bottle mostly empty, they filled the tub with half a foot of water and pulled down the curtains and piled the unburned towels nearby.

"We can't use the bed," he said with some regret. "What if I set the sheets on fire?"

"You won't," she said, and sounded sure. "You wouldn't hurt me. It'll be fine."

Several hours later they agreed practice was excellent, and being quiet was exciting in its own way, and they should continue as soon as either one of them could move again.

Nothing else went up in smoke.

* * *

Once Lelet had collected their dinner and fled back up the stairs, one of the men at the bar tossed down his drink and began to get to his feet.

"Seems like she's tired out the first one, I'm going to see if she needs some company, cold night like this. Anyone with me?" A few men laughed, but the innkeeper stepped behind the bar.

"Here." She slid another beer his way. "Leave 'em be. I've already sent word to Beb and the boys, they'll be here in the morning. We'll let them deal with those two." She pulled a stout wooden club with a nail driven through it from under the bar. "And if there needs to be trouble, Beb'll see to it."

Between the club, the drink, and the name, Jef sat back down. "It's just they seem like a bad sort. No need to wave that thing around."

The woman laughed and returned the weapon to its spot under the bar. "Just wanted to make sure I got your attention."

"Undivided." He lifted his beer. "To Beb, then, and his swift arrival."

Chapter 5

Eriis

FOR SOMEONE WHO had grown up without knowing the meaning of privation, Ilaan thought he was adapting to his new life in quite a dignified style. Instead of his much loved turret room with the view of the towers and the city wall, his new single room, tucked away in the Quarter itself, had one window which looked out onto another window an arm's length away. The scrims across the alley were heavy and always drawn down. He didn't know if anyone lived there. His library was reduced to what he'd carried away under his arm. His books were ash and his family no longer spoke his name. His fine white tunics all left behind, he now only wore brown, the cheapest kind. He'd never even gotten to wear a Mage's robe, much less gotten a look in their secret books.

On the other hand, he no longer felt his father's eyes on him, and he could quit pretending the Mage's life would suit him. Every time he thought of the Raasth or of the great stone table, the one scored by nameless clawing fingers and stained with blood, the table that was to be Rhuun's final destination, his throat closed. He refused to think his new life was anything but a fair trade. Those first days, though, that had been bad. He'd tried to explain to Aelle why Rhuun had to go, but she refused to listen. She blamed him, and when he told her what the Mages wanted, she called him a liar. When he told her about Rhuun's human father, she simply refused to hear it. His mother had not been able to pour water on his father's anger, and his home was now this little room.

He missed Aelle terribly, and he knew she missed him. This was the longest they'd gone in their lives without seeing each other.

And what the queen revealed, he was still working through it. She claimed to have no great love for Rhuun, but only wanted to use him in a game she played with his human father. It seemed a little clever to Ilaan. A little obvious. She always had a strange way of showing affection, and her relationship with her son was not an easy one, but he wagered she'd walk through the Crosswinds to protect him, if for no other reason than he was hers. It wasn't like her to leave Rhuun to his own devices. Until that conversation he'd assumed she felt her son couldn't lace his boots without her intervention. Well, he didn't expect to hear from her again, at least until she wanted something else.

As for Rhuun himself, Ilaan could barely stand to think of the trouble he'd flung his friend into. Certainly he was working, he was never without a plan, but this particular plan had too many moving parts for his liking, and too many lies. Relying on the fears and weaknesses of others, with their egos to be stroked, their little secrets to be learned, it made him uneasy. Too many factors. But what choice did he have?

Niico stayed away as well, and that left him with an ache in his heart. He knew Niico loved his life, his celebrity, and his position in society. He still thought his *shani* would be willing to give it up for him, and he hated that he was wrong. He started to make new acquaintances here in the Old City, but it wasn't the same. He felt they were afraid of him and unsure of what he had to do with the strange news coming from the royal quarters about the Prince, the Queen, and the Mages. *Wasn't young Ilaan a Mage as well? Or was he?* He had a lot of work to do, if this idea of the queen's—this notion of tying together the prince and the rain—would come to pass.

So when the knock came on his door several weeks later, he counted a number of reasons to be happy.

"It's just too dull without you," Niico said, "and besides, I always loved spy stories. And now I'm in one." As they embraced, their fire lit the little room with its radiance.

Chapter 6

Mistra

WHEN RHUUN NEXT opened his eyes, it was barely light. He held still and waited for the burns and bruises from the night before to start their complaining, until he remembered where he was and with whom he had slept. There was nothing to repair and no injury or insult to put away. He set his feet on the old boards and considered a life where every morning started with something other than degrees of pain.

Looking back at her, still asleep with her arms thrown over her head, he thought about waking her and having her again. But he could hear her snores, kitten snores (she'd been so charmed by his thinking cats were "angry little dogs" she let him walk around calling them that for a full day before she told him what they really were) and decided to let her sleep. It was the first time they'd slept together under a roof, in a bed, and he'd chased her across the sheets until she told him he was making her too hot (and, as it turned out, that could be good or bad. Context) and she couldn't sleep with him lying all over her.

He considered the scorched towel laying in the copper tub. His people didn't manifest as adults, it simply never happened. But it happened to him, a late-arriving gift from his mysterious father no doubt, and he would have to figure out how to control it, or risk burning a house down. Or not do the sex with Lelet. Once again, he wanted to talk to Ilaan.

He decided to go downstairs to the main dining room—by himself—and get her a cup of her beloved coffee. He could smell it now. Maybe he'd get some for himself while he was at it, he hadn't met a human that didn't like coffee. He'd keep his head down. How many of them could be about so early, after all?

He found their clothing stacked and folded just outside the door. Her dress, while no more flattering, was at least clean. He laid it over the chair for her. Once dressed, he quietly made his way to the bar, where the coffee steamed in a cracked old silver canister. Cups were set beside it. No one was about.

He was on his way back towards the stairs when he heard two women speaking just outside. One of them was the innkeeper. The front door of the inn was closed against the cold morning air, but the window next to it had the shutters cracked open to let in some light.

"He'd be back by now, he's never this late," said the younger of the two. "You know my Beb don't like me to worry."

"Well, he might have come across something that got his interest, Barbara. What did he say?"

Beb? There was only one Beb, and he was a charred corpse at the bottom of the Gorda River—he'd put the man there himself, along with his two villainous friends. And this woman was waiting for him? She'd be waiting until the moons fell.

He could just about see them through the slats in the shutters, and when they came inside, they couldn't see him at all. Pressed against the dark stairwell, he had a frantic moment when he realized the coffee cup was floating in midair and rested it on the windowsill in case one of them glanced his way.

"He said he and his boys had spotted a pair of burglars and he was going after them. A man and woman. I'm worried, what if they had weapons? Or what if they were traveling in a bigger group?" The woman gnawed her thumbnail. "Tell me about the two from last night. You think it's the same ones?"

"Don't know. Traveling rough, they were, no bags, but they had gold on them, see?" She held up one of Moth's rings for inspection. "And where' there's one, I'll wager there's another. The man was big, but there was something funny about him, and that girl! What a slut. Howled like a cat for half the night and strolled out wrapped in a bed sheet for her dinner, just as proud as the Queen of the Fairy People! When they come down for breakfast, you can talk to them. But be subtle-like. She says her man is simple, but he's the size of an ox."

"If they've done something to my Beb, I'll subtle them into the ground." The pair headed back into the kitchen and Moth exhaled and rematerialized. Time to go.

He hurried back to their room and set the coffee on the bedside table, and shook Lelet's shoulder. She grumbled and rolled away from him.

"*Shani,* we have to go. Get dressed. Here, drink your coffee and get dressed."

She sat up and blinked sleepily at him. "What's going on? Oh! You brought me coffee, you're so sweet."

He pulled the covers off and threw her dress on the bed. "Get dressed and stay quiet."

She set the cup down. "What's gotten into you?"

"Beb's woman? The one you told me about—Barbara? She's downstairs." Lelet gasped. "She's talking with the owner of this place. They are looking for us. I don't know how much he told her, but we ought not to wait around and find out." She paled and nodded, wiggling back into her dress.

"Is there another way out?" she asked, tightening the belt and sliding into the too-large slippers. "We have to get back around to the stable and get the horse." They tried to recall the layout of the big main room.

"I think there must be a back door, since there's a kitchen." Moth only knew this because he'd seen the back door at Lelet's own house on one of his many trips to their kitchen. The layout and functions of human dwellings were still largely a mystery.

"Okay," said Lelet. "Here's what we do. I'm going to talk to them." He began to protest, but she said, "I'll just tell her we're on our way south and make it a short conversation, and while I'm doing that, you'll have been out the back door and gotten the horse and cart ready. You'll probably have to give the stableman the other gold ring, I'm afraid."

"What if she knows about your hair?" She rooted through the leather bag until she found his hat, and neatly tucked her hair up under it. He wasn't convinced. "What if she—"

"Sweetheart." She took his hands in her own. "It'll be fine. You can do this. Just... keep your head down." She took a look round their room. "Back to the stars and the bears, I guess." She gave him a quick kiss and squeezed his *yala*. "If you have to, think of me and set something on fire. Okay. Here we go." She hoisted the leather bag over her shoulder. He slipped out the door and vanished into the shadows on the stairs.

Moth, keeping to the shadows, crept past Barbara, who was nursing her coffee at the bar and staring out the front window. The innkeeper was outside, Moth could hear her sweeping, and had a jolting memory of an old woman and an even older broom. He couldn't quite place the face, and then it was gone. He shook his head and quietly opened the door to what he hoped was the kitchen, and was relieved to find himself in a small, sunny space full of well used wooden cutting boards and dominated by a long stone fireplace. He couldn't find a shadow to hide in, but that was fine, no one was tending to the big kettle coming to a boil on the fire. The griddle was cold, but a bowl of eggs sat out, ready to be cooked, along with several loaves of brown bread. He grabbed one, stuffed it in his pocket and continued out the back door.

There weren't any shadows in the courtyard leading to the stable, but that didn't matter either, since he'd need help getting the horse and cart put back together. He found the stableman smoking around the side of the barn, upwind where the horses wouldn't smell it.

"Good morning, sir," Moth said. "Glad to see you are awake. I'm afraid we're making an early start of it, and I'll need some assistance." The man looked him over. He would have made a fine Eriisai politician, he was absolutely expressionless. Moth couldn't guess the man's age, he had bristly brown whiskers that began nearly under his pale blue eyes and vanished into the collar of his faded checked shirt. His skin was almost as dark as Moth's own, but creased and rough looking. The man blew out a stream of smoke and stubbed his cigarette out against his boot heel.

"In a hurry?" Was everyone suspicious, or was he just jumpy? Moth couldn't tell.

"I'm afraid so. Oh," he remembered. "Perhaps you'll find a use for this?" He held out his gold ring. The man's hand moved and the ring vanished.

"No use hanging about, then," said the man. It was as if the gold woke him up. *Coffee and gold,* Moth mused. *I must remember that.* The man lit a lantern on a post inside the barn, where even with the front door open it was quite dark, and motioned Moth to come in. As he followed the man inside, the three horses threw their heads up at the sight of him and began to back away within the confines of their stalls. "Horses don't like me," he told the man. "I don't know why not."

The man shrugged and slipped into the stall to calm their horse. "Horses are funny," he said. "Sometimes they don't like folks. It's like they can see something riding on your shoulder. Or maybe you have a smell they don't feature. Just stay quiet there, they'll calm down." He led the still nervous horse out of the stall and Moth helped him line the cart up behind the animal. He watched closely as the man fastened them together. The man talked as he worked, and somehow his voice calmed both the horses and Moth. He drew closer to watch the man, and learned that what he'd privately called "metal thing" or "strappy part" had names like girth and trace and bit. The horse watched him, its huge eye showing white at the corner.

From the main building, there came a crash, and the sound of women shouting. One of the voices was Lelet's.

"Moth! Help me!"

At the sound of her call, Moth took a step back, and knocked the lantern off the post and onto the dirt and hay strewn floor. The man swore, and shouting, "Help! Fire!" ran back towards the main building.

"Wait! What about—" but the man was gone and the horses were all screaming. He took a step towards the barn door, but he couldn't leave the animals. He opened the stalls, stomping on the fast moving flames as he did, but the horses, out of fear of him or fear of the fire in the barn, backed away and refused to come out. Moth opened every door he could find and slapped the rump of his own horse as hard as he could. As it bolted towards the door, he raced after it.

* * *

After counting to one hundred, Lelet ambled down after him as if she had nothing much to do and all morning to do it in. As she'd expected, the pair of them, the innkeeper and another woman with a long salt and pepper braid down her back, were waiting for her.

"Lovely morning," she smiled, pushing past them to refill her mug.

"After the night you had, I thought you'd sleep in," commented the innkeeper.

"Where's your man?" asked Barbara, for who else could it be? She wore faded men's breeches and a leather vest over a grey and white striped man's shirt. She was a smoker; her fingertips were stained yellow. "The big one. I want to talk to him."

"As I told you, Ma'am—" she nodded at their hostess, "he's a bit shy. Is there a special reason you wanted to speak to him?"

"My man, my Beb. He was due back two days ago. I think maybe your shy friend knows something about it." She narrowed her eyes. "Maybe you do, too."

She furrowed her brow and made a show of thinking hard. "Beb, did you say? Beb." She tried not to choke on it.

"No. He's missing? How dreadful. You must be awfully worried. Well, if we see anyone on the road we'll be sure and ask after them."

Barbara smiled a flat and dangerous smile. "Them?"

"Him," Lelet said, cursing her stupid mouth. "Him. Dangerous times. That's why we're eager to get an early start. We'll be on our way in a moment." She was sure she heard noises from the stables and headed for the door.

"Where's your man, dearie?" Barbara asked again, stepping in front of Lelet, barring her way. Lelet shifted the leather bag to her other shoulder, wondering if it was heavy enough to knock the older woman down, when Barbara's hands flew to her mouth and she began to shriek.

"Murderer! Thief! That's Beb's knife!" She flew at Lelet with her hands like claws and Lelet swung the bag at her, more out of reflex than any sort of plan. The innkeeper ran to the bar and ducked out of sight.

The two women circled each other until Lelet looked back past Barbara towards the kitchen and shouted, "Moth! Help me!" The other woman looked away long enough for her to duck under Barbara's upraised hands and shoot out the door.

Now what? she thought in a panic. Barbara was on her heels. Lelet tripped on her overlarge slippers and stumbled forward. The older woman ran into her and fell into the path of their horse, pulling the cart. Barbara rolled out of the way with a shout and lay in the dust, teeth bared and reaching for her leg.

The horse slowed enough for Lelet to get to her feet, grab its lead and pull herself up into the cart, throwing the hat and her bag in behind her. She smelled smoke, and the horse was desperate to get as far away from the place as possible. But where was Moth?

The innkeeper came out into the courtyard with a club with a nail driven through the end of it.

That looks familiar, she thought, We are in a bad part of town.

The cart shook and she looked back to see Moth hurling himself into the back. She didn't need him to tell her to go. She went.

Chapter 7

Mistra

"NO ONE IS following us," Moth told her after they'd run hard for a mile or so. They stopped to let the horse take a rest. "Because I set the stable on fire. I didn't mean to. What if the horses got burnt up?"

"Tell me what happened." She couldn't believe that neither of them were hurt. She couldn't believe their bad luck, either.

He leaned against her. "I gave the stableman the other ring, and he got our horse, um, roped up to the cart. The horses were upset that I was there, but he said not to worry about it. Then I heard you call me and I—"

"You were able to make fire, like you did in the room. I knew you could."

"No." He looked miserable. "I turned when I heard your voice and knocked a lantern over." He rubbed his face. "I pulled all the gates and doors open, but what if they couldn't get out? Should we go back?"

"Barbara knew who I was. She saw this." Lelet pulled her dress away from the belt and the knife. "Because I'm an idiot and I forgot to hide it. This is my fault, not yours. The lantern, it was an accident. I'm sure the stableman got everyone out. We can't go back."

They sat in silence by the side of the road.

Finally, Moth said, "I think—"

"No," she said. "You can't go home. Not yet."

There was a long pause. "I wasn't going to say that. I don't want to go. I don't know how to go. But I can't stay here. Look what I've done to you." He touched her face. "You're dirty again."

She wrapped her arms around his neck. "I don't care. I'll sleep outside with the bears. I'm not afraid."

He sighed. "We can't keep doing this. We need to go somewhere safe. That's what I was going to say. We have to get off the road, those people and their friends will be looking for us now. I wish I could talk to Ilaan." He helped her down from the cart and they led the horse off the road to a small stand of trees, out of sight. They walked the short distance through the brush to the river and sat side by side.

"I thought of something," she said, "I'm pretty sure you're not going to like it."

"Go ahead." He picked up a pebble and rolled it between his fingers. It was pink and yellow.

"Well, you said just now you didn't know how to go back, and you said you wanted to talk to your friend. But Scilla must know something, too. She didn't do this on her own." He had to agree. "She may be angry at me, but why take it out on you? You said her behavior, the way she spoke to you—"

"It was like she knew something about me that made her hate me. Most of the time. Sometimes she was looking for someone to talk to. Your people are very confusing." He tossed the pebble in the water and they watched the ripples.

"But she knew things. She was expecting you?"

"It certainly seemed that way at the time," he said.

"She knew where you'd be, and how to do that binding thing. I guarantee they don't teach that at the Guardhouse."

"Someone from Eriis taught her, well, I knew that." He watched her, curious.

"Had to be. And who from Eriis knew where you'd be, and when? And how to catch you? Who is keeping you here—without a word, in the dark—until they're good and ready to use you? Moth, who sent you here in the first place?"

"No," he said instantly. "Not Ilaan. He is more than my brother."

She shrugged. "Scilla is my sister, and look where we are. I know you love your friend, but who else could it be? All you've told me is how smart and powerful he is. Maybe he's got a good reason, but it seems like he decided your life was on the table."

"The table..." He shuddered and stood to walk away from her.

She caught up with him. "What happens? Say we go and we see my sister. What happens?"

"I gather she'll signal someone—the people who want me back haven't been napping. They managed to corrupt your sister. It's possible they may have figured out how to get The Door open even without my blood."

"Without your . . . did you say *blood*?"

"I told you. It's my human blood that opens The Door, since it was humans that locked it. I think they mean to blow it down completely. That would take a lot of blood. That would take all of it."

She turned pale. "Blood? I mean, you said you were in trouble, but I thought. . ." "She pushed her fist against her forehead. "That's why you're here. The real reason. If you go back they'll kill you."

"What did you think I was talking about?" She realized she hadn't seen him angry before. "The Order built the locks and sealed it with blood. No one could leave Eriis because our keys didn't fit. Until the Mages found out about me—well, until Ilaan figured it out. They don't need keys if they have me. And he sent me here. And he's one of them, now." He looked down at her, deflated. "What is the word for *rushta* in your language?"

"Shit," she told him.

"That."

"Moth, if your friend is there when that Door opens, even though you love him, don't go to him. Don't go through."

* * *

They sat on the back of the cart, passing the loaf of bread back and forth. He held her hand, rubbing his thumb absently across her wrist. *There's something*, she thought. *It's important. It's right on the edge of my brain. I just have to wait for it to come back*. Then she had another thought.

"Blood, right?" she said.

"Hmm? Yes. That's the way it works."

"Does it have to be your blood? Or is it any human blood?"

"I...don't know," he said.

"Is that what my sister wants me for?"

He pulled her close. "It doesn't matter. We don't have to go there. We're free—I am free. I can go anywhere. Maybe I'll never go back. Come with me—I still need a tour guide. I need to learn the proper names of things. And the ocean, and the bo-hats, we should go look at them, right? We can turn around and leave and never go near the Guardhouse and never go near that inn place again."

"You're going to want to go to the Guardhouse, though. We should go see Scilla right away."

"Why? That's the last place we should go."

Lelet smiled at him. "I just remembered why I recognized your author's name. Do you still want to meet Malloy dos Capeheart? Because I know where you can find him."

* * *

The only thing left was to deal with the horse.

Lelet released it from all the tack and traces. It stood quietly, swishing its tail and looking at her with its huge, mild eyes.

"I think you'd better tell our friend here to move on," she said to Moth. "He'll listen to you."

He nodded and stood close to its head. It regarded him warily. "I hate to just leave you like this, but we're walking the rest of the way. Lelet's sister wants to meet us off the road at a place called the Stumps, and the path isn't safe for your feet. I imagine you have places to go—maybe you'll be able to go back home? I'm sure your master will be happy to have you back. Thank you for your service, and for not biting my hand off. Or stepping on me, or breaking my bones, or throwing me in a ditch. You have been a faithful and excellent companion, and if I ever get back home, I'll tell my friends Eriis won't be truly civilized until we have horses like you."

The horse, by now accustomed to this not-right smell (*Fire! Burning! Run! Oh, it's this nervous creature. No need to run, despite the stink*) leaned forward and rested its long forehead against Moth's shoulder. Then it ambled off in the direction they'd come. It felt pretty sure it could find its way home. Same length, straight line.

Lelet pretended not to see the shine of tears in Moth's eyes.

Chapter 8

Eriis

ILAAN CRACKED HIS neck and wiped the chalk dust off his hands. He set the slate on the floor in the corner. Another day, and done with it.

"Remember, tomorrow is history and letters," he called after the handful of children as they raced from his room—his new home, classroom and place of exile—into the alley towards the boulevard beyond. Their parents couldn't pay much, but he didn't need much. The last few weeks had been a bitter lesson in need and want, and the valley between them. If he started counting what he wanted, the list would never end.

Niico waited around the corner, scarf drawn over his face, until the children's dust had settled.

"The fat one shows some promise, I think," he said, hanging his scarf on a hook by the door. "But that meat-vendor's brat needs his head separated from his body." He set a parcel on the single table and pulled Ilaan into an embrace and a lingering kiss. It had been over a week since he'd managed to sneak away, and that was five days too long.

"I'll pass that along to their parents, just as soon as I am paid," Ilaan replied. He looked over Niico's shoulder at the package. "What's this?"

"Let's see." Niico turned and used one hand to peel back the paper, the other twined through Ilaan's long hair. "*Sarave* from your father's own cellar—without so much dust in it, and dinner direct from inside the Arch. I have standards, you know." He pulled Ilaan's head back and kissed a line of sparks down his throat.

Ilaan took a breath and pulled away. "You take risks. If my father—"

"Yes, yes, off to the Crosswinds. But he pays me no mind, he's occupied these days with your ex-colleagues down in their hole. And Aelle wouldn't notice if you set her hair on fire, poor thing." He let Ilaan go and began poking through his small collection of plates and forks. "So no one will miss a few scraps and one bottle."

"Thank you."

"You haven't tasted it yet," Niico laughed.

"That's not what I mean. Aelle—"

"She just needs some time. And a distraction. I have something in mind." He poured them both a glass and set the table. "I suppose I should say someone." Ilaan sat and sipped his drink and stared at the floor. Niico sat beside him, silent for a moment. Then he said, "I think they've found him."

Ilaan's head shot up. "Rhuun? The Mages found him? What happened?"

Niico shook his head. "I thought that might get your attention. The rest of us just walk behind—"

"Oh, stop it with that nonsense. If you were alone and lost? Light and Wind knows I would break the mountain's back to find you. Should I do less for him?"

Niico sighed. "He's alive and well, as I told you he would be. That one always manages to land on his feet, even without wings."

"Tell me exactly what you heard."

"I took dinner with your family last night. Also attending was the Zaal—now, there's a sour piece of work. Quite puts me off my meal, but your father receives him as if they are old friends."

"Niico."

"One must set a scene. Allow me to continue. Drink your drink. So, I might have done a tiny bit of eavesdropping after dinner. They were talking about a quarry, and then about some girl. They are also looking for the queen. There's something funny going on there, I don't know what. It may be that your father is using the Zaal to track her down. Did you know they don't like each other? I thought it would come to flames for a minute."

"Niico, did they find him or not?"

"Right. Sorry. Well, we knew they were both looking for Rhuun, and they've found him."

Ilaan drew his hand back. "And you learned all this just last night?"

Niico folded his arms and said, "Thank you Niico, for watching over my mopey sister and my delusional mother. Thank you for risking your reputation—at the very least—by trotting down here to *Rushtaville* whenever you can steal away without drawing suspicion. Thank you—"

"Oh, all right. I apologize. You're right, I am ungrateful and simple." He refilled their glasses, his mind buzzing. Rhuun safe, and with the humans. "And thank you most particularly for this, the stuff they sell down here gets caught in your teeth."

"Well, you're welcome. There's more."

Ilaan ran his hands through his hair. "I suppose you'd better tell me."

"They've found him," Niico said again. "And they're going to try and get him back."

Ilaan frowned. "That's not new. I mean, we know the Zaal went on a tear when I sent Beast away. He and my father both." He waved a hand at the little room. "Thus my accommodations. I gathered they've been trying all along. Knowing where he is and bringing him back are two different—"

"Ilaan, you're not listening. They know where he is and they *do* think they know how to bring him back. And it's going to happen soon. Very soon."

"We have to warn him," said Ilaan at once. "We have to get to him first. And I know how to do it." The room faded away as he visualized his plan. He had to write a little note. "There's one thing I need, to make it work. I can...I can try to shimmer into my father's study; it'll still be in his desk. It's a long way, but—"

"Obviously, I am going to get this thing for you. Once I do—"

"No, *shani*, this isn't a spy story. The Crosswinds are a real thing."

"Once I get you what you need, are you going to know what to do with it? Because you don't have more than another day to figure it out."

"Why would you do this? I know how you feel..."

"If you know how I feel, then you know why."

"I am yours." Ilaan's eyes swam with tears.

"Same. And don't you forget it. Now." Niico cleared their plates and put the slate flat on the ashboard tabletop. "Here's your father's study." He took the chalk from Ilaan's hand and drew a rectangle "And here's his desk. Let's talk about what's inside."

Chapter 9

Mistra

LITTLE SISTER, ARE you there?

Of course I am, I'm right here.

We have fallen behind schedule, or at least it seems so to me. I begin to worry.

I don't understand what could have happened. I had it all arranged. The criminal and his minder should have been here days ago. I don't know what could be keeping them.

You made the creature understand it was not to harm the human you've chosen to accompany it? Because the beast is impulsive and if it thinks it is in danger, it might very well lash out at whomever is closest to it. Perhaps I wasn't sufficiently clear in describing the dangers it poses.

I did tell it, I told it to come straightaway and no funny stuff. And I made sure it wouldn't harm me, I did that first.

We are worried, my sister. We are worried we might have made an error in judgment entrusting such a dangerous adversary to one so young. You are untested. Your skills may not be as developed as you led us to believe.

That's not it; I did everything you told me to! I know the binding spell was perfect. I'm afraid.

What do you fear, sister?

I'm afraid I may have chosen poorly in picking the creature's companion. She's not so smart and is easily distracted, especially if someone is being nice and attentive to her.

This is a foul beast who belongs in chains, a depraved monster. If it speaks a pretty phrase surely any human could see through its wiles.

I thought so as well, but what else could be keeping them?

If the human you chose is particularly witless, the creature might see its chance and attempt to escape. Of course if that were the case we would be most disappointed. We have put much effort into this endeavor, sister. I know from your own words you want this to succeed. Unless you no longer wish to join us here on Eriis? If you've had a change of heart, I would mourn the loss of my most treasured companion, but I would understand. After all, Mistra is your home and it can be frightening to imagine new horizons, no matter how tempting those horizons might be.

No, that's not it! Not at all! Mistra is not my home, not my real home. I want to go, it's all I want. They have to show up. They have to. I will go to the appointed place again today. Open the Door. I know they will arrive today. I know it, I can feel it.

We cannot wait much longer. Soon we will not be able to open The Door at all. Resources are limited. And our patience is also reaching its limit. We will open The Door as you've requested. I sincerely hope we find you waiting there. You, your human companion, and our prisoner.

I won't disappoint you.

* * *

Dear Littlest,

I hope this letter finds you snug and warm and more clever than ever.

The weather has been delightful, just a bit of a snap in the air—isn't it fun at this time of year? And the garden is still hanging on, although I think your rose—the yellow climber outside your old window—is due for a great big haircut in the spring. Perhaps we can schedule an emergency pruning visit for you? Surely your teachers would give you leave for something that important!

Pol writes to ask after you constantly, I told him he ought to set down his script and just go see you already! His show opens in two months' time and all he does is rehearse. (Is it rehearsing if you're doing it by yourself?) I know he's in just one scene, but you'd think he was Elfraim Littleton back from the beyond to trod the boards! It's a pleasure to hear him so happy and excited, though. Rane says he knows every word so if anyone should fall ill (or tumble down the stairs, or eat a bad whelk, or, well, I trust you get the idea)—including the fresh faced young ingénue—he could step in without missing a beat. He also says Pol would only be happier if it was a one man show! Personally I think what he really wants to do is direct (Pol, that is, not Rane). Rane is making trouble and has a chorus of sad-faced sighing young girls following him around, so he's in an exceptionally good state of mind. The fresh air seems to agree with him. Father is overjoyed that he's got all his boys around him and now he's after me to make a visit. Imagine us all relocating to the great outdoors! (I am trying to put my visit off as long as possible, but it's probably going to be at midwinter.)

Stelle sends her love, did I tell you she's come to stay? The old place is just so big; I can't stand an echoey hallway!

Darling, I don't mean to worry you, and honestly it's probably nothing, but have you gotten a note from Lelly? She was supposed to be visiting some friends at the coast, but I haven't gotten a word from her in over a week, and you know she loves to keep us up to date. Like I said, she's probably found a new boy and is having the time of her life, (what is it with your brother and sister? they're just the same, no wonder they fought all the time!) but if you hear from her please do let me know. But don't worry, I'm certain she's fine.

Let me know if you need any school supplies or another emergency box of chocolates.

All my love and more,

May

* * *

Dear Biggest,

You'll be happy to hear that I made a fort out of my blankets and hid in my fortifications until the chocolates were vanquished. It's colder here than back home, I'm guessing because we're so close to the ocean. My classes are going well, and I am making lots of friends. I haven't heard anything from Lel, she'd write to me last anyway. I'm sure she's fine and will turn up sooner rather than later with some nasty creature in tow (just kidding. But I'm sure she's fine).

Go ahead and cut the roses back, as I am busy with my work and I don't know when I'll see home again. I have a lot to do and it's all wonderful and exciting. I don't want you to ever worry about me. I'm glad you have a new roommate, Stelle is very nice. She can help you decide on a proper husband out of all those Firsts and Seconds (ick).

Please tell Pol and Rane and Father I love them very much.

More than all my love,
Scilla

* * *

Scilla set down her pen and stretched her aching fingers. She'd gone through every fingertip gathering the blood that cracked open the Door and her hands were a swollen mess. The simple act of holding the pen and writing a letter was terribly painful. It was a good thing she had become indifferent about taking notes in class.

It had all seemed so simple—the demon grabs her silly sister, and they arrive at the stumps three days later. The Door opens, and the demon is led off to whatever appropriate fate awaited it. Then, and this was the part Scilla could see the most clearly, the Voice holds out his hand (her hand?) and Scilla herself steps through The Door to her new friends and her new life in glorious, gorgeous Eriis. And

Lelet is left all by herself for a change. She'd be in so much trouble.

The idea that the creature might have hurt her sister was out of the question. No, it wouldn't have hurt her, it had been funny all along about causing a human to come to harm. And Lelet might be a silly cow, but she was at least bright enough to see that the thing holding her captive was dangerous, untrustworthy, and rude to boot. So what if it resembled a pretty human man—it obviously wasn't one. It would be like marrying a dog that happened to have learned to walk upright. No one could be that stupid.

And the rest of them? Well, May always poured out some sugar with her words, but it was clear no one would miss Scilla when she was gone. They all had each other, even Rane and Lelet made a strange sort of pair, and where did that leave her?

Eriis, Scilla said it to herself over and over, an incantation of a sort of paradise, otherwise why would her teachers make it sound like nothing short of hell? If everyone knew the truth, they'd burn the Guardhouse to the ground and join her on the other side.

Now it was the morning of the sixth day, and she was in danger of disappointing the Voice, who had been so kind, the Voice who was her only friend. They had to show up, and it had to be today. It would be.

It was all going to be fine.

* * *

Down three flights of stairs and half a mile of stone corridors, Brother Blue was getting his daily news report.

"Olly, what have we learned?" The old man settled into his creaky leather chair and waited as Olly thumbed through his notebook.

"Well sir, there was a farmstead robbed inside a week ago and the place turned upside down. It was one of the small holdings back towards the city."

"Terrible thing. And the farmer and his family?"

More thumbing. “Nothing to tell. They just vanished. But when the postman came through this morning he said he passed,” and here he quoted his notes, ““a damned big fire done got put out. Day’s ride from here.” Looked to him like a campsite got away from some folks. But,” and here Olly cleverly answered what he knew would be the follow up, “no one at the site and no trace of the campers. Good thing we’ve turned wet, weather-wise, the whole forest could have gone up.” Olly looked expectantly at his master. “Think they’re connected?”

“In my experience, everything is connected, if you wait long enough.”

“Maybe,” Olly speculated, “somebody was burning evidence.” He paused. “But of what? And why not just burn down the house?” He set down his notebook and rubbed the back of his neck. “Not that I’ve planned crimes, sir. Or thought about disposing of a body. Or how not to get caught robbing a house...”

While Olly backtracked, Blue thought about Scilla, and fire, and demons, and wished this whole nasty business had never begun. The last time they’d checked in on her “extracurricular activities,” Scilla had arranged for her pet demon to bring her sister to the Stumps. She’d hinted at something on the other side of The Door, and it smelt to Blue like a prisoner exchange. But that didn’t make sense either. She had a great whopping demon at her beck and call, and even though it appeared to have a terrible temper, who would give such a prize away? What could she be trading it for? What did they have over there that she might want? And why did she want her own sister in the creature’s company? Scilla was a deep dark lake, indeed. But she’d packed her candle away and with it the only way Blue could keep an eye on her. They couldn’t risk having the demon loose in the countryside, particularly after it had resulted in Scilla’s brother cutting his hand. The only way to get the creature back where it belonged was to let the voices call out to Scilla, as they called out to so many members of her family, and hope for the best. So it was agreed to lower the Guardhouse’s ancient charms of protection and let her communicate once again with the other side. Truly, it hadn't worked out so well for her mother or her brother, but Scilla seemed to be made of harder clay.

"Oh," said Olly. "I should have said this first. The postman also said he spotted a man and white haired girl at the Split Tree the inn yesternoon. That has to be them. The, uh, demon. And Scilla's sister."

Blue frowned. "The Split Tree? What were they doing there?" The place had a bad reputation, a nasty creature like a demon might pass unnoticed. But a well-bred human lady? That would raise an eyebrow.

Olly looked at his notes. "They appeared to be having lunch," he replied. "But if they're heading this way, they should be at the stumps by the end of the day."

"Well then." Blue extended a hand and Olly scurried to help him to his feet. "This whole unpleasantness will be over by first moonrise. He chuckled and shook his head. "Dining with a demon. That young lady is lucky to be alive. Olly my boy, let's go talk about places in the trees, and go quietly unobserved, shall we? It may be a long day; do pack us some lunch."

Burned places and robbed places and places no human should ever go. Blue was anxious to get some answers at last.

Chapter 10

Eriis

"WE EARNED THIS house," Niico's father would say when into his drink, and slam his hand on the ashboard dining table. "We earned it and we stay." Sometimes he would croon his late wife's name, and sometimes he would cry, which made Niico feel sick. She was gone, all the nice things were gone, but from the house she earned on her back, his father swore, they would not be moved.

Niico grew to realize what he was good at: he was quick and strong, and that made the other children at school keep a civil head in their mouths no matter how used and faded your tunic was. No one called his mother sdhaach twice.

He was quick; he learned how to take the nice things he wanted, not like the Ugly Prince who had everything set before him, who only wore the finest clothing, went well fed and happy, and always with that beautiful little companion by his side.

He thought sometimes about his mother and the old king, and when those thoughts turned to white flame he made sure to take something nice for himself.

He was only caught once.

* * *

"Are you certain you won't come out later?" Niico asked Aelle.

"Have you gone simple?" she replied. "I said no five times. I'm going to take a nap, the heat's slamming my eyes shut."

The heat, thought Niico, *and the bottle of sarave I practically poured down your throat*. She'd sleep the afternoon away. Siia was locked in her room chanting over her stones, although whether she prayed to Light and Wind for the safety of her children, or simply used it as an excuse to absent herself, he didn't know. And Yuenne was out for the day as well. He had been in fine spirits when he'd set out with the Zaal, calling to Siia not to set a place for either one at dinner.

"We might be quite late coming back," he said to her as he came out of his study and reached for his scarf. "Put in a good word for me with your little rocks."

That was good. That meant he had some time. But it also meant they were nearly out of it.

Now Yuenne's house was quiet, other than the ever present wind in the eaves. The window scrims were closed against the dust and it was almost cool. Niico quietly closed Aelle's door and stood in the hallway. He closed his eyes and saw Yuenne's study. He opened them, and he was there. He wished he had more time to look around, for it appeared that Yuenne did not practice austerity when it came to his own comfort. The desk was real wood—no, there were two wooden desks. A marvel. One nearly black with age, it looked to have been well used for things that burned or melted or leaked. The other was gorgeous red-gold, finely veined in a whorled pattern, and like glass under the hand. This was the desk Ilaan said would hold Yuenne's most prized treasures.

Niico lit the small crystal lamp that sat on the desk and quietly pushed back the great, overstuffed armchair. Yet he couldn't help but take an extra second to run his hand along the seat. It was as silky as flesh against his fingers. Peering closely, he could see tiny pores. This was leather. He had read about it.

The drawers were locked of course, but Ilaan had spent enough hours playing under this desk to know that the keys were on a hidden hook. Niico reached under the desk and groped around until his fingertips found them. The noise when they hit the stone floor was deafening.

He heard footsteps and for the first time felt envious of Rhuun—he couldn't disappear into a shadow. Until that moment, he'd never wanted to. He made himself crouch small and hid under the desk, quietly rolling the chair in after him.

The door opened, and a voice said, "Counselor? Are you back early?" A pause. "Anyone in here? Miss Aelle?" He watched the maid's feet go by as she adjusted the window scrims. Satisfied, she headed for the door. But she paused, hand on the latch.

"How did this..." Her voice was right above him.

Do not get caught. As Niico prepared to shimmer out of the room, it went dark. The maid had put out the glowing stone. More footsteps, and then the door shut.

Once his heart slowed to something like normal, Niico counted to fifty and crawled out from under the desk. "Like a jumpmouse," he whispered. "Like two jumpmice." Not daring to relight the lamp, he tried key after key on the bottom right hand desk drawer until, with a tiny click, it unlocked. He opened the drawer and reached inside.

Chapter 11

Mistra

FINALLY!

Scilla spotted the pair heading her way down the forest path. But something was wrong. Something was very, very wrong.

Instead of her pet demon leading her sister, cold and disheveled, with her hands tied by a piece of twine, with her eyes red from crying, and her hair full of twigs, she saw something quite different.

They were walking slowly—strolling—there could be no other word for it—strolling towards her, and they were holding hands! Her sister, although wearing the ugliest dress Scilla had ever seen, looked as if she had not a carc in the world. And *her demon*, her toy, her pet—the one she'd personally dragged through the Veil—was gazing at Lelet with nothing short of adoration. It took her a minute to place his expression. He looked happy. And despite the chill in the air, they both looked rosy and warm.

This was intolerable.

"What is this?" she snapped. "Demon, step away from her."

Moth looked Scilla in the eye and placed his arm around Lelet's shoulder. "No, I don't think I will."

"But you have to! I bound you! Get away from her. Do as I say."

"What did I tell you?" Moth said to Lelet. "She's an absolute slave driver. I don't know what they're teaching at that school of hers, but your family should look into it."

Scilla felt the blood draining out of her head. The Voice had warned her again, only this morning, that the demon might try to escape at the last minute. It was obviously using her sister's lack of wits to try and gain its freedom. Well, they'd both be in for a surprise. Scilla had carefully said the words the Voice had taught her, and as soon as she saw them, a flash of color far away through the trees, she'd stabbed herself in the finger. She could no longer make a fist—she was a great believer in the discipline of practice—but it was a small price to pay. Soon, she'd be on her way and the demon with her, leaving Lelet to tidy up. And her slut of a sister wasn't going to ruin her plans by taking her demon away, not when she was so close.

"I bound this creature," said Scilla, "and it belongs to me. You can't have everything of mine. Whatever you did to him, give him back."

Lelet smiled. "He's not mine to give. If he feels like it, he can tell you how your charm got broken." The pair exchanged a look, and the creature's hand crept to a scar on his throat, one faint silver line among many. "But he belongs only to himself." He leaned down and whispered something in her ear and she fairly glowed. Then she looked back at Scilla. "Look, I'll tell you what. I won't murder you with my bare hands for arranging this little adventure—or ask Moth to do it, and he's got plenty of reasons— we won't hurt you. But we are going to have a conversation."

Scilla fumed silently.

"This is serious, Scil. This," Lelet said, squeezing the demon's shoulder, "is a person. Not some sort of puppet. And whatever I did to make you so angry—"

"This creature is a monster, it's not a person at all, and if you had any brains you'd know it," Scilla said. "You wouldn't be standing there slobbering all over it."

"Why do you say these things?" asked the demon. She glared at him and said nothing. He continued. "I told you when you bound me there would be repercussions. I think we'll meet them today." He took a step towards her and she remembered the burning creature that had fallen into her cell. She backed away and he shook his head. "Not from me, I told you I would never harm you and I meant it. Would a monster hesitate to take its revenge? Would—what else did you call me? A base criminal? What did I do to you, Scilla?"

"You'll find out," she answered, "The Voice told me, the Voice told me what to do, the Voice loves me, it's my true friend and it told me all about you. You escaped from Eriis and they will have you back. The Voice told me how to bind you and they're coming for you. Soon."

Lelet and Moth shared a glance, like they were the oldest, best friends.

"Whatever happens," Moth told her quietly, "stay well back." Then to Scilla, "I see this Voice is your good friend. I think he might be my friend as well, I think there must be a misunderstanding between us."

"You think the Voice is also your friend? You have funny friends, demon." Scilla took her notebook out of her pocket and flipped the pages, full of her most recent correspondence. *"...a well-known corrupting influence..."* she read, *"...degraded creature ....this monster ....A beast."* She snapped the book shut and tucked it back in her pocket. "If that's your friend, what do your enemies say about you?"

She was satisfied to note that he looked less happy now and more as if he'd been slapped. Scilla glanced around nervously, not sure what she was supposed to look for. The Door had never actually opened in her presence, despite the words and her blood. The agreed upon hour was almost over. All she'd ever felt was a rush of heat in the air, almost as if someone was taking a peek, or a sniff, and then it would fade away.

Lelet was tugging on the creature's arm. "Come on, this is pointless. She doesn't know anything. We'll meet dos Capeheart another way. Try the front door or something."

Scilla frowned. That name again.

The air behind them began to shimmer with heat, and Scilla leapt back and hid herself behind her sister from the blast of baking hot wind that rushed through the open Door.

It looked like a regular door in any home on any world, but instead of the stumps and the forest and the Guardhouse looming behind it, there was a vast grey brown desert, dotted with distant firewhirls. Off to the right under the low, dirty sky, there rose an ancient, heavily weathered sand colored city hard up against a ragged line of cliffs. In The Doorway stood a man, small and slight in stature, with a dirty, torn tunic that had once been fine white silk. His long black hair, only slightly touched by grey, hung around his dark crimson eyes, which were tilted like those of a cat and heavily lined by many days under the hot skies of Eriis. He had a smear of dust on his face and a fresh burn on the back of one hand. He was out of breath and held up a hand to compose himself before he could speak. Scilla gasped. Was this her Voice? A man, he was a little man old enough to be her father. She bit back her disappointment, because the man looked to be in distress. Oddly, her demon addressed the little demon man as if they were acquaintances.

Moth took a step towards The Door. “Yuenne? Counselor? Are you all right?”

“Alive, thank Light and Wind,” gasped the man. “I’ve found you at last. Our work is not in vain.” He dropped his hands to his thighs and continued to gasp for breath.

Moth drew closer. “What’s happened?”

“It’s your mother. Terrible...terrible...”

Lelet took Moth’s arm. “What’s going on? Who is this? It’s not—”

“This is Counselor Yuenne. He is my mother’s advisor and father to my friends.” He frowned. “I don’t know what brings him here in such disarray.”

Lelet took a step towards him. “Are you well, sir? Do you need our help?” Moth took her arm in a firm hold to prevent her from getting any closer.

Yuenne stood up and looked through The Door at the scene. “But where is my Scilla? She ought to be here.”

He said her name. He knew her. Whatever he looked like, he was her Voice. Scilla peered around Lelet’s shoulder. “I’m here.” She slipped past her sister and Moth. “But it looks all wrong. Where are the rivers? Why is it all sand? And are those fires?"

"I only have a few moments," Yuenne told them. "Scilla, I'll explain everything, but I need you both to come now. Prince Rhuun, it's your mother, she's in terrible danger. The Mages have risen against her, she needs your help." He gave an exhausted laugh. "It seems only you can help her, after all. Finally, your chance. But there's no time." Something exploded in the air above and behind him, and they all jumped. "The Mages—she needs you. Hurry!"

Lelet hauled Scilla back. "You don't intend to go with him, do you? What's he told you?"

"That Eriis is beautiful and I'll be happy." She addressed Yuenne. "Why did you call him the prince? He's a monster."

"He is the prince, and as he well knows, he is also a beast. Am I mistaken?"

"He is not mistaken," Moth said.

Yuenne nodded and continued. "But now it seems he may redeem himself in our world, if he is brave enough to do it." The edges of The Door buckled and shimmered. "Please, both of you...the queen and our city are in desperate need."

Moth and Lelet spent a moment pawing at each other. Scilla tried not to watch, but she heard them say 'It's your mother,' and 'I wish we had more time.' There was some kissing. Yuenne, for that was the Voice's name, eyed the pair with the same disdain she felt. She noticed he changed his expression to one of relief and gratitude when Moth broke away from Lelet and joined him. He walked through The Door without a backward glance. Scilla also wished she had more time, because some parts of this weren't adding up. But Moth knew the Voice and trusted him, and the Voice seemed to genuinely need Moth's help—and her own.

"Scilla, hurry!" cried Yuenne. The Door warped and sparked, it was collapsing. "Will you come and help us, my sister?"

She pulled away from Lelet's grasp. "Let me go, I promised."

"That you did," Yuenne said. He held his hand out. "And we must be quick."

Scilla took a step towards him as Lelet reached for her again, but as she did Scilla's eyes widened. She gasped and held up her hands. Something had bitten her under her gown; it was still stinging, and it was burning her arms. As she shook her sleeves, the dark brown fabric stuck to her wet skin. She looked down at the rapidly spreading bloodstains on her bodice, and began to whimper. Lelet pulled off her soaked robe, and gasped at the sight of her writhing, moving flesh. Scilla stood with her arms out as the words began to form, carving themselves into her arms and chest. She began to scream.

LIES DON'T GO HE LIES DON'T GO DON'T GO DONT GO YUENNE LIES DON'T GO DON'T GO DON'T GO LIES ITS LIES DON'T GO YUENNE LIES DON'T GO DON'T GO DON'T GO DON'T GO DON'T GO DON'T GO DON'T GO DONT YUENNE LIES DON'T GO DON'T

"No! Moth! No!" Lelet screamed and scrambled to pull him back through, but was left with a handful of sand. All that remained was the smell of dead ash from where The Door stood. It was gone.

Chapter 12

Eriis
5 hours earlier

THIS IS IT?" Ilaan asked.

Niico had handed Ilaan the flat, narrow box and collapsed onto the bed, where he remained on his back, his scarf still hiding his face. He was out of breath and shaking.

"It had better be," Niico replied, his voice slightly muffled. "Nothing else looked even close. I take it back about spying, by the way. I am too delicate."

Ilaan put the box down and sat next to Niico, untying his scarf and putting it aside. "You are as delicate as a rock wall. And as strong." He opened the box. "Let's see what we've got."

He held up a slim cylinder made of the common stone of Eriis, smooth and pale yellow, blunt at one end and ragged and rough at the tip. "It's gotten a workout over the years," he said. "I remember it being longer."

"What is it? It looks like a pen."

"It is a sort of pen. It...one might say it pokes a hole in the Veil and lets you talk to the humans. I used to play with it. I didn't know what it was for, back then. I was only five, maybe six. I was in my father's study. I climbed onto his chair and found it in one of the drawers. I remember being angry, I wanted sweets but Mother said it was too close to dinner. I drew pictures of my sweets—little circles—on his blotter, and then wrote "Eat them up" or something. Then he came in and took it away, said it wasn't a toy." He twirled the stone pen between his fingers. "He locked the drawers after that. So, someone over there is connected to the stones. I wonder how that happened." As Ilaan held the pen up, his eyes became hazy and unfocused, and his voice sounded both softer and deeper. "Magic is literal," he said. "You were right. This is a pen. It makes words. Words want to be heard. This pen will find something to write on, be it a piece of paper or a brick wall, or a mind. It wants to be heard. My father was talking to someone. Someone heard his words. If we want our words to be heard, I must see who is listening." He pointed at his shelf. "That bowl."

"The bowl is listening?" Ilaan just stared at him. It felt strange, to be stared at. "Oh, sorry."

Niico scrambled to set the stone bowl in front of him. It had a glossy grey outer surface, but the interior was coarse and unfinished. Ilaan took the rough end of the pen and began to grind it into the mortar.

"What are you going to do with that?" Niico asked. "Eat it?"

"No. The pen is to speak. The dust is to see." Ilaan poured the grit into his hands, and before Niico could cry out or try to stop him, he crushed the handful of sand into his eyes. He dropped his head and ground his palms against his face, rubbing hard and wailing in what might have been pain. Then he went quiet.

"Ilaan?" Niico wanted to pull his hands away and see what damage he'd caused himself, but was afraid to get too close. There was a smell of dust and blood in the room. It smelled like the Zaal, bitter and strange.

Ilaan looked up. His face was a dusty whitish mask, dotted with blood from where the grit had scraped the skin. His eyes were completely blank and dirty white; the bright red irises gone. "Ah. There they are."

"There who are? Are you all right?" Niico was nearly frantic, and Ilaan's serene smile and calm voice made it somehow worse.

"I can see them, like little lights. The brightest light is Rhuun, like a star in the sky." Niico felt the old pain in his heart. He might have been a star in his *shani's* sky as well, but he'd never be the brightest. He had always struggled with the notion of a sky big enough for many stars.

Ilaan picked up the stone pen and pointed it up. Tiny lights flickered on, dotting the low ceiling. "You know there are stars above us every night? We just can't see them. But I can see them now." He twirled the pen again, and the constellations overhead slowly drifted and spun. "And there are humans with him. Two of them, close together. One big and one small. They are connected to the rock and bone of Eriis. I wonder how? Ah, look—two more. But they aren't—no. They *are* all important. I don't know how, yet, but they are."

Niico tore his eyes away from the lovely spinning lights above them and leaned over Ilaan, who stared blindly around the room. "Okay—four humans and Rhuun, little lights, now what?" *If this goes wrong, who do I call?* He had to back away, Ilaan was putting off waves of heat, far hotter than even the flames of joining. Niico could see the fire of his True Face flickering just below his skin. "Ilaan, can you hear me? What happens now?" *If this goes wrong, how do I stop it?*

"Why are there so many?" Ilaan squinted at the scene only he could see, making the white dust on his face crack and flake. "There are too many. I don't..." Then he gave a long, shuddering sigh, and the stars overhead winked out. "My father. He is in Mistra and in Eriis and yet not. He is in between. He does not fear the Veil. Where is the Zaal?" He was becoming less composed. The bitter smell was fading, and tears joined the blood running down Ilaan's face, making golden tracks in the white dust. His clear red eyes swam up through the filmy haze. "I have to let them know...but who?" He looked around wildly, but Niico didn't know if he saw the room or the scene unfolding on the other side of The Door. The great heat had receded slightly, he drew as close as he could to Ilaan.

"What's happening?" Niico asked.

"I'm losing them. I don't know which one to warn. This pen talks to a human, I thought there'd be only one. What if

I tell the wrong one, or what if it's too late? His star is moving away. He is fading away."

Niico swallowed his fear and gripped Ilaan's arm. His hands began to smoke. "I'm going to help you." He guided Ilaan's hand until the pen point touched the table. "Do you see them still? Rhuun, and the four humans?"

"Yes. They are drifting apart. But yes, I see them. Big and small." Ilaan shivered. "Young and old. I don't know..."

"The small one," Niico decided. "Pick the smallest one and warn them. Do it now."

"But who...I don't know..."

"They will kill him." Niico knew they were nearly out of time. "He's the brightest star in your sky, and they'll kill him. Pick one and warn them."

Ilaan settled back into his seat, and began to write.

Chapter 13

Mistra

OLLY DIDN'T WAIT for Brother Blue when the screaming started. By the time the old man reached the two young women and his assistant, the boy had Scilla wrapped in his own cloak, and he and the sister were frantically trying to stop the blood that seeped from the myriad of scratches on Scilla's arms and chest.

Blue knelt next to Scilla and gently examined her arm.

"I believe these look worse than they really are," he told her in a low and soothing voice. "See? They are stopping already. Shallow." How the marks had gotten there and what they meant could wait until she—and her sister—were back in the Guardhouse.

Olly lifted the girl and they made their way back through the trees. Scilla's sobs had tapered off, but Lelet's had not. She hadn't wanted to leave the stumps at all.

"He might come back. He might escape," she said, referring, Blue assumed, to the bigger of the two demons. But ultimately she didn't want to leave her sister either. "We have a lot to talk about." At that, Scilla turned her face to Olly's shirtfront and began to sob again.

Blue shook his head at this foolishness. Demons. Bad business, the lot of them. They would have quite a lot of sorting out to do.

* * *

Once the group had gotten settled in his study, Blue decided to question the two girls together. It was too much trouble to consider separating them at this point. Scilla's wounds now seemed to be fading—corrupt magic from the other side, no doubt. Only her youth and vitality had saved her from more blood loss. Strong human stock would always win out over whatever nasty business came from over there. That was good, at any rate. What was less good was the display of emotion going on in front of him. Hysterics. Olly had wisely retreated to the chair in the corner.

If there was one thing Blue couldn't abide, it was hysterical women.

First it had been his mother so long ago, weeping and howling over his 'disgrace.' Well, she'd been proven wrong, hadn't she? His disgrace forgiven and a damned fine life to show for it, here at the Guardhouse. Now he had two new ones. He'd get one calmed down and the other would start back up. At the moment, the white haired one, the older sister was leaning over his desk. He had Olly give her a blanket to wrap over her ridiculous dress, but she'd thrown it on the floor. She had a big leather bag slung over her shoulder which she refused to put down. She was also armed. He kept one eye on the knife shoved into her belt. Its blade was stained with rust. It had to be rust, he thought. Rust or mud.

"Why aren't you listening to me? They're going to kill him! We have to open The Door!"

Blue sipped his tea. "We will do no such thing. And I assure you, that creature is perfectly safe, if you can call a life in that squalid hole safe. Don't you see how you were fooled by its wiles? How you both were?"

"It? Stop! He is not an 'it', stop saying that!" she shrieked.

Yes, thought Blue, another victim of these seductive villains. Another hysterical woman.

"His name is Moth," she continued, "and he is a good man. He saved my life, we have to get him back."

"Well, that is how they work. I'm sure it told you a lot of pretty stories, my dear. But you may rest assured they were all lies. That is all they know how to do." He set his cup down. "I certainly hope you did not allow it to...take liberties with your person."

Lelet would have launched herself across the desk if Scilla hadn't grabbed her by the back of the ugly brown dress.

"Brother Blue," Scilla said, "I can explain."

"Oh," he smiled, "I most heartily doubt that. But you are welcome to try. Let's begin with who is a liar and where you were advised not to go. Someone went to marvelous lengths to warn you. Friend of yours, I gather?"

Scilla held up her arm—the scratches were now just a maze of red lines, as if she'd stumbled into a berry patch. "I don't..." He recognized her expression; it was the look of no longer being sure.

"We've been keeping a close eye on you since the Veil incident. Did you think it was forgotten?" asked Blue. She did think we'd forgotten, he thought. As if the lot of us haven't spent our lives keeping The Door shut, and this little chit thinks she can waltz through it whenever her demon friends call her name. va'Everly. The whole family, he thought, looking at the two women, Well, we'll probably have to return the endowment. It was a risk accepting someone with that name to begin with. "Once we realized you were in contact with one of those creatures, it was only a matter of shoring up our defenses. We were interested in what you were doing with that big one, though. He was rather different than any demon in our records, we thought perhaps you'd somehow recruited a human to torment your sister."

"She made Moth her slave," snapped Lelet. "You should throw her out the window."

"It deserved it, and so did you. It was just a criminal," said Scilla.

"Stop. Saying. It." gritted Lelet. "Who told you he was a criminal? Was it the one who warned you not to go?" She gripped Scilla's wrist and held it out. "Or was it the one who tried to take you? What did that man tell you, that it was all sunshine and roses over there? Scilla, what is wrong with you? You never used to be so stupid!"

"Stupid is you believing anything that monster told you. Did he tell you he was in the house? In your room?"

"Yes. He told me everything. Everything you made him do." Lelet was crying again, blotting her face on a white gown she'd pulled from the leather bag. Blue sighed. More hysterics.

Scilla had gotten her color back and looked more herself. Blue had to admire the girl, she was already onto her next scheme.

She asked Blue, "How did you know? That it was a demon, I mean. How did you know we'd be there today?"

"The candle, dear. You did a fine job of charming it, it showed us everything the demon saw. A perfect record. When we get this sorted, we'll be adding it to our library, so please do not lose it. We were sometimes looking over your shoulder, so to speak. We finally decided enough was enough after your brother's incident with the broken mirror—we didn't intend to let things escalate to actual bloodshed. We let the creature's folk contact you again. And look! It's gone, no harm done to the Order, and everyone back in their place. Door shut. Now, what to do about you?"

"Yes, it's shut," said Scilla. "I have to stay here and help keep it shut. Those people are a nightmare, that place is a wasteland. Please, let me stay. I broke a promise to that man, the one who took Moth. If he gets back through, he's going to come for me."

Blue looked at her appraisingly. "So no more deals with demons? And this time you mean it?"

Her eyes shone with the dedication of the newly converted. He recognized that look as well. "Nothing," she said, "is more important."

Lelet looked at her sister with disgust. "But it's not shut. There's something you don't know. About him."

Blue cut her off with a wave of his hand. "I assume you still refer to the big one. We know more about The Door and certainly much more about demons than you, my dear. Even one of their own took it on itself to send a warning, so the ones we saw today must be particularly notorious. They don't want us meddling any more than we want them coming here. Just because they were having one of their little fights doesn't have anything to do with us. I gather they're breeding them bigger now. Obviously it's to be regretted that one of them had a great effect on you, and I suppose we should thank you for your sacrifice, since it's led us to new information. You can't really be blamed, though. They are a race of seducers and you didn't know any better."

"You're wrong," she said through her tears. "He wasn't a liar." She held up the dress. "He fixed it, just like he said."

Blue spent a second trying to imagine what she was talking about, then gave up. "How many years of study on the topic of those monsters have you done?" Blue asked her. "What are you, a Third? Hmmm? You don't seem to have the wits of a First; I don't see you running a Family business. And if you were a Second you'd most likely be properly wed by now and not running wild all over the countryside with...well. This was an exciting adventure, but it's time to take your pretty dress and go home, back to your friends and parties."

"I am a Fourth, and he came here to see you," said Lelet. "We came here even though we knew there was a chance The Door might open, because of you."

"Well, that's highly unlikely, but if it got him back where he—it—belongs—"

"He read your stupid book, old man." Blue gaped at her. "All the way over there on Eriis, he somehow got a copy of *The Claiming of the Duke*, and thought you were some kind of genius. He told me your book changed his life. Just because he has crap taste in literature doesn't make him a monster."

"My....what did you say his name was?" Had the room gotten colder? Blue felt a chill.

"He told me his name was Moth, but that isn't his real name. I don't know it and it doesn't matter. But he did tell me who his mother is. He's the Prince. His mother is the Queen."

"And who is this prince's father?" Blue asked faintly.

“He doesn’t know the man’s name. But he does know one thing and that does matter. His father was a human.”

“Lies,” Blue whispered, “Lies.” Hellne...did you figure it out after all? That little escape hatch I came up with a hundred years gone, you gave it to your son, and he came here...he’d be a man by now....it cannot be... He passed a shaking hand over his face.

Olly stepped in front of the desk. “Can’t you see he’s ill? This day has been too much for him. You both need to go.”

“Go?” Lelet pushed the boy aside. “There’s only one place I want to go. You want to keep your precious Door in place? Because pretty soon, it’s coming off the hinges. That’s what he’s for, that’s why they want him back. He’s not a monster or a criminal or a key. He’s not a beast. He’s a weapon. Now, I don’t care if there’s a Door or not, but I’m not going to let him die if there’s even a chance I can save him. And you’re going to help me.”

Brother Blue had gone quite grey. “Is this possible? Is it true?” *Hellne, what else were you keeping from me?*

Lelet looked at Scilla and at Blue. “You’re both so clever, aren’t you? A whole building full of clever people. Well, now you’re going to figure out how to get me there.” She slammed the dagger on the desk. “You’re going to figure out how to hide my face, and I’m going to Eriis and I’m bringing him home. And then both of you and this place and that damned Door can go straight to hell.”

Blue caught Scilla’s eye. *She might be of use after all*, he thought.

“It is not impossible...” he began.

“Is there precedent..?” she asked.

“Olly,” said Blue, “I am going to need some books. I’ll make you a list.”

The white haired sister, who had finally stopped her wailing, curled up in the corner in Blue’s good chair. She held the ugly dagger up and stared at the light on the blade. Blue thought she looked a little mad.

“Hurry,” she said.

Chapter 14

Mistra

IN THE END, they'd sent Lelet home.

"Don't worry, my dear," Brother Blue would say, "we'll get this figured out. But you must understand it's quite complicated. There is no room for error. They will know a forgery in an instant. If we get anything wrong..."

Scilla said, "Quit looking over my shoulder, you're driving me crazy."

Nearly a month of drifting up and down the hallways of the Guardhouse, ignoring the stares of the young novices and the outright contempt of the older brothers and sisters. She was the girl who laid down with a demon, they told each other, not kidnapped at all, but by the side of that foul creature on purpose—worthy of nothing but scorn. No one could understand why Brother Blue was letting her stay, much less lock himself away with her for hours. And Sister Scilla? She had the rest of her life to prove whose side she was on. It was a mystery the residents of the Guardhouse couldn't unlock.

"Nothing to do with you," Olly would say to those who asked. "Brother knows what he's doing. Let that girl alone." As Blue's right hand, he felt obligated to try and explain his master's initial dismissiveness. He tried to apologize to Lelet, reminding her that after all, no one knew this one was a good demon—no one knew any of them were good, really. She'd said nothing, but put her hand on the knife she carried everywhere. He gave her as wide a berth as possible after that, and advised everyone else to do the same.

* * *

Whenever Lelet tried to sleep, her last moments with Moth played on an endless loop behind her closed lids.

The stumps, the trees, the Guardhouse in the distance, and the smell of the sea. Then only the smell of the other, burning world, and they were saying goodbye.

She threw her arms around his neck and they kissed. "You are not a beast," she whispered pressing her lips against the dark silk of his hair. "You are my beautiful darling. Never forget it. But it's your mother. I understand." She brushed tears off her cheeks. "I wish we had more time. Go save the world."

He pressed his forehead against hers. "*Shani*. How could I ever forget? I'm sorry you never got to show me bo-hats," he said. "But you are an excellent tour guide, for a wench." He smiled, the smile she would carry with her for the rest of her life, and he kissed her again. And then he turned and walked through The Door and out of sight.

But it had all been a lie, and every moment she spent in ease and comfort brought Moth another moment closer to his death—if they hadn't murdered him already.

She didn't sleep much.

* * *

She'd been stirring the normally placid waters of the Guardhouse for a full month when Blue called her into his study. She took the good chair in the corner, but immediately got up to pace.

"You've got something?" she asked. "You found the answer?" They'd found dozens of old volumes devoted to life on Eriis before the war, books that had been locked away as possibly corrupting influences, books Blue hadn't seen since his youth. They answered questions like how tall and what shape and what color, but as to the act of transformation, there was no clue.

"That doesn't mean it isn't there," he reassured her. "They tried to tell us, the demons, they explained it over and over, so I know it's there, we just haven't found it." He thought perhaps it was also locked in his memory, somewhere behind a wall of beatings and grief.

"And once you do? Will it work?" She looked exhausted. Worry had taken its toll on her, and he'd gotten numerous reports of her wandering the hallways in the hours before dawn.

"Well, you've threatened to string me up and make a necklace of my eyeballs on several occasions. I think it's in everyone's best interest if it works."

"That's not an answer, old man." She would not be placated. But Blue had been dealing with young people, some of them nearly as angry and frustrated as this one, his entire life, and wouldn't be intimidated.

"Lelet, I think it's best if you go back to the city. Your sister has written to ask after you and I would like you to reply and tell her you'll be home soon." She opened her mouth to argue but he cut her off. "We will continue our work, Scilla and I, and when we have the answer, you will know. Remember, time runs differently on Eriis. It's likely your young man has been back there only briefly."

"He could be dead by now. And—"

"And I am to blame for allowing that little man to contact Scilla, yes, I believe we've established that." Blue had not told Lelet his suspicions regarding the big demon's parentage. It was so long ago, and if it were true (and it certainly seemed likely to be true) he had a lifetime of ignorance to look back on, much to answer for, and many questions he knew would probably go unanswered. But tell the girl? The recrimination he'd see in her eyes, that would be too much to bear. "But you are a distraction to Scilla, and the other students are asking difficult questions. You understand we are in the business of keeping The Door shut, not marching through it. We will get more done with you safely home." She glared at the floor and he said, "Lelet, we have already made arrangements. You'll leave tomorrow. Please." He pushed a notecard and pen across his desk.

"Inform your sister you are on your way back to the city." The girl bit back whatever argument or insult was on her tongue and did as he asked, tossed the pen on his desk, and left without a word. *We will figure this out*, thought Blue. *She may never come back, but at least my...at least the prince won't die alone.*

* * *

Lelet returned to her little stone room and looked at her possessions. It wouldn't take long to pack. All she had was an ugly brown dress, a knife, and her white party dress, which, as she discovered, had been meticulously repaired.

I will come for you, she promised, and for the hundredth time held the fragile garment to her face. She could smell wild woodsmoke, faintly. She folded it and put it in the leather bag, along with the hat, which she decided she would keep safe for Moth's return. He hated that hat.

The trip back from the Guardhouse to the city was considerably less exciting and much quicker than the one she'd taken in the other direction. When they passed the inn she'd visited with Moth, she smelled smoke from the stale fire, but she didn't look out the window, and they didn't stop. Sometimes she stared out the window of the carriage, seeing nothing. Other times she stared at the ceiling and pictured the stars and the moons crossing the sky, and the glow that a pile of stones might shed. She looked at her own hands and wondered what it would be like to be him; to use your hands to make rocks turn to flame. When they passed the remains of a house, long destroyed by fire and barely claiming a roof, she realized she had no tears left to cry.

Chapter 15

Mistra

MAY MET LELET at the front door with a warm embrace and a good deal of confusion.

"Darling, your note—we couldn't make any sense of it at all! You look a fright. Go have a bath and get into your own clothes and we'll sit and have a nice talk. I'll call for some lunch." May didn't mention the knife at her hip or the unusual brown dress. She couldn't help but see the pain in Lelet's eyes. Her sister looked to have aged ten years.

"Do you want me to go upstairs?" asked Stelle. "Perhaps you two ought to talk privately."

"No." She took Stelle's hand. "It's the three of us, now. Stay."

x x x

When Lelet came down for their lunch, May thought she looked a bit more herself. Although, the dark blue, plain cotton dress and sturdy, flat shoes were hardly her sister's typical attire. More disturbingly, she'd let her hair grow out so you could see the dark roots. If nothing else, this alone was cause for alarm. But May thought she'd best not jump in with questions. Lelet would come around to telling her story in her own time.

"Have you heard from Father? And Rane? How did Pol settle in?" Lelet asked between bites of cold curried chicken and toasted wheat loaf. She ate like she hadn't seen a proper meal for weeks.

"Father is fine, and tells me that Rane says he hates it, but he's got some color in his face and has even found a pack of hoodlums to go around with. He's learning how to ski, of all things. Pol is still trying to get used to not having to do paperwork." May thought Pol might change his mind about life in the country. "He has a part in a play that opens next month and plans to take the stage by storm. They have a nice little community out there."

"I've missed you," Lelet told her. "So much has happened..." her mouth tightened and she took a sip of tea.

"Your note, love. You said you met someone. You said everything is different." May's thoughts returned to the sad-eyed beauty she'd shared an afternoon with; the disappearing, reappearing ghost who liked port and said his name was Moth. Although it was silly, she found she was sorry that Lelet had found someone else, presumably someone with a pulse. She wondered if the ghost's next thing made him happy.

"I want you to understand that everything I am going to tell you is true." Stelle and May looked at each other curiously. Lelet was not a notorious liar, why should they doubt her? "Let me think how to begin," she said. "It all started when I was kidnapped by a demon."

May took Lelet's hands between her own. "I know it must feel overwhelming right now, but we will love you no matter what you decide. It doesn't matter who the father is."

Lelet gave a muffled shriek. "May. I am not pregnant!"

"It's just not Billah, is it? I mean, if he is the father, I suppose—"

"May! Not pregnant!"

"Well, darling, when you tell us something like that, what are we supposed to think?" She hadn't been angry until this point, only worried. "First you were staying with friends at the coast. Then, no, you were with Scilla. Then this note— If you weren't doing something foolish, why make something up?"

"Why would I make up something that sounds so absolutely stupid? Okay. Let me start again." She raked back her dark and light hair. "Magic, all the things we think are children's stories, it's all true. But we have it all backwards."

May perked up. "Ghosts? Ghosts are real, though, right?"

Lelet frowned. "Probably? I guess?" She shook her head and tried to get back on track. "But it really all starts with Scilla. She's so much smarter than we thought, but she's as gullible as any little girl. And she's so, so angry with me."

Lelet did her best to explain how The Door and the world beyond were more than legends, and how their little sister had captured a demon. "She still won't tell me exactly what happened, but they—the demons—they contacted her somehow. She called the demon she talked to The Voice, she said she spoke to it, and it spoke to her. It made her promises. It turned her against us."

May frowned. Hearing voices, Scilla wasn't the first member of the va'Everly family to claim unseen voices spoke to them. Scilla might be the first of the clan to talk back, though. Their mother, for instance, had called it her Gentleman. May spent many hours as a little girl hearing her mother talk about her mysterious friend The Gentleman, until her mother stopped talking to May and then stopped making sense. Finally, May recalled, she'd stopped talking at all. And then the pills. She turned her attention back to Lelet, coldly aware both her sisters might be heading in the same direction. She herself was the only one spared.

That was when she thought again of the ghost. No, he was real, she recalled that Rane saw him as well. Rane saw him. Yes, Rane, who chatted with dogs, a reliable witness. May forced herself to return to Lelet's tale.

"...and that's when Scilla had him kidnap me. It was the night of the Quarter Moons party. I was with him for over a week."

May was horrified. This was the last thing she'd expected. Was it possible they were talking about a real person after all? "Lelly, did he hurt you? How did you escape?"

"It wasn't like that," she said. "And I wasn't afraid of him. It was like an adventure, at first. He was...is..." she broke off.

"He's what?" asked May. "Lelly, you know how this sounds, don't you?" So far none of this made any sense to her, least of all Scilla's part in it. Maybe it wasn't the same affliction that carried off their mother, but that gave her little comfort. A real man could do as much damage as an imaginary one, more. She was still leaning towards Lelet running off with some handsome boy, and hadn't completely ruled out a pregnancy. Perhaps the man was married? She looked like she'd been through something terrible, not like a girl who just had a whirlwind romance.

But Lelet stuck with her story. "I know what he is. I know for sure. He can do things regular people can't."

"Like what? Break your heart and leave you stranded? Any man can do that." Stelle put her hand on May's knee. She took a breath. "Sorry, Lel, but it has to be more than 'he told me so'."

"He can disappear, he can step into a shadow and just vanish. Can any man do that? Can you?"

May set down her cup hard enough to splash tea into her saucer. "Like literally disappear? Like if he stood on the dark side of a door he'd turn invisible?"

"Yes. I saw him do it, that's what—"

"And he was here at our house?" May's heart began to pound.

Lelet nodded. "And he has the most beautiful eyes I've ever seen. They weren't blue or brown or like regular eyes at all. They were—"

"Red. They were red, weren't they? Lelly, tell me his name."

"His name is Moth," she replied, "but why—"

"Holy hell, *you're* his next thing?" Neither Lelet nor Stelle had ever heard May swear, and they both gaped at her. "He was here! We had port. He's the ghost! I mean, he's not a ghost at all, I *knew* it."

"He liked you, Lelet, I could tell." Now it was Lelet and May's turn to stare at Stelle, who smiled at them over the rim of her teacup. "He would follow you from room to room, it was sweet. Oh, don't look so shocked. Of course I could see him. Poor thing, I didn't want to upset him so I never let on. He *thought* he was invisible, I mean of course part of the time he was. I think he just wasn't very good at it. May, I thought he was a ghost also, so don't feel bad."

"Pol couldn't see him, either," May said. "Rane could, though."

Lelet was mystified. "Why didn't he tell me any of this? He never said any of you ever saw him. May, you *spoke* to him?"

"You make it sound like you can't ask him yourself, Lelly. Where is he?"

And now she had to describe the awful afternoon at the stumps, The Door, the burning desert, and the horrid little man who had lied to them and stolen Moth away. She had to figure out a way to go there, find him in all that sand, and bring him home safely.

"Well, we have to go get him back, don't we?" She was so relieved her sister wasn't destined for the same end as their mother, she would have set out that very moment.

Lelet threw her arms around her sister's neck. "Oh May, thank you. But you have to understand, I can't just go there. I think it's still too hot for humans. And they'd grab me and kill me for my blood in a second. Human blood is the key to everything. That's why I'm getting a new one of these." She pointed at her face. "Instead of throwing her off a bridge, I'm letting Scilla make it up to us by doing some real magic. She's figuring out how to disguise me as one of the demons, and I'm going to go over there and rescue him."

By the time it was all laid out, May was ready to call for dinner. *So my ghost who is not a ghost is actually a prince. And he's half a human as well. So there could be children*...she was already planning the ceremony. Despite the danger and uncertainty, and despite what was undoubtedly the single worst plan she'd ever heard, May had no doubt she'd see Moth again and under far different circumstances. She was a great believer in happy endings.

Chapter 16

Mistra

IT HAD BEEN long enough, it was time to rejoin society.

May practically had to shove Lelet out the front door, after ordering her into a prettier dress.

"You are not going anywhere this evening that requires running through the woods," she'd said. "So why not leave the hiking boots home? Just this one time? And put on a dress not designed for combat?"

The post had already come and nothing new to report from the Guardhouse, so Lelet couldn't use that as an excuse. And it had been nearly two months—Lelet's friends no longer believed she was recovering from a fever contracted the night of the Quarter Moons party. They thought she was snubbing them. So she accepted Althee's dinner invitation, combed and pinned up her freshly bleached hair, put on a green velvet dress, black leather and silk heels, her favorite iron and pinpoint diamond choker, and then the hardest part, a smile on her face and a quip in her mouth.

The cab took her down streets she knew well, she'd been up and down them her whole life. So why didn't it feel like home anymore? She took a deep breath and resolved to give it a chance.

Althee had a cottage at the end of a chic block of shops and cafes. She was one of the few of their group who knew how to cook and in fact had no staff, and the aroma of roasting meat drifted down the front walk (it was something of a joke that they all had to help wash the dishes at the end of the night, so the meal had better be worth the effort). The room was cozy and full of people she knew—people who couldn't fly, disappear, or make her cry. She had to confess, it felt good to be back in a smart outfit with friends she knew and understood. There was drama sometimes, there was the usual amount of petty silliness, but there was no mystery and that felt like a relief. Her friends received her more kindly than she would have expected.

Althee opened the door, releasing a rush of warm, herb scented air, and tugged on her hair. "You're back to white. I have to tell you, I much prefer it."

Lelet pushed a dark coppery curl from her friend's brow. "I don't clash with you anymore."

She took Lelet by the shoulders and looked her over. "And you've gotten thin, you miserable cow."

Lelet laughed. Maybe this would be all right after all. "You look just the same, thank goodness. Is this new? I love it!" Althee favored unusual flowing thigh length dresses over heavy knitted tights rather than gowns or long dresses for evening. The trip she'd taken to the southern provinces as a child had made an impression on her and she was constantly on the hunt for exotic embroidered fabrics that might look garish on anyone else. Tonight it was Ever Blue and gold in a peacock feather pattern over a rich espresso brown. The bright shades complimented her pale skin and dark red hair, and her seamstress made sure the outfit flattered her curves. Lelet took her arm and headed into the little house. "Now make me a drink and tell me everything I missed. It's like I've been locked in a dungeon!"

Her friends had lots of questions, and she had a carefully rehearsed story.

* * *

"It was awful," she told them as they sat down to dinner. "I had this raging fever, walked out the back door and ended up wandering around past the Greenleaf Gate! I could have fallen in the canal! Can you imagine? Per actually found me out thumping around in the mud and had to carry me inside. That's twice he's come to my rescue, I must remember to do something nice for him." Her friends snickered. "Oh, shut up, you people are perverts. Anyway, I barely remember a thing, in bed for all those weeks. And after I just got back on my feet after my fall, I tell you, I feel like I lost a whole season! The only good news is I lost some weight." Althee made a face at her. "And no more smoking!" She took a sip of white wine (she was off the red) and smiled and nodded, agreeing she was lucky to have survived. Yes, it was a pleasure to be out in public. The theater next week? She would check her calendar. A platter of braised rabbit in a mustard cream sauce, fragrant with thyme, came around and she only hesitated for a moment before helping herself.

"So a fever makes you tear your own dress apart?"

Billah. Althee hadn't mentioned he might show up. She hadn't seen him since the night she'd broken it off with him, and now he was standing behind her, uncomfortably close. He'd brought the cold in with him and she thought she could feel his breath on her neck. Her knife, she recalled, was locked in her bedside table. Well, it was unlikely to come to that.

"Billah, how lovely to see you. It's been ages. What are you saying about my dress? I'm afraid as usual I don't know what you're talking about." Her friends all exchanged looks—he'd been telling everyone who'd listen she was lying about being sick. They knew a confrontation was inevitable. Would it end in reconciliation? Or would it get ugly? The atmosphere became charged.

Billah reached into his pocket and pulled out something small, the size of coin. A stiff, white satin rose, dabbed here and there with mud. "This is from your dress. I should know, I've taken it off you often enough." There were some hushed gasps and some laughter, quickly silenced.

"Billah," Althee said warningly. "Don't make me regret the invitation."

"No, its fine," said Lelet. She took the rosette out of his hand and tossed it next to her plate. "You've been carrying this thing around all this time? How sweet. Yes, I suppose I must have pulled it off."

"And does a fever make you fly? Because there were footsteps, and then there weren't."

She kept her face still. "Go ahead and tell us what really happened, Billah." She had her fork gripped in her hand under the table, just in case.

"I went down there the next day, after you didn't show up at the party. I saw your footsteps heading away from the gate, and I saw the roses. Then no more footsteps. Not yours anyway. A man's. Yours stopped and his started. And none of them led back to the house. So how'd you get there? Did you fly?" He crossed his arms and nodded triumphantly.

"No," she said. "I went wandering off with a lovely tall man who picked me up and carried me away with him. I wasn't sick at all, I was roaming the countryside. You're a terrible detective." Billah looked stricken and she felt a sudden stab of sympathy for him. Her fear had been his presence when Moth had taken her; that he'd heard her screams. But he hadn't been there. He didn't know anything. She set the fork back on the table.

Althee excused herself to answer a knock at the front door and Lelet took the opportunity to take Billah by the arm and lead him away from the table. "Come. Let's step outside." Their friends would just have to be disappointed that there was to be no further performance.

They stood on the back steps, which opened from the kitchen onto a well-tended herb garden, now touched by frost. The kitchen door had a small round window made of tiny mullioned panes of glass. She recalled a party less than six months earlier, standing on this very spot, sharing a cigarette with Billah and then lifting her dress for him. Squeals of laughter and whiskey and tobacco flavored kisses. It had been nothing but fun, back then. Now she could see frost like white lace on the burnt edges of the sugar-be-gones, and she could see her breath. "Billah, you mustn't spy on people. You could get into trouble."

"So you don't even deny that you're lying? About the whole thing?"

"And you shouldn't go around telling tales. It just makes you look...weak."

His finger, shaking his finger in her face. That had made her decide to cut him off the first time and here it was again. "I know you took up with someone else. Just tell me."

She pushed his hand down. "Even if I had, it's not your business. We are not wed, not betrothed, we were never even exclusive. Billah, we aren't even friends anymore." She wanted a cigarette for the first time in weeks, she could practically taste it. "I was sick. I tore my dress. Now I am well. Leave it." The look in his eye told her he knew she was lying. She wearily realized she didn't care. She missed Moth with an intensity that bordered on physical pain, and relished it, because it was all she had left of him. It was time to go home. She reached up and tucked the trailing end of Billah's handsome heather and smoke wool scarf into the collar of his fine black pea coat. "I think it's best I don't overdo it, my first time out of the house. If you'll excuse me..." she left him on the stoop and went back inside to make her apologies to her hostess, but Althee was already coming her way. Lelet lingered near the stove, relishing the sudden rush of warmth.

"Sorry about the surprise," Althee said. "He begged me—literally begged me to not tell you. I hope you aren't too angry. He was really quite worried, underneath all his theatrics." She looked at Lelet searchingly. "We all were."

Lelet shrugged. "I was bound to see him eventually. I hope he understands now. Al, I'm sorry but I'm a bit tired. Maybe a little too soon to be out. I—"

"You know, just because we didn't argue over the dinner table doesn't mean I believe you," she said. "Billah was right, wasn't he? I was at your house too many times, asking for you. May was frantic, but she wouldn't say a word. You didn't show up at the party, and I know you weren't home the whole time. Darling, where were you?"

"I was sick. I had a fever," Lelet said.

Althee sighed. "Very well. You'll tell me when you tell me. Here, this just came for you." She handed Lelet a letter.

Inside the envelope was a folded piece of paper, torn out of a notebook.

Come back. We have something.
-Scil

"I have to go," Lelet said, crushing it into her pocket. "And I may be gone a long time. I'm sorry, I can't explain. But when I come home, I promise, you'll understand."

Althee nodded slowly. "I see. Another 'illness'." She paused. "Did you get your pirate after all? Is he worth it?"

"A pirate." She gave a short laugh. "No, not a pirate. He's not what I ever expected." She was filled with the desire to be gone, but forced herself to answer. "But he's the most 'worth it' man who ever lived."

"Well shame on you for keeping a secret! I should be angry with you for not sharing. Unless he's....a deposed foreign prince! And there's a scandal! There's a scandal, isn't there?"

Lelet laughed. "You have magical powers of observation, Al." She paused and chewed on a fingernail. "Listen. If that's the story that gets put about...if people think I maybe went south..."

Althee embraced her in a crushing hug and said, "Whatever you're really doing won't hold a match to the story I'm going to tell. So, go and hurry up and come home. I want to see this one for myself." She took her friend's chin in her hand. "Do I need to tell you to be careful? And eat something! You're starting to look like a bicycle!"

* * *

Billah joined Althee on the front walk as Lelet's cab pulled away.

"What was that all about? Where is she going this time?" He paused. "It's no use, is it?"

"Sorry B," she answered. "I think that girl is in love." She turned and took him by the arm. "Now, let's have some dinner. Did I tell you my cousin's best friend is coming for a visit? Sidra's been stuck out on her family's farm for ages and she's desperate for some civilized conversation." Althee pulled the door shut behind them and reaching the table, slipped the dirty silk rose into her pocket, to be prayed over or thrown away; she'd decide later.

Chapter 17

Mistra

"A PRINCE, A foreign prince, that's what she says...." Billah couldn't recall calling a cab, but he must have, otherwise how was he rattling down a cobbled street on a cold leather bench? And who was sitting across from him? He shouldn't have drunk so much, but Al set a fine table, it would be rude—damn rude not to indulge. "And don't I have the right to take a drink, after the way that woman treats me?"

The man, for it was a man, he was certain, despite the fine dark wool scarf covering his face— the man nodded. "What else did she say? Anything about her family?"

"Family? They all hate me. va'Everly. Snobs." He suddenly felt sorry for himself, his heart ached over the injustice. "I took good care of that girl. Gave her anything she wanted. But she..."

"Heard voices?" The man sounded...greedy? Was that the right word?

Billah choked back a sob. "What? What voices? Oh wait...you mean her mother. That old lady heard voices right up to the time they put her in her last dress." He frowned. Who was he talking to? "Shouldn't have said that."

"No, you're quite right," said the man, handing Billah a silver flask. He instinctively raised it to his lips. "You've gone through a lot for that girl. Where is she now? Who is this so-called prince?"

The liquor, oddly, made Billah feel more clear-headed. It had a minty flavor and a fine heat. Cut nicely through the cold air in the cab. "Gone off someplace. Again. Left me. Again."

"Any woman would jump at the chance for a foreign prince. If that's really where she's gone. What else did she tell you? What about the voices?"

"Are you calling my Lelet a liar?" He moved from melancholy to belligerence as the drink heated his belly. A fight, maybe that was the thing to do. "That girl will come to her senses and come back. You'll see." A fight! That would be just the thing. Then Lelet would understand. But his arms felt so heavy, and maybe he'd just close his eyes for a moment instead. At least the man stopped talking, even if no more of the minty drink was offered.

When he woke up, he was in front of his own apartment and the driver was shaking his arm, demanding the fare and swearing if Billah hoinked in his cab, he'd find himself in pieces in the street. Along with his wallet, Billah pulled a card out of his pocket. He simply gave the whole wallet to the driver, who took his fare, added a healthy tip, and tossed the wallet onto the stoop. Billah ignored the driver's show of disrespect, he'd paid that way often enough. The odds of giving too much were just as high when you couldn't quite see the bills as when you let things work themselves out. He tried to focus on the card, but the letters swam around most sickeningly. He gave up, shoved the card and his wallet back into his pocket, and thumped up the steps to his suite of rooms, throwing his fine coat and long scarf on the floor. He slept in his clothes and dreamt of Lelet's mint flavored kisses. She was laughing and walking away with a huge dark shadow at her shoulder.

The next morning Billah, holding his head very still, tried to recall the man in the cab's face, or voice, or anything he'd specifically said. He seemed to remember the man asking about Lelet's family. He hoped he hadn't said anything foolish. He looked at the card again. It was on a cheap cotton stock, no embossing or any design, plain black ink. It read *The Inner Order* and underneath had a street address in a part of town he did not frequent—mostly warehouses and for-hire storefronts. On the back, someone had written *When you are ready to find her*.

He shook his head (at once regretting the sudden motion) and tossed the card in the trash. Inner Order, it sounded like some sort of cult. Had the man said something about hearing voices, though? How did he know that? The va'Everlys kept their family secrets close to their fancy silk shirtfronts. If the rest of the lot knew what Lelet had told him while in a less than sober state, they'd toss her out on her narrow ass. Billah fished the card out of the trash and put it in his wallet. Then he went off to get some breakfast. Something greasy for his stomach, and lots of coffee for his head. And then he'd take another look at the card.

What had the man said about voices?

Chapter 18

Mistra

"'**COME BACK, WE** have something.' That's it? That's all she wrote?" May tossed the crumpled page on the big cherry and ebon desk and threw her hands up. "What is going on in her head?"

May was waiting for Lelet in the front room, the curtains drawn, a fire laid in the grate, and a pot of tea steeping. The man with the letter had come to their house, and May, not wanting to wait, had sent him to Althee's. She'd picked up and put down her knitting five times waiting for Lelet's arrival. It had to be a message from the Guardhouse, no one else sent notes in the middle of the night. She didn't know what would be worse—the news that there was nothing to be done (which was as good as a death sentence for one and a life of guilt and grief for the other) or else she'd be sending her sister into who knew what kind of danger—fires, blood, a desert wasteland. Privately, she blamed herself. If she'd been able to convince Moth to stay, none of this would have happened, and he'd be here with Lelet now. It would have been easy had he really been a ghost—after all, what's time and place to an immortal visitation? 'Ghost business', like *that* was plausible. But she'd been careful of his feelings and hadn't pressed him on it. He'd gone his own way and walked into something terrible, and Lelet with him. And then there was Scilla. The voices she heard may have been real, but that didn't convince May she'd never hear the other kind.

"I told you," said Lelet. "She's angry at me, and the fact that she's the one who...well, I'm sure she doesn't like being wrong. It's still mostly all my fault to her, because I missed that dinner."

May sighed. If Lelet really thought that was the only reason Scilla was in a rage, she hadn't learned a thing. "This is all just so hard to believe. But we have to be careful with her now." She poured herself another cup of tea. "I'm going to float away if we have many more late nights like this," she muttered. "I know you're caught up in getting to your friend—no, don't get upset, I'm not saying you shouldn't be. But there are people involved outside of you and him."

"Fine." Lelet threw herself into an overstuffed armchair and held her bare soles up to the warmth of the fire. "What are my crimes against Scilla?"

"Crimes?" She knelt next to Lelet's chair. "Let's think about this. What is her life? She lives in a drafty stone fortress and writes charms and things at a desk all day. For fun she makes friends with monsters on the other side of The Door. And for what? She just wanted you to pay her some attention, Lel, she adores you. And you just never noticed. I can't believe I have to tell you this."

"That's not...that can't be true. She hates me. She would have said something."

May shook her arm. "Ugh! You can be so blind sometimes. Said something—she practically took out a notice in the paper! She had you kidnapped and dumped at her feet. Why? So you would finally have to see her. The fact that her pet demon became your pet demon was just one more thing you just casually took away from her." Lelet tried to head for the stairs, but May pulled her back down into the seat. "In her mind, Lel. That's what it looked like to her. And stop with this running off when you get upset business, it doesn't become you."

Lelet shifted uncomfortably. "Why are you taking her side all of a sudden? I thought you were with me."

"There are no sides, there is just us. You are putting your life—and Moth's—in her hands. I think you'd better approach her with a different attitude than 'you owe me'.

You are defensive and in need of help. She's defensive and can give it to you. Someone has to back down. And from what I gather, if you approach this wrong, she can cause you even more harm. You'd better be careful in your choice of words."

Lelet folded her arms. "I'm listening."

"She's angry. Apologize." She raised her hand to stop Lelet's reply. "I know, just like with Rane, it's not your fault, you didn't do anything. And look where your brother ended up. If you waltz in there and expect her to wave a magic wand or whatever it is you want her to do, you'll never see Moth again. Is that what you want? No. I don't want that either. I intend to sit down for a nice dinner with that young man. And Stelle likes him, so it's settled. Now, what to do. Treat Scil with the respect she feels she deserves. She's got a great mind, you said so yourself. But she's also a child, and she is also fragile. Let her know you appreciate her help. Let her fix her mistake without rubbing her nose in it. Make her feel special. I know you want to kill her, but if you expect this plan to work, you need her to know you love her and trust her."

"Well of course I love her. Trust her?" She sighed. "I guess I have to. I could bring her some nice things from here. The cab comes early, but I do have a little time to make up a box for her. Some things to wear. Are they allowed to wear their own clothes?" She looked shamefaced. "I should know that. Well, some things to wear, and pretty soaps, and hand lotions, and stuff. A nice quilt—that place is cold. And a new notebook and pen, she's always got her nose in a book. Maybe she'll let me color her hair?"

"I don't think that will be necessary," May said quickly. "But this is a good start. Listen to her when she speaks. My heart says she wants to make this right. Let her. Now shove over."

Lelet made room on the fat cushions. They stared at the fire for a little while. May sipped her tea.

"If this works, I don't know how long I'll be gone," Lelet said "I...you know we really don't have a plan yet. I know one name and one word from Eriis."

"What's the name?" May asked.

"It's his best friend's name. Ilaan. He's supposed to be some kind of genius. He's the one who'll help me. I hope." She sighed. "I thought he might be this Voice person Scil was talking to, but instead I think he was the one who warned us. I...He's involved somehow, but I don't have a choice. I have to find Ilaan."

"Ilaan." May drew it out. "That's pretty. And what's the word?"

"*Rushta*. It means 'shit'."

May laughed. "One name and one word. I suppose kingdoms have been conquered with less, although frankly none come to mind. You will be careful. You'll be careful and smart, and you two will come home. Oh, I found something in a shop today, something new for the spring season. I thought of you and had to buy it." She ran to the big desk and pulled out a small package wrapped in bright foiled paper. "I wanted it to be a surprise for when you come back, but I can't wait." She handed it over.

Lelet peeled away the paper. She found a pair of stiff, curved wire pieces attached to two ovals of smoked dark grey glass. "I've never seen anything...." May showed her what do with them and she put them on. "These aren't for me, are they?"

"I'm sure he'll let you borrow them. They look quite smart! They are called 'eyeshades'. The shop keeper told me that come spring everyone will be wearing them."

Lelet wrapped them carefully back in the paper. "When we come home, you can give them to him yourself. And he'll know you are the best person who ever lived, just like I do. One name, one word, and you. How can we fail?"

Chapter 19

Mistra

"**HOW CAN YOU** *not* fail, is the better question." Scilla had an oversized book, mildewed and mice-gnawed sitting next to an even older and more abused looking box on Brother Blue's desk, which at some point she had taken over. Brother Blue stood near the fire. He hadn't had much to say, but he looked around at the two young women now.

"If you don't think this will end well, we don't send her at all."

"With respect, Brother, it's not your decision." Lelet reached for the box, but Scilla slapped her hand away. "It's my choice and my risk." She caught and held Scilla's gaze. "If Scilla says it works, then it does. Even when she's wrong, she's usually right." Lelet noted the high color appear in her younger sister's cheeks and hoped May would approve. She'd been twisting herself around like a hooked fish trying to compliment Scilla without overdoing it—the girl would see through her in an instant if she sounded insincere.

She'd arrived near second moonset a day earlier and was forced to once again spend a sleepless night in a cramped stone cell, and then take a silent breakfast of oatmeal, grainy bread, and tea with newly ordained brothers and sisters who were less than delighted to see her. At least the tea was strong. *Demon business*, they whispered to each other. *Bad business.* She and her luggage were then escorted back to Scilla's room to sit and wait through errands, and duties, and pot scrubbing, and morning devotionals, and whatever else these pinch faced creatures did all day.

When Scilla finally finished with whatever was keeping her and showed up, Lelet was having fits of frustration—the room was almost too small to successfully pace. She was a little surprised at how fiercely her little sister hugged her. Was she glad to see her after all?

It did turn out to be a pleasure to watch Scilla go through her gifts. Lelet was reminded how young she really was. She lit up at the new notebooks with the gilt painted birds on the covers, instantly put the ribbons in her hair, and wrapped the quilted silk blanket with its white and pink rose pattern around her shoulders. The dresses, she left undisturbed.

"They prefer we wear the robes and clothing they provide," she said, gently stroking the yoke of lace decorating the bodice of a blue day dress. "The rest is nice, though. Thanks. Why'd you bring this? I told you I'd help you."

"I know, Scil. But it seems like a sort of grey place up here, and I thought you might like some pretty things to look at."

Scilla frowned at her. "You're afraid I'll send you to the wrong place. Or turn you into the wrong thing."

"No! Not until right this second, actually. Good lord, Scil, would you do that?" Scilla said nothing. Lelet slid off the little bed and joined her sister on the floor under the quilt. She put her arm around the younger girl's shoulder. "You wouldn't. I know I wasn't the best sister in the world. I could have spent more time with you—"

"May told you to say that." But she didn't move away.

"May helped me see how I didn't appreciate you. And she was right. And now we're going to do something really amazing together. It's going to be fine."

Now Scilla did wiggle away, and stood with her back to the room, quite close to the fire in the tiny grate. "How is it going to be fine? You'll get your boyfriend back and I'll get kicked out for consorting with demons. Or you'll never come back and it'll be my fault." She sniffed. "It's all my fault anyway."

"No, darling. No, come back here and sit by me." When she moved the rug so that they could both sit near the warm little blaze, she was confronted by a pair of footprints scorched into the wooden floorboards. She ran her hands over them with a whispered promise, then looked back up at her sister. *Tell her it's fine. Tell her you aren't angry.* "There's no more fault. Lots of things happened. At the end, the part that we're left with is that I found two special people." Scilla looked at her curiously. "Well, the second one is you, obviously! I would never have known you were so smart! Or that you cared about me so much. I'm so lucky to have you." Scilla leaned against Lelet.

"I don't want you to go. What if I do something wrong?"

"We will be slow and careful. I'll do exactly as you say. And Brother Blue will help us, right?" Scilla nodded. "Do any of the other teachers know what you two are doing?"

"No. It's very secret. I'm taking you a back way to Brother's office." She picked the bird notebook up and turned it in her hands. "I think I like this best of all." She picked up the matching red and gilt pen, opened to the first page and wrote:

1. Turn my sister into a demon.

2.

"What's the second thing?" asked Lelet.

"A secret," Scilla answered.

Lelet nodded and rose to her feet. "Let's get working on your list." They tossed the pretty quilt over Scilla's cot and hung the ribbons over her lamp. When Olly came to collect them, they were ready to go.

Chapter 20

Mistra

"**SCIL, WHAT HAVE** we got?"

Scilla knew her sister was in a hurry, but the long-ago people who wrote these charms refused to be rushed. They demanded attention. She opened the decaying book and slowly flipped through the pages. When she'd found what she wanted, she turned the book so Lelet could see it. Olly peered over her shoulder from a safe distance.

"This, for starters." It was written in elaborate script in black ink with red and gold loops and flourishes. Men, women, and fanciful animals, chained to each other with tiny glittering ropes, marched around the margins of the page. The print was not only small and faded, but heaped in irregular piles of verse. Lelet squinted at the page and then looked at her sister expectantly.

"Do you remember the binding spell?" asked Scilla.

Lelet took a deep breath. "The one that you used...yes, I remember it."

"Well, the one I cast was given to me by that Counselor man." She had at least given up on the idea of the whole thing being a misunderstanding. The Counselor was the Voice. He wasn't her friend. He'd lied about everything. She still had white lines on her arms and chest, they ached in the cold. If someone—she didn't know who, and that made her even angrier—if someone hadn't warned them, she'd probably be roasted and eaten by now. Lelet had ignored and underestimated her, but this was much worse. This was **betrayal**. In Scilla's mind, the word was red and black and dripping with flame. If Lelet could take away something The Voice found valuable, she'd make sure her sister at least got the chance. "This is a different one. Binding spells don't work on things you'd consider natural. I mean, I can't cast one on you. Moth is considered supernatural, and so I could bind him; if they wanted to they could bind me." She saw what Lelet was about to ask and added, "The human thing doesn't matter. He was born on a different world and so it worked."

"And this—" Lelet nodded at the page, "points the spell in the other direction?"

"Sort of."

"Why do we need a binding spell anyway?" Lelet asked. Brother Blue hadn't said a word, just stared unhappily at the fire in the grate.

"Well, it's not the binding part I want to use. When you've bound a person, they can see where everyone is, like little points of light. The original idea I guess was to make it easier to serve. But with this spell, we get a map. Of Eriis."

"That's...Scil, that's really smart!"

Scilla rolled her eyes. "It's not a secret; I just had to find the right book. Olly helped me."

The boy blushed and shrugged. "It was more carrying things up the stairs than anything else."

"Do you understand what your sister has in mind?" Blue joined them at his desk. "I wonder if you'll think she's so clever after you hear it."

"Well, I assume she wants to use it on me so I can find where I'm going."

Blue snorted and turned back to the fire. "Go ahead and tell her your brilliant idea, Sister."

Scilla looked up, grinning. "It's not for you. It's for me. I'm going to bind myself to the city. The whole city. I'll be able to see where everyone is. I'll know everything."

"Oh no. May will kill me. No, Brother Blue, is this as dangerous as it sounds?"

He didn't turn. "If anyone on Eriis feels her presence, she could potentially become bound to them. Imagine the damage one of those creatures—the Counselor you spoke of—could do to her, to all of us. And I think we all know the way to break the binding spell in Scilla's case, would be permanent."

Scilla shook her head. "But no one will know, that's the thing. I cast it from right here, and I'll be able to find Moth. How else are you going to get him back? You don't know a single thing about Eriis. Plus I can keep an eye on that Counselor. I can even watch you."

"So you cast this thing on yourself, and you can communicate with Ilaan and let him know I'm coming?"

Scilla rubbed her arm under her sleeve, where any message would be scratched. She wondered if it would appear in Eriis on another person's skin. "And I'll make sure The Door opens in front of him, not in the middle of the desert or under a building. Or in the Crosswinds. Do you even know what that is?" Lelet admitted she did not. "Hmm, if it didn't have to do with your boyfriend, I guess you just weren't paying attention."

Lelet took another series of deep breaths. "You're right," she said. "I really have a lot to learn. I do know I can't go looking like this." She held her hair out with both hands. "I look a fright!" Scilla laughed. "So this is dangerous, but you'll be clever and I won't have to have an awkward conversation with May and Father?"

Scilla leaned back in her seat. "I won't get caught. You, on the other hand, well—all we can do is try." She smiled. "How do you feel about sand?"

"Sand?" Lelet frowned. "I don't mind it on the beach. I know there's lots of it on Eriis. Why?"

"That's the rest of it. See, once we have a contact and know where to put it, opening The Door is easy."

"It is not easy, it should not be easy." Blue wrung his hands. "I have doubts. I know you are determined to reach your friend, but I fear we'll find ourselves with an open Door and our Sister Scilla here bound to someone on Eriis. And you a captive or worse."

"They won't want her as a captive, though. They have no use for demon blood over there." Olly pointed at the box. "Show them what we found, Scilla. I think this could work."

"You *think?*" Blue snapped. "Scilla, what have you been telling my assistant?"

"That he's good for more than pouring tea and carrying things up stairs, is all," Scilla answered mildly. Olly blushed in a shade that looked potentially fatal and found something to look at on the bookshelf.

The only thing stupider than girls, thought Scilla, are boys.

* * *

"Are you serious?" Lelet looked at the several threadbare bundles of sand Scilla had carefully taken out of the dirty old box. They were tied at one end with ribbons that had once been brightly colored and resembled nothing so much as filthy baby's socks. "Explain this to me again because I could swear you said I have to *eat* these."

"Exactly!" Scilla bounced in her seat. "It's so perfect—well, if it works, I mean. See, these things are called klystrons."

"Not kelstrons?" asked Olly.

"No. I translated the pages myself. Klystrons." Scilla turned back to Lelet. "The demons give them to their children to help them bring along their magic powers, right? They're sand from outside the city walls of Eriis. The little demon children would hold them in their hands and they would amplify whatever ability the child had. Very powerful."

"And very dangerous," added Brother Blue. "I fear you two—three—will carry on no matter what I say, but these things caused several deaths when we brought them here for study. That's why they were locked away."

"Brother, weren't they just handed to human children?" asked Olly. "Little ones that didn't know what they were? To see what would happen?"

"I must see about separating you two," said Blue, but he sounded only tired, not angry. "This is true, though. The little ones didn't develop any gifts. They turned into...I can only call them monsters. We had to send them all home; some went home in little boxes. Of course, that was a long time ago. We don't know why or why they don't work on adults. We suspected it must be something lacking in our blood. Or in our minds. In any event, the subject has been closed for many years."

"Okay," said Lelet, "but back to the 'eat them' part?"

"That's the beauty of it." Scilla's face was shining like a candle. "You don't need the right kind of mind or blood or anything else. The sand's job is amplification. It does that to the demon children, we knew that. But like Brother said, it does something different to humans—transformation. Eat with one hand, hold my hand with the other, and I'll guide you. Just follow my voice, I'll do the charm, and we'll get you into the right shaped body, not a hideous freak monster like those other children."

Lelet poked one of the bundles. It was about the size of a man's thumb. "How many do I have to...eat?"

Scilla shrugged. "I would say until you have red eyes and black hair, and then you can stop. Oh, and I think you should unwrap them, that cloth or whatever it's made of looks sort of dirty."

"Are you enjoying this?" asked Lelet.

"I will be. Start eating."

Chapter 21

Mistra

IT TURNED OUT to be seven.

The first little bag of sand had been easy. Well, not easy, but easier than the second, or the third, or the seventh. Lelet's tongue felt parched and shriveled, her throat began to burn, and she could feel each sharp edged grain of sand as it ran its busy errand through her body. After the second bag was gone, Olly had to guide her hand clutching the spoon to her mouth because she could no longer see through the white haze. She hung on to Scilla's hand as hard as she could, feeling herself shifting and sliding inside her own body, following the trail Scilla's words laid down. Her hands tingled and finally went numb. Her feet felt freezing cold and as if they were across the room. Her stomach felt like the morning after a particularly long night. She kept going, but her mouth was so dry, were her lips cracking? Were they peeling back?

"Don't hoink it up! You'll just have to swallow it again." That was Scilla speaking, probably.

"Stop this. She's had enough." That must be Brother Blue. Scilla would never think to stop.

"Catch her!" Someone's hands guided her to the floor. There was a scream, not her own. She smelled something burning; this time she thought it was herself. She couldn't remember the last time she'd had a breath; the sand had stoppered her like a broken hourglass. But nothing hurt and nothing seemed wrong; so why was everyone making so much noise? She figured she'd just close her eyes for a minute or two and then set everyone to right. But when she'd opened them to total darkness, she panicked.

Can't breathe...can't...

She opened her eyes—she was blind! She couldn't move. It had all gone wrong. After a few dizzying moments, she realized her dress was wrapped around her head, and she pulled it free of her face and sat up.

Olly, Scilla, and Blue gasped and drew back like a string of puppets. Scilla nodded at Olly, who held a hand mirror out to Lelet, keeping himself well out of reach.

Golden skin, the color of perfect toast, the color of the expensive caramel candies May used to bring her, the same golden color of *his* skin. Deep garnet eyes, almond eyes that tilted up at the corners like a cat. And black hair, long and as silky as a cats. An absurdly dainty nose and a rather ordinary mouth. Not her mouth. The new little teeth looked startlingly white against the dark skin. She peered at herself, fascinated. She'd gotten tangled in her dress because she'd lost nearly a foot in height. And her shoes had fallen off. She wiggled her kitten sized toes: her dream of darling little feet had finally been realized. She glanced down, no, her breasts weren't any more impressive. Well, it would have been out of proportion anyway.

Olly reached into his pocket and solemnly gave Scilla a silver coin. "I should never bet against you, Scil," he said. She nodded and tucked it in her pocket.

"You're so tiny," Scil marveled. She reached over and touched her sister's newly darkened hair. "And it's so soft! Um, are you okay? Can you talk? You had us a bit worried."

She cleared her throat. "I'm okay, Scil." They all gasped again. "What?" She gathered her now-huge dress modestly around herself and slowly stood up.

"Your voice," said Olly. "It's not your voice. Scil, what do you think?"

"Well, she's a different size, so that may be why. Or they maybe have different vocal parts?"

"Just like her..." They'd forgotten Brother Blue, who slumped in the chair in the corner. He had gone grey. Olly rushed to his side with a cup of cider spiked with rum. The old man sipped and then waved his assistant away. "I'd almost forgotten. How they look. You know, they all look rather alike, it was my gift that I could tell one from the next, or so my master told me. That's how I got this job, that's why I spent so much time with them, that's how I met her. And you look just like her..."

* * *

"Are you really, really okay?" Scilla took Lelet's hands in her own. They were nearly eye to eye. "You don't feel dizzy? Or like you'll swallow your tongue? Or boil your own blood by accident?"

"No, stop Scil. I feel... I feel really well." Ever since her fall from the horse, she'd had a lingering ache in her ankle. It was gone. She held out her arm. "Pinch me!" Scilla complied. "Harder."

"Well?" Scilla asked.

"Barely felt it. Stand back." Scilla retreated to the far wall, and Olly did his best to shield Blue with his body. Lelet turned towards the fireplace. She held out her hand and closed her eyes. Now she could see it, like a path she could follow that had fire at its end. It was so close, an alley behind her eyes, a place to turn and push...

A tiny shower of sparks leapt from her fingertips and drifted to the floor. She trod them out with her bare toes. A slight warmth.

"Did you see it? I did it!" She was shocked to see Scilla with tears on her face. Had she ever seen her sister cry? She went and gathered her in her arms, as she so often had (but apparently not often enough) and with their new equal height, they pressed their foreheads together. "What's wrong, Scilly? It worked."

Scilla rapped her lightly with her forehead. "I know it worked. I know it's all going to work. We're going to do this and it's all going to be fine. I know it."

"How do you know?" Lelet asked.

"Because you trust me," Scilla said.

"Well, of course I—"

"No, you're not just saying it. You mean it. You trust me and I can do this."

Lelet smiled and touched her sister's cheek. "You seem pretty sure all of a sudden. How do you know?"

"Because you never asked me if I could change you back."

* * *

"Well, she can't stay here!" Brother Blue alternated between staring raptly at Lelet's new face, and muttering and shaking his head with his eyes turned back to the fireplace. She was growing uneasy under the intensity of his scrutiny. "We devote ourselves to keeping them out, not sheltering them." What to do with their newly made demon had turned out to be a problem none of them had foreseen, because none of them expected the spell to work so efficiently.

"Very well, Brother. I'll escort my sister back to my cell; she can stay there with me."

The old man is going to be a problem, Lelet thought. *And without him I can't get where I'm going.* She wasn't sure if Blue understood who she was, that she was a counterfeit, despite the fact that he'd witnessed her transformation. He was wandering in his wits more than any of them realized. Perhaps Olly was correct—the shock had been too much for him.

"Escort her? Walk her down the hall?" Blue's color was bad and his voice had a reedy timbre. "Why not sit her at the head table at dinner? Why not have her lecture the class?" He reached out for Lelet and snatched her upper arm. "Why didn't you tell me? Did you know he was mine all along?" Lelet had no idea what the old man meant, but the way he grabbed her put her in mind of a day in a forest, and blood. Without thinking, she held her hand palm out in front of his chest. His ratty old robe began to smoke. She gasped and leapt backwards as Olly pulled the scorched fabric away from Blue's body and smothered the sparks with his hands.

"I'm...I'm so sorry, Brother, are you hurt?"

Olly helped him into the comfortable chair in the corner. Scilla examined the burned edge of the fabric. "Lucky you don't know what you're doing, Lel. You could have burnt him to a cinder. What got into you?"

"I just...he grabbed me and..." she shook her head. *Please don't hurt me.* "Never mind. He's right. I can't stay here, and it's not safe for me to stay with you, either, Scil. We're halfway there. I have to go, now, today." They left Olly to tend to Blue and went back to the desk, now a jumble of papers and dirty rags and stray drifts of sand.

"You can, though, can't you? Turn me back?" Lelet asked. Scilla dragged her finger through the sand. A circle, dots and lines. The sand became airborne and floated in front of their faces, glowing red and green and blue, its grains performing a dance too intricate to follow.

"I can. All you have to do is walk back through The Door, and you'll be back in your bony old body." Scilla snapped her fingers, and the patterns of color and light dropped to the desk, sand once again.

"What else have you lied about, Hellne?" Blue said. "Scilla, my dear, step away from that creature. She lies and calls it love. We must send her back."

"Whose Ellna?" whispered Scilla.

Lelet shrugged. "He thinks that's my name. He called me a creature. Maybe another demon?"

Scilla crouched next to his chair. "We must send her back, Brother Blue, and we need your help. How do we open The Door? Can you help us?" He waved her away, closing his eyes. "I know, you are tired. I know it is shocking and awful that...uh...Ellna is here. So let us send her away."

Blue was asleep.

Lelet put a cushion on the chair facing the desk, and climbed up. She propped herself on her elbows and watched Olly fussing with the old man. She would have been surprised if Blue leapt to help them, but she felt a strange restlessness that said, 'Go, move.' Whatever happened next, it would have to be soon.

Scilla joined her, taking the desk chair and sitting on her feet so she could see over it. "I can open it, but only halfway. The...the person I was in contact with on Eriis did the rest of it. I don't know how to open it all the way, but he does." She indicated Blue, who twitched and snorted as the past replayed itself behind his eyes. "But it's all out of order anyway. I need to cast the binding spell first so we know where to send you. I have to find this Ilaan person. Then The Door. So let him sleep. Olly, can you let Brother Maron know he's taken ill and needs someone to lecture at midmorning?"

After Olly tucked a blanket around his master and slipped away, they made sure the door to Blue's study was securely locked, and turned back to the moldy old book.

"Are you scared?" asked Lelet.

Scilla thought about it. "No," she finally answered. "I'm not the one going there." She had the book opened to the correct page. "Lel, I can still stop this. It's not too late. You don't have to go." She took her sister's hands again, now tiny, dark skinned and perfect. "Are you sure you want to do this?"

Lelet gripped Scilla's hand tightly; then touched her sister's brow, pushing back a lock of hair that had come unraveled from her braid. "When we were traveling together, me and Moth, we were attacked by three...very bad men." She paused and swallowed hard. "They killed him. In front of my face. They killed him and I couldn't help him." At Scilla's confused look, she said, "He was only killed for a minute. Or not completely killed, I guess. His people heal really fast, that's what he told me."

"That's what broke the binding spell," said Scilla.

Lelet nodded. "They left him on the ground and they took me with them." Scilla gasped and covered her mouth with her hands. "No, that's the thing. He came for me and he saved me. They didn't hurt me, not really, not like they hurt him. But he rescued me. And now I have to rescue him. I have to go." She was surprised, there were no tears. They'd been replaced by resolve, and by the desire to burn something—or someone—to the ground. It definitely wasn't safe here, for any of them.

"You love him," Scilla said.

Lelet smiled. "Can you love someone after only a few days?"

"That's a stupid question. Of course you can!" Scilla was indignant. "You love him. I can tell."

"It doesn't matter, though. I'd have to help him even if I didn't love him. I owe him my life. But I think you're right. You're turning out to be right a lot of the time, Scilly," she paused. "Hey, what's the matter?"

Scilla had gone red in the face and was rubbing her fists against her eyes. "I never meant any of this to happen. What if those bad men had hurt you? It was my fault. I just wanted you..."

"Shhh, I know." She drew the sobbing girl against her chest. "Nothing bad happened. It'll all work out." Lelet realized she meant it. She used the sleeve of her huge dress to wipe her sister's face. "Now, look at me. You did this."

Scilla peered at Lelet's new features, touched her nose, drew a finger along her dark, fine eyebrows. "Are you still you? I thought you'd look more like yourself, only smaller. And different."

Lelet began to say, 'Of course I am still me,' but she hesitated. "I'm not sure," she finally answered. She looked at her hands. "I want to use them," she said. "I want to..." she shook her head. "I don't know. But I think it's best I go, and soon."

Brother Blue said, "He's mine, he's mine," but did not wake. They turned to look at him for a moment.

"Who do you think he's talking about?" asked Lelet.

Scilla shrugged. "Some demon or other, probably. I bet he knew lots of them, back in the old days. I'm glad he's sleeping; he'd try to stop us. He wouldn't, though." She turned back to her book. "I think you'd better sit over there," she said, pointing towards the window. "I'm going to cast the binding spell, and I don't want you accidentally getting bound...Lel, your hands!"

She looked at them again. They were on fire. She shook them out as if they were oversized matches. "I'm sorry, Scil, don't be afraid."

"It's because of me binding Moth. Just thinking of it. You want to burn me up." Scilla huddled at the far side of the big desk chair.

"I want you to fix this. And you are. Do the spell."

"Are you sure—"

"Scilla. Cast the binding spell. I can't stay here."

Scilla took a deep breath, and rooted around in her teacher's desk until she found a candle she was satisfied with. "I need you to light it," she said. "Can you do that?" Lelet held out a finger and the candle caught an odd blue flame. "Now, like I said, go back over there. Don't come near me until I'm done."

Lelet watched as Scilla painstakingly recited the verse. She didn't have to eat sand or cut off a finger or even hold her breath—it struck Lelet as somewhat unfair. Then she remembered the risk Scilla was about to take, and felt ashamed. She recognized the word 'Eriis', and she heard Scilla say her own name. A faint blue glow hovered near the ceiling, slowly lowering itself over Scilla, the book, the candle, and the desk, until it formed a sort of shimmering globe. When the sphere around her was complete, Scilla blew out the candle. The blue light vanished.

"Did it work?" asked Lelet.

Scilla's eyes were wide, but she didn't seem to be seeing the room around her, and she didn't answer. Lelet wanted to go to her, but what if it wasn't finished? Moth said it felt like a rope tied around his mind, it sounded terrible.

"I can see them..." she finally said. "I can see everyone." Scilla blinked rapidly and shook her head. "And they can't see me." She climbed down from the chair and took Lelet's hand, pointing it out the window and up at the blue sky. "There they are, they are waiting for you." Then her eyes rolled up and back and she slumped to the floor.

Lelet propped her against the wall and grabbed a cushion off a chair to put behind her head. Her sister's heart was strong and her eyes moved behind closed lids. She tried to speak; her hands fluttered. Lelet simply didn't know what else to do.

"She is looking at the city, I think," said Brother Blue. He leaned over Scilla and passed a hand over her brow. "I can only hope the city is not looking back at her." He put a hand on the small of his back and straightened up. "We will resume this adventure when your sister has returned to us. I will have Olly bring up something for you both to eat. I strongly recommend you do not leave this room."

"Who is he?" asked Lelet. The old man raised a brow curiously. "You kept saying 'He's mine.' Who were you talking about? And who is Ellna?"

There was a long pause. "I'm afraid I don't know who you mean," he said. "It was a long time ago." And he left without another word.

* * *

Blue went to the roof; he could still make it up the stairs, a feat of which he was justly proud. He stood and looked out towards the ocean; the cold wind whipped his cleric's robe around his thin legs, and he took a deep breath. *Not too many more times,* he thought, *but maybe that's not such a bad thing. I've lived too long.*

When he'd gone to the study of magic under the old cleric, back when he'd been young and thought he'd live the natural span of days, he learned that power was no gift—it was a bargain, made carefully and paid without exception. And at the time, a drop of wit meant nothing—he was the wittiest fellow he knew. He would run out of life well before he ran out of wits. It was important to strike a deal, because magic would take what it liked if you did not.

Back then, with a full company of clerics all working together, the effect had been minimal. And as the years went by and their numbers dwindled, well, no one performed magic any more, anyway. Until now. He wondered if it were the same on the other side of The Door, and what became of the secretive Mages he had never seen. What did they sacrifice? And were they even still alive? He supposed he'd find out soon enough. Or the sister would, at least.

This would be the greatest act of magic he'd performed in many years, and he had no doubt what the price would be. The sister would go to Eriis, but after that she was on her own. And with that act of magic, and the next of bringing her home—should she somehow survive—he feared it might be his last. He wondered if Hellne would find it amusing, if she would laugh at the thought—he'd finally meet his son, and not understand who he was.

Perhaps our debt might be settled, Hellne. Perhaps you'll let me sleep.

Chapter 22

Eriis

THE SMELL.

That was how he knew where he was, the dry stink of ash and the dust that gathered at the back of his throat.

Rhuun sat up, spat out a mouthful of grit, and looked at the sand, the low clouds, the firewhirls in the far distance, and Eriis; home, right where he'd left it.

"Did you see that? The positive *menagerie* of human persons he had following him around?" Yuenne accepted a fresh white silk tunic from a robed and hooded Mage who had hovered just out of sight of The Door, and a second handed him a cloth to wipe his face and hands. He wiggled his fingers, and the burn on his hand faded to nothing.

As soon as Rhuun walked away from Mistra, he'd been somehow frozen in place, and thrown to the ground. It must have been one of the Mages, there were four of them in a loose circle around him, looking down with bright, greedy eyes, and then there was Yuenne, who smiled his little smile. "Well, we'd better get him home."

The Zaalmage looked close to tears, such was his excitement. "Away from here, in case they want him back." He nodded at the thick line of glassy, scorched sand where The Door had stood.

"I agree." Yuenne squinted out at the burning desert and adjusted his immaculate cuffs, "Did any of you see what caused my little Scilla to cry out like that? No? A shame. Another day, then. Anyway, no reason to linger."

"We have made our Raasth ready. How long have we waited for this—"

"Oh my goodness. I'm so sorry," said Yuenne. "Did we not discuss this? It must have slipped my mind in all the excitement. He'll be under guard in the Royal Quarters."

"Absolutely not," hissed the Zaal. "We need him where we can use him, and no preparations have been made..." the other Mages looked at each other and shrugged and pointedly did not look at the Zaal.

"Your brothers here were most helpful in charming his room. Please don't be angry with them, there may have been some misunderstanding about where the orders came from. In any event, it's all ready."

While they spoke, Rhuun got his feet under him. Obviously, he'd been tricked. The Door was gone and Mistra was out of reach. It was a long way, but he thought if he could get to the Old City or the Quarter...he made it about three steps before one of them lifted a hand and his feet flew out from out under him again. His legs felt as if they had turned to stone.

"Shall we continue this conversation off the sand, gentlemen?" asked Yuenne. "The important thing is we have him back."

"Where is Ilaan?" asked Rhuun. "Let me talk to him." The five looked down at him as if they'd forgotten he could speak. "And my mother, Yuenne, I gather is only in danger from you. I'll see her as well."

"I don't think you understand the reality of your situation," said Yuenne. "You will be accommodated and, probably for the first time in your life, you will be of use."

"But the Raasth..." whined the Zaal.

Yuenne ignored him. "Shall we, gentlemen?" The air around them blurred and for a few seconds, Rhuun was alone. He had no time to even think about where he might go, because one of the Mages reappeared with Yuenne at his side. "I forgot about your...disability. Well, you and our friend here are in for a nice walk," he said, addressing the Mage. "We'll be waiting at the Great Hall."

* * *

The Mage walked behind him. The few times Rhuun turned to speak to him, the man vanished and reappeared out of his eyeshot. He said not a word. When they finally reached the hall, they found Yuenne, looking refreshed and tidy. "You should thank me, I'm sure you'll be a great deal more comfortable up here. Might even extend your expiration date."

"I want to talk to Ilaan," Rhuun said again. The great hall was full of people, a shifting sea of greys, whites, and tans, pausing in their errands to turn and watch. He recognized many of them. None would meet his eye, but he could feel their gazes following him. At least Lelet was safe. He'd think about that later. Right now he spotted a familiar face and gave a sigh of relief.

"Aelle. Thank Light and Wind." She stopped on her way to wherever she was going and looked him up and down, taking in the grit and dust on his face, his dirty human clothing and tied back hair. Her white silk tunic was immaculate, her hair tightly coiled and intricately woven with white beads, brilliant against the black gloss. He could see a filigree of new tattoos in black and gold peeking out from under the cuffs of her wide sleeves and reaching towards her fingers. She had lined her eyes with green and gold, which made her look older and mysterious. Her hand was lightly resting on Niico's arm. "Aelle, I have so much to tell you..."

She tipped her pretty head forward and spat on the ground at his feet. Then she turned to Yuenne. "Father, I will see you at dinner." She glanced up at Niico, who was looking studiously at his nails, and they continued down the corridor.

"Burned that bridge, as the humans say," murmured Yuenne. "Well, she was bound to come to her senses. So!"

He clapped his hands and looked brightly up at Rhuun. "What may we expect? I'm sure you're wondering."

"Why do you want me up here? Instead of the Raasth?"

They pulled ahead of the Mages, who were engaged in an argument of one low voice and several hisses.

"Simple. If we keep you up here, the people will remember who caught you and how much they owe our family. It's the least you can do for poor Aelle."

They made the left turn at the end of the hallway, as Rhuun expected. The corridor leading to the long row of doors to his family's quarters seemed darker than he recalled, and dirtier. They came to his own room, but the carved ashboard door he'd grown up with had been replaced with an exquisite slab of what looked like real wood, chased with silver. Yuenne nodded at one of his white-clad household guards, standing to the side.

"The door is charmed, of course," he said to Rhuun. "Don't touch it, and you'll be fine."

"State your business," said the door.

Yuenne smiled and said, "We have brought Prince Rhuun home." It swung open.

They filed into the small room, and it felt like a crowd. It was just as he'd left it three months earlier, counting the days as they did on Mistra. It felt like a lifetime. He had no idea how long he'd been gone from Eriis. The book he'd been reading before going to Ilaan's party lay on the bedside table, the three little relics from before the war hung on the wall; there was even sand on the floor from a thrown bottle just before he'd entered the Veil. Oddly, his dresser had been ransacked, the drawers open and clothing scattered about.

"The windows have been sealed against the dust. For your own protection of course." Yuenne turned to the Zaal. "Well, I'll leave you to it. Keep me updated. Rhuun, what a pleasure to have you home where you belong."

"This is not finished," snapped the Zaal. "After all these years my brothers and I will have a return on our investment."

"I'm the one who threw the stick and made this drunken fool limp home after it. You and your brothers were still sweeping the floor and working on your stone lighting technique when I struck this agreement with the old Zaal."

"Yes, and we have gotten quite good. In fact, That Which Pierces the Veil and Calls to Kin ought to be back safely in our hands when you're not...playing with it."

"So fancy." Yuenne chuckled. "It's a pen, and I'm hardly playing. Tell me, which of your Mages has been contacting the humans all along? And who sent the chlystrons to the humans in the first place?" He paused, and after an uncomfortable silence, the Zaal admitted it had been Yuenne who whispered the idea in the ear of the old king. "And as far as our friend here, you've got full access, he's all yours. What more do you want? And what about keeping him fed and so on? I'll have to find someone to clean up after him. Do you want some girl barging down into the Raasth?"

Rhuun was already sick of being spoken about like he was invisible. He made a leap for the door. A second later, he found himself on the floor with scorched hands. He swore under his breath, using the human words he'd picked up: "Cock. Piss. Shit."

Yuenne made an 'I told you so' gesture. "That foolishness must come from your father's side." The door opened again and he left Rhuun with the Mages.

The Zaal said to his fellows, "We will talk about giving orders and taking them once we are back in the Raasth. If they don't come from me, they probably don't come from me!" He calmed himself with some effort. "However. It cannot ruin a great day. Let us begin." One of them pulled a long, thin knife from under his robes. Another had a shallow silver dish.

"Now," said the Zaal, "I really must apologize, Prince Rhuun. Normally, of course, the Ceremony of *Laa Na* is performed under much more dignified circumstances. This is irregular to say the least."

"Well then, don't do it," Rhuun replied. "Maybe it won't work, anyway."

The Zaal shrugged. "That is a chance we are willing to take. We've been waiting a long time for you." He nodded at the Mage holding the knife. "You belong to us, now."

Rhuun backed away. "You're wrong." *Dinnertime*, he thought, *and I'm the meat.* He found a shadow and stepped into it. The mages paused in their advance. There was some hissing. The light in the room increased rapidly, until there were no shadows left. Rhuun, visible again, shielded his eyes. They turned the light back to its previous soft glow.

"*Laa Na*," said the Zaal. "At last."

One of the robed Mages held out his hand, and again Rhuun found he couldn't move. They circled around him, sniffing. He watched in horror as his arm held itself out. Then there was the knife, and then there was blood.

It lasted only a few moments, and they capped the bowl and left him. One of them came back a few minutes later and unfroze him. His arm began to heal, and instinctively he put the pain away. He sat on the edge of his bed and looked around.

He was alone.

He got up and began to fold his clothes.

Chapter 23

Eriis

***"SHAN*, YOU'VE BARELY** touched your dinner." Yuenne kept a close eye on his daughter. Niico, her constant companion these days, watched her as well.

Siia poured her a touch more *sarave*. "It's for the best. You know that, don't you?" she said.

Aelle forced a tiny smile and took a sip. "It was strange seeing him today. Of course. But, I knew you'd bring him home eventually, Father."

Did her lip quiver? He was sick of her tears, sick of her soft heart, and thoroughly sick of her making excuses for that great beast. He was so sure he'd gotten her past it. Well, this was just one more dune to march over.

"Aelle, you may hear things, you know how people like to talk." Yuenne watched her struggle with how much to say.

"I've heard...some things. About the Mages. About, um, blood." She had gone pale and clenched her fork as if it were the only solid thing left.

Ilaan, again, speaking where he ought to keep still, he thought. Ilaan, his son, his hope, puts a foot through all his plans. He'd deal with that in due course. "Oh, poor darling. This is why you must come to me. You must be terribly upset. No, the Mages are there only to protect Rhuun and make sure he doesn't leave us again."

She looked up. "Really? Because I heard—"

"People love to talk about things they know nothing about. No one is going to harm him." He used the same soothing voice he'd used when she was a child. *I'll be back soon*, he'd say as she wept and clung to his leg. *I'll bring you back a treat.* Had he ever? He couldn't recall.

"When will he be released?" she asked.

"Well, he spent a long time on the other side, we have to be absolutely certain he didn't bring anything back. You know, diseases like the Choking came from Mistra." Aelle nodded slowly. "And he has much to tell the Mages about what happened to him while he was there. Of course, he broke our laws when he opened The Door, and there must be consequences for that as well. So we'll see." He took a small bite of his dinner. She nodded again. This was a critical moment, he had to tread carefully. "Not that you'd want to see him anyway, of course."

"I...well, I thought to talk to him..." she looked confused. It was time.

"I would have thought you had more pride than that, Aelle. You've been listening to the gossips, you seem to know so much, what else have you heard?"

She opened and then closed her mouth, baffled by his sharp tone. Not ready to cry, yet, though. "Only about the Mages...and his, ah, his father...what else is there?"

"His father, well, you heard from your many sources about that. His human parent. Blood calls to blood, as they say, and in this case they were correct." He paused. "So no one is talking about his woman, yet?" Siia was staring at him, wide eyed and near panic. Niico looked as if he wished he were anywhere else, Crosswinds included. Yuenne ignored them and pressed on.

"His...what?" Aelle still looked merely confused. "Did you just say he had a woman with him? Over there?"

"I know it hurts to be replaced, but consider how the Prince must have felt, among his own people for the first time in his life. What a relief for him."

Aelle was breathing rapidly and her pallor replaced by high color in her cheeks. "Speak plainly, Father."

Siia shot a dark look at her husband and said, "You are a strong girl—a woman now, by Light and Wind. You will be fine—better off by far."

Yuenne continued. "When I found him, there in the human world, he had several of them by his side. One of them, a young woman almost as big as he is, hung on his arm. He had her hand in his. I don't know how those creatures comport themselves, but I know what it looked like to me."

"I see," Aelle said faintly. She took a bite of dinner, chewed, and swallowed. The rest of them watched her effort. "I see," she said more loudly. "Well then."

No tears. Well done. He had never been more proud of his daughter. If she had made a fuss he still had all that kissing and longing glances and extended farewells to talk about. Best to keep that in his pocket, just in case. *Perhaps Siia is right and she'll be fine after all.* "I'll need someone to tend to him—bring him meals and so on."

Aelle nearly choked on her drink. "You can't imagine I would—"

"Light and Wind, no, certainly not!" That was all Yuenne needed, having that creature seduce his daughter a second time. If he had his way—and he generally did—she would never lay eyes on him again. And his Aelle, a servant? Not in his lifetime. "I'm sure you must have a friend, a schoolmate, who might be appropriate?"

She pursed her lips. "There might be someone."

"The girl ought to be...immune to his charms." Aelle looked sick. He silently cursed himself, he'd gone too far.

"When you were children, you were good for each other," said her mother. "You have nothing to apologize for, *Shan*. How could anyone have known he was...he isn't...Help your father find someone who can properly attend to him." Yuenne knew his wife once had a warm spot for Rhuun, although he'd fallen out of her good graces as they grew older. She said she thought he'd gotten rather strange. Strange, that was putting it mildly! Well, he had the example of his mother. Even back in the old days, Yuenne maintained that the old king and even the otherwise sensible heir, her brother Araan, had let that girl run wild. But taking up with a human? Honestly, who could have guessed that Hellne had it in her?

"We went to school with a girl named Daala. You remember her?" Yuenne shrugged. "Her husband is...well, I think the family would be grateful for an opportunity like this. They—she and Rhuun—they didn't care for each other, but she's clever enough and a hard worker."

Yuenne was glad to have that settled; he couldn't tell one giggling girl from another, and as long as she kept Rhuun from starving and didn't try to smuggle him out under her dress, it didn't matter to him. He turned to another topic. "It would do his mother good to know he's been brought home safely." Siia gave Yuenne a sharp look, but held her tongue.

Aelle set her fork down. "Father, you can ask me every day from now until the moons fall into the sand, and my answer will be the same: I don't know where she is. I saw her the night of the party, I saw her leave with those awful Mages, and then I never saw her again. I. Don't. Know. But I'll tell you who should hear this, and it's Ilaan."

Yuenne slammed his hands against the table. "I will blame your mouth on the shock of seeing Rhuun again today. Because why else would you mention that name in my presence?"

Niico pushed back from the table. A muscle twitched in his jaw. "A walk in the evening air will cool all our minds."

Father and daughter glared at each other over the table for a long moment. Aelle dropped her eyes. "Forgive my harsh words, Father. It was the shock, as you say." Then she turned and left the room with Niico in her wake.

"He is still your son," said Siia quietly.

"He is not. He can eat sand in the Quarter with his band of ragged peasants. He is not a member of this house anymore."

Siia let it go, but Yuenne knew his wife well enough to know that just because she kept her thoughts to herself, didn't mean it was finished.

* * *

Several nights later, as they lay side by side, he knew the subject was still on her mind. Or something was. He watched the silk scrims in the windows bellow in and out, in and out, feeling her restlessness, until he couldn't take it any longer.

"You might as well tell me," he said.

"It's Rhuun." This was a surprise. He hadn't realized she had a thought to spare for him. "Don't let this continue."

He propped himself on an elbow. "How do you mean?"

"End it quickly. Finish with him and call it done." This was more than a surprise—he'd always thought she was the tender heart of the two of them. Had she been hiding something more ruthless? He found this idea arousing.

"The longer we keep him alive, the more we can collect. The better it is for Eriis," he pointed out. "But you think we should kill him now?"

Now she sat up. "No. You misunderstand. Take what you need, what the Mages require. Take as much as you can without killing him—I'm sure it's quite a lot. He's very large. Then send him back."

He was disappointed. Soft hearted after all. "*Shani*, we went to a lot of trouble to get him back here to begin with."

"He is bad luck. Everyone who comes near him suffers in some way, himself most of all. I can feel his sorrow; it's like a cloud, I can almost smell it. Take what you need and send him away. I fear what will happen if you don't."

He rubbed her shoulder. "Is that what your stones are telling you?" He reminded himself to put a stop to that little habit of hers.

"Yu, send him away. Let him try his luck with the humans. Didn't you say he even had a woman over there?"

"Well, not so much what you or I would recognize. More like a shrieking *daaeva* hillwife." He held his circled fingers over his eyes. "And like this." As he intended, that made her laugh. "And her hair? Was white."

"It was not! You didn't tell me that!" They rearranged themselves and she laid her head on his shoulder. "There is one more thing."

He groaned. “A good and proper wife knows the time is never right for one more thing.” He knew what was coming.

“I’ll remember that when I want to be good and proper. You must reconcile with Ilaan.”

He was silent.

“Yu, listen to me. You know this business with the Mages will come to bore you. And you’ll want to strap your hiking boots back on and head back to the Vastness. I’ve seen the way you look out from the terrace; you wish you were there right now. I want my children nearby when you are gone. Aelle walks as if she is asleep; she says the right things but she’s not right, not yet. And Ilaan will not come where he is not welcome. Let him come home, for her sake.”

He still had no reply.

“Admit it, you’re more angry that he kept a secret from you than that he helped Rhuun escape. You hate when you don’t know everything.”

“I? Madam, I am an open book.” She laughed. “The truth of it is this. If I hadn’t brought Rhuun home, we would have had a debt to the Mages we never would have been able to repay.”

She rolled onto her elbow again. “I don’t like how that sounds.”

“I was hoping to avoid this conversation,” he sighed, “because I knew it would displease you. Long ago, I made a deal with the Zaal. One for one, we agreed. They’d take Ilaan and I’d give them the human blood they required. Those were the terms, and as far as the Mages are concerned, they were met. That Ilaan has disappointed us—and them—matters not at all.”

“You traded Rhuun for Ilaan.”

“Hellne was hiding something; that was obvious. Her behavior with those humans was disgraceful. And I knew the child wasn’t like us the first time I saw him; I just didn’t have any proof. I thought once Ilaan was a Mage, he’d be able to see it. They can smell things and so on. I was right, but the timing was all wrong.” He looked at her carefully in the faint light of the nightstones.

She nodded. “A fair trade.”

He let his breath out explosively. "Then you should also know that Ilaan thinks he was able to negotiate the terms on his own."

She frowned. "Terms? You mean with the Mages, his coming and going—"

"Everything they agreed to let him do. That's what Rhuun's blood is worth to them, they abandoned generations of tradition for it. I'm afraid Rhuun's fate is simply out of my hands. They'll never let him go. And as far as Ilaan, well, he thinks he got his way because he's clever. He got it because of me."

She looked sick. "Why do you tell me this now?"

"Say he comes home. Say I bring him back to you. Can you keep what I told you to yourself? Will you tell him I traded his friend for that Mage's robe he wanted? Or that if it was up to him, he'd be down there in the dark with the rest of them? Or should we let him find his own way back to us as a good and proper son?"

She had no response. She lay back down in the darkness and stared at the ceiling.

So far and no further, Siia, my princess, my pet, he thought. I knew you'd see things my way.

Chapter 24

Eriis

ILAAN SAT ON the stoop at his front door, watching the lights of the Old Quarter rise behind the walls all around him, as his alley settled into darkness. Directly opposite his door was a blank stone wall with a plate propped against it. He watched it intently, as he had for much of the day, and as he had the previous three days.

He'd nearly jumped out of his skin on seeing the words after his dinner that night, scrawled onto the bottom of his plate: *Thanks for warning. Sending help.* He didn't know how long the message had been there, but he had a good idea of who had written it. That swarm of little human lights. Niico had quietly returned the stone pen to his father's desk; he had no way to answer. He could only wait.

Beast had found himself some friends on the human side who were ready to risk a trip through The Door to help him. For the first time, Ilaan began to wonder about the stories he'd been carefully spreading, about the prince, about rain. Stories that would be useful should they need to turn to the residents of the Old City for help. It was hardly worth considering they might have any truth to them. But Rhuun had done something over there so profound he'd called an army, perhaps, to his side.

Ilaan nearly gave up, ready to go back to his books and his cot, when the smell told him magic was about to happen, or was happening, or never hadn't happened. It was bitter and metallic, like blood. He knew it well.

The plate he'd propped against the wall began to glow and seemed to change perspective it was no longer a plate, but a quickly widening hole. Then The Door swung open and a young woman stumbled through. He caught a quick glimpse of someplace vividly green, a whiff of cold, wet air, then The Door shut and the smell of bitter magic faded away. No army, then. Just one woman.

"Is he alive?" she asked immediately.

He stood up and slapped the dust off his robe. Reaching past her, he picked up what was once again just a dinner plate. "He's alive. Come inside." She followed him into his neat little room.

"My name is Lelet. I'm the one who contacted you." She paused. "I suppose there's not much choice in telling you; I am a human person from Mistra. I've been charmed by someone quite skilled and given this new face. I'm here to rescue the prince." She took a breath. "So if you're one of the, um, bad guys, I've made a terrible mistake." She waited.

"The prince is my oldest friend and I welcome your help. You haven't made a mistake, not yet anyway." Not an army, but maybe she would be of use. She extended her hand. He looked at it, perplexed, and she quickly lifted it to pat her hair, which was long and unbound, like a child. She carried herself too loosely, she stared at him like she was simple, and her robe was light blue which of course wouldn't do at all, but in every other respect she was a remarkable forgery. Seeing her confusion, he added, "I'm Ilaan. I sent the warning. I'm sorry it was too late."

She nodded. "You saved my sister; my family is in your debt. But I know who you are." She looked at the worn stone and then out the door at the dirty sky. "It's just like he said. So, he's alive." She gave a sigh of relief. "Have you seen him? Is he well?"

"Comfort yourself with knowing that the Mages intend to keep him alive and in good condition. Their current work demands it." He didn't tell her what that work involved. He wasn't completely sure and didn't want to put it in his mouth or in her ear. He handed her a cup of water, and stopped her before she drank. "You must take three small sips, and then I'll do the same. Then you can drink the rest." He sighed. "A lot to learn. I guess Rhuun didn't tell you much."

"Ruin? That's his real name? I thought that was what that awful man called him. Why would someone name their child—"

"No, it's like this." He flipped over the paper he'd been writing on and spelled it out for her.

"Rhuun...it's kind of beautiful that way." She turned the paper over. "What languages are these?"

"That's Mid-Eriisai, and that's your language, but from many hundreds of years ago. I'm working on some things."

"He told me you were clever. He talked about you all the time."

Ilaan colored and shrugged. "Language, it's my main study. No, don't stare. That's really important. Never stare."

She stood and walked to the window. "Nice view." She paused. "Three sips. Am I going to be able to do this?"

"You've got a new face and you've made it through The Door. A little late for hesitation. Lelet," he said thoughtfully. "First of all, we'll need a better name for you."

"My own name, isn't that good enough?"

He laughed. "No. No one would ever name their daughter that. It's too close to Lelee. I imagine it was common enough once, but it's fallen out of favor."

"Why? It's just a name."

"I'll tell you a story about the first Lelee. It happened ages before the war, before anyone even knew about the Door, in the earliest days of the Regency. Lelee was a beautiful young lady whose parents made a marriage for her with a wealthy, older farmer. He doted on her and she at first was happy for the attention. Their little daughter was their blue sky. But Lelee was spoiled and restless. She found herself bored with her husband and with life on the farm. Her little daughter began to grate on her nerves. She wanted to escape. She began to dream about the court. Soon all she could talk about was going to the city and being presented before the king. She prayed every night to the Fire Moon—"

"Is that the big or the small one?" Lelet asked.

"The smaller one is the Fire Moon. 'Take me to Court', she prayed, 'I would give anything.' And the Fire Moon heard her prayers and found her boredom attractive and her fickle heart interesting. He appeared to her in the guise of a handsome young man, and she did not hesitate to join with him."

"That little slut!"

"He asked her, 'What would you give to be presented at Court?'

"'Anything,' she said. 'Everything.'

"He asked her three times on three nights, and every night she gave the same answer, 'Anything. Everything.' On the fourth he did as she desired and took Lelee to the city. Still wearing a young man's face, he presented her to the Court, but as they stood before the King he dropped his mask and showed his True Face. And he said, 'Look! I give you Lelee. I present to you an unfaithful wife, I present to the Court a murderer.' Of course she didn't understand until he explained that when you care for nothing, everything can be taken away. Her husband lay dead in his bed, and their farmlands had been put to the torch. Lelee was never seen again. The Fire Moon took her daughter to raise as his own, but that's another story. And that's why we can't call you Lelee."

"How very...um...instructional. Okay." She thought for a moment. "What about May?" She drew it out. "Maaaaaay."

"Maaya." He nodded. "A pleasure to meet you, Maaya. My father is the awful man you mentioned earlier, by the way."

She looked horrified—the way she screwed her face up was like a stage parody of emotion. He began to see the scope of the job ahead of them.

"He said Moth's—Rhuun's mother was in some sort of terrible danger from the Mages. But that was a lie, wasn't it?"

Ilaan nodded. "He always knows what to say to get a job done. He's been planning this for a long time. Rhuun is sequestered in the royal quarters, under my father's control.

He nodded. “That’s right. A perfect day. Don’t cry, we have little enough water as it is. We’ll get him back. I have a plan, Maaya. Remember that, I always have a plan.”

No one goes in to see him without his approval, and approves no one. We've tried to get friends in, but it's no u The only ones to see him are my father and the Mages. A his server. Now, the serving girl, Daala, I hear she compla of overwork. I hear she grinds the stones to dust abo caring for him to anyone who'll listen. The burden, you se

"They might need to hire another serving girl. One wh listens more and talks less."

It was Ilaan's turn to sigh with relief. This strange hybr creature was brave enough, maybe, to be of some use. "M father is the one who'll talk to you about the job. He's got n reason to think you're anything other than an unlettere girl--with that old-fashioned name and your accent, yo might be recently moved in from the Edge. We'll talk a lot you and me, that'll help your diction. And before I let my father see you, we'll make sure you're no different than any other girl in the city. Once you're in, you can let Rhuun know we're getting him out of there."

He could see she was struggling to remain composed. "I am grateful," she said.

"He's my best friend and has been my whole life. I am the one who is grateful." He hesitated, then said, "I haven't seen him since he's been back. They won't let me talk to him; I don't know what you are to each other..."

"He called me *shani.*"

Ilaan raised a brow. I have to keep this girl well clear of Aelle, if nothing else. "Do you know what that means?"

"I assumed it was the same as sweetheart, or something like it."

"Not really. It's more than that. You see, *Shan* is wha you call someone you are fond of. A parent says it to a child an older person to one younger. It means sunshine. You' notice we don't have much of that here, so it's a special thing to call someone."

"And *shani*?"

"The literal meaning is a blue sky untouched by clouds.

"A perfect day." She blinked back tears.

Chapter 25

Eriis

DAYS TURNED INTO weeks and Maaya wandered the streets and alleys of Eriis, mainly staying close to the alleys in the Quarter she knew by heart. She kept her eyes down, but quickly learned to mimic the way the Eriisai slid their gaze across your face, taking the measure of you without even appearing to notice you. Back home, women (and some fashion forward men, Rane included) wore earrings, and of course a necklace or a bracelet was nothing special, but here the people used their features as a canvas. They had hoops and rings and studs of gold, silver, black, or white in noses, eyebrows, lips, tongues—and of course she knew there must have been a feast of ornamentation beneath their drab tunics.

Ilaan told her tattoos that anyone might see were coming into vogue, and she sometimes caught a glittering gold and black design on a hand, throat, or the back of a neck. He said since The Weapon, tattoos and ornaments were strictly kept out of sight. But, he added, things were changing. Even their clothing was changing, which was good news as far as she was concerned. Noticing no one in the Quarter wore any garment but the drabbest shades of brown, she asked why and he gave a shrug—it's always been that way, he'd said. The people coming and going from the palace—which she learned was now called the Councillary—often wore white. No one wore black. Ilaan explain that by wearing black you displayed your allegiance to the royal family, which was no longer considered a wise sartorial choice. It was even said that you might find yourself sent to the Crosswinds if the brown in your tunic was too dark, but of course people liked to gossip. Still, he said, handing her a tan robe with white stitching, why take a chance?

One afternoon in the market, she caught a glimpse of a man surrounded by white clad guards. He wore a brown robe with the hood thrown back, and it was trimmed at collar and cuff with bright green. It felt like a splash of water. She thought about her family's famous Ever Blue silk, it would knock these people over.

She was learning not to stare, but it was a hard lesson when someone on the street in front of you would stop walking, sprout wings and sail away, or simply appear out of thin air. They seemed to have a sense of where objects in their path might be, and didn't materialize half inside a wall, at least, not that she'd seen. She knew they all had fire, even she had that, but rarely did she see anyone use it. They were unfailingly polite to your face, but she shuddered to think what might be said about her clumsy attempts to fit in. She knew she smiled too much, walked too fast, and her accent was deplorable. It sometimes seemed overwhelming, and then she would think of Moth, and how he was so close, and she would grit her teeth and get back to it.

* * *

She sat across from Niico and Ilaan, the scant furniture pushed into a rough triangle. She looked forward to Niico's visits, finding him amusing if sometimes a bit blunt. Ilaan seemed to wilt a bit without him. Back on Mistra their relationship would have raised eyebrows, and she wanted to ask Ilaan if his father disapproved, or if he knew, but felt it would be another rude human blunder to add to her list. Sometimes having a glass of the awful swill they called *sarave*, sitting and listening to the two of them joke and tease, she was reminded of home. She tried to remember the friends Moth had told her about and decided Niico was the one who could fly, Ilaan of course was the smart one. If there was another who could change her face, Maaya hadn't met her yet.

"Whoever made you did a fine job," Niico told her. "If you never speak or move, you'll fool everyone. Now, what was your name again?"

"Maaya," she told him. They'd run through this many times, and she knew there was a long way to go. Still, it was hard not to be impatient. "I've just come from the Edge."

"Really? The Edge?" Ilaan looked unimpressed. "What cross alley do you live on? Who is your father? What do you think of the Mages?"

"I lived on Crags Pierced By Sun near where it crosses Waterless. I've just gotten here—"

"Got here, I think you would say," said Niico.

"I just got here. The Edge will be a fine place to live one day, but my father Iool told me I should take my chances in the city. My mother Maala—rest her now—always wanted to live in the city, but the Choking took her first. She used to say the Mages would make it rain one day. I am pleased to serve in any way I can." She kept her eyes demurely on the floor. "I am not afraid of the Beast."

She at first flatly refused to call Moth that, and it still felt like dust in her throat.

"She's getting there," said Niico. "If I just bought fruit or something from her at a stall, I wouldn't think twice."

She adjusted the collar of her plain tan tunic. It crossed in a flat V over her breasts and knotted at the hip. "I've been wondering..."

"Well, now's the time to ask," said Ilaan.

"Did that hurt?" She pointed at the slender golden ring in his right nostril. "I see most everyone has them. Noses, lips, everywhere. I've never seen them anywhere but in ears before." Of course she had, but she had no desire to talk about the fate of those little gold rings. And as for the golden balls that had brought her so much pleasure, that was no one's business but her own. And Moth's.

"Hurt?" Ilaan looked confused. "I don't..."

"When they put it in, did it cause you to feel pain?"

Niico and Ilaan shared a glance. Niico said, "Put out your hand." She didn't want to. This was going to be a test. She held out her hand and stared at it so intently she didn't notice where the flame was coming from until a pinhole appeared in the center of her palm. Ilaan had shot a concentrated beam of fire directly through it.

"Does that hurt? Are you experiencing pain?" he asked.

"No!" she breathed, amazed. "No, it just feels warm. It...it doesn't feel like anything at all. That is so weird." As they watched, the hole closed. The little circle was red, then pink, then silver, then gone. It took only seconds.

"Does that answer your question?" Ilaan asked.

"It answers a lot of questions." She held her hand up, examining it front and back. "But you can feel things. You must."

"It seems to take a greater degree of intensity," said Niico. "Instead of here" he separated his hands by an inch or so, "like you humans, the sensation must be here," and he moved them a few inches further apart. "It makes us less vulnerable to things—it's how I can compete. If I had to stop and cry over every burn, I'd still be doing training runs with new fledglings."

"It saved us after the War," added Ilaan. "It kept us from burning up in the heat. It wasn't always so hot here."

"Yes, I wanted to ask about that, too. I was expecting it to be hotter," she said. "Isn't that a big part of the problem?"

They looked at each other, trying to decide how to say it.

"It is still too hot for human persons," Ilaan told her. "But in the last few months it's gotten cooler." He looked away from her. "What the Mages are doing, it appears to be working." He tried to spare her from too much detail, but it was in every mouth: the blood of the prince, the magic of the Mages.

"Oh! Well, that's...oh, no." She twisted her hands together. "I have to be ready soon. Otherwise..."

"Otherwise the very people we will turn to will wonder why they should help us. There are other ways," Ilaan told her. "At least, I think there are."

“What if they make it rain? What if they use him and it rains? No one will help us,” she said.

“Then you’d better be ready and soon. Now, hold out your hand, I want to see your flame.”

She did.

Chapter 26

Eriis

AFTER A LONG, dry afternoon of lessons (arrange your tunic around your knees like so when you sit; look at me as if we are old friends—no, let your eye slide off to the right, not the left; Galiina's Bluff is a card game, Galiina Bluffs is a place near the city) Maaya's throat was dry and her head thumped (*at least,* she pondered, *I won't get a headache*). Niico rose and went to the door, throwing his scarf over his head.

"I am expected" he said. "I'll see if your father has anything more to say about another server. Look for me in two days' time."

She politely looked at a book (she thought she was holding it the correct way) while they said their goodbyes. She thought it was time to find her own little room, here in the Quarter. *Maaya,* she thought. *Yes, I live here in the Quarter now. Maaya. Nice to meet you. I've got a little place just off Waterless.*

After Niico had gone, she said, "Is he like a spy or something?"

Ilaan nodded. "He is exactly like a spy. He puts himself at risk coming here. Fortunately, my father thinks I am hiding out and trying to come up with a plan to get back into his good graces. It does not occur to him, what we do here. He thinks the story is over; he has Rhuun and the Mages in his fist. So he doesn't pay much attention to Niico. He has become close to my sister. She, unfortunately, is not close to me right now. But I'm glad he's there for her."

* * *

Ultimately, their story was how Niico had run into a woman, late of the Edge, who worked at a fruit stall and asked him if he knew how a young lady might find better employment than in the market.

"I told Yuenne you want to work inside," he told Maaya, finding her on her own in Ilaan's little house. "I said you must have seen me walking with Aelle and figured I was connected to the family of the Counselor. I said you looked polite, at least. And Yu said he'll see you, if only to get that Daala to stop her mouth. So," he said, accepting a glass of water and watching as she sipped thrice, properly, as he'd taught her, "You'll meet him tomorrow morning."

"I'm not ready." Her placid face was at odds with her panicked tone. That was fine. "What if he recognizes me?" Niico looked her over. She was in every respect an average girl of little means, simply trying to better herself.

"Unless you remind him, it's highly unlikely. Yuenne has a great deal on his platter. You know he named himself Chief Counselor?" He rummaged through Ilaan's tiny kitchen, finding cups and a bottle.

"Is that something like Prime Minister?" she asked.

"No idea. But with the queen...wherever she is, there is no one to stand in his path. We always thought he wanted to take the High Seat, but it appears he intends to toss it aside in favor of something new." He handed her a cup of *sarave*.

"Thank you. I don't do the three sips with this stuff, though, right?"

He knew she knew that one, but was letting him instruct. After so many years of deferring to his clever Ilaan in all things, he found he appreciated that. "That is correct. Only with water." She sipped and swallowed with some difficulty. "I gather our favorite drink is an acquired taste?"

She made a face. "It tastes like a rusty nail stirred in water. With some ash thrown in for texture. You all really like this stuff?"

"I would remind you, it wasn't our idea. We'd love to be drinking your *birr* all day, but mostly all we have is sand."

She sobered and took his hand. He raised a brow, but said nothing. "I am honestly sorry. I wasn't thinking. It's all so much to learn, but that's not an excuse."

"Accepted. Here's one more thing to learn." He withdrew his hand. "Unless you have an established relationship, it's considered in poor taste to touch someone's hand. Any bare skin, really. There are many who think it's rude to touch a casual acquaintance at all. In fact, there is an element of...invitation to it."

"Light and Wind." She dropped her head into her hands. "I just insulted your drink and made a pass at you."

"Well, you got 'Light and Wind' right."

She groaned, then straightened and smiled and took a sip of the *sarave*. "Yum! Now. We were talking about my future employer. You said something about the High Seat. That's where the king or queen sits, so how was he planning on taking it over? Is he somehow related to Moth? I mean Rhuun? Or does he think he can maybe marry the queen?"

Niico laughed. "His wife would have something to say about that. Siia seems sweet, but she's made of rock underneath. No, it was through Aelle, of course. He planned on her taking the seat, and convinced Aelle it was as good as foretold."

"Aelle...is she the face changer, or..."

He wasn't surprised Rhuun hadn't talked about Aelle with this human. It would have been uncomfortable, not expedient. He expected no more from the Ugly Prince. He said, "Aelle is Ilaan's sister. Rhuun might have mentioned her. Of course, what Yuenne really wanted was for Rhuun to marry her and *then* disappear. From what I gather, Yu promised him to the Mages a long time ago. The way he vanished through The Door that day was most inconvenient." Niico shook his head. "Aelle on the Seat, the queen disgraced and out of the way, and Ilaan assuming control of the new Peermage. He aims high, Yuenne. Rhuun put his foot through those plans, for fair." He frowned. "I don't know what he intends to do now. I just hang around and listen. Aelle needs me. She is not...she is no longer quite herself."

"Wait. This girl—Aelle. She and Rhuun..."

"They were together since they were children. Everyone thought they would wed. She certainly did. Part of the plan."

"She's the peach. Huh."

"The what?" So he had mentioned her. But given her an unpleasant human name.

"Ah, nothing." Maaya darted a look into his eyes and then slid her gaze down the right side of his face, deftly ending the conversation. But just when he was about to compliment her, she raised her head and continued. "But if I may ask, why didn't they wed?"

Niico sipped his *sarave*. Too bad, but it would have to do. Neither one of them, nor the prince himself had days enough to train the girl in proper behavior. "I'm not sure it's my story to tell. But Rhuun is...he wasn't a good match for Aelle. Maybe Ilaan can tell you more."

"You don't much like him, do you?" she asked.

He sighed. The Ugly Prince was the brightest star in this woman's sky, as well. "It's a long story and goes back many years. The thing of it is, he and Ilaan were so close, I thought they were together. I didn't have friends, not those kind of friends anyway, and I didn't understand what it looked like. I used to think they were laughing at me. I used to watch them, always talking, always smiling. And Rhuun with his head bent down so Ilaan wouldn't have to strain to hear him. I would think, 'that should be me.' I just couldn't understand how Ilaan could be with someone so ugly. No offense. I didn't know how to talk to someone as clever as Ilaan—you understand we were so young—and I was only good at one thing. So I took it out on Rhuun. I'm not sure that he's forgiven me."

"Who? Rhuun or Ilaan?"

Niico smiled. "You cut right to the heart of things, don't you? That must be a human thing. No, we are not friends.

But it's important to Ilaan and so it's important to me. But Aelle...I think she'd see him dead. I think she'd hold the knife. Stay away from her. You'll know her—she's very beautiful, and wears only white. And she never smiles."

Chapter 27

Eriis

"SOMETIMES I WISH they'd just drain him and get it over with." Maaya hurried through the Old Quarter marketplace, racing to keep up with Daala, who grumbled as she walked. The taller woman frowned at the lengthening shadow on the side of the War Tower. "*Rushta*, we're going to be late."

"Why don't they?" Maaya asked. She juggled the heavy silver pitcher from hand to hand nervously.

"Oh, give me that," said Daala, trading her basket of food for the heavier pitcher. "What did you say your name was?"

"Maaya," she said, forcing herself to be calm. "Why don't they?"

"The best vessel is one that's alive, isn't it? They can take as much as they want and there'll still be more. Until they're ready—but that's got nothing to do with me. I'll be glad to see the back of this whole thing, though. Night and day, beck and call. Like he's still some sort of prince. Like I'm some sort of errand girl. I don't know what made them think this was a job for one person. Just come in from the Edge, did you?"

"Yes," said Maaya, "my family, they thought it would be better for me in the city, there'd be jobs. We tried and tried, but the Edge is nothing but sand. I've never seen so many people in one place."

"Well, you're lucky to have this assignment. Not that I'm not grateful—I can use another set of hands and a bit of free time. All he does is drink and complain, and my husband is starting to do the same." Daala paused and looked her over, "Now, you know what to do? When we get there?"

Maaya gnawed briefly on a fingernail. They'd had this conversation dozens of times, she, Ilaan, and Niico. An unlettered country girl would not leap to answer. She might even be a bit suspicious of her new city raised superior. "The Counselor mostly said not to talk to him, and to do what the Mages tell me."

"And me," added Daala. "The Mages, and me."

Maaya nodded and looked at her feet.

This seemed to satisfy Daala, who led them through the ancient stone gate, the Royal Arch, onto the palace grounds. She snickered.

"They'll need to change the name of the gate," she said as they entered the Great Hall. "Stay in the back, don't speak, do what you're told."

Here at last. Maaya gazed up and around at the satiny stone walls of the great, wide hallway, mostly black flecked with grey and white. There were dozens of baskets of rocks, suspended from nothing, glowing and throwing overlapping circles of warm light on the floor. Taking stock of everything around her kept her from fainting from nerves. Instead of listening to her pounding heart, she counted windows, many of them, and high off the ground. They were all covered by heavy, dark silk curtains—the dust got in anyway, but it would have been worse inside than out, without them. The floor did not shine like the walls, as generations of feet had ground decades of dust into the tiles. The sound of moving feet over the gritty floor was constant, like an interior wind. She saw scores of servants with baskets of sand, and with sand transformed into loaves of bread and squares of something—she couldn't tell—food? There were many people in groups and by themselves, strolling and chatting; many of them all in white, which looked quite smart against the dark stone walls.

"So don't talk to him. And try not to stare; he's even uglier than he was when we were children." Daala smiled unpleasantly. Maaya had taken an instant dislike to the woman, and along with hiding her fear, she also worked on masking her distaste. "You know, he used to chase me all over when we were in school. Wanted to join with me in the worst way. Like he even had a chance, that great beast. Of course I said no—politely. One had to be polite, back then. Not anymore. He's losing his wits faster than sand through a screen. He won't remember his name, soon."

"I thought he was with that Aelle girl? Wasn't he?" At Daala's look, she continued. "Even at the Edge we liked to keep up with the Royals. It was all so...glamorous. And we heard that girl had him all to herself. I guess we heard wrong?"

"Oh, Miss Stick thought it was a done deal! Like that ever stopped a man. Don't let anyone tell you otherwise." Despite her hectoring tone, Maaya thought Daala looked pleased to be correcting her impression.

The corridor ended in a T shape, and there were four robed men waiting for them at the left-hand arm. Daala swore under her breath.

"Daala. Why are you delayed? Who is this?" The Zaal, as Maaya had learned, was the only one who spoke. He had a fingernail-thin band of green on the border of his hood.

"This is Maaya, the new girl." said Daala. "She got lost and made us late."

The Zaalmage leaned in and gave Maaya a sniff. She fought an impulse to back away. "Very well. Take the pitcher, stay in the back. Head down, mouth shut. We will instruct you. This is a day of collection, and there may be some...unpleasantness. If you feel you must cry or you become discomforted, leave at once."

"I am honored to assist. I will do as I am told," Maaya said, keeping her eyes down. She followed the group down the corridor, which was darker than the main hall. There were bowls of stones set on the floor, but only every third one was lit. The windows were covered and looked as if they had been for years. Unswept sand gathered along the edges of the tiled floor. They reached a door which looked to be made of real wood, intricately inlaid with loops and swirls of silver. Maaya thought it looked like clouds racing across a dark sky. She had been warned not to touch it. Two of Yuenne's household guards, clad in white, stood on either side of it.

"Very well. Let's get this over with." The Zaalmage leaned forward and blew on the door.

"State your business," said the door.

"Would one of you please re-charm this thing? It's supposed to recognize me," the Zaal snapped.

"State your business," the door said again.

The Zaal sighed and said, "The Mages are here for the Ceremony of *Laa Na*." The door swung open.

They filed in. It was even darker inside, and one of the robed Mages lit the stone bowl that hung from the ceiling. The room was small in contrast to the grand scale of the main corridors, and a bit stale. It contained an outsized rumpled bed, a desk, and a low dresser with a mirror hung over it. Maaya noticed three square places on the wall where the paint was several shades darker—whatever hung there had been there for a long time, but was now gone. The windows were sealed with dark silk and more silver. A pair of dusty boots lay in the corner and several books sat open on the various pieces of furniture. A tray with bread and cheese sat untouched, the edges of the cheese curling slightly. Next to the tray, two bottles of *sarave*, both empty. Sand had gathered in many places along the walls. Other than that, the room was empty.

"What's *Laa Na*?" whispered Maaya.

"They give everything a fancy name. It means Waterfall Cascades into a Silver Sea." Maaya looked confused. "It means they're collecting his blood, you nit. Don't they teach you anything out there?"

The Zaal gave them a sharp look over his shoulder. The two women looked studiously at the floor.

"Prince Rhuun," said the Zaalmage, "let's not make this any more difficult, shall we?"

Nothing.

"Need I remind you of your family's wellbeing? And your friends? They are counting on you, as are we all—of course. Your sacrifice—"

"Fuck you and all your little hooded friends." The voice came out of nowhere.

He remembers a few words, she thought, and bit back a hysterical laugh.

"Ah, that human greeting again. We are educated. Your sacrifice goes towards a better future for Eriis. The advancements we've already made—"

"Ugh, fine. Just don't make me listen to your *scorping* speech, *again*." A tall man with long, tangled hair appeared, sitting on the bed. He was thin and his eyes were strangely bright, as if in the grip of a long fever. His tunic, which hung off of him, had the sleeves sliced off. Maaya gasped, caught herself and lowered her head. *Hold your face still, hold it still, everything depends on it...*

"Prince Rhuun, if you please?" The Zaalmage nodded at his two brothers. One produced a shallow silver bowl from under his robes and set it on the bed. The other handed the Zaal a long, thin knife. The Zaalmage turned it in his hand and Maaya blinked at the sliver of light on the blade. There was no need to test the edge. Rhuun folded his arms and looked away. The Mages shared a look. One of them lifted a hand and twisted it in the air. Rhuun flinched and went rigid. His arm pried itself away from his body and hovered over the bowl. The result of many earlier 'sacrifices' was evident from his wrist to nearly his shoulder.

Now that things were in place, the Zaalmage quickly collected enough blood to fill the bowl, and in exchange for the knife, the third Mage handed him a silver lid—it wouldn't do to spill a drop. As they watched, the slash on his forearm began to knit. The three filed out, leaving the Zaalmage, the two women, and Rhuun.

Once the bowl was safely out of the room Rhuun was released.

"You don't have to do that," he said quietly. His voice shook.

"You knocked the bowl onto the floor, if I recall. You tried to take the knife. We do what is necessary for the good of Eriis. And we thank you for your sacrifice. Your family and companions will be well rewarded."

"I want to talk to Ilaan," he said.

"Yes, well, he does not wish to talk to you. I have asked him as you've requested, many times. He is busy. He has friends and family of his own, now. Ah! But. Your mother sends her regards and thanks. She is well." Rhuun rolled his eyes and vanished. "We will see you again in a few days' time. Your books will be delivered tomorrow." The Zaalmage waited for a reply, and when it became clear none was forthcoming, he turned to the two women. "Clear out the mess, see that he eats, don't talk to him. Daala, we have discussed punctuality."

"I was explaining to the new girl what she had to do. It won't happen again."

"Hmm." The Zaalmage glared at the two and left.

Daala went about straightening up the room, turning the sandpiles into little cubes that could be retranslated into something else and putting them in the now empty basket, straightening the mirror, bustling about as if there wasn't anyone there with them. She set a fresh platter of bread and triangles of tan and white cheese on the desk, and as she worked, she closed every book she came across. Finally she turned and said, "I know you want *sarave*, but you're getting water. Finish the water and we'll see about the *sarave* for tomorrow."

"Thank you, *Mother*," came the voice from thin air. "And see about the books arriving in the morning, why don't you? The Zaal wants to keep me happy, after all. And I want a new tunic. This one is too big."

"If you ate what I brought you, it would still fit."

"Once you've eaten food on the other side, you really notice the sand taste. It's all a bit gritty. But you know about that, don't you, Daala? Everything turns to sand in your mouth."

"If you love it so much, why don't you go back and live there with your disgusting humans?" Daala had given up the pretense of cleaning and stood with her hands on her hips, snarling at the unoccupied bed.

"Oh, believe me, I would. Open the door and watch how fast I leave. You'll never have to wait on me again." He reappeared, still sitting on the bed. "Hey, who's the new girl?" Maaya was trying to be inconspicuous, but the room was small. She poured fresh water from the silver pitcher into a ceramic jug set next to Rhuun's meal, and then waited by the door for this to be over. She couldn't tear her eyes away from the stripes and slashes up and down his arms. "Hey, new girl? Did Daala tell you about how I tried to get under her dress? It's her favorite imaginary story. Ask her, she'll tell you I was on her like grit on glass." He vanished again. "It's a really funny story." Daala turned red and gnawed her lip.

Maaya whispered to her, "I thought we weren't supposed to talk to him."

Daala snatched up the jug and with a sweet smile, poured the water on the floor. "Oops," she said. She nodded at Maaya. "Let's go. We're done here." She slammed the door, making the inlaid silver vibrate and whisper. As they walked away, Maaya thought she heard a voice.

"Hey, new girl."

She turned, but there was no one there.

* * *

Daala was a bit longer in the leg than Maaya, and she had to struggle to keep up with her, which was fine because it precluded conversation. Maaya had no desire to revisit what they'd just seen. When they arrived at the kitchens, Daala slammed the pitcher onto the great stone slab of the counter. The cook shouted at her to mind herself and that just made her angrier. She whirled on Maaya.

"I would quit. I would tell him to eat *rushta* and die for the rest of his sorry human life, may it be short."

"Why don't you, then?"

She sighed and Maaya could see some of the fight drain out of her. "To work for the Zaal and the Mages is an honor.

What they are doing will change our lives, and it's important. It's already started, hasn't it?" She smiled thinly. "Plus I get to see that beast get what he deserves. I just wish they did it more often." She wiped the dust off her hands and patted her tightly coiled hair. "That doesn't mean I want to see him every day, though. Tomorrow you can clean up after him." She twisted her mouth. "Books in the morning, pick them up at the library. And I guess *sarave* if he wants it, which he will. The Mages will not attend, but that doesn't mean you can be late. Find me after and let me know he's behaving himself. And don't talk to him!"

* * *

As the evening dust rose outside the city walls, Maaya navigated her way, following the streets she had memorized from the Royal Arch towards the heart of the Old City and on into the Quarter. She wandered through the maze of cobbles and courtyards, past the little school with the scorch-marked walls, past the fruit stands and the fabric stalls, until she at last came to a blind alley. She looked both left, right, and above to check if anyone was following her. Once she felt confident she was alone, she slipped inside. The buildings were close enough to touch on both sides, and in the dark she did just that. At the end of the alley, she climbed a narrow stair into complete darkness. If she didn't know there was a door, she would have walked right into it. She knocked once, twice, paused, again, again. As the door opened, she stepped into the square of light and shut it quickly behind herself.

"Did you see him?" asked Ilaan.

Her only answer was to fall into his embrace and sob as if she would never stop.

Chapter 28

Eriis

THE NEXT MORNING, Maaya stood outside the door of Rhuun's prison and tried to figure out what to do. She bore a basket with his meal that she'd collected from the kitchens—a bowl of fruit and a meat broth along with bread and cheese, a bottle of *sarave*, and a pitcher of water. It was heavy and she'd have to make another trip to get his books later. But she'd been instructed not to touch the door, and there was no point calling out—he couldn't open it from the inside anyway. The guards were still there, although today they looked bored and barely glanced at her.

She leaned forward and blew on one of the silver swirls. *Blood and breath*, she thought. *To make magic work, blood or breath. Not all that different.*

The door said, "State your business."

Maaya, feeling a little foolish talking to the door, said, "I'm to clean the room and deliver a meal. I'm here for Daala."

The door opened, and as soon as she was inside, shut itself behind her.

It appeared much as it had the day before, an empty room in need of airing out, the bed unmade, and sand on the floor. The food was picked at. The lamp was lit—the Mages hadn't put it out before they'd left. She imagined it had been glowing all night. She set the tray down, poured a glass of water and held it out.

Rhuun appeared sitting on the floor at the foot of the bed and gratefully accepted it.

"Thank you, new girl. You're a lot nicer than that rat-face Daala."

She watched him drink. "You've gotten very good at disappearing," she said.

"Yes, well I've had time to practice." He yawned and stretched. "Could you turn the light out when you're done? I threw a bottle at it, but it wouldn't break. Got sand all over the floor, though. Sorry." He looked at her more closely. "Why are you crying? I'll sweep it up myself, don't worry about it."

"It took me so long to get here," she said. "I'm so sorry."

"You're sorry? About what? And 'got here' from where?" He took in her puffy eyes and anguished expression. "I'm sorry, but do I know you?"

"Yes," she said. "Yes, you know me, Moth."

He lunged off the floor and pinned her against the wall by her shoulders. One hand found her throat. "Who are you? Who told you to call me that?" Rather than try to free herself or pull away, she stared at his outstretched arm and he followed her gaze. The most recent slash had reopened and was slowly filling with blood.

She took the edge of her sleeve and gently wiped off the arm that held her. "You did. You told me it was your name. In the cart. Back home."

He took a step back, still holding her at arm's length. "No. Don't say that. You're the new girl. The Mages told you to say that. What are you? A spy?" He shook her hard enough to bounce her head against the wall. "What do you want? Why don't they just kill me?"

"We robbed a house, and you vanished, and I flew through the air."

He stumbled back and away from her. "You're not her. You're one of them. Why are you doing this?"

"You gave me orchids. I gave you fire. I got a new face so I could find you. Did you really think I wouldn't come for you?"

"Lelet?" He gripped her by the arms again, as if to see if she was really standing there.

"We ate a pear, you and I. And we joined...don't you remember?"

"Lelet...How is this possible? Are you real? If you're not real...If you're not real, it's almost over."

She reached up to touch his face, stroking the scrubby short beard he'd allowed to grow in, tracing with her fingertips the bruise-purple shadows around his eyes. "You aren't taking care of yourself," she whispered. "It's a good thing I showed up. I've come to take you home."

"How? How are you here?" But she couldn't answer because he was kissing her, and she could feel his tears on her face—or maybe they were her own. And it was as if all his grief and fear and loneliness transformed into something else, because now there was nothing between them but need. It poured off him like water, and as his kisses became more urgent her sorrow fell away and she matched his desire. As they kissed, she fumbled with the laces of his leggings, he was so thin they would have slipped right off, but instead got caught on his erection, which made him yelp. As his *yala* sprang free she caught a flash of gold, hot and bright, and then it was gone.

He pulled hard on the hip tie of her tunic, and when it wouldn't come loose he simply rucked her dress up to her waist, and she kicked off her sandals and was out of her leggings and linen in a flash. He was thin, and reduced in some ways, but he was still strong enough to lift her. Now she was pinned to the wall again, but this time by the length of his body. She locked her legs around his waist and gripped him by the hair and cried "Yes" and "yes" and "yes," arching her back against his thrusts. He couldn't last long, and he finished with a shuddering gasp with his face buried against her neck. He carefully set her down and then collapsed on the floor beside her.

They straightened themselves and dressed in silence. She sat with her back against the bed, and he sprawled with his head in her lap.

Finally he said, "This wasn't what I wanted for us."

"I know." She was trying to tease the snarls out of his silky hair with her fingers, but it was no use. *He'll need a haircut*, she thought.

"I've thought about it—you and I, what it would be like. I've thought about it quite a lot, what would happen if I ever saw you again. This...was not it."

"Funny," she said, "it was exactly how I pictured it."

He laughed, and then they were all right. He rolled onto his back so he could look up at her.

"There's something going on. No one will tell me anything. But listen, you have to find Ilaan. They say he won't see me, you have to get a message to him."

"Sweetheart," she said, "Ilaan sent me to you."

He had to get up and stand with his back to her for a few minutes. His story came out quickly enough; he thought everyone he knew had turned their backs on him and left him alone. He'd been locked away here for many weeks, he'd lost count. He thought every day he was going to die. Many times he wished they would just hurry up and kill him. He never dared to hope he'd see her again.

"I suppose I ought to start by asking how you got a new face," he said.

She stood on her toes to fix her hair in his mirror. She sighed, her dress was hopelessly wrinkled, but at least they hadn't torn it. She slipped her shoes back on and picked up the tray.

"It'll have to wait—they'll wonder what we're doing in here. I'm guessing your friend Daala doesn't linger and I have to go tell her you're still alive. I'll be back with your books later today. And if you don't eat, I'll be very angry."

He pulled her into his arms and kissed her. "Whatever you want."

"*Shani,* I have to go."

He smiled. "You learned a new word."

"It's an important one. I will tell you everything. But you have to know, you are not alone." She kissed him again, and the door shut itself behind her. She'd only taken a few steps, when she returned, opened the door, and found him sitting on the floor drinking water.

"I can turn the light off, if you still want me to."

"Leave it on," he said. She kissed him quickly, then more slowly, and wouldn't leave until he set the tray on the floor by his side and began to eat.

As she made her way back towards the main hallway, she again thought she heard a voice.

"Her eyes, her eyes..."

But again, there was no one there.

* * *

"So," she said, "what's the story with you and Daala?" She sat on the edge of his bed and transformed the sand on the floor into cubes, which he gathered and put in her basket.

"Well," he said, "she's responsible for this." He pointed at a faint, curved scar on the top of his foot. "Or maybe it was this one." He lifted the edge of his leggings and showed her another thin line, this time on the back of his calf. "I didn't actually catalogue them. But at least one. Then when we got older, she wanted something else." He rubbed the back of his neck and looked a bit embarrassed. "She was pretty upfront about it, but at that time there was only one girl for me. Then she said Aelle would never have to know." He paused. "I, ah, well. I laughed at her."

"Women generally don't like that," she pointed out.

"It was nerves! But you can't take it back, can you?"

"The women in your life fall into two rather distinct camps, I've noticed." He tossed the last chunk of sand in the basket, sat on the floor next to her and leaned against her leg. When she'd brought his books, she'd been pleased to note that he'd eaten everything on the tray and drunk all the water. He'd also gotten rid of the beard, and she thought he'd even made an attempt on his hair. The *sarave* remained unopened. "Now, tell me about this room."

"This? Is where I grew up. I could've moved to a bigger one, the hall is nothing but empty family quarters, but I guess I was used to it. And I had it fixed so things were the right height." She'd noticed the bed was cobbled together from several sources; it was longer than her own bed back in Mistra. "But it's not mine anymore. Now it's full of charms. I can't open the windows or the door, and they've done something to the stones so I can't light them or extinguish them. I haven't been able to make fire since the inn. All I can do is this." He vanished and reappeared.

That's not nothing, she thought. Then she remembered the Zaal's irritation the day before. "There's something wrong with the door, though. It didn't open for the Zaal."

"I think it's because Daala keeps slamming it. You're not supposed to touch it."

I'll make sure to give it a good whack on my way out, she thought.

He continued. "They've also charmed the room against harm. I tried to take the knife away from the Zaal and I even got my hand on it. But I couldn't do anything with it. And once I broke the mirror and tried to use the glass, but..."

"On the Zaal?" He didn't reply. "You tried to use the broken glass on the Zaal? Moth?"

"I tried to use the glass, but it didn't do a thing." He lifted his hand and looked at his wrist. "Not a thing. They just cleaned up the pieces and hung a new mirror. It's too low, but I don't have any way to rehang it. I got in a lot of trouble for that—the mirror was pre-war and made of real glass. This one? It's transformed. There's nothing real in here anymore." She wondered how many things he'd tried to break, and rested her forehead against the top of his head.

"I'm real," she said. Then she hopped off the bed and sat facing him, cross-legged on the floor. "So. Would you like to hear a story?"

"What's it about?" he asked. "Does it have horses? And is there a beautiful girl in it?"

She laughed. "You would ask about the horses first. I'll put one in for you. All your friends are in it. Everyone who loves you is in it."

"How does it end?"

She leaned forward and kissed him. "Happily ever after, *shani*. At least, I hope so."

Chapter 29

Eriis

"YOU'RE LOOKING a bit lazy today," said Niico.

He hung upside down from the handgrip on the ceiling of the aeronasium. At one time, the whole ceiling had been interlocked panels of crystal and richly polished, inlaid wood imported from Mistra, with braided silk and golden ropes for the athletes to swing from, but since the Weapon, it was just another yellow-grey stone building. The panels had been replaced with ashboard, and plain rough twine made for serviceable grips. A section of the benches where the roof had caved in had only recently been replaced. It was a symbol of the improving conditions that athletes now came to practice and matches were enthusiastically attended.

Eriis now had some time left over for leisure.

Hollen stretched his wings and joined his sparring partner at the roof. He preferred not to hang upside down, it made him light headed. He knew that would ultimately prevent him from ever being truly successful, so he was glad for the opportunity to train with Niico, who felt nothing and held nothing back. Everyone looked lazy compared to Niico.

"Do you still go to the Night Cafes?" Niico asked. This came as a surprise, since Niico rarely made small talk. Perhaps since he'd broken with Ilaan, he was looking for companionship. It would be something of a coup to show up with Niico; he was as close as Hollen knew to a celebrity. Certainly they'd gotten much closer since that night, the strangest party Hollen had ever been to. First their queen had shimmered in, and Ilaan had his head down with her, then Ilaan said something to Aelle he hadn't overheard, but made her laugh in a way he recognized as fear. That was when the Mages, the legendarily reclusive Mages had pushed past Niico into the great room and demanded to see Prince Rhuun. Anyone could have told them they were too late—a combination of a crowded room and too much *sarave* had sent him home. The Counselor had taken Aelle by the arm and told everyone it was time to leave. She looked upset, but there was no good excuse for him to try and approach her. Later, he'd heard the prince had vanished through The Door without a word to her. Rhuun's behavior would have been inexplicable, but for the fact that he was—astonishingly—half a human. It was all anyone talked about, how that explained his appearance (unusual, if you were kind, appalling, if you were not) and his behavior (a drunk, it was said. A cripple. A shame). And poor Aelle, she'd been nothing but kind to him, and now, such a betrayal. Fled back to his own kind at the expense of those who had raised him.

Hollen waited and watched for Aelle's pale, composed face, but after the night of the party she had not returned to the Night Cafe. And now Niico wanted to talk about it.

"Of course." he replied. "Want to come with? There's one next week, they're holding it—"

"Ah, no. Best not to say. No. In fact I think perhaps you ought to be busy that night." Hollen knew Niico often took his meals with the Counselor—the *Chief* Counselor's family. This was more than likely not idle gossip. While not exactly forbidden, the Night Cafe was understood to be not openly discussed. Hollen thought it was interesting that now that little flashes of color had started to appear in public places—he'd seen a Mage, which was remarkable enough in itself, and this one had a narrow band of bright green embroidered on the hem of his robe—the Cafe was coming under new scrutiny. He wondered what sort of trouble the party goers would find themselves in. A stern talking to, most likely.

Orders to disband. Rhoosa, as the organizer, she might find herself swimming in sand, though. Now that he thought of it, he hadn't seen Rhoosa lately.

Hollen asked, "Did you tell Aelle to stay home as well?"

Niico dropped like a stone from his handhold and plummeted towards the dirt floor of the arena before flaring his wings and pulling out of his dive with seemingly inches to spare. Hollen took off after him, shooting fireblasts at his heels. He led with his feet and opened his wings a split second later, but it made for a noticeably slower decent. All but two blasts missed, Niico was too quick. They did another circuit around the giant room, this time on the horizontal plane and with Niico firing away at Hollen (with a greater degree of accuracy), before heading towards the roof and the handholds again. This time they faced each other.

"Aelle told me, Holl. She asked me to let you know. And asked you keep it to yourself."

There was a pause. Hollen decided to take the offered bait.

"How is Aelle?" he asked. His face felt a bit warmer than exertion would explain.

"Aelle, I am sorry to say, still pines for the prince." Niico let go of the rope with one hand and stretched out hanging from the other. He opened his wings to make the stretch greater. "I think she would benefit from the sort of company I can't provide."

He had seen Aelle and Niico walking together often enough, laughing and talking together, and couldn't help but imagine her on his arm instead, looking up at him, smiling at him. Perhaps touching his hand. "You think I should call on her?"

Niico laughed. "I'll make it easy on you. Come to dinner tomorrow, and she'll come as well. We'll talk about our upcoming bouts and how much faster I am and how things are improving. We'll talk about the weather and the dust. Bring *sarave*."

Hollen frowned. "I would prefer not to serve as a distraction to her, you understand."

"Holl. She asked after you. She is desirous of your company. I've arranged a meeting. Would you like me to also hold your *yala* for you?"

Hollen blushed and let go, completing a long, graceful turn around the arena and touching down lightly. He headed for the first row of benches, where he had left his kit. Niico was right next to him, Hollen hadn't seen him descend. He sometimes thought Niico had invented a way to shimmer from place to place while flying. They were quiet for a moment as they opened their kits and wiped off the dust with their towels—Niico's was white with a black border, Hollen's grey. During actual matches, when there was an audience, the fliers wore the briefest garments modesty would allow, making it easier for the judges to spot scorches and burns. Hollen had never flown in a judged match, but he had his grey outfit set aside, for he knew he'd have his chance one day.

Hollen said, "You mentioned the prince..."

Niico shook his head. "Don't ask. I won't have any more to say on the subject. And when we all sit down for dinner, I highly advise against mentioning him." Niico tossed his towel into his kit bag. "Ilaan made his choice. I'd hate to see Aelle make the same mistake."

Chapter 30

Eriis

"UGH, NO! WHY?" Aelle flung herself backwards onto the couch. She'd retreated to her room after getting the news that she was expected at dinner the following night.

Niico tagged along after her. He had affected a look of surprise which he thought would entertain her. "I thought you liked him."

"He's fine. I just don't want to sit through a whole meal." She had her arms over her face and sounded a bit muffled. "You did this on purpose, Ratface."

"I do everything on purpose. I hate to see you so pouty all the time. It's been months, Ratass, it's starting to make me sad."

She threw a tufted grey and white silk pillow at his head and sat up. "If I could just see Rhuun for a minute, if I could just talk to him...."

"Here we go." He tossed the pillow back at her and went to the cabinet in the corner, pulling out a bottle of *sarave* and two glasses. "Hmm, just like *not* in the old days, there's actually something in this bottle. Okay, let's go through it again. Why do you want to see him? Do you want to be unhappy?"

"No, of course not. I just want to know why." She took the glass from Niico and stared into it. "You say, 'I do know why'. And I say, 'I want to hear it from him'. And you say—"

"Your father will have my head if I encourage you, and you say—"

"I'm not overfond of your head anyway." She sighed and took a sip. "A human girl. A big, nasty—and did you hear? They say she had white hair!" She took another sip, this time more of a gulp.

Niico was well aware that 'they' was her father, the only one who'd seen this alleged other woman, and he didn't hesitate to fill the ears of every gossip at Court—what was now called the Counsel. Yuenne was careless of what Aelle felt, but very exacting in what she heard. As far as Aelle was concerned, Rhuun had been detained for the crime of opening the Door and confined for his own safety. The Mages, the blood, well, her father told her it was a lie, and so it was. And how easily Rhuun had abandoned her for a human more to his liking? Some things were hard to hear, but Yuenne knew she could handle it. Niico knew which parts of the story were lies and yet he almost believed Yuenne's version himself, so persuasive was the Counselor. He knew the truth of the story because the white haired human woman was currently a proper black haired Eriisai girl, living across the alley from Ilaan. He'd never been able to figure out how Rhuun managed to claim the hearts of people like Ilaan and Aelle, but there must be something to him, because the human girl had risked her life to try and save him. Niico was determined to help her, because she'd sworn to take the Ugly Prince back to Mistra and out of Niico's life.

"Anyway," Aelle continued, "I don't need a reason. I'll just ask him how he likes human women, and then I'll set him on fire. And not the good kind."

"Aw, that sounds fun! So, Hollen will arrive before second moonrise, why not put on some of that gold eye paint we got you? It makes you look less tired."

She finished her drink and held out the glass. "You are a deeply unpleasant person." She paused. "Did you tell Hollen to stay away? From the Night Cafe?"

"Yes, that was when he asked after you. He was so nervous, it was adorable." He took a drink and then asked her the same question that had troubled Hollen. "What will happen? How much trouble will there be?" He leaned forward. "Does it have to do with your father? He's up to something, isn't he?" He was on a short list of those who were allowed to ask about Yuenne, he tried to be judicious.

She continued to stare into her glass, not meeting his eye. "We shouldn't be making color like that. It isn't up to us, we're little more than children ourselves. When it's time for color to come back to Eriis, older and more experienced minds will let us know. It was wrong all along, and now it will cease."

For the first time, Niico felt afraid. "You told him. You told your father about the Cafe." And he immediately began to retrace every word, every step he'd taken with Aelle, praying none of them would lead her back to the little alley, or to Ilaan, or to the human woman they now called Maaya.

Aelle stood and opened the tall glass doors to her courtyard. It was a still afternoon—there were more of them now—and let the air and light in, along with the ever present dust. Nothing stopped the dust. "Someone has to guide us, now that the queen is...wherever she is. And how can he guide us if he is in the dark? If I'd told him what Ilaan and Rhuun were doing with that book, none of this would have ever happened." She gazed out the door at the low clouds. "Everything got ruined."

Niico put his arm around her shoulder. "Oh, *shan*, I'm sorry. I know. It's hard. But your father, he'll just tell them to stop, won't he?"

She pulled away and turned to face him with a little laugh. "What else do you think he would do? Send them to the Crosswinds?"

It had occurred to him.

* * *

Niico's trip back to the Old City normally was brief and uneventful—with his scarf thrown over his head, he was just another veiled figure out for a stroll. He never flew in public, it drew too many eyes and his style was easily recognized.

Today, he took a long, twisting route, doubling and backtracking over his own path. He could hear his heart in his ears and felt a hand fall on his shoulder at every step.

"You have to see her, Ilaan," he said after he'd calmed down. "We're losing her entirely. And get rid of that before someone sees it!"

Ilaan had decided to color one wall of his little house deep red. It wasn't a wall you could see from the street, and it gave the eye something to do, since the window remained a blank square. Maaya had nearly wept when she saw it, and raced home to color one little corner of her own room. If you pushed her cot away from the wall, you would find the floor a bright blue. Niico had been indifferent to it at the time, but now he saw nothing but disaster.

"Can you bring her here?" Ilaan asked, then shook his head. "I wonder if that's wise, now that I think about it. Maybe I should meet her somewhere. It's past time she and I had a conversation. You're certain she doesn't know you are here? Or that you've ever been here?" Niico knew keeping so much from Aelle made his *shani* feel ill, but if Yuenne found out about Maaya, well, if there was anything left of her to feed to a firewhirl, it would be a miracle. Between the theft of the stone pen and plotting to steal Rhuun away from the Mages? His own life, Ilaan's, all forfeit. They had to bring her to their side. "I think I know what I have to do," Ilaan said. "And it's all up to Aelle. I have to be as persuasive as my father, because everything depends on it." He laid his head on Niico's shoulder, and Niico wondered how many more unguarded moments they'd have together. "Can you bring her to the Old City tonight? Bring her to the place that used to be a plaza, the one next to the War Tower. The nose." It was all rubble, never rebuilt. It was dark. "Bring her after first moonset."

"Do you have a plan?" Niico laced his fingers at the back of Ilaan's neck. He already knew the answer. Ilaan blew sparks against Niico's lips and traced a line of flame down his back.

"It's all up to her. But if it works..."

Niico knew what went unspoken. *If it works, you'll follow your bright star, and I'll be alone.*

Chapter 31

Eriis

"...AND THAT'S HOW I wound up hanging out of a third story window!" Aelle took another sip of *sarave* and leaned back on her cushion. This was turning out to be more fun than she'd anticipated. Hanging out a window would have been more fun than she thought this evening would be, true, but Hollen was quick and clever once he got over his nerves, and Niico laid an excellent table. Plus any evening drinking with Niico was bound to at least not be boring.

"I had to fly up and rescue her. Again. Ratty, how is it that you can neither fly nor shimmer?" Niico asked.

She smiled. "Maybe I can and I just don't want to."

"Well, it's lucky you had Niico to retrieve you. I've never seen anyone fly like he does." Hollen's hero worship of Niico was sort of sweet, Aelle supposed. "Will you be attending the matches?"

Aelle hesitated. "I...ah, I need to look at my calendar."

Niico came to her rescue. "She's busy doing the thing that evening—aren't you? Didn't you tell me?"

Hollen didn't pursue it. "When you are free and it is convenient, I hope you'll consider allowing me to escort you to a match."

Aelle nodded thoughtfully. He sounded as serious as if he was addressing the Counsel, and it had taken all night for him to finally come out with it. But an evening with a nice, normal young man might serve a purpose. "I will absolutely consider it." He lit up, and she had to admit, the attention felt...appropriate. She liked Hollen better when he wasn't quite so formal, like when they'd attended the Night Cafes. She thought about how he'd looked coming off the floor, flushed and out of breath. She thought she might like to see that again.

"Well played, Hol," said Niico. "Aelle loves a grand gesture, so make sure you bring her when I'm flying." He gave Aelle a pointed look. "And it would be nice to see you in the stands again."

"A truly grand gesture would be watching me beat you in a match," said Hollen, and they all laughed. "One day," promised Hollen, taking no offense, "you'll see."

Aelle reached for the bottle, but Niico moved it away from her and replaced her glass with cool water. "It's getting late," he told her. "Hollen, thank you for visiting this evening. I hope we might dine together again soon. And are you training tomorrow?"

Once they'd sorted out their schedules and were alone, Aelle said, "What's on your mind, Ratty?" Usually they drank until there was nothing left to drink and one helped the other fly or stumble home.

"He's nice, don't you think?" Niico put the plates and cups away and straightened the cushions around his table. "I hope he gets to compete soon. He's pretty good, he just needs more nerve. Sometimes he flies like he's afraid his wings are going to fall off."

"Well, not everyone is like you. You had one fall off so you know they grow back," she replied.

"Yes, hmmm. Good times. Thanks for reminding me. We'd gone almost an entire day without referring to our dear absent friend."

"Ooops. Sorry." She reached for the *sarave* again, and again he moved it aside. "Would you mind? *Rushta*, what's gotten into you?" He sat next to her and took her hand. "Niico! What—?"

"Shut up. Listen to me for a second. We have to go out. Tonight. Now. So get your scarf and put your sandals on."

"What? Now? No, I don't want to—"

"I know you don't want to. You never want to. But we are going out. Someone needs to see you; they're waiting for you right now." Hope and fear flared in her eyes. "I'm sorry, *Shan*, I'm not taking you to see Rhuun. But you do have an appointment."

He wouldn't tell her where they were going, or who was to meet them, but she had a pretty good idea. As they walked together through the arch and past the play yard towards the Market Square, she shivered and he took her arm.

"I wouldn't have brought you out if it wasn't important. I hope you won't be angry with me later."

She sighed. "This was going to happen eventually. He can't stand it when he doesn't have me around to torment. He'll tell me something awful about Father and I'll tell him to look at his own behavior. We almost don't need to see each other, it's like it already happened."

Niico took her to the shadow of the War Tower and kissed her cheek. "Listen with both ears, Ratty. See you tomorrow."

She stood alone in the dark for a few minutes, leaning against a chunk of stone which once formed part of a huge sculpture —of what, she didn't know. She walked past it almost every day back when she liked to be out where everyone could see her, and had never given it much thought. It was just a part of the Old City that had never been repaired. She thought it rather resembled a nose.

Finally she said, "Ilaan, you might as well come out, I'm not going to stand here all night. It's late and I'm getting bored."

He shimmered in right next to her and she leapt back. "I had to be sure you were alone," he told her.

She gave him a dramatic death stare and smoothed her scarf down around her throat. "You know how much I love it when you do that. Whom did you think I was bringing?"

"Some moron in a white tunic, maybe?" She snorted and he continued. "We have to talk, and it's long overdue."

She took a closer look at him. "You look like you've been eating sand. What's going on?" He didn't reply, he just looked sad. "You know, this could all be over if you'd just apologize to Father for helping—for what you did. You could come back home. He shut your room up, but it's all still there, all your books and stuff. Now that…" she took a breath, "now that Rhuun is safely home, it's over. Maybe you could even go see him. If you wanted to. Ilaan, I can't bear this, please, can't you just come home?"

"What exactly do you think is going on? With Rhuun? What did Father tell you?"

"Well, he did break our law, you know that. I told you it was wrong, opening the stupid Door; it's only because Father is so understanding that I'm not locked up myself! Or living in a hovel down here with the sand trash. And who knows what Rhuun did while he was there? There are diseases and things; he could have brought something back."

"It's for his own safety, right? It's only until we get this sorted out? And since he's not cooperating, well, who knows how he was corrupted. Is that about right? Is that what Father says?"

"I suppose as usual you know better," she sneered. "I suppose it's all a big lie and I'm so stupid I can't even tell the moons from the sun? I didn't come here so you could tell me lies about Father. He's doing important things, and—"

"And what? With the Mages? Aelle, why don't you go to Niico's matches? You used to."

"None of your business," she snapped.

"And why don't you go out to dinner? Or to your friends? You go to Niico's because it's around the corner, and other than that you stay home. Why don't you go out?"

"I don't have to justify my comings and goings….and how do you even know?" she asked. "Are you spying on me?"

"I am worried about you. And not only you. Aelle, why don't you go out?"

"Maybe to avoid meetings like this!" she replied.

"Why are you afraid of going out? What happens when you do?" he asked again.

She pressed her lips together hard. "They all talk," she said, "they all talk; they all have something to say. If I go to the matches or to my friends, or sand forbid sit at a table in public, I hear how sad my life is and how I was tricked and abused. Poor Aelle. Right to my face! We're *so sorry* for you." She wiped her eyes furiously. "And if I go to the Old City or the market, do you know what I hear?"

"Tell me," he said quietly.

"That the prince is some sort of magical hero, that he'll make it rain and open The Door. That he loves someone else. That he's dying." He pulled her into an embrace and she only resisted for a moment before hugging him hard. Then she pulled away. "I'm tired of crying and I'm tired of thinking about him. I wish he never came back."

"Well," said Ilaan, "from what I hear, he wishes that, too. I'm sorry. I don't know about making it rain, but he's in trouble and we are out of time. Father—"

"Is not part of this," she said firmly. "Ilaan, I won't hear it. The queen walks away, Rhuun runs away, and who's left? Father is taking care of everything when no one else would."

"I'll keep repeating this until you hear it. I know you love Father. I know you trust him. I know you think he makes it rain. But Father and the Mages are working together." He took her by the wrist so she couldn't leave. "Father wanted to run things all along. Think, Aelle. Why did he push you together with someone he thinks is beneath you?"

She laughed bitterly. "He thinks everyone is beneath us, you and me. What did you expect; he'd be satisfied if we grew up to labor at a transform farm? So what if he encouraged me to be with Rhuun, why wouldn't he? If Rhuun had any sense at all we'd be wed by now; you thought so too, don't tell me different."

"I did want him to marry you, because I love you both. But surely, you see you would have made each other miserable. Aelle, be honest."

She smiled. "We didn't even have to bother to wed for that to happen. So much trouble saved." She paused. "You know, I think I could have forgiven him for his father being...not like us. I didn't care that he never manifested, or had no fire. Or I was used to it. And I was used to the way he looks." She struggled to remain composed. "Is it true? Did he meet someone else, over there?"

"Yes. I'm sorry. But I will not lie to you."

Aelle nodded. "I wasn't sure about the rest of it, I'm not deaf. And I'm not stupid!" Ilaan started to speak, but she continued. "Even though Father told me one thing, I heard so many others...But that I had been replaced, I think that much at least Father was happy to tell me. He absolutely forbade me to see him. I thought he was looking out for me."

"Father generally looks out for himself, and the rest of us walk behind."

She considered this. "But you decided all on your own to join the Peermage, Father had nothing to do with that."

"He had a hand in it. It was my idea to study for the Peermage, but not for me to wear the robe and snuff out my voice; he wouldn't let me go until they agreed to my conditions. He wanted you on the High Seat and me the next Zaal. With his careful supervision, of course." She didn't reply. "This is the *scorping* worst. I keep wanting to tell you about this stupid fight I'm having with my sister. How is Mother?"

"Nervous." Aelle was glad to change the subject. "She and Father disagree about something, I don't know what and it's none of my business anyway. I think she prefers when he takes those long 'vacations'." She frowned at him. "It appears I don't have to tell you how Niico is."

"He's been in touch," he said. "I'm exiled, not dead!" That made her laugh. "I am going to ask you to do one thing, and I'd like you to do it tomorrow. Once it's done, you can pretend I am dead, if you chose to. But do this one thing first."

She sighed. "You can't know how much I've missed you. The only way this whole thing would be worse is if you really were dead. Even when I want to set you on fire, I still want you around. What do you want me to do?"

Thanking Light and Wind, Ilaan said, "It has to do with Daala. Here is what will happen...."

After she'd finally agreed, he said, "I'll leave first, you go later. Be careful. I'll be waiting." He stepped into the street, looked around, and shimmered out of sight.

* * *

Half a block away, Hollen watched the figure he knew to be Niico—scarf or no scarf, there was no mistaking that walk—step out from the shadows of a ruined statue. He was probably coming from an evening with Ilaan, that's the only thing that could have taken him into the Quarter, and Hollen had seen him coming and going from there often enough. It had been pure chance he'd noticed him at all, that first time, and someone who didn't train with Niico nearly every day wouldn't have been able to pick him out. But there he was, striding casually among the workers and vendors in the Old City, obviously going somewhere. Hollen wanted to call out to him, but for some reason he didn't. He fell in behind, and watched as Niico stopped to chat with a girl who looked like she'd just arrived from the Edge. And then a door across the alley opened, and Ilaan called him inside.

Hollen thought about what he'd seen and grand gestures. He nodded to himself and flew home.

Chapter 32

Eriis

AS SOON AS Rhuun heard voices in the hallway, he left off making his bed and vanished, pressing himself as close to shuttered windows as he could.

They filed in, the Zaal, two Mages, and Daala behind, toting a heavy basket and looking uncharacteristically flushed and breathless. The Zaal seemed to be in a worse mood than usual. Good.

"Which one of you is responsible for charming the *scorping door*?" he asked. The guilty party's hand crept up. "We will have a conversation later. And you," he turned to Daala. "I'm certain whatever kept you was terribly important."

"Sorry, I'm sorry." She never looked up from the floor. "The kitchens were busy and I had to wait. Sorry."

"Hmm." The Zaal turned back to the room, addressing the empty bed. "Prince Rhuun, it's a day of collection. Shall we begin?"

"Don't really feel like it today, Assleak." He had few joys these days, practicing Mistran words was one of them.

"Ah, the prince delights us with his human language lessons." The Zaal's smile was a bit forced.

"I want to talk to Ilaan. And I want to see my mother."

"And I want the rains to come again," answered the Zaal. "But guess what? I might get my wish, while, as we've discussed, Ilaan does not wish to see you and your mother is otherwise occupied. You know this. Now, let's get this over with."

The light in the room rapidly grew brighter, but Rhuun had been practicing things other than swearing—he had little else to do. He found shadows in the folds of the bedcovers and in the pages of his books.

The Mages turned to the Zaal for instruction. "Fine," he grumbled. "You have no one to blame but yourself for the untidiness."

From the ceiling came a fall of fine black dust. This was new. It smothered him like a weightless sheet and made him cough, and his outline was instantly observed. He reappeared and steeled himself against what came next; being stilled, watching the mages make his arms move, and then *La Naa*. Which was the worst part? He didn't know.

Daala began to gather the dust, but the Zaal stopped her. "This is hardly the time, Daala. What is the matter with you today?" She backed into the corner. "*Laa Na*, again, and we approach our goal. We are grateful for your sacrifice."

"Kiss my balls," said Rhuun, but his arm was out, and the knife, and the bowl.

As before, the knife was traded for the lid, and the Mages released Rhuun and filed out. Rhuun examined his arm, which slowly formed a new scar.

The Zaal watched him. "What's wrong now?"

Rhuun looked up. "It's taking longer. Longer than it should. I think you're close to using me up. I hope you get your rain soon, because once I'm gone, you'll have to go back to slicing up jumpmice."

The Zaal folded his arms. "Once we have what we need from you, a steady supply of human blood will no longer be a concern. The only worry will be where to put it all." He turned to Daala. "And you! Have you come over simple in your wits? You know better than to distract us in the middle of *Laa Na*. Clean up this dust and see that he eats. We need him for a little while longer."

After the Zaal was gone, Daala said, "Is it true?"

“Is what true?” He’d vanished again, and got a mean little pleasure out of watching her not know quite where his voice was coming from.

“Is it true that you’re not healing right?”

He laughed and reappeared and held out his arms, a patchwork of weeping wounds and swollen scars. “What do you think?” She stared for a long moment, but had no reply. She just went to work on gathering the dust. “What, no smart remarks? No joy? Daala, I’m surprised. And where’s the new girl? I thought it was her day today. Although she’s not really new anymore, is she?”

Daala said nothing, finished transforming the dust and set out his meal. She finished as quickly as she could with no scornful parting comments, only an oddly searching look over her shoulder before she left.

* * *

Rhuun reappeared and leaned back on the bed. He was tired. He’d put back on some of the weight he’d lost once Maaya—Lelet—had made herself known to him. But his arms ached all the time, as fast as he put the pain away, it seemed to rush back. He felt like a cup, filling and filling with water. Whatever was going to happen, it had better be soon. He closed his eyes and thought about the river and the birds. He thought perhaps later he’d remember the party and the music. And maybe later he’d see Lelet with his dinner.

The door flew open, and Daala raced in. “*Rushta*! The Mages been and gone? And look, I get to see you in the flesh. This is a special day after all.”

This is interesting, thought Rhuun. “You’re too late,” he told her. “They were not pleased. What kept you? A long breakfast with your many admirers?”

“Ugh, it was so stupid. I got a message that the Counselor needed to speak to me, but when I arrived at Court—I mean the Counsel—he wasn’t there. I have no idea what it was all about, but I had to wait forever before they even told me he’d left.”

"Well, I'm sure it was your fault." He took a chance. "Maaya already cleaned up and brought me something to eat. Something about that girl gives me an appetite."

She looked around the room with her hands on her hips. "I bet it was her. She has a sweet voice, but there's something nasty in her mouth. She's trying to get me in trouble."

"Don't ask me," he yawned as she stormed out, "I just live here."

He sat still on the edge of the bed. There was only one person he knew who could change her face so flawlessly, who might want to see him, who had a part in this. But was she there to help him? Or was she there to hold the knife?

Chapter 33

Eriis

IT WAS COOLER in the evening; almost cool enough for a human person to walk about without discomfort, if they didn't mind the heat.

On the one hand, Maaya felt happiness for her new brothers and sisters of Eriis. They had suffered a great deal and deserved a kinder climate. On the other, she knew the cost of each degree, every warm breeze, each cloud that seemed perhaps not quite so threatening. For every dust storm that never materialized, another bowl of blood. Soon, she thought, there wouldn't be anything left to take. Even when he wasn't trying, she thought he was fading in and out of sight. No matter how bright she lit the stone lamps, he was always in a shadow. She was losing him, drop by drop.

That morning, she'd replaced one untouched meal with another, and no amount of kissing or teasing could rouse him. He opened his eyes and seemed confused about who she was. And when he realized it was Lelet, and that Lelet was the same as Maaya, he gave a sleepy smile, and told her to come back later.

But as much as she wanted to grab Moth and lead him out of the palace and back through the Door, she knew she'd be struck dead for her trouble and he'd be no better off.

She sat on the stoop in front of her own little room off of Waterless and contemplated the water in her cup. She'd been told it was possible to make the water freeze, but hadn't had any luck. As Rhuun had told her (back when he was Moth and she was herself) heat came more easily to the Eriisai, probably because they had enough and more to spare. And so she made the cup of water steam.

She liked her stoop, it was in the shade (or whatever the equivalent was, when you never saw the sun) and she even liked her room, although on Mistra it would have scarcely been large enough to be called a pantry. She'd never lived alone (on Mistra women of the Fifty Families rarely lived without their relatives, or husbands, or children, or all of them) and it oddly suited her. She was at first afraid it would be too quiet, but there were voices up and down the street from before the sun rose behind the clouds until after the second moon had set behind those same clouds.

Ilaan and Niico had found her a long grey robe—a traveling robe, they'd told her, don't wear it around the house—and she'd gotten a few tan tunics, plain brown leggings, linens, and sandals. The pretty blue robe she'd worn through the Door was folded and tucked away out of sight. Tan was understood to be an unaffiliated color, binding her to no house and drawing no attention. In other words: one of the working poor. And finally, and importantly, a scarf with a little white stone sewn to one corner to keep it weighted down. Wear it when you go out, particularly past the Royal Arch. Wear it when you go to work at the palace—and make sure you call it the Counsel, not the palace anymore. If you're not sure, they said, wear it. It had felt awkward and rubbed against her neck, catching the hair on the back of her head, until Niico showed her how to properly pin her long black hair into coils and wrap the scarf correctly under it. After that, she understood the freedom she'd been granted to walk around and see the city, the people, the market, and the desert past the city walls. She looked like everyone else; she looked like no one. At first she kept close to her alley and the streets she had come to know, but curiosity made her want to explore.

She thought often of how Moth had been dropped onto Mistra, informed of his terms of service, and left to his own devices. She hadn't appreciated his bravery and resourcefulness, and she felt embarrassed at how many people eased her path through this strange city. Of course they all had their own reasons to help her, but without them, she'd have been lost the first day.

In her room she had a cot pushed against one wall and a swath of blue—her best attempt at Ever Blue—underneath, which she saved like a treat to look at once every evening. That had been the hardest thing for her, harder than the tasteless food and the baking heat, the lack of color ground against her nerves. Everything was yellow, harsh shades of sand, with greys and browns and white mixed in. Ilaan told her that lately, and only very lately indeed, some high ranking folk in his father's counsel had taken to adding a narrow stripe of color to the hems or collars of their garments.

"The Mage," he said, "you saw him that day in the market. The Zaalmage has a green band on his cloak. And my sister wears green and gold paint around her eyes. If they're doing it, so will everyone else." Because neither one of the two of them took a step nor a breath without his father's expressed approval.

The lack of color made her eyes ache, but the lack of taste had almost gotten her in trouble. One went to great lengths, here on Eriis, not to offend.

Ilaan had taken great pride that first day, the day she'd arrived, in running to the market and picking out the nicest things he could afford. His family had cut him off, he explained, and he was getting by through teaching the children of the Old City their letters. He had little enough, but he wanted to make her properly welcome. She sat at his tiny table and at first didn't understand what he'd placed in front of her. It was on a plate, so she assumed it was food, but it looked like squares of shiny paper. He waited for her to eat and react, and she waited for him to show her what to do.

Finally, she picked up a tan square and nibbled off the corner. It tasted like fine sandpaper, but with a trace of something that might have been cheese. The look on her face must have said enough. She'd offended him.

"I'm sorry I can't offer you the fare you are used to," he said, rather stiffly. "It won't kill you, at least."

"I'm the one who should be sorry," she said. "Our food looks different, that's all. I am completely at your mercy, Ilaan. Show me what to do. Pretend I'm a visitor from another world. A world with simple-witted people."

He chuckled. She'd turned the slight onto herself. "Fair enough." He made a stack of tan and white squares. "You can use your fingers for the squares. Use the knife and fork for the light brown swirled ones. Cut it into four smaller squares."

She did and took a bite. After a moment of chewing and tasting, she said, "Peas?"

"I don't know what that word is," he confessed. "It's just called greens."

She shrugged and smiled. "I've had worse," remembering May's insistence she eat her broccoli as a child. She paused and pushed the 'greens' around with her fork. "Is all your food like this? Shaped into squares?"

"Well, no. Fruits are round. And meat is in cubes."

Some food was round, some was square, and meat was in cubes as advertised, but to her it all tasted like the paper the original food had been wrapped in. She wondered how these people managed to keep themselves alive until she noticed they all ate and drank with gusto, commenting frequently on how tasty and fine the meal was. And they all seemed healthy; she'd never seen anyone who looked sick—other than Moth, of course.

This evening, Ilaan was off on some errand and she was feeling proud of herself for negotiating two round small fruits and some bread and cheese for her own dinner. It was considered rather low class to sit on the steps and eat, but enough people around her did it anyway, and this was where the breeze would be, if there was one. It gave her time to think. The Zaal, dressing himself up prettily with a new green hem on his robe; the Mages, all coming up and out into the light, like bugs. She thought about *La Naa* and knives and she thought about fire.

Use me, said the fire. She agreed that would be a fine thing to do.

The little girl was back, watching her through the window. Maaya had spotted her before she'd even moved in, flitting in and out of the house so quickly she could only be shimmering, as it was called. The girl was too young to attend classes, but was old enough to play by herself in the dusty front yard (the yard was a patch of dirt with a neat white fence around it. Maaya didn't have a yard, only a step). The little girl came out onto her own steps, playing with a small white and brown striped ball. She bounced it into her yard, but the ground wasn't level enough to return it to her hands, and it rolled to a stop at Maaya's feet. Maaya picked it up to toss it back, but when she looked up the girl was standing right in front of her.

"You're new," the girl solemnly informed her.

"Yes, I am. My name is Maaya. May I know your name?"

"Mine is Thayree. My mommy is called Kaaya. Maaya, Kaaya, that's a rhyme." She took her ball and fled back into her house (on foot for once), but Maaya spotted her peeking through the curtains in the family's front room. Then they played the 'I see you/I'm hiding' game for a while. Maaya smiled and thought about Scilla. They'd played this game when she was small. She couldn't know how her sister fared, but she knew if anyone from Mistra was watching over her, Scilla was.

The air shimmered and the little girl was sitting on the steps next to her. Like all the demon children she'd seen of both sexes, the girl had silky black hair worn loose past her shoulders, and the same gorgeous golden skin. Their eye color seemed to be where most variation took place, and this child's eyes were dark garnet. Maaya guessed she was about 3 or 4, and tiny. The temptation was great to scoop her up for a cuddle.

"You're good at that for being so small," Maaya told her.

"Mommy says I mini festered early. I can shimmy me plus a friend, too. Mommy says I'm special."

Maaya's heart twisted. "One of my best friends is also special. I hope we can be friends, too, Thayree."

The girl giggled and began a new game of tracing shapes in the dust with her bare toes. "You're new," she said again. "Mommy says you are."

"She's right, I am new. I came here from the Edge. Do you know what that is?"

The girl frowned. "It's far. It's farther than I'm allowed to go by myself. Is it nice?"

"It's far away, that's right. I think it's nice."

"Is your mommy there?"

Maaya didn't know how to answer. She settled on a version of the truth. "My family is there, yes. I have a big sister and a little sister. My little sister is bigger than you, but not much. And I have a serious brother and a funny brother."

"How do you fit all your brothers and sisters inside the house?" Maaya laughed. "Is your funny brother funny looking or funny acting?"

"He's funny acting. He's very nice looking." She leaned forward and whispered, "Sometimes we fight and then we get in trouble."

Thayree's eyes got wide. "Fighting isn't proper. Mommy says so."

"Well, your mommy is very smart." They sat quietly for a few minutes, the child drawing stick figures in the dust. She drew one that might have been Maaaya herself, and added a wide pair of wings.

"Did you mimi fester your wings yet?" Thayree asked.

Maaya realized she'd entirely forgotten about them. How was it possible? She'd been on Eriis for weeks, seen many others take to the air, and it had never occurred to her to try it for herself. Well, she had a lot on her mind.

She said, "Let's find out." She stood and looked around in her mind until she found the right places to flex, and she tightened and pushed and it felt like when you stretch a muscle just to the point where you get a cramp. Instead of a cramp, something popped and then relaxed and her own wings, pink-tan, soft and leathery, poked out from the back of her tunic. Looking back over her shoulder, she could see they were not quite as wide as her outstretched arms, and they felt like a pair of expensive gloves. All their garments were tailored with slits to accommodate wings, and again she shook her head at simply forgetting to look. She gave them a stretch and it felt good in an entirely new way. *I have to show him*, she thought at once, but then wondered if he'd be hurt. She gave them an experimental flap, and to her astonishment found herself two feet above the street. She was so shocked she forgot to follow up and barely landed without falling on her backside into the dust of the alley.

Thayree fond this hilarious and through her giggles suggested she start to practice. "Mommy says practice is better than wishing."

"Your mother's a smart woman," she agreed. She folded the little wings away (they seemed to somehow hug the insides of her shoulder blades) and sat back down. She was glad the water cup was still there, feeling out of breath. She pulled her scarf from around her neck and wiped her face, more out of habit than necessity. But a breeze chose that moment to catch the scarf and blow it down the alley towards the boulevard. With a sigh Maaya rose to retrieve it, but before she was even on her feet, Thayree had shimmered away, appeared for a split second at the corner, and then reappeared, scarf triumphantly in hand.

"You're a marvel, but would your mommy be angry if she saw you appcar in traffic like that?"

The girl's eyes widened. "I forgot," she said.

"Well, promise me you won't forget again and we'll forget it now. Thank you for saving my scarf, Thayree." She leaned down and gave the girl a hug.

"You'll need it," Thayree whispered. "You better practice wings, too. If you're going to save the prince."

Maaya was so startled she dropped the girl and sat bolt upright. Thayree didn't seem to notice her shock and went back to drawing in the dust. "Thayree, why do you say that?"

"Mommy says that's why you're here. Everyone says so."

A new voice over her shoulder said, "What does your mommy say about the prince?"

Ilaan dropped onto the step next to Maaya, his face impassive.

"He's good. He's nice. He's funny looking, but nice." She looked up at Maaya. "Not like your brother, funny looking, *not* nice looking. But nice inside. Mommy met him and she says so. She says it's going to rain one day." Thayree threw her arms around Maaya and loudly whispered, "But it's a secret! Bye, I have to go now." She shimmered away, Maaya assumed back into her own home across the alley.

Chapter 34

Eriis

ILAAN COULD TELL by the look on Maaya's face that he was in for it. And sure enough, once the little girl was safely out of earshot, she turned to Ilaan and hissed, "Is that true? Does everyone know why I am here?"

Ilaan answered, "I wouldn't say everyone. But yes, a lot of people who live in these alleys know who you are."

"Ilaan, they'll take me to the Mages!" she looked frantically up and down the alley, as if expecting white robed guards to appear all at once.

"Settle yourself. They don't know everything, they don't know where you come from, other than the Edge. And put that away!" Her hands blazed with flame and she shook them out. He looked around as well, frowning, and pulled her inside.

With the ashboard door shut, he sat her down on the edge of her cot and pulled her chair over for himself. "I haven't told you the rest of it because it wasn't in place."

"The rest of what? Why are you spreading rumors about me?"

"The people around here think you had an affair with the prince while he was visiting a transform farm, and you've come to the city to try and rescue him. Everyone who has ever seen them together knows he did nothing but fight with my sister, so a sweet, poor, honest, unaffiliated girl appeals to their sense of romantic tradition and helps cement Rhuun as identifying with the people in the Old City. Most of them have relations on the farms and at the Edge. That he never in his life went out there, they don't need to know that. And how you got here, they certainly don't need to know that. But a romantic tale of a noble and commoner, yes, that's the tale they're telling. Haven't you wondered why everyone around here is so accommodating? Do you have any idea how much you paid for that meal?" He indicated the remains of her lunch sitting on the table.

She groaned. "I thought I was just doing really well."

"You're doing well enough to not draw the attention of my father's household staff when you go to the palace, and well enough to make your neighbors think that Rhuun would find you appealing. So I'd have to say you're doing well enough to be part of this particular story." There were other stories being told, about the Mages and the secret experiments they did on children. About the days to come, when the prince would lead them through The Door. About rain. But she didn't need to hear those, not yet anyway.

"*Rushta,*" she muttered, rubbing her forehead. "You're making a mythology. What happens when they find out the poor but honest farm girl is actually a human and an enemy?"

He shrugged. "It might be even better. Bringing warring camps together, I haven't worked it all out yet. But Maaya, I have worked out the first part. It's time."

She gripped his hands. "We're getting him out of there."

He decided if there was ever a time to excuse her crude human behavior, this was it. "We're getting him out. Are you ready? Your part will be the hardest."

"This part," she said, looking around the little room, "the part where I'm walking around free and he's in a cage, this was the hardest part." He nodded. "I can't believe you convinced her, Ilaan."

He sighed. "She's angry, of course, but now she's angrier at our father than at Rhuun. She's got a long path ahead of her."

"Because of your father."

He nodded. "Nothing but lies. And I know how he is with her, he'll explain why he lied to her, and how it was all for her good, and he'll make it sound like the truth. But I think she's strong enough, or at least angry enough, to hold her own. We may have a new neighbor, here in the Quarter."

After seeing *La Naa* with her own eyes, Aelle could no longer pretend their father's words were true. She understood that helping Rhuun meant also helping this human girl—her replacement. Ilaan wondered if he'd be so willing if it meant passing Niico on to another.

"It might be better for everyone if Moth did wed your sister and take the High Seat." Maaya was looking at him strangely. "Your friend, your sister, your father, all happy. And you. Wouldn't it be better for you?"

"No. It would be a disaster," he said without hesitation. "Rhuun would have found himself in exactly the place he is right now, thanks to the Mages. And that would leave Aelle in a dangerously exposed position. The only one to come out ahead would be my father."

"And you," she said again, "if you wanted."

"Yes, if I wanted to bend the knee and be his errand boy." He leaned back in his chair and narrowed his eyes. "You think I'm playing a deeper game than I really am, Maaya. We're getting him out. Isn't that why you're here?"

"We're getting him out and he's leaving with me, Ilaan. As we discussed."

"I cannot speak for the prince. You say he'll leave with you, I'm sure that's where he'll want to go." They went over it a final time, their plan, and he left her to it. He couldn't help her suspicion, humans seemed to have minds that raced around like jumpmice, and hers had decided to be suspicious about him. He supposed it was less frightening than the other dangers she was about to face. Well, she was on her own for now.

As for him, he had a meeting to prepare for. He wasn't looking forward to it.

Chapter 35

Eriis

ILAAN LOCKED HIS door and sat at his little table. He sipped his *sarave* and nibbled his dinner and finally got up to pace. He folded and unfolded the sheet of paper that had appeared on his desk that morning. No matter how many times he read it, it said the same thing. 'Be at your dwelling by first moonrise, we must talk.' He'd written his acceptance on another piece of paper and set it in the same place the first one had appeared. Within seconds, it had vanished. Well, it was past first moonrise and he was home. So he waited.

He was rewarded at last with the rank smell of magic, and without the customary shimmer Hellne stood in the middle of his room. She looked around, her face as usual a mask.

"Is this the best you could do?" she said. "Rather small."

"I wasn't left with much of a choice, was I?" he answered darkly. "I told you not to call on me."

"Yes, thank you for the invitation. I know it was under duress. But remember, what we do is not for my own benefit, nor for yours."

"I gathered you aren't here to catch up on gossip. What am I called upon to do for him now?" She sighed and patted her coiled hair. He took a moment to notice her dark, well-worn robe over an unadorned black tunic, and oddest of all, dusty boots. He didn't think he'd seen her in anything but the daintiest of sandals ever before. "You look tired, Hellne. In fact you look dreadful. What's going on?"

"Traveling, so hard on a woman," she murmured. "That's why I'm not there with you. So don't fret, there's no need to offer me water."

He ground his teeth. "My apologies. Where are you? What's so important?"

She walked to the cot and perched on the edge; he could now see her outline was just slightly out of phase with the rest of the room. She was sitting on something, but not his bed. "I am in the Vastness, and can't tell you more than that. I have seen...well, there are things here that prevent my return."

"Yes, the Mages and my father among them. You've left a vacuum, and the jumpmice are scrambling to fill it."

"There's no vacuum, Ilaan." She smiled. "There's someone who will do very nicely on the High Seat, until I get back."

Ilaan shook his head. "Don't try that on me again, I didn't believe you the first time. It certainly won't be me, and it won't be Aelle, either. It's most definitely over between them. She's all but dragged Rhuun off to the Crosswinds herself. Plus, he loves another." He was expecting an explosion, rage, delight, anything, but Hellne barely blinked.

"Hmm, we'll get back to that. I was quite serious about you, by the way. And I haven't completely ruled you out. No, it won't be Aelle, and it won't be your father, although I understand he's busy changing all the signs. Good. It's keeping him busy. Now, everything is in place? The door and the room? And with the human girl?"

Ilaan's jaw dropped. "How do you know about this? No one knows where she's from."

Hellne laughed. "That story about Rhuun having an affair with some peasant, it's charming. 'He loves another.' Ha! He'd only have gone out there if the Edge served *sarave*. But nice work, just vague enough to be believable. Now, once you have him out, what next?"

"Well," he said, "we have a plan to get him to a transform farm, where he can recover his strength. And then the human girl intends to take him back to Mistra." At her look, he added, "I assume we have a new plan?"

"A transform farm. That's an interesting choice. You've been there? To the Edge, have you?"

He shifted uncomfortably. "Not as such. But I've heard—"

"Mostly shift work, they do out there. A few small settlements, family farms in the process of blowing away, but generally temporary housing. It's dangerous, tiring work, transforming. So they don't stay out there very long. Dormitory style, most of it. So, please tell me. How do you intend to hide Rhuun out there? Throw a sheet over him?"

Ilaan fumed. "We won't be there long."

"Once Yuenne realizes what's happened, he'll come here first. And he'll go out there next."

He had to admit she was correct. And according to Maaya, Rhuun was in no condition for extended travel. "Fine. Where do I take him?"

"Did you know my family used to have a little *dacha* in the hills? No? I didn't either, until I went through my father's things. Rest him now. I suppose he took his special friends out there, before the Weapon. A place he called the tents. I gave it to an old friend of mine to look after." She moved her hand and a sheet of paper fluttered down from the ceiling. It landed at Ilaan's feet. "I didn't know a thing about it, and neither does your father. Go to your transform farm if you must, but don't tarry. Go to the tents. You are expected."

"And the human girl?"

She waved her hand dismissively. "He already had his vacation among the humans. Now it's time for him to grow up and take his place on the Seat, until I return." She paused. "The girl should go home, though. She'll be a distraction and he'll be busy. And, obviously no one from *that place* will ever sit on my Seat."

"It falls to me to convince him to stay at the scene of his imprisonment, take the Seat he doesn't want, and break with the woman he *does* want. Some friend."

"Would you want anyone else by his side during this difficult time? And as I said, things will be different." She smiled. "Hidden things brought to light."

"You are being annoyingly unclear, Hellne."

That made her laugh. She reached for something he couldn't see and nodded at someone standing behind him. "You've come so far since we hid my little book. You were scared to sneeze in front of me." She paused and took a sip of water. Her image vibrated slightly. "I'm told weather is happening, it's so tiresome. I've been as clear as I can. Get Rhuun away from the Mages. Follow the plan, get him to the tents. And don't let that girl get too comfortable. We'll talk again soon." She blinked out of sight.

"Rushta." He bent to retrieve the sheet of paper. It was a map. Well, he told himself, one thing at a time. Maybe I'll get lucky and we'll all earn a trip to the Crosswinds tonight.

Chapter 36

Eriis

"ABSOLUTELY NOT. COMPLETELY out of the question."

Rhuun leaned heavily on the dresser. He looked up at the mirror and saw a drawn, hollow eyed stranger looking back at him. Behind him, Maaya frowned and fidgeted on the edge of his bed. She'd been there for the better part of an hour explaining how he was to walk out, free as a breeze, and leave her as a hostage in his place. It was an insult to think he'd consider putting her in such danger.

"This is the plan, Moth," she told him. "Everything is in place."

"And without even consulting me? How could Ilaan think I would go along with this? How could you?"

She sighed and came up behind him, he felt her head against his back. She slipped her arms around his waist. "How much longer do you have? If you don't go today, will you be strong enough to go tomorrow?" He knew she was right; he'd lost more weight and had trouble raising his arms. And all he wanted to do was sleep. It frightened him to realize he didn't look forward to her visits as much as he was starting to look forward to the day when the Mages would finish the job. Then he could rest.

She said for the third or fifth time, "How long can you remain unseen?"

He closed his eyes. "I don't know."

"How long? It has to be long enough to get you into the market square. Can you do that?"

"It doesn't matter because I'm not going. What kind of person would I be to let you stay here when I go free? Ilaan has to come up with something better." He found himself wishing she would leave so he could go back to sleep.

She turned him by his waist (she avoided touching his arms) and gave him a gentle shake. "This is the plan. I know you're tired, but you have to go." She reached up and brushed his long hair back out of his face. "*Shani*, look at me. You can't stay here. I came all this way; do you know how many parties I'm missing?" She waited for him to smile for her, so he did. "It'll be fine."

"I can't help but notice, you keep saying that."

She planted her hands on her hips. "I'm starting to get a little bored with the accommodations," she said, looking around. "And you never take me anywhere nice. You have to go heal and get your strength back. I have needs, you know." She said it with a smile, but he knew it was not a joke. They'd stopped joining and he hadn't even noticed. When was the last time? She was right—if he didn't go now, he'd probably never see the outside of this room again. He'd never see her ocean, or taste chocolate, or hear birds again. He'd never see her face when she found her pleasure. But it couldn't be as easy as simply walking away.

"What about the door?" he indicated the wood and silver slab that kept him captive. "It'll call the Mages."

"It won't, though. That's what I'm trying to tell you. The door is smart, but the room is dumb. The door asks the room, is my prisoner inside? And the room says, yes, there is one person here. And the door goes back to sleep. It doesn't care who that person is."

"How did Ilaan figure all this out?"

"Niico. Niico's always at the Counselor's house, I guess he and Aelle are tight these days. And he's kind of famous, so people like to brag when he's around. The Counselor likes to talk about pushing the Mages around, and he's always complaining about that door—no one can get it to work right. He said something about it having its own agenda, although I don't see how that's possible. Niico says they never bothered to give this room eyes, however they'd do that, all it can do is count to one. As long as it counts one, no alarms to the door. The door is supposed to be able to tell who's using it, but like I said, it keeps breaking down. They think it's the wood; it doesn't like the Mages any more than the Counselor does. Any more than I do, ugh, what a collection of creeps." She handed him his boots, and he bent to put them on. "I guess it feels funny to wear shoes again."

He straightened back up and became lightheaded. He leaned against her, and realized she was waiting to see if he would lead her to his bed, perhaps for the last time. He considered this, but when he further realized she was actually holding him up, he decided against it. He didn't want her last memory of him to be his expiration mid-joining. Even so, his boots were on, and that was something. "I think I can go unseen to at least the Arch. I'm just not sure." He looked around his room. "Remember when we were outside all the time? You were scared of bears. We never did see any, though."

"Maybe when we go back, we'll see some. There's so much to do! I still owe you chocolate, don't I?"

"I'm holding you to it, even if I have to come back from the dead. Again. No, don't do that, I'm sorry. I meant it as a joke."

She wiped her eyes. "What do we say about jokes?"

"Mainly that I shouldn't tell them." With some difficulty, he put his arms around her. They looked worse than they felt (and they felt on fire most of the time). He'd repaired a tunic by sewing the sleeves back on so she wouldn't have to see them. But he had to have her close. "What happens to you?" he asked. He was just stalling now, afraid of what might happen next. He wouldn't just be letting her down, he'd be placing her in terrible danger, and everyone involved. He couldn't fail.

"Don't worry about that. If you don't know, you won't tell if something...goes wrong. But it's all taken care of, so don't worry. I'll be with you soon."

"To the market square? That's it?" A short walk, he'd done it a million times.

She nodded. "You will be met. They're waiting for you right now. You should go."

He pulled her closer and kissed her, hating himself for agreeing to this awful plan. "I don't want to leave you."

"You're not leaving me; we're just going to be in different places for a little while."

He smiled. "It makes sense when you say it like that. You turned out to be the best person I ever kidnapped."

"Hey now," she said, "I thought we agreed that wasn't entirely your fault."

He slowly faded away, keeping his arms around her. When might he touch her again? But he let her go and she opened the door.

"I am yours," he whispered in her ear. "I'll love you until the moons fall into the sand."

The door closed.

Chapter 37

Eriis

ONCE HE HAD faded from view and she was certain he could remain unseen, she opened the door. She felt his kiss, and a fierce whisper against her ear, "I am yours. I'll love you until the moons fall into the sand."

She threw her arms out, but there was nothing there. One of the white clad guards glanced over his shoulder at her through the open door, and she nodded at him and pulled it shut.

She wiped her face again and took a deep breath. The first part of it was done, and she couldn't do anything but hope he had enough strength left to go unseen until he was past the Royal Arch and into the market. The next part was up to her, and she wasn't looking forward to it.

"Just like we practiced it," she told herself. "Pretend you're in Ilaan's room and we'll have a big drink when we're done. You just have to live long enough to tell him you love him, too. It'll be fine. It'll be fine."

She'd never been so afraid and so full of joy at the same time; deep calming breaths did nothing to slow her heart. "So let's get this over with."

She took a scrap of paper out of her pocket and unfolded it; it was covered with Eriisai script, but spelled out so she could read it. She didn't need to understand the words. She held the paper up with her right hand, and with her left, firmly gripped the ornate silver doorknob. She began to read aloud.

She concentrated so hard on sounding out all the words properly, she at first didn't notice smoke rising from her fingers. She paused to take a breath and swallow, and saw that her hand was on fire. She pulled the sleeve of her tunic away and kept reading. The page burned above her fingers, there'd be no using it again. As she got toward the bottom of the page, she started to feel pain, something she hadn't experienced in any capacity since Scilla had changed her into her current form. Whatever she was doing to the door, it was fighting back. At first the sensation, pain, was interesting, and she pushed it aside. She kept reading even when the skin on the back of her hand turned black, cracked and flaked off, when her hand fused with the silver of the handle, even when she had to gasp out the words so she wouldn't scream and bolts of agony shot up her arm, making her good hand shake violently. Finally she got to the bottom of the page and said the final words; the paper turned to ash and crumbled. She pulled her charred hand off the doorknob, noticing with sick fascination that the pinkie finger of her left hand stuck to the door and broke off.

She stumbled to the bed and sat, holding her hand up, the pain receding and the skin already sloughing off its dead black surface, revealing new, golden pink skin underneath. Her pinkie, however, stayed missing. She wondered if it would grow back.

Part two was done. The door was locked. Ilaan told her the Mages and the Counselor would eventually figure out how to get it open, but it would buy Rhuun some time. It would also be that much longer before she went from anonymous serving girl to suspect, or fugitive, or criminal.

She sat on the bed and watched her hand heal and prepared to wait.

Hours later and she was still waiting. The charm she'd cast on the door had drained her and she drifted in and out of sleep. She sat up and came full awake—there were voices outside, angry voices. The Zaal and probably the Counselor. She also heard the door itself, which although it seemed unlikely, sounded both bored and irritated as it repeated, "State your business," and occasionally, "It'll be fine."

Finally they abandoned traditional opening charms and simply began shouting through it.

"Which one of the girls is in there?" came the call. She guessed the guard didn't know her name, or hadn't cared to learn it.

"It's me, Maaya," she called back. "There's something wrong with the door."

"What do we say about jokes?" said the door.

"We need to open it; we need to speak with the prince." That was interesting, so they weren't sure.

"He won't reappear, he's in a mood," she said. "I haven't seen him since lunch. I need to go home; can you open the door for me please?"

"I love you," said the door. "I am yours." That caused some raised voices in the hallway outside.

After another hour of hissing and swearing, shouting, and cursing, (and the door occasionally repeating bits of her last conversation with Moth) the Zaal finally got the door to open. He was red faced and looked furious. Yuenne was behind him, not a hair turned. Smiling his little smile.

"Maaya," he said. "Where is the prince?"

She shrugged and pointed at the ceiling. "He's in a bad mood. He won't show himself. Usually he says thank you at least." They had her stand with them in the doorway and caused the rain of black dust to fall. In the past, it had unfailingly revealed his outline, but today it just landed on the furniture and the floor.

"He's not here, is he, Maaya?" asked Yuenne. "What have you done?" He looked genuinely curious and not particularly angry.

"He's here," she insisted. "I brought him lunch. Where could he go?"

"You're the new girl, aren't you?" Yuenne asked, still simply making conversation. "From the Edge? First time in the big city, of course. So many new things to see and do, and a real prince to serve every day, very exciting for you." He gave her a conspiratorial smile. "Something to write home about, befriending a prince. And lots of time to get to know each other. Did you feel a little sorry for him, finally? Did he tell you that you were special? Did he make you promises?"

"I just bring his lunch," she insisted. "Daala said not to talk to him. There's something wrong with him, he's so big."

The Zaal stuck his nose in her face and took another sniff. This time she did back away. "This one is involved. She smells like human."

Yuenne crossed his arms and looked at her thoughtfully. "Crosswinds?" he asked the Zaal. "I think not yet." And back to Maaya. "We still have so much to discuss. If you just bring his lunch and you're not allowed to talk to him, why do you smell like him?"

The Zaal shrugged impatiently, eager to go look for his missing prize. "Leave her here, the room's still charmed. And she'll be willing to share more of her story with us. Surely she had help." He sniffed at her again, the air around her head. "There's something strange...Shall I look inside?"

Yuenne made a face, but nodded. "So intrusive. Well, be quick." And to Maaya, "If you'd like to tell us anything, now would be the time."

"I just bring his lunch, I don't know why I smell—" The Zaal took her by the arm and drove his fingernail into the meat above her elbow. Though it didn't hurt the way it would have if she were herself, she felt stripped bare and turned inside out. The room and her stomach lurched like the morning after a night of hard drinking and she felt her knees begin to give out. The Zaal's mouth was on the wound he'd made and he held her up by the arm. After sucking and licking for a long minute, he let her fall to the black, gritty floor. She turned her face away and threw up in the corner.

"Well, the prince was all over her." He licked the blood off his teeth. "Human. I can taste it on her. They were...intimate." He gave a little pout of distaste. "I don't think she can shimmer, I didn't taste that, and hasn't manifested face shifting, although I sense it's there. She's got a lot of fire, though. Quite a lot." He looked down at her;

she'd crawled into the corner and wiped the vomit off her face with her hem. "Fire won't do you any good in here."

Yuenne shook his head and laughed. "What is it about that boy that turns the head of otherwise sensible young ladies? Maaya. Can you stand? Good. Maaya, you understand that the prince used you and left you here. He knew you'd be in trouble and left you anyway."

She burst into tears. "He said he'd put me on the High Seat. He said we'd be together."

"Of course he did." Yuenne patted her shoulder soothingly. "Now, who helped you? Who else knows what's happened?"

She shook her head. "No one, just me and him."

The Zaal made to respond, but a guard in a white tunic came up behind Yuenne and whispered something in his ear.

"Well!" he said. "This has been enlightening. We are called away, and I imagine we'll have the prince back here where he belongs before first moonrise. Then we can talk some more about how you helped him and who else knows about it. You'll be staying here, Maaya, so you might as well clean up."

The door complained, but ultimately they locked her in and left.

She sank back to the floor and waited for the spins to stop. Then she got to her feet and poured herself a glass of water.

"In different places," said the door.

"You've got that right," she replied. "Part three," she said. "So far, so good."

Chapter 38

Eriis

RHUUN WAS PRETTY sure he'd told her the truth of his heart, but he knew there was the chance he'd merely dreamed it. No, it felt like he had told her. And he was out of the room, too. None of this was a dream. He'd been meaning to tell her, waiting for the right time, and felt such a bold admission would get a nod from the Duke. He looked back, waiting, but she simply glanced at the guard and pulled the door shut. It would have been nice to hear her reply, but there would be time for that, if they all survived to the next moon rise.

He got his bearings, ignoring the guard (who stared through and past him, idly twirling the ring through his lip) and looked up and down the hall. To the right, more empty royal quarters and at the end of the hall a large courtyard, once used for parties and informal gatherings. The last time he'd been there, he'd flirted with an actress. Aelle had been furious. If she were able to shimmer, she'd go to the courtyard. No, this wasn't about Aelle, this was about him. If he could shimmer, it would be one jump from the courtyard to the Old City. Then he could wend his way back through the alleys to the Market Square.

Rhuun turned left and walked in a slow, straight line right down the middle of the royal quarter's hallway. His fists were clenched and he was breathing slowly through his nose, as if he were carrying a great weight. Every few seconds he'd look down at his hands and feet, and seeing nothing, continue on. He wondered why he couldn't see through the inside of his eyelids, and why his clothing disappeared along with him, but if he was carrying something it remained visible. All good questions for Ilaan, once this was over.

Yuenne's household guard brushed past him, serving men and women ran busy errands with trays and platters, couriers with bundles of papers; in the new Counsel, there was much industry and a job for every hand. He felt as if, compared to their light feet, he was moving in slow motion. And always, the voice in his mind, right at the edge of panic, *Don't leave her behind, it'll be the Mages or the Crosswinds and she'll be gone forever; don't be the coward and the joke everyone thinks you are; what kind of man leaves his woman behind; would the Duke go along with this idea? You'll never make it anyway, well at least you'll die together*. He ran his hands through his hair, realizing too late that his hands and his hair were now both streaked with blood. *The voices in my mind*, he noted, *are not especially helpful*. He tried to put them aside, still his brain, concentrate. He looked down and saw his shadow on the floor, and with great effort made it fade away. He was now at the T shaped junction where the royal quarters branched off from the main hall. The Great Hall was busier than the smaller hallway he just left, and brighter, fewer shadows, fewer places to slip between.

This is me talking now, he said to himself. *And I have to keep going. For Lelet. For Ilaan. And Aelle. For myself. It'll be fine*. He moved from pillar to stone bowl, finding the darkest places. It was getting steadily brighter, no way around it, he'd have to cross from the Great Hall into an open courtyard under the sky, through the Royal Arch, through the play yard of his school, and only then pass into the Market Square. Someone would be waiting, but who? Niico, to fly overhead and set him alight? And how long could he wait? *Just keep going*. He was doing fine. He was almost through the entrance of the Hall. He looked down and saw he was leaving a trail of blood, his arms leaked, dripped and spattered onto the tile. No one appeared to have noticed, and already many feet smeared and trampled and erased the marks of his passing. He kept going, feeling the heat of the day for the first time in many weeks, and now he was through the Royal Arch. He held his head up and quickened his pace through the dusty play yard—he'd run its length often enough as a child, usually because he was being chased. Finally the market square opened before him. It was thronged with people, mostly in brown or grey or tan, and of course a few showing their optimism about the future of the Councillary by wearing white. As he passed into the crowd, he recognized faces, the sand seller, the sweet maker, and was that Diia? They all brushed past and around him, pointedly not looking in his direction. He wondered at how strange it was to be among so many people, and how odd it was to be outside, just as it had once felt strange to be inside—he remembered the little room they'd shared at the inn, that certainly had begun well....

"Isn't that the prince? But what's happened to him?" someone behind him said, and he looked down and to his horror realized he'd allowed himself to come back into view, and at a head and more taller than everyone else, he instantly drew all eyes. He tried to vanish, but the light was bright, the dust was in his face, and hands were on him, many hands pulling him into a crouch. Someone threw a scarf over his head and hands propelled him forward. He had to hold himself up by grabbing at the legs of those who moved him forward, or pushing against the ground. Once or twice someone stepped on his hand or kicked his arm and he saw white lights behind his eyes and struggled to stay on his feet and put the pain away. He trusted the dark brown and grey clad legs weren't ushering him back to the royal quarters, he trusted this was Lelet's plan. Shouting behind them, but they were already into the warren of alleys where the Counselor's guard hesitated to go. It got quieter and shadows returned, and still he was moved along. He thought about the water in the river, and being a fish in the water. His legs were starting to cramp from the bent over crouching walk.

Finally the hands stopped and he sat back on his heels, sighing with relief as the blood flowed back into his legs. He pulled the scarf off his head. They were in an anonymous alley in the Old City. There were people on every stoop and watching from every window and rooftop. The street behind him was crowded. No one said a word. The group of people in front of him were stone faced, although there were also gasps and anger. Blood ran down his arms and soaked the sleeves of his tunic; he could hear the slow drip into the dirt. *I've frightened these people,* he thought. He wanted to tell them he was sorry, but still no one spoke.

The crowd parted to let through a child. A tiny girl, no way she was fledged yet, and here she was, as he sat on his heels she was just the right size to smile in his face. Her dark eyes were merry and her black curls bounced against her shoulders. She didn't appear to be afraid of him or notice that he was covered with dust and blood.

"My name is Thayree," she told him. "Are you the prince?"

"I am the prince, and it's nice to meet you, Thayree." He was too exhausted to wonder why everyone around them seemed to be holding their breath.

"Do you want to go for a ride?" she asked, and stuck out a chubby hand. He held out his own hand just as the air around both of them began to shimmer.

* * *

Within ten seconds, the crowds had filled the empty space in the street; within twenty the bloodstained dust was gone.

By the time the Counselor and the Mages showed up, there was no one around and no story to tell.

Chapter 39

Eriis

AFTER THE COUNSELOR and the Mages left her locked in, Maaya's first order of business was seeing to the bite mark on her arm. She knew human bites were the nastiest, worse than dogs or cats, but she didn't know what the Mages had lurking in their mouths, or if they even counted as 'human.' She didn't want to lose a finger and an arm in the same day. But by the time she'd settled her stomach and looked, her arm didn't have a mark on it. Her finger, though, that seemed to be gone for good, and she wondered if it would reappear with her human face and grey eyes when she walked back through The Door.

She didn't know how long she'd been in Moth's room, there was no way to see outside. The windows were covered with black silk and sealed with silver. Around the edges, there were scratches where someone (she assumed Moth) had tried to peel away the silk, but without success. A small cruelty, because Eriisai told the time by looking for shadows out the window, the dust tides, and by the moons' rise and set. Without a window, it was neither day nor night.

Well, enough of lying like a lump on the empty bed. She was curious of how he'd spent his long days here without completely going birds and bats. He had a few books lying around and she picked up the one nearest at hand. Her own language was enough like Eriisai that she could navigate his beloved *The Claiming of the Duke* without too much trouble, but she found it difficult at best to follow their written script. The pages revealed words and letters she knew, but they were mingled and mixed with little stars and wiggly lines that moved when you looked at them. Flipping through, she stopped.

There was a drawing in the book, not part of the book. Someone had taken their pen and drawn over the text. It was a drawing of a girl, a pretty, smiling girl with something in her hand, lumpy and oval. It might have been a pear. She was holding it out, an offering. It was a human girl with a suggestion of white hair. She slowly turned the page. "Oh." Her hand crept to her mouth.

Horses, horses and cats and pretty white haired girls, walking and leaping and laughing with each other as they wandered across the pages, and a river flowed along the bottom. All were drawn in a simple hand; the way you draw something you wanted to remember, something you thought you'd probably never see again.

She gently closed the book and put it back where she'd found it.

What else had he done here, to keep his mind occupied and ward off the fear of the next *La Naa*?

Rummaging through the large dresser, a hulking slab of dark wood crowding the small room, was the next thing she decided to do. She knew wood was a tremendously valuable commodity, and it was strange to see such an obviously expensive piece shoved against the wall in what had been a child's room. She had grown up, as Rane put it, 'devastatingly middle class.' Not that she'd ever missed a meal or seen a dress she couldn't take home, but the va'Everleys didn't command the kind of wealth that let them vacation in the Southern Provinces every winter, like Althee's family. Still, this display of casual extravagance, a museum piece that no one would ever see, left behind in the room of a prisoner, she found that slightly shocking.

In the big dresser she found stacks of the dark, loose woven leggings everyone wore. Holding up a pair, they came nearly to her chin. In another drawer, tunics in black silk; all the same except some of them had their sleeves neatly cut off, and some, at the back, were for a broader, heavier person. She held one to her face; it smelled of woodsmoke, faintly. She found a palm sized box made of ashboard with a picture of a bird scratched into the top. Looking at it more closely, she realized it was actually a mouse with wings. Moth told her illustrative arts were not highly regarded, but someone had a neat hand, it was charming. It turned out to be a sewing kit, old and well used. She wondered if the person who gave him the box taught him how to draw as well as sew. She slipped it into her pocket.

At the back of the right bottom drawer, she found a scrap of brightly colored silk. For a few minutes she sat mesmerized by the shine of the blue and red herringbone. The pattern and bright colors made her homesick; the unexpected flash of color made her almost dizzy, and she traced the old weave lines with her fingertips. It was wrapped around a shard of mirrored glass as long as a finger and thin as a blade. Experimentally she tried to draw blood from her only recently healed hand (the pinkie still showed no signs of growing back), but as soon as the tip touched flesh it stopped, not penetrating or even denting her skin and going no further no matter how hard she pushed. The room was charmed against harm, and against self-harm. Well, she couldn't be angry about that. She rewrapped the glass and put it back in the drawer, out of sight.

The dresser was too heavy to move away from the wall, but thinking on her own secret swath of color under the bed, she laid on her back and looked underneath, looking for clues. There was nothing but a small stamp indicating the piece had been assembled in Mistra. She knew the factory, had been there as a child; her father had sold them bolts of silk to cover chairs and couches.

Bolts of silk. She scrambled out from under the dresser and threw the drawer open and pulled the silk scrap away from the glass, which she tossed aside. Of course it felt familiar. It *was* familiar; it was the same pattern as one of her mother's scarfs. The colors, she knew those too: carmine and Ever Blue. Before everything had gotten boxed up and given or thrown or packed away, she'd played dress up with it. How had the same fabric gotten here? Had some long ago relative traded with the Eriisai? The more she learned, the less she felt she knew. She tucked the fabric in her pocket with the sewing kit. Lots of questions, assuming they all survived.

She wondered and waited and still no one came to the door.

Voices woke her. She could hear a woman talking to the guard. The door opened, and it was Daala. Maaya looked past her, the corridor was dark, most of the bowls of stones extinguished, and no one went by before it swung shut. So, quite late. Daala stood just inside the room and stared at her.

"Daala? Are you all right?" Daala sighed and wriggled her shoulders.

"I am neither all right nor am I Daala." At the end of the wriggle, the woman's whole body gave a shudder, like someone pulling a sheet off a table in a magic show. Maaya did not recognize the person she became, but she was the most beautiful of any of the Eriisai women she'd met, even if she looked tired and unhappy. She had a hint of gold around her pale rose eyes and her white silk tunic was spotless.

"Aelle," she said, attempting to arrange her wrinkled, plain brown tunic as she got to her feet, "Thank you for coming to see me." Maaya wondered if she'd live through the meeting. Aelle's face revealed nothing.

"So you're the one everyone's talking about. Maaya, I am to call you?"

Maaya nodded, and then remembered. "Please, may I offer you some water?"

The girl barked a laugh. "Is that what they told you to say? To be polite? No need. Sit." To Maaya's surprise, Aelle sat on the bed next to her. "So. Maaya. Who made you? They did a decent job." She examined Maaya with the expert eye of a collector of flaws.

"My sister made me. She used a very old spell and a bunch of these little sand packages wrapped in fabric."

"Like so big?" Aelle held her finger and thumb an inch or so apart.

"Yes. I don't remember what they're called but I had to eat like 10 of them."

"Eat?" She laughed, astonished. "You ate the sand from our desert? And you went through The Door, and found my brother, and tricked my father, and here you are." She gave Maaya an unreadable look. "If all the humans are as devious as you, no wonder you won the War."

"I know you'll find this hard to believe, but it was over a hundred years ago, where I'm from. Time is different there. In fact most people don't think you exist over here, if they think about it at all. They think you're a story to frighten children. It's just my sister and a handful of old men, keeping The Door shut. On the other hand, yes, when there's something important to us, humans fight to win."

Aelle raised a brow. "You sound like the Duke in that stupid book!"

"It is an exceptionally stupid book, I'm afraid." They both laughed. "I mean, so stupid."

"I knew there was no way it could be true. Honestly, rivers? Of water?"

"No, that part is real," Maaya replied.

Aelle looked suspicious. "Water that fills a valley? Please. And what were those things called? Rhuun was obsessed with them. Big, animal things." She held a slender hand up like a long snout.

"You mean horses, I think. And they're real also. You should come visit."

Aelle gave a tiny shudder and brushed a stray hair from her brow. The way she'd said his name, as if it didn't hurt her to say it; was there still an element of possession? Maaya looked again at the other woman's hand. It was a delicate, fine boned hand.

"I think not, this is—is something wrong?" Aelle nodded at Maaya's own hands, which were on fire. Startled, she gave them a shake and they went out.

"No, I was just reminded of something. It's not important."

"What happened there? That's unusual." Aelle pointed at Maaya's left hand.

"Ilaan taught me how to lock the door. To, um, buy more time. After he left. And the door wasn't happy about it." She held her hand up. "It doesn't hurt, but I don't think it's going to grow back."

"You charmed the door? This door, that the Mages made?" Aelle shook her head, amazed. "You're lucky you only lost a finger." She looked at Maaya speculatively. "If you knew, you would have done it anyway. Wouldn't you?"

"Wouldn't you? Isn't that what you're doing here right now? You stand to lose more than a finger."

Aelle looked at the floor. She finally looked up and said, "What else can you do? What do you have? I mean when your sister made you. Do you know?" Before Maaya could reply, Aelle leaned in and said, "I couldn't ask that of a real Eriisai, you know. One doesn't just ask such things. It's considered quite vulgar."

"How refreshing for you I don't know any better," said Maaya. "I assume you mean can I fly and whatnot. I really don't know. Ever since I got here I've been trying to stay out of sight, not practice fire or flying. Wait...the Zaal. He did something to me. He said he was going to look inside me."

Aelle looked shocked. "He did that to you? Why? He was questioning you about where Rhuun went, I assume."

"Yes, and the Counselor—um, I guess that's your father?" Aelle gave a terse nod. "He said to do it, to look inside. And that freak bit me!"

Aelle wrinkled her nose. "What he did would have nothing to do with getting information. It only would tell him what you manifest towards. He did it because he wanted to, and he was curious, and because he could."

"Your father—"

"Leave him aside for a moment. What did the Zaal say?"

"He wasn't sure if I could shimmer, and I had face shifting although I had never used it, or brought it forward or something. He said I have a lot of fire. A lot. He was pretty specific about that." Maaya touched the place on her arm. "I almost think the Zaal felt like having a snack of my blood."

"I've heard the Zaal has an affinity. It would appear that proper Eriisai blood tempts him almost as much as human blood. It's well that he didn't see anything unusual about you, other than all that fire. He might have set you aside for further study. There has been talk in town about what they do down there in their Raasth, I always dismissed it as gossip...my father always assured me it was gossip." There was a pause. "Will you take him away with you?" Aelle asked. "I mean, will you take Rhuun back to your home with you? If this is successful? If you both live?"

"I know who you meant. If he wants to come back to Mistra with me, yes. I hope he does." She rummaged through the desk until she found the bottle of *sarave* she'd delivered earlier in the week. Like making love and talking and eating and anything that wasn't sleeping or waiting to die, he'd given up on drinking. She couldn't find any glasses, so she shrugged and took a long drink and handed the bottle to Aelle, who accepted wordlessly. "I really hope he does. I'm sorry. I know you two—"

"We were children together. I thought we would be adults together. I would prefer not to speak about it." Maaya could hardly disagree, although she got the impression Aelle wanted to talk about nothing else. Perhaps she wasn't the right person to listen, though. They sat and passed the bitter drink between them. Finally, Aelle said, "*Klystrons.*" Maaya looked at her curiously. "The little bags of sand. They're called *klystrons*. They're toys for children to help them manifest. They are said to tie the child firmly to Eriis, where we draw our fire. Certainly no one eats them!" She frowned. "What would that do to a person? And so many! You say you ate ten of them?"

"I lost count, I wasn't feeling very well at the time. But it was five or more."

"Eriis is part of you, now. Whether she knew it or not, your sister made you well." She squared her shoulders. "Would you like to hear more about the Mages?"

Maaya smiled. "Like where they can be found? And how many there are and what they can do?" Aelle smiled back, the first time an expression Maaya recognized crossed her face. It only lasted a moment.

"The Mages call their lair the Raasth, an old word in our language. It means Free from Harm, or Free from Blame, I can't recall which," Aelle had said. "Either way, down there they are free to do whatever they like, and that's the way it's been since I was a child. Before, I suppose. They used to be the guardians of all the knowledge of our past, and they worked to improve our lives."

"They've made it cooler," said Maaya.

"Yes," said Aelle. "I find it uncomfortable. But when it would have mattered, they didn't protect us from the Weapon, and since then no one really knows what they do. They never speak and they never come up out of there. Until now, when one of them has set up shop at my father's table. I'm afraid I don't know how many you'll see—no more than ten. You understand most of what I know is from my father."

"Aelle, we must be clear. You know what they're doing? How they made it cooler?" Aelle looked at her hands, then back up to meet Maaya's eyes. Holding her gaze, this in itself was difficult for her, Maaya knew.

"We both know what they do," Aelle said. "I saw what they did. I saw *LaNaa*. It is barbaric. They are barbaric. And even though I—even if I hated him and wished him dead, Rhuun is a Prince of Eriis, not a bucket of sand. They have no right. They should pay. I put on Daala's face, you know that. I had to see for myself. I couldn't believe Ilaan when he told me. I saw them take the blood... from Rhuun. As Ilaan said. And other things. A week ago I would have called it idle talk." She took a breath. "But not anymore. I've heard..." She dropped her gaze. "I've heard they experiment on children. I've heard they are raising *daaeva* to do their bidding. I've heard..." she paused, her lips formed a hard line.

"What else have you heard?" Maaya gently touched her shoulder. Aelle leaned into her hand.

"I've heard they go at the beck and call of my father. He told me not to listen to idle talk. That's what he calls everything he doesn't like, idle talk." She looked again up at Maaya. "But it's not, is it? They do those things, down there.

For him. It's all true." She sat up taller and took another long drink of the *sarave*. "If you go to them, if you go down there, they will kill you."

Maaya looked at her hands. "I think they've never met anyone like me before. I think they may not kill me at all. And if they do? I still did what I came here for."

"You rescued him." Aelle sighed. "And I sat in my room and let my father fill my ears, and I wanted it to be true."

Maaya knew what it felt like to have a parent lie to you, although her mother's lies were never anything but fear and delusion, while Yuenne lied as casually as slipping on his boots. "Aelle, I didn't do this alone. I'm just the stone. You and Ilaan are the ones who threw it."

Aelle smiled thinly. "And the Raasth may find itself paying with more than just a broken window."

Maaya said, "Your father is in this, up to his neck. Does he also have to pay?"

"Leave my father to me," she snapped. "And I'll leave the Mages to you and your fire. Even if you see my father, if he trips and lands at your feet, if he draws you aside and begs you to forgive him, turn your face away and leave him to me. Are we in agreement?"

"I have a feeling I'll be pretty busy without bringing the Counselor into it. He's all yours and best of luck to you."

"Do you know what happens now?" asked Aelle. "If it works properly, I'll never see Rhuun again. Or you." She paused, her face a perfect mask. "I think its best this works properly."

"Aelle, I know there's no way I can thank you—"

"See that he lives. There, you see? I still care for him; not that it matters to him. Make sure he lives through this. As for anyone else you come across, well..." She shrugged, stood, and smoothed her white silk tunic. "Stand up, now."

Chapter 40

Eriis

SINCE HE OBVIOUSLY couldn't do it himself, and being able to shimmer with a partner was very rare indeed, Rhuun never had the singular experience of being in one place and then, with no effort, no long walk or hike or run or climb, being somewhere else. He now understood why his mother had always been so fond of it.

He blinked the dust out of his eyes and found himself sitting in the middle of a road, surrounded by people. It was a different road than the alley from a moment ago, and the people were different, too. The only thing that was the same was the anger and dismay on the faces of those who stared at him. Well, people glaring at him; that proved he was still on Eriis, if nothing else. The little girl, the prodigy who shimmered him out of the Old City, let go of his hand and ran to a handsome woman in a plain brown tunic. The woman wore a very relieved expression.

"Mommy! I took the prince for a ride. He's funny looking but nice, just like you said!" The woman snatched the child up in a fierce embrace.

He got to his feet. "Thank you," he told the woman.

"You don't remember me," she said. "I knew you when you were a boy. I have the kite stall in the Old City." She watched him swaying on his feet and frowned. "Perhaps you ought to try not to move." Calling over her daughter's head, she said, "Where is he? Someone go get him." A boy took off and ran to a collection of weathered, small stone houses at the end of the road. Past the houses hunched a huge, low ceilinged structure, open on all sides and busy with people coming and going, shimmering in and out with bags and baskets. A piece of the hillside behind the building was gone, like some huge mouth took a bite out of it. This could only be a transform farm. Other than the farm and houses, the road and a low range of hills under a low sky, there was nothing to see. He realized he was at the Edge, and with no little amazement, that he was alive.

"You're leaking," Thayree told him, and he was, his sleeves were saturated with blood and his arms dripped onto the street.

"Light and Wind," came a familiar voice, "that must have been the worst vacation ever!" Ilaan was right there, smiling up at him. His plain dark brown robe flapped in the constant wind, and his hair flew in and out of his face. Rhuun tried to remember what he wanted to ask. There was more than one thing, but how could he be sure?

"Ilaan?" he said. "Ilaan? I have to ask you..." he took a stumbling step and pitched forward. Ilaan did his best to prop him up. "I have to know..."

"Just take it easy, Beast. I've got you. You're safe now."

"No, it's really important." He shook his head urgently, blood splashed the ground around him. "Ilaan, why can't I see through my eyelids?"

"Okay, well, you've got me there." He sagged against Ilaan, who staggered under his weight. There was a time not long ago when he would have knocked his friend down instantly. "Can I get some help please?" It took four of them to help Rhuun into one of the little houses, and by the end they were simply dragging him. He tried to apologize to the men, but his mouth no longer wanted to obey him. There were no chairs or cots big enough to accommodate him, and by the time they finally laid him on the floor he forgot about questions and horses and girls, and gratefully closed his eyes.

The workers who lived in the little dormitory house gathered outside. They had already collected the bloody sand.

Ilaan knelt next to Rhuun and examined his slashed, ruined arms for a long time.

"I'm going to kill my father," he said.

* * *

"Is the prince going to die?" asked Thayree.

"Hush," her mother scolded. "Certainly not. Go outside and play for a few minutes. Don't shimmer off!" The girl began to gleam, caught herself, and ran out the door. Kaaya watched her leave and repeated the question. "Is he?"

Ilaan rubbed his forehead. They sat at the table in the front room of the little house, where they could see both the child playing in the street, and Rhuun's boots in the second room. "There is nothing that shouldn't simply heal. I think, I hope, he just needs rest. Your girl has one more trip. I don't think we should wait for him to wake up." He didn't think this was true at all, that rest alone would cure Rhuun, but didn't want to alarm Kaaya, who had been so accommodating. And if they lost Kaaya, they lost Thayree, and that would be the end of them. Also, one night at the transform housing had been enough. The sounds of the wind up and down the alleys back home, he was used to hearing that. Here, with nothing to stop the wind or stand in its path, it was uncomfortably like voices, sighing, demanding, pleading. He was eager to leave.

Kaaya sighed. "One more trip. This is a bag of sand all the way around. If word gets back to your father, I don't think there's a farm far enough away to hide her." It was not even an open secret that Yuenne had a particular interest in those who manifested in, as he called it, unusual ways. If it helps the realm, Yuenne would say, it belongs close by my side. Neither Kaaya nor Ilaan intended for Yuenne to get word of this gifted little girl.

"You might consider staying with us, then," he suggested.

"No." She shook her head. "I don't want to disrupt her life any more; take her away from our clan and her friends. I just have to make her understand the difference between a secret and a really big secret. You know, she's proud of herself, she'll want to tell everyone in the Quarter she saved her prince."

"She should be proud. And hopefully she'll be able to tell her story sooner rather than later. But you really should think about the tents. All are welcome, from what I've heard." He felt more than uneasy about the last part of this trip. He'd heard about the hidden *dacha*, the sort of 'tent city,' how to reach it, and the help that might be offered, in his last communication with Hellne. Of course, she never lied or arranged the truth to suit her purposes. But any idea he'd had about staying at the remote transform farm while Rhuun recovered flew out of his head when he saw his friend's condition. Clearly *La Naa* wasn't the only thing that had happened to him, and that in itself was bad enough. Ilaan knew he would be weak and tired, and Maaya told him he had grown thin, but there was a cold shadow over him that filled Ilaan with fear. He simply didn't know what to do. His plan was no longer entirely his own. And as far as the human woman, he wished her well, but she was also on her own, as they had agreed. He wondered how her meeting with Aelle had gone, and if they both walked away from it.

As he waited at the transform farm, those shimmering in began to bring back reports from the city that there was a rumor that the prince had been spotted in the Market Square. It was hours later that it became official. The Counsel promised a reward for information, and the Crosswinds were mentioned for those who withheld what they knew. Ilaan thought it was likely his father didn't know that when the people of the Old City talked about the Counsel, they usually finished by spitting in the street. Many had taken to wearing black tunics hidden under their light tan robes. He wasn't likely to get much assistance from them. Since the alarm hadn't been sounded for several hours regarding the escape, he had to assume Maaya had managed to lock the door—he could only guess at what cost.

The girl was either astonishingly brave or completely uninformed. He'd explained what she had to do and what might happen, and she'd just looked at him with the proper mixture of boredom and impatience. Was she afraid? For once her Mistran emotion hadn't been written across her Eriisai face. He was a little ashamed of himself for thinking she would end up being the hole in their plans. In fact, he had no doubt she would show up at the tents, grab someone by the hand, and demand to see Moth, as she insisted on calling him, at once. He shook his head. Humans.

"There's no point in waiting," he said, "We've imposed on these people enough. And we must impose on you again, as well. You and Thayree."

Kaaya nodded. "One more trip, and then we leave you to it. I'd hate to try to explain to Thayree why she didn't get to save her prince. He may be ugly, but I think my little girl has fallen in love. And there are the stories..."

"One day she may tell her children with the sound of rain on the roof."

"Thayree? Come inside, *shan*," she called. "It's time to go for another ride."

* * *

Why is everyone talking about tents? Rhuun wondered. His eyes wouldn't open, he was too tired to move, but he could hear voices, and it sounded like everyone was going on a camping trip. Was he back on Mistra? Were they tenting in the yard at Lelet's house?

"Tents, Thayree. That's what we're looking for. Just like before, take hold of his hand and follow me when I shimmer out." He was comforted to hear Ilaan, who knelt on one side of him, and he could hear the little girl on the other, talking over him as if he were a table. He felt himself rising to the surface. He didn't think he was in Mistra after all. Too bad.

The little one yawned. "Want to go home. Mommy? I want to go see Dolly."

Another voice, an older woman. "One more trip, and your friend will be safe. And then we'll go home. We'll have a big dinner with Dolly, right?" The woman added, "Dolly is her doll."

"Okay. Wake up prince!" The girl poked Rhuun's arm.

"Ouch, stop." He coughed and tried to sit up. He looked at the girl, then the two tense faces. Both Ilaan and the woman had snatched away the child's hand. "Hello. Um, where am I? Where's Lelet?" He tried to rake back his blood stiffened hair, but his arm wouldn't obey. "*Rushta*—um, sorry, Mother." The older woman looked familiar but he couldn't place her. He looked at the child more closely. "I remember you. We were in the city."

Thayree beamed. "We went for a ride. You're the prince. You're not going to die."

"Well, that's good news. Ilaan," Rhuun asked carefully, so as not to alarm the child, "was there some question? Where's Lelet? I mean Maaya?"

Ilaan didn't answer at first. Rhuun couldn't put his finger on what was wrong, until he realized—his friend was afraid. He'd never seen that before. Ilaan finally said, "It's just so good to see you. But you look like you've had a building fall on you. How do you feel?"

"Like it was a big building. My arms...aren't working right. And I'm kind of tired. Where is she? Oh, thank you for rescuing me. I guess I should have said that first." He paused. "I missed you. I had better not d -i -e, because we have a lot to talk about."

"Your eyelids, yes, I know. You have a lot of people to thank, so start repairing yourself. We're going to the tents. Did you ever hear your mother talk about that? About tents?"

"Tents? No. I don't think so. Where is my mother, anyway? Speaking of people I'd like to talk with." Rhuun couldn't decide if he was dreading or looking forward to that conversation. Just talking exhausted him; he couldn't imagine what it would take to confront his mother. He hoped she wouldn't show up right away. He was happy about camping, though. Tents might be fun, if Lelet was there. He felt himself sinking again, and it was a relief. Ilaan was speaking. He struggled to listen.

"There's more than I can tell in a few minutes, and your friend here is getting a little sleepy. We'll meet at the tents, and you'll heal. And we will talk."

"And Lelet will be there?"

"We'll talk when we get there." Ilaan looked to the little girl, who snapped to attention and took Rhuun by the hand.

"Tents!" she said. And with two bright spots and one much darker, they were gone.

Chapter 41

Eriis

LONG AFTER SECOND moonset, the door to the prisoner's room opened and a slender beauty in a white tunic glanced at the guard—he was nearly asleep and did not look up at her—and walked calmly towards the Royal Arch. The halls were nearly deserted, and other than a few more white clad guards who nodded at her (she ignored them), no one noticed her make her way out the great hall and towards the school yard.

"Aelle! Slow down!" A young male demon appeared from the shadows of a stone column and joined her as she walked. She got the impression he'd been waiting for her—for Aelle. "You're out late. Is everything all right?"

"Of course." Maaya knew she had to keep her conversation to an absolute minimum and get free of the young man. He gave her a look she recognized from many, many cocktail parties, and she allowed herself to relax, just a little bit.

"You are looking well," said the young man, "It's a nice evening. Well, technically I suppose it's almost morning. Dust isn't up yet. Not too dusty, lately, so that's good, anyway. So."

"Hmmm." She decided to do Aelle a favor and smiled at the man. He was quite nice looking, with large clear red eyes, and more heavily muscled than many of the Eriisai men she'd seen, and his attempts at small talk were sort of charming. "It is indeed a nice morning."

"I'm glad I happened to find you out and about," he said. "I have to ask you something." She gave him a wide eyed look and invited him to continue. "If someone was to hear something, or see something...unusual—"

"You don't refer to the prince? Because I hear he is missing," she said. If he knew where Moth had gone, that could be a problem. At least he hadn't seen where she came from. Her hands tingled and she put them behind her back.

"Not exactly. But if one were to see something, or hear something—"

"Unusual, yes you've established that," she said. What was he talking about?

"Well, I think there are some things some people are doing that might find them swimming in sand. Things that go against the Council."

"How unlucky for them," she said slowly. If this was a friend of Aelle's, neither Ilaan nor Niico had ever mentioned him. She had to assume he knew nothing about what they'd conspired to do. And so he probably knew Aelle only as her father's princess and the jewel of the family. That Aelle, the old one, would go right to her father. "If something has happened, then those we trust to take care of us should know. How can we be expected to always know what is correct?"

He looked vastly relieved, and made so bold as to reach towards her hand, but lost his nerve and dropped it at the last second. She wondered what exactly she'd given him permission to do.

"Have you considered my invitation?" he asked.

"I get so many invitations. Please be a dear and remind me." She wanted to smile again, but remembered what Niico had told her and kept her face still.

He laughed. "You are in a funny mood tonight. This morning. The matches, I was hoping you'd join me. Remember? Niico is flying." The matches could only be the aerial events Niico was constantly training for and talking about. Sport was just as dull on Eriis as on Mistra, but according to Ilaan (and to Niico himself, should you ask him) Niico was a sort of genius in flight and it seemed like the sort of thing Aelle might want to do. It would be good for Aelle, she decided, and would get her mind off other things.

"I believe I'd be delighted." He looked so pleased, she was certain she'd made the right choice. Aelle would thank her. Well, maybe not, but with any luck she'd be long gone before this hypothetical date took place. "Yes, I'll attend with you. I'm so pleased you asked. I look forward to it." And she reached out and lightly stroked the back of his hand. He looked about to faint and she figured it was time to say goodnight. "I am a bit tired. May we continue this conversation later?"

As he was unable to reply, she simply gave him what she hoped was a charming smile (Aelle would just have to deal with the fallout of so much smiling) and took off towards the Arch and the winding stair that Aelle promised would lead her to the Mages.

She went in search of a special old door, a door carved into the rock face that helped divide the old city from the royal quarters. The Raasth, Aelle had called it. Free from Harm. Not today.

She looked up and saw the top of the War Tower. It was true morning and the dust was rolling back. Now that it was brighter and easier to see, she quickly spotted a hole, a bite gouged out of the rock wall, not a door at all. The mouth of the tunnel was on the inside of the royal arch, but half hidden by a weathered stone sculpture of an Eriisai warrior. The statue made the helmeted man out to be taller than a human, and what he'd held out in front of him was gone, along with his hand and the lower part of his face. His cat-eyes were still visible; he had once been beautiful. She skirted the base of the statue and found her destination: a stair that wound around a corner and down out of sight. As she stood in the entrance, a gust of rank air came up. It smelled like blood and grief, it smelled like magic, and after smelling it, something that was waiting in her mind lifted its head. She held up her hands. While she had been admiring the statue, they had gone back to being Maaya's; mutilated, nine fingered, not Aelle's delicate, fine boned hands. Her head buzzed and swarmed, voices shouted from far away, deep inside her mind. She knew if she wanted, she could open her little wings and fly halfway across Eriis, to the Vastness and back, and be home in time for breakfast. She pointed at the rocks at her feet and they liquefied and splashed across her sandals and ran in a miniature white hot river down the stairs. She gave a shaky laugh and turned back to the stone soldier. His face was complete and he smiled at her serenely as he lifted his hand to show her the way.

Use the fire, said the statue.

She followed it down.

After arriving at the first landing down, she had to ask herself—Stairs, why bother with stairs? Maaya looked down the shadowed stairway, thought for a moment about where she might like to be standing, and with the shimmer her mind had been hiding, found herself there. She smoothed her tunic over her thighs and looked at the seething puddle at her feet. The corridor dead-ended at a stone wall which she gathered was also the door to the Raasth itself.

Use me, said the fire.

She glanced at the hot stone river, the liquid rivulets of rock playfully lapping at her toes, and then back at the door. At once, the rock wall liquefied and fell like silent burning rain to the floor. The flaming river ran between her feet and disappeared into the cracks between the stone tiles.

Her hands were on fire, white and clean.

What is happening to me?

The big round stone room was brightly lit, although by what source she couldn't say, and all around her, niches in the walls rose out of sight. It looked like each gap had something different in it; a stuffed toy, a bundle of letters, a child's tunic. The wooden worktables placed around the room looked like any busy library in any of Mistra's neighborhoods, or at the University itself. Instead of students flirting or working or passing the time, robed and hooded Mages bustled about, carrying scrolls, books, glass tubes, and silver bowls. She couldn't see what the tubes or bowls had in them, but it wasn't hard to guess, especially considering the smell. None of them had yet noticed her.

She cleared her throat.

Books hit the table and bowls were fumbled and carefully set down as the robed men, perhaps ten in all, looked up to see who had come on them unannounced. None spoke.

"Is the Zaalmage here in the Raasth?" Maaya asked. She pointed to one of the figures standing close by, her arm like a dripping star. "You will answer me."

The figure shook his head, *'No.'*

"That's good. Good. Tell me, which of you participates in *La Naa*? Is it all of you, or just a few? Those who do, please raise your hands." To her surprise, they did as she asked and three of them slowly put their hands up. The close one, the one she'd chosen as the spokesman, was one of them. "Do you know why I'm here? Who I am?" They glanced at each other, unsure of how to proceed. "You," she said to the one she'd picked. "Let's start with you. Put down your hood."

Moving slowly, as if under one of their own charms, he did.

"What's your name? I'm giving you permission to find your voice, today. I think you'll come to need it soon."

The man held his hand to his neck and make a gacking sound. He coughed and tried again. "Coll. My name was Coll." The others hissed their outrage.

"Quiet," she told them. "You will all have a chance to speak today. You have some decisions to make."

One of them near the back, taller and yet also somehow more stooped than the rest, lifted his hand and she felt the beginning of a rush of stiffness in her hands and face. But she threw her own hand up, it flared white and blue, and the Mage's charm withered and fell apart. "You know what *klystrons* are? Yes? Well, I ate five of them. Maybe more." At their hissed reaction, she said, "Ate them. The power of Eriis is in me." Maaya had only the faintest idea what she was talking about, but also felt the sand had not stopped working through her when she'd changed her face and form. Maybe it was guiding her hand now. Maybe the sand itself wanted this place cleaned out. “Which of the three of you held the knife?”

Coll stepped forward. “I know you,” he rasped. “You attend the prince. I myself escorted him out of the Vastness, from The Door to the palace, er, the Counsel, when he returned home. *La Naa* is the greatest gift he could give Eriis. It is our hope that in time he will come to understand that.”

She laughed and they winced, some clapping their hands over their ears. “Coll, before you came here, did you have a family?” He nodded. “Would you consider it a gift to have *La Naa* performed on your mother? Or your brother?”

The taller one in the back hissed, “Do not speak to her. This is dirty women’s magic, nothing more. She is not of the Peermage and does not have the capacity. Woman, leave this house at once and we will say no more of it.”

“How generous of you. Tell me,” she said, directing her question to the angry figure in the back, “Was it you who held the knife? Or did the Zaal only trust you with the bowl?”

“I held the knife,” he replied, “and will do so again, until the prince is as an empty pail. He is no proper Eriisai and only worth what little blood remains. He’ll be dead soon, and so, I expect, will you—sand or no sand.” He threw both hands up, palms out, and a sheet of stinking grey flame raced at her head.

It was like playing lawnball, Maaya would think later on, but instead of little wooden balls with bright feathers, she used chunks of flaming glass. As impervious as they were to injury and as quickly as they healed, it took a lot of glass to incinerate the Mage.

When it was over, she stood ready to defend herself, but after two or three of the remaining Mages raised their hands and then thought better of it, they made no move against her. They circled the heap of burnt cloth and slagged glass.

“His name was Eiith,” said Coll. And all of them, in creaking, croaking, rasping voices said, “Rest him now.” One by one, they dropped their hoods and dragging their hands through the ashes, made long marks on their cheeks and brows.

"The prince is free by my hand," she told them. "Eiith, rest him now, is dead, by my hand. Would any of you care to join Eiith? Or would you take the example of your prince and live in the open air? Because this place—" she looked scornfully around, "is about to be gone."

"Madam," said Coll, "Madam, why? Eiith spoke in....regretful terms regarding the prince, but all of Eriis knows our work is important. Soon we will be able to open The Door and revenge ourselves on the human world. Don't you want that? Doesn't the prince?"

So it was true, what Moth had suspected. They were doing more than tinkering with the atmosphere. "How close are you? To making it ready?"

"Very. So, again, and with no disrespect—why?" He nodded to himself, figuring it out. "Of course. I have been long removed from the world of men and women. I saw you with him. You attend the prince and wish to protect him. Perhaps you have grown attached to him. Think of it this way. What greater legacy could he have than lending his very blood to the Weapon that will take from Mistra what the humans stole from us? His name will live forever."

"It will, I think," she agreed, "but not like this." The men, now with their faces exposed, frowned and whispered together. "Tell me," she said, pointing towards a stern faced man on her left.

"You are from the humans. We can smell it on you. At first we thought it was from attending the prince, but it is your own. You are from the humans, somehow with a demon face. Your manifestation is corrupt, your power is warped. How else could you walk into our Raasth and strike us down? Well? Have you come to finish the job the Weapon started?"

"Oh, no," she said. "Very far from it. If I could bring back the rain I'd do it right now. But war upon war is not the answer. Yes, I attend and protect the prince, but I also protect everyone on the other side of The Door. You'll stop your work. That's why I'm here." They stood silently. "Do you have families to return to?"

"We do, some of us," said Coll, "but they may not show a kind face when they see us."

"Then you'll make new families, or convince the old ones. But you can't stay here." She looked around again. "I will not be remembered as the girl who burnt down the library, though. These books should be saved. And you must have things you love, even down here in the Raasth. I will count to fifty. And then whatever's left..." she shrugged. "Oh, and if any of you go directly from here to Yuenne or the Zaal? You'll meet Eiith on the other side. And that's a promise made by a human."

They gaped at her and at each other.

"One. Two. Three..."

They went from frozen to frantic in a heartbeat; raising so much dust in grabbing volumes and artifacts that she didn't see one of them, the stern faced one, quietly gathering every tightly lidded silver bowl he could lay hand to.

The last one fled past her at the count of forty-five, giving her as wide a berth as possible. The white flame of her hands now reached nearly to her shoulders.

Use me, the fire said.

She did that last thing, the thing she didn't know if she could do, the thing that revealed her True Face and set the fire free. And as sand boiled into glass, she shut her eyes and pictured the place neat and dry and clean; smelling for a while like ash, but the stink of blood and pain, that would all be gone.

Chapter 42

Eriis

AELLE LOOKED AGAIN around Rhuun's room—his prison, she now supposed. He'd been locked away here for months, and she'd actually agreed with her father; wholeheartedly believed in the good and right and proper treatment the prince received. After all, he had transgressed against Eriis, against them all. Against her. Shouldn't he be made accountable? House arrest, well, it's not so bad when you call it that. You're safely tucked away in your own house, where else would you want to be? Servers brought you food and drink, and you had books to read while you sat and thought about what you'd done. While you counted your regrets like grains of sand.

She thought about her self-imposed house arrest and gave a little laugh. "We were both my father's captives. At least now one of us is free."

She touched the places on the wall where the three human artifacts had hung, they were gone now and good riddance. Other than that, the room was more or less the same as when they'd shared it, first as whispering, gossiping children, then sharing flame as adults.

But, she reminded herself, he had no flame. And now he was gone, maybe forever. She would have liked to see him again, despite everything. She wanted to hear from his own mouth why a life with no power and among strangers was finer than spending his life by her side. As soon as she thought this, she knew it was foolish. He never had any power, and she *had* seen him. She had to thank Ilaan for that, although she didn't feel grateful. While she was accustomed to Rhuun's strange appearance, anyone could see that even for him, he looked wrong. It had taken all her composure not to run to his side, or run away. Diseases like the Choking rarely struck those in the city, and almost never among the royal family and their circle. Transform farmers and those living out on the Edge, they got the Choking or were damaged beyond repair by the vast swaths of Change that turned the sand to any of the hundreds of goods that keeps them alive and in comfort here in town. She had never seen a sick person before, but she knew he wasn't sick. He was being murdered in slow motion. The choice was no choice: she would help her brother and the human woman, or Rhuun would die.

She had to admit—if only to herself—that he'd found a warrior among the humans. The girl called Maaya, whatever her real name might be, appeared to have no fear and no regard for her own safety. Aelle wondered if the human girl would serve better as the High Seat's champion than as its queen. Obviously there was something between the human and Rhuun, he must have promised her the Seat. What else had he given her? She couldn't bear to ask the details of their relationship, out there among the humans, although she was desperate to know. Niico would have reminded her this sort of behavior only served to make her unhappy, and he was right. But didn't she deserve to know who—or what—had replaced her? She could practically hear Niico's voice, he would have told her no one really belonged to anyone else anyway, to find someone to give her pleasure, and to release her past. Easy for him to say, that rat-faced bag of sand, that *scorping* liar had been with Ilaan the whole time! Everyone she loved and trusted—from Rhuun himself to Niico to her father, they'd all lied. Her mother must have known the truth and even she turned her face away. She realized it was only Ilaan who had been honest, all along. And strangely enough, the human girl as well. Aelle sighed. She should have been brave enough to ask the girl what she and Rhuun were to each other when she had the chance. She could guess; it wasn't merely friendship that compelled Maaya to eat sand and risk her life. She should have asked. The High Seat, and what else?

Aelle herself had given up on ever holding the seat when Rhuun went through The Door, and it had been so many months since she'd enjoyed his embrace it was becoming difficult to recall what she'd craved so much. He'd have done anything for her, but as she'd finally told Niico after much *sarave,* he never asked for anything in return, because he didn't want anything she had to give.

She knew her father still scrambled to reassemble his plan of holding the seat and the Mages, but her brother had removed himself from the arena, and now? They would have a conversation, she thought. She and the Counselor.

She glanced at the mirror, this time instead of Daala's pinched visage, she was wearing Maaya's plain, calm face. It had been surprisingly easy for Maaya to follow Aelle down the correct mental pathway—she suspected it was the *klystrons* the girl had eaten. Eaten! How did the humans come up with these things? She'd taken Aelle's face and form, and set off to wreak Light and Wind alone knew what havoc on the Mages and their Raasth.

The humans, Maaya swore, did not hold grudges beyond reason, but if you endangered them or their loved ones, best sweep your sand and say goodbye. Maybe the stupid book wasn't so stupid after all.

Now she sat and waited as they had agreed. In case for some reason her father's household guard looked inside, Maaya would still be there. As the morning dust rolled back she'd shift back to her own face. That part was simple. And the next part would be too, because the room was charmed against everything Rhuun could do, which was almost nothing, but not charmed against what a normal person could do. A normal person could just shimmer away. A normal person might simply shimmer out of this little room to the now-unused courtyard at the end of the hallway, and finally out into the Quarter beyond the high stone wall, that would be...less simple. She knew the route, she'd done it in the past, but she couldn't shake the vivid image of rematerializing half in and half out of a wall, or drowning in sand, or in midair. And of course she couldn't fly. She laughed bitterly. If Rhuun had no power, at least it wasn't from cowardice. No, she figured she still had a little time to settle her nerves. It wasn't like she had a choice. The Zaal and her father would waste no more time on Maaya now that Rhuun was gone, and if they found Aelle in his room, they'd have the truth out of her in a flash. One more thing she couldn't do—lie to her father. The door would more than likely raise an alarm, although from what she'd heard it seemed to be operating according to its own inscrutable wishes. But either way, the room would be empty and she would be gone. Back home? She'd decide when she was out of here.

She took another sip from the bottle of *sarave* and sat on the edge of the bed, hoping she could judge when morning arrived in her head. She began to feel...odd. Uncomfortable. And there was a funny smell. It was when she realized she was the thing they called 'cold' that a door swung open—not the door to the room—a Door. And icy air rushed through it along with a giant, hideous monster with hair like sand and flesh like spoiled, white fruit. It grabbed her.

"Lelet! Thank goodness. We've got you, let's get out of here."

Before she could cry for help, she found herself pulled off her feet (the monster was twice her size) and hurled through The Door, which slammed behind her. It couldn't have taken more than three heartbeats. Without thinking, she leapt to her feet, ran to the hottest thing in wherever she was—a fire!—and changed back to her own face.

"Olly," said a young female voice, "I think we got the wrong one."

Chapter 43

Eriis

THE SKY WAS blue, clear and cloudless, and a gentle breeze blew dust in her nose. Maaya sneezed and it woke her up.

She had been sleeping the hottest part of the day away wedged under a huge, brick colored rock which itself was half buried in the sand. The danger was getting buried yourself, but at least, she thought, there were no snakes. Or bears, for that matter. The sky was the same dirty, grey-brown she'd come to loathe since she arrived on Eriis. Behind the ugly clouds, the sun was hovering above the jagged mountains to what she had decided was the west, the direction she was traveling. It was time to move on.

She'd left the city on foot with no one calling after her and not even smoke or ash to mark the transformation of the Raasth into dirty glass. The Mages had all dropped their robes and fled, most, she assumed, into the Old City. She wondered if she might meet one or two on the road out of town. Once well outside the city walls, she'd stretched her wings and flown until it was dark, and then she'd walked some more. She'd left the transform farm behind two days earlier.

"The prince? Our prince?" they'd asked. "No. Never met him. Hear he's a funny looking sort of fella." Ilaan had promised to take her to visit these farms, since her cover story had her growing up here in the place called The Edge, but he never had. It wouldn't have mattered, it was nothing but a lot of sand and some suspicious workers gathered around shabby stone huts. A woman alone asking questions? And with the strange and stranger news out of the city? No one was willing to admit Moth, Ilaan, or Kaaya and Thayree had ever been there. In a way she was grateful, if they wouldn't tell her, they more than likely wouldn't tell Yuenne's guard, either.

After the third or tenth blank faced Eriisai shrugged and turned away, she felt the familiar frustration and anger, the desire to strike out, and she hastily looked at her hands. They were just hands. Whatever the sand had given her had slipped below the surface of her mind, content to sleep until she needed the fire again. Apparently it did not think itself needed now. Instead she thought about the face of the statue smiling down at her. Now it had Moth's beautiful eyes and a mouth like hers. *May would be so happy,* she thought, *even if it had red eyes. We would love it no matter what it looked like, wouldn't we, Moth? But oh, I hope it looks like you.*

It didn't matter who told her anything, because nothing would stop her from finding him. It was just sand, and she knew the way. As the sky grew dark, she opened her wings. She didn't understand why more Eriisai didn't fly, it simply felt so good. She wondered if she might have a special talent for it, like Niico. She wondered if she'd ever get to ask him. Despite his tart tongue, he was devoted to Ilaan and the way he helped both her and Moth was proof of his good heart.

It was too easy to daydream while soaring over the cracked and darkened landscape, and she slammed her knees into an up thrust finger of rock she hadn't noticed. She supposed flying at night was like sailing at night; strongly discouraged. So, time to walk. This far from the city, past even the last cluster of farm houses, it was as dark as she'd ever seen it. The low clouds normally cast some light back even after second moonset, a dim smear of light through the haze. Ilaan had been clear in his directions, and she felt like time had somehow slipped past her. The gullies and sudden rifts and cracks made an obstacle course, but she felt neither tired nor sore from exertion. It was time to walk, so she walked, climbed, slid, and scrambled, sometimes on hands and knees, through the rocks and sand.

Eventually, there was a soft glow past a tall outcrop of shattered rock. It wasn't the dirty yellow morning. It was the light from the Tents.

As a young girl, Lelet had gone every season to the Performance of the Great and Divine Creatures of the Southern Provinces, held in huge tents on the Grand Lawn of the Families' Archives. Her favorite was the *Lyonne*, a fierce looking beast with long and tangled yellow locks around its face, but mild golden eyes. It and its mate, who had less hair but a more ferocious expression, would pace and circle their iron barred cage, and you could buy a bag of tasty bits to toss inside. The creatures would reward you with a look at their grand, enormous teeth, and she and her friends would shriek and laugh and jump away from the bars. There was so much to see; they would wander about pointing at the long necked giant of a beast that resembled a cow with great, curving horns—how did it hold its massive head above its spindly neck?—and marveling over the huge bird with the eyes of a man and a woman's voice. It spoke to her, once, and said, 'You'll go there! You'll go!' She assumed it meant its own far off homeland, a steaming southern jungle, or nothing at all.

The tents that held the Performance were a child's toy of paper and sticks compared to what lay before her as she stood atop the broken, rocky ridge.

The Tents were almost the same color as the sand around them, a tawny gold like the eyes of the *Lyonne*, but as big as a village. It, or rather, they, because it looked to her like many tents, tucked against each other, overlapping edges and corners, stacked and folded around each other, moved in the constant wind like the sails of many ships. It was beautiful.

It took another half an hour for Maaya to reach the entrance; at least, she hoped it was the entrance. This close to dawn, there were few people about, and no one paid her any mind, other than a glance and a nod. The child minding the door—or flap, she wasn't sure what to call it, sat and watched her approach, a bucket between his knees.

"My name is Maaya. I've come a long way. I'm here for the prince. May I see him?" she asked the boy. There was no point in pretending this was anything else, because if Ilaan hadn't made it, if Moth hadn't made it, then her journey would begin again. To where, she didn't know.

"I'll tell Mother you are here. First," he indicated her feet, "those must come off. They will be returned to you when you leave." She obliged, happy to take off the heavy boots. He passed them with a murmured word to someone inside, just out of sight. She made a note of which direction her boots went, just in case. He raised the bucket and bade her stand on a square of silky grey stone. As he poured, she watched the sand turn to water. "Mother is particular about her rugs," he told her. "Come with me." She followed the boy into what was nothing short of a small city. The pointed roof, held up by tent poles she couldn't see, soared many stories above their heads. Somehow there were people living and working above the ground. *A multi-story tent*, she thought. *Why not*? The bronze silk walls let in air, and kept out most of the dust. She wondered if they guarded the entrances carefully for that reason; the air was much clearer inside the tents than inside the palace. Halls and walls and alcoves and vast rooms opened and closed and pulsed around her, it never stopped moving. Bowls of stones cast the soft light she'd seen from the hillside, and the floors were entirely covered with soft woven mats, the rugs the boy had mentioned. It was like being inside a golden sea creature, she thought, swimming in place in the sand.

She'd never been a good judge of distance, but she figured they'd gone as far as her home on Mistra to the public stables, not an insignificant distance. The boy stopped in front of one of the little side rooms. A shivering curtain served as a door. Light came through it, but she couldn't see in.

"Stay here," said the boy, and he ducked inside.

As he pulled back the curtain, she saw a very familiar pair of boots sitting just inside. Later, she would give herself credit for briefly considering doing as the boy asked and waiting. Briefly, though.

"Get away from him," she said. "What are you doing?" A child was crouched over Moth, who was stretched out on the floor, with only the thin rugs to keep him off the sand. She saw the rapid rise and fall of his chest; he was alive, but whatever the child was doing was obviously causing him great distress.

"I'm sorry! Mother, I told her to wait," the boy said. The child turned and looked up. It was not a child, but a woman. Very old, fabulously old. Her eyes, nearly lost in the seams of her face, were milky and blank. She looked up, but not at anything in particular. She smiled.

"Leef, please escort our new friend back to the hall. If my boy wishes to see her, he will see her." She turned her back and continued her ministrations. She heard Moth gasp and she took a step forward. Without turning, the old woman raised a hand, and it was as if a large man took her by the shoulder and marched her back out into the hall. The boy followed her out.

"Mother Jaa doesn't like to be interrupted," he said by way of apology. "Please, sit."

There was no furniture, in fact she realized she hadn't seen any chairs at all, and no tables higher than her knee, only fat cushions and stacks of rugs. She sighed and settled herself on the ground just outside the door. The boy sat on the other side of the curtain; she gathered to make sure she wouldn't try to go back in before the old woman was finished. He darted back inside and came out with a cup of water. They passed it back and forth.

"What is she doing to him?" she asked.

"Mother will let you know."

"How long has he been here? Is Ilaan here? Can I see him?" The boy just smiled politely and nodded and hummed to himself.

An eternity later, Mother emerged and said, "Leef, we've arrived at another day." The old woman was correct. Maaya could now see light coming in through the silken walls as the glowing stones, in response, slowly dimmed. Without another word, she strode off, and Leef said, "She'll see you now." Maaya looked shocked and the boy laughed.

"If I was to take offense," said the old woman, wagging her walking stick at them, "I'd never get anything done. And I can see you well enough, young lady."

They followed Mother Jaa (who kept a surprising pace for her age and apparent fragility) to another curtained doorway. This time, all three went inside. It was a simple room: cushions and a low table, mats on the floor, an ancient broom propped in the corner. A white porcelain cup sat on the table. Maaya wondered where it came from.

Maaya sat across the table from the old woman with her legs tucked under. The boy poured them water and retreated to a pillow near the door.

"Now," Mother said. "Who sent you and why have you come here?"

"Ilaan sent me," she replied. "Didn't he tell you? I'm here for the prince. Ilaan can tell you."

"He told me many things," said Mother. "He told me a woman who can change her face would come from the city. But which woman and what face?"

"Well, my own face, of course. My name is Maaya—"

"Is it? Names are a funny thing, aren't they?" She began to realize this old woman thought she was a spy, or an assassin. And with good reason: if she could change her face, she could be anyone. "How did you get here?"

"I walked. And I flew." The woman frowned. "I did. It was difficult at first, but I did what Ilaan said—at light I would find a spot under some rocks and dig into the sand so I wouldn't get too hot or be seen. And at moonrise I flew until I couldn't see, and then I walked."

"You mean you shimmered," Mother said. "Because that trip should have taken you over a week, and from what I have heard, a city woman left the transform farms two days ago."

"No," Maaya shook her head. "No, I can't shimmer." Then she remembered her trip to the Raasth, is that what she'd done? This wasn't going as planned at all. She was supposed to get to the Tents, find Ilaan, and then see Moth.

And when he was well, they'd go home. "What were you doing to him? You were hurting him. Why?"

The woman smiled slyly. "You know perfectly well none of our people can experience pain."

"You called him your boy, are you the queen? Is Moth your son?"

Now Jaa laughed. "Me? The queen? You have gaps in your education, whoever you are. No, he is not my son. Nor is he yours, either. Why are you so invested?"

She clenched her fists under the table. She wouldn't cry in front of this awful woman. "He is my friend. He saved my life."

"A long way to walk for a friend," the old woman mused. "And if you are who you say, your debt is paid. He lives."

"No," Maaya replied. "Love is not a debt to be collected. And as long as he's alive, he belongs with me."

The old woman nodded happily. "Love! Now that is interesting. Tell me, since you can't shimmer and aren't sure which is your real name, or his for that matter, how did you get him out from under Yuenne's nose?"

"He walked out. I took his place as hostage. But you must know this if you've spoken to Ilaan."

Mother disregarded her. "And the Mages just let you wander away when you were done?"

"Then you don't know everything. There aren't any Mages anymore."

The old woman's brows shot to her hairline. "This is new news. Explain."

"I went down to that rathole they live in, and I gave them five minutes to gather what they felt they couldn't live without. I made them talk. And then I burned it down." The old woman went pale and at last looked every bit of her years. Maaya felt bitter satisfaction in telling her something she didn't know.

"And the Zaal?" she asked, when she had composed herself.

"He wasn't there. I imagine he and Yuenne are still both out looking for Moth—for the prince. They won't find him here, will they?"

"Not unless you gave them directions they won't. The Zaal without his Raasth, the Mages uncloaked. This will be dangerous for you. Rest assured my boy is not the only one they now seek."

Maaya was suddenly exhausted. "Please, can I see him? I won't disturb him."

Mother Jaa steepled her gnarled fingers in front of her face for a moment. She said, "Perilous times. Leef, please see that Miss Maaya doesn't have a knife in her pocket to take another drop of blood, or a rock to chunk me in the head. I can only imagine she'd like to."

Maaya didn't answer. She stood and allowed the boy, who murmured "sorry, sorry," to look through her clothing. He handed something to Mother Jaa.

"Where...where did you get this?" The old woman held the little sewing kit in her hand, running her fingers over the winged mouse scratched onto the lid.

"It belongs to the prince. He's had it forever. He can sew better than anyone I've ever met."

Mother Jaa smiled again, but instead of suspicion or cynicism, there was only joy. Her blind eyes disappeared for a moment, so broad was her grin. She had perfect, tiny teeth, except for one grey incisor. It gave her a rakish air. "You are the one Ilaan told me to expect. I hope you can forgive the fears of an old woman. My lovely boy would be precious to me even if he wasn't the heir." She stood. "Let us go see him. When he speaks, it's only to call your name." She paused. "Names."

Chapter 44

Eriis

"HOW LONG HAS she been in there?" Yuenne asked his man at arms.

"Well Sir," the white clad guard replied, "the morning dust was just rolling back when we brought her in." Yu glanced out the window of his front room and up—the Tower, broken off at the top, was just starting to cast its shadow.

"Very nice," he replied. "She should be ready to chat. Don't go too far. You are dismissed." But the man had only taken three steps when he added, "Oh, Bremm, do bring us a pitcher of water and glasses. The girl in the kitchen will set up a tray for you." The man departed with a nod.

Yuenne took a quick glimpse in the mirror and brushed back his hair. It had been a long and fruitless night on the sand with the Zaal at his side—certainly not the companion he would have chosen. And from the looks of the dried-out, suspicious faces at the transform farms they visited, not one to travel with if you wanted answers. He should have gone by himself, or with one or two of his men. But the Zaal would not be denied a chance to hunt for, as he annoyingly continued to call Rhuun, the 'quarry.' If the man had stayed in his Raasth where he belonged, there might still be a Raasth. Even now, the Zaal was trying to sort through what was left, and gather up those Mages who hadn't dropped their cloaks and fled. Yuenne thought perhaps he might offer sanctuary to a stray Mage or two. It might do to have someone like that close at hand. But first, he still had the problem of the prince. He sighed. It seemed like the problem of the prince was all he ever dealt with. It had seemed like such a good idea, all those years ago. Ilaan a Mage, and Rhuun a sacrifice. But everything that young man touched turned to sand.

He put a smile on his face and opened the door to his study. "Daala! Thank you for being so patient. You know how busy it can be around here. Always something to do." He eased himself into his fine leather chair, and wondered if she'd taken the opportunity to look at it more closely, or if she knew what the skin of it was made of at all. She herself was seated on a worn ashboard stool with no back. It was a low seat, it made her look up across his lovely Burled Birdseye Maple Wood desk at him.

"I am pleased to serve," Daala replied. Yuenne thought she was perhaps not so pleased, although thus far she was properly composed. "Have they found him?"

"They?" Yuenne asked mildly. "I assume you mean me. I assume your intention was to remind me that I have lost a very fancy piece of property, and that I require your help in getting him back. Or did you have something else in mind?"

"I have nothing in mind, Counselor." The girl, smiling blankly, looked at the floor. Yu admitted he was rather impressed. She was as impassive as a stone wall.

"What did you have in mind the last time you attended the prince?" Yu asked. "My guard reports that you made two visits during the day yesterday, and left in quite a huff the second time. And then another visit near dawn." The guard had seen her enter the room, all right, but he'd reported it was Aelle who left not much later. After further, rather more aggressive questioning, the man agreed he must have been mistaken.

That got to her. She frowned. "Three...Your guard must be mistaken, Counselor. I attended the prince only once, and he told me—"

"I did not ask what he said. His words are like blowing sand. I asked what you had in your mind, leaving, as my guard reported, in a huff. And what drew you back in the early hours. A tiff, I gather, happily resolved?"

He watched her squirm a bit, trying to figure out how to justify her actions without bringing Rhuun's comments into it.

"I...was informed a meal had already been delivered. I was late, and I was angry with myself." She cocked her head. "I was late because of you. Counselor."

"Because of me? How remarkable." The man at arms shouldered the door to the study open, and Yuenne smiled at him. "Bremm, at last. Set it there, on the sideboard. Wouldn't do to get the wood wet." The man nodded and left them with the tray, water, and glasses. "Do you know why you shouldn't get wood wet, Daala?"

"Well, I don't have anything made of wood, and I don't have extra water to splash around, so no, I do not." He laughed to himself. She was still trying to be her usual, mouthy self.

"Leaves a mark. Water. It leaves a mark." He knew from the guards that Daala liked to dump the prince's water on the floor. Sloppy, he thought. Rude. And it got her nicely coiled up, wondering if she was in trouble for that as well. But he didn't intend to pursue it. It had done its job. "But let's go back to why you were late. Because of me? Please, enlighten me."

"Well," she said, "I got a message to meet you at the Court—at the Councillary. And when I arrived, you weren't there. And by the time I got to his room, he said—"

"Who sent you the message, Daala?" She was blinking too much, he noted. He thought she was telling the truth.

"I don't remember. I don't know."

"He said, he said—you put great stock in what the prince tells you, don't you?" She looked up and he saw something flare in her eyes. Yes, there was something there. "You two practically grew up together. Good friends, old friends. Did it bring you distress to see him in such a state?"

"What? No!" More blinking. "It was that Maaya, she had a flame lit for him, pardon my language. She's the one you should be talking to." She shifted on the stool, her back was probably starting to get tired. "I remind you I am a married woman. And the Beast was no friend of mine. Maaya, her and..." And here she stopped, snapping her mouth shut.

"Maaya, and?" But she had her mouth tightly shut, and folded her arms. "Daala, there are a variety of outcomes for you today. One of them involves you and your delightful husband moving inside the Arch and into a nice new home. Would you like to hear the others?" She hunched on the stool and tried to remain composed. "We will have the prince back, and soon. If you think he will protect you, I assure you he will not be able to."

"Protect me? Him? He can't even protect himself."

The girl spoke with such venom, surely there was something between the two. If she didn't care, she wouldn't speak so. "So it fell to you to protect him, perhaps during an early morning visit. It becomes clear. Now, will you—"

"Aelle," she snapped. "Your precious princess, she had something to do with it. Everyone in town is talking about it. You didn't know that, did you? Well, look to your daughter if you want to know where Rhuun went. Do you even know where she is?"

Yuenne carefully poured himself a glass of water, and watched Daala's face as he drank without offering the cup. It was a shocking breach of courtesy. "What an interesting thing to say. I'm going to give you one chance to take it back. I understand. You are tired. Perhaps you heard gossip. So let us ask ourselves, do we really intend to accuse Aelle of acting against the Counsel?"

She raised her chin. "You don't know where she is. No one does, not even Niico, and he's her pet jumpmouse these days. Both of them gone, and where is Ilaan?" She actually laughed. "And here you are talking to me, as if I would lift a finger to help that freak. You've got sand in your eyes, Counselor. Look to your children, and you'll find Rhuun hiding behind them. Just like always."

"One more time, Daala. Do you accuse Aelle?"

"Obviously. As does everyone else." She leaned forward. "I am on your side, yours and the Mages. You should have drained him when you had the chance."

Yuenne nodded. "You may be right about that." He called out, "Bremm, please join us." The man stood behind Daala's stool. "Daala will be our guest at the Councillary for the time being. And what luck! We already have a room prepared."

He leaned back in his seat, listening to her shouts, her threats, her accusations receding towards the street. She'd tried to shimmer away, of course, but he'd taken precautions. No shimmering in and out of this room. He'd speak to the Zaal, get her stilled, and then he supposed it was up to Bremm to deliver her to the Crosswinds. Yes, he really ought to have a Mage in his employ.

She might be right, and she might be lying, but Daala would never have Aelle's name in her mouth again. And if it was the Crosswinds for every filthy peasant in the Quarter, it would be no great loss to him.

The house was finally quiet again, and he thought he might take his rest, when the maid knocked on his study door. He motioned her in.

"A young man to see you," she said. "A friend of Miss Aelle. He says there's things you ought to know. His name is Hollen."

"Hollen," repeated Yuenne. "Things I ought to know. Well, you'd better see him in."

As it turned out, Hollen was correct.

Chapter 45

Eriis

MAAYA FOLLOWED JAA back down the billowing hallway, and said, "You called him your beautiful boy. Then you don't think he's ugly or crippled or any of the other terrible things people say about him?"

"How would I know what he looks like?" Mother Jaa asked. "He looks as he must, like his father, I assume. Like you, when you're wearing your own face. Leef, please describe Miss Maaya to me."

The boy said, "I think she's going to faint."

"I am not going to faint," she told them. "Ilaan says more than he should."

Jaa gave a cackling laugh as she pushed the curtain aside. "That may well be the case, but he didn't tell me. That story he's been putting about, the prince and the farm girl?" She nodded at Rhuun, who frowned in his sleep, but didn't stir. "My boy always wanted to go adventuring, but his feet never took him to any farms. At least, not here on Eriis."

Maaya knelt next to Rhuun and took his hand, which was cool and weightless. The room was small, almost as small as the one they'd escaped from, and like that room there were no windows here. But unlike it, there were no locks, not even a proper door, just a billowing silk curtain to keep eyes away, and no furniture, outsized or otherwise. It appeared to be a sort of storeroom, with piles of old rugs and fabrics lining two walls. Maaya supposed the smell of mold would have been overwhelming back home, but here on Eriis, that wasn't an issue. Some of the rugs had been arranged to create the suggestion of a bed, cradling Moth against the warm sandy floor.

"Who are you? What is this place? What were you doing to him?" She had more questions, but felt it would start to sound foolish.

"My name is Mother Jaa. I've known this boy since he was a child. I taught him to sew. Oh, don't look so shocked. Ha, I was right, good guess."

Maaya was glad the old woman couldn't see her blush. "So you lived in the city? In the royal quarters? Were you his tutor?"

"Royal?" She laughed again, as if they were trading jokes over a bottle of wine, as if the conversation was nothing of consequence. "No, I spent my years in the Quarter. He came to see me when there were too many eyes on him. I can see where things go. And I taught him where to put things. That's what you saw. In order to put the wounds of *La Naa* away, one must first find it, re-experience it, and then cause it to vanish." She reached down and patted his other hand. "He is young and his body wishes to heal. See?" She lifted the blanket thrown over him and Maaya sighed with relief. The slashes and marks were starting to knit and fade.

"Then you can heal him? Or help him heal himself?"

"Oh, no," she replied. "He has a shadow over him. You can feel it, even if you can't see it."

The old woman's matter of fact tone startled Maaya. "What do you mean, a shadow? How do we get rid of it?" *A shadow*, she thought. *He can vanish into a shadow, and now he has one following him around.*

"It's an odd sort of thing, a shadow cast by nothing. I don't think it intends to harm him. But it will. I will consult Light and Wind." A strange look passed over her face. "Perhaps they will reply." She sat back and beckoned Leef to bring them some water, her expression brightening. "His mother sent me here many years ago. She gave this place to me."

"The queen gave you a hidden outpost. That's an interesting gift."

"There are those who lost favor, who decided life in the city did not please them, and even the transform farms may lose their luster. Those people needed a place to go. I came between my boy and the way his mother wished him raised. But she saw value in what I taught him and in having a little place tucked out of sight. She agreed I could keep watch over him as long as I didn't interfere, and as long as I kept this place—in case she needed it."

"I assume she did," Maaya said.

"She is not here. She travels, as well. But look! My tents were of use after all. And our Counselor, he has sent many people my way. He may not know it yet." She sipped her water. "Tell me about the man my boy has become."

Maaya nodded. "He is the bravest person I know. And he is honest even when it would serve him not to be. I don't understand why someone so good should have had such a painful life. I don't know why everyone called him ugly. He's beautiful." Again, Maaya was glad the woman couldn't see her wipe away tears.

Jaa cocked her head, looking at her, or looking towards her—Maaya wasn't sure. "Do you know the story of Aa?"

Maaya shook her head, then flushed and added, "No, I don't—"

"It is a story as old as Eriis itself, perhaps older."

Maaya looked up. "Like the story of Lelee?"

Jaa snorted. "Lelee? That *sdhaach*. Older by far. At the beginning of us, when there was only fire, Aa came to be aware of itself. And like all alone things, Aa longed to gaze upon another's face. So Aa lit a new flame as beautiful as its own. And this face, once made, was perfect, the perfect mirror, and it was called Iaa. Even so, Aa was quick to passion and just as quick to boredom, so it created another, hot new flame, called Oaa. And these two flames together were the first demons and the first Eriisai. But they shrank from the blazing heat of Aa; they turned away and looked to gaze only at each other. And from their flame, we are all descended. Now Aa, in a rage, decided to create the perfect opposite of itself, one so ugly it would never seek its own visage and never turn away. And so Aa created Tr, and that was the first human. But even Tr grew exhausted under Aa's constant gaze, and Tr escaped Eriis and made a whole world as ugly as itself."

"Tr. Mistra," said Maaya. "That's um...okay."

"So you see, all of us on Eriis consider ourselves three steps from divinity. From perfection. And anything which strays from that will not be celebrated."

Maaya looked down at Rhuun. "He strays pretty far from that."

Jaa nodded. "Most of us, we don't often think on the story of Aa. But since the Weapon, much store is placed in things being as they were; as if we were still the mirror of Aa. Something that looks out of place, which cannot be explained, something different, we turn away from that. To those who remember the story, he falls too far from Aa. And to those who don't, he is a reminder of what we've lost. Do you understand?"

"It was too hard to be kind to him, when Eriis wasn't kind to you." The old woman nodded and smiled as if she'd solved a child's riddle. "I can, though. I can be kind."

Jaa snickered. "Kindness? Is that what they're calling it in town now?"

"He owns my heart. We joined. Should I be ashamed?"

Jaa bent over and addressed Rhuun. "A warrior, you've found yourself. Well done." She patted his cheek and waved for Leef. "I will leave you. If he wakes make sure he eats, and do the same yourself. Take some rest; no one will disturb you. Ilaan will want to see you when you are refreshed." She held out her hand for Leef's assistance.

"Mother?" Maaya asked. "What if I hadn't had the sewing kit with me? What if you thought I wasn't really the woman from the city you were told to expect?"

Jaa's eyes vanished into the maze of wrinkles as she grinned. "Why, the Crosswinds, of course."

Leef helped her to her feet and escorted her out, pulling the curtain shut behind him.

She was so tired it was making her feel nauseated. It had been a day and a night since she'd slept. Or more? She wasn't sure. She curled up on the pile of rugs next to him, making sure not to disturb or lean on his arms. "I'm here, Moth. We made it. Did you hear what I said? You own my heart. I'll love you 'til the moons fall into the sea." She closed her eyes.

"Sand."

"What?" She sat up. "What did you say?"

His eyes were barely open, glowing red crescents, and he had a faint smile. He'd never looked less to her like a human man. "Sand. That's the expression. We don't have seas. You know that." He blinked rapidly. "What time is it? Did I miss lunch?"

She was momentarily at a loss for words. Finally, she said, "Moth, do you know where you are?"

"Because I'm kind of hungry." He carefully propped himself onto his elbows. "This is not my room." Light reentered his eyes. "Lelet? Where...what is this?"

She leaned forward and kissed him. His mouth was cold and he tasted like ashes. "You're at the tents. Mother Jaa is taking care of you. Ilaan is here, too." He took the water she offered and drank the soup, but pushed the bread aside.

"Mother Jaa...I thought I dreamed her. She must be a million years old." He took a deep breath and poked at his arms, and flexed his fingers, looking uncertainly at the places where the ugly wounds had been. "We put everything in its place. Um, tell me the part about the moons again?"

"You mean, that I will love you until the moons fall into the sea, or the sand, or onto your head?"

"That's it. Me too." As they lay back down and she finally closed her eyes, he muttered, "I miss your white hair. Maybe we'll see it again soon."

He wants to go, she thought, and her happiness for a moment overcame her exhaustion. *Sunshine will drive away the shadows. We're going home.*

Chapter 46

Mistra

AELLE STOOD IN front of the fireplace in a large, dark room—actually, she stood *in* the fireplace—her hands alight with blue flame and held out in front of her. The yellow headed giant hung back behind someone—a child?—of nearly her own size. A wrinkled, white haired man-monster was collapsed in a big chair in the corner.

"What is this place?" she demanded. "Why have you brought me here?"

The girl took a step forward and said, "My name is Scilla va'Everly. You are at the Guardhouse on Mistra. We intended to bring my sister Lelet home, but it appears," and here she shot a sharp look at the yellow giant, "we have made an error. We won't harm you in any way. Um, would you like to get out of the fire?"

The giant said, "Are you sure she's the wrong one? She looks just exactly the same!"

"How dare you!" Aelle snapped. She stepped out of the fireplace and they both took a step back. "Send me back to Eriis immediately!"

"I'm sorry, um, Miss, but we can't do that. Not today, anyway." The girl pointed at the old monster. Maybe he was dead. No, he gave a snore like stones rolling down a hill. Just sleeping. "Our teacher, Brother Blue, is the one who can work The Door, and he's in rather delicate health. We can try tomorrow, or the next day at the latest. It was a great struggle for him to open The Door at all."

Aelle extinguished her hands and folded her arms. "I am to be your prisoner?"

"Not at all," said the young girl. "You are our guest. Can we get you anything?"

"Make it warmer," she said. "A good deal warmer. How can you all just be standing there?" She could control her temperature, all her people could, but this was ridiculous. "And why is it so dark in here?" She rubbed her forehead. "I am actually on Mistra?" She laughed sourly. "I was the only one who didn't want to go."

"May I ask your name?" the girl said. "Olly, get her a blanket from the trunk. And light some candles, please." Olly found a folded blanket and gave it to Scilla who handed it to Aelle. The boy immediately retreated to the corner.

"My name? I am Aelle, daughter of Yuenne the Counselor and Siia of the White Flame. Who did you say you were?"

At Yuenne's name, the child made a strange face, but quickly composed herself. She handed Aelle the blanket. "I am Scilla va'Everly, sister of Lelet, the face changer. You're a face changer, too."

"Maaya," said Aelle. "You're the sister who made Maaya." She pulled the blanket around her shoulders. It was a blanket for giants. "So you may know Rhuun as well."

"I don't...who is that?" Scilla asked, although Aelle was pretty sure she knew.

"Rhuun, the Prince of Eriis. The heir to the High Seat. The half a human. The reason she is there. And now, why I am here." Aelle glanced up at Olly, who was lighting all the candles he could find. "Chair," she said, pointing at a spot close to the hearth. He raced to oblige. "Scilla of the Guardhouse, let's talk about your sister and the prince."

* * *

"He never told me his real name, he said to call him Moth," said Scilla. She and the child sat with knees nearly touching close to the fire. Olly hung back as far as he could while still being able to listen. "And he didn't talk about you at all."

"And you met him as he came through the Door?" Aelle asked. "You were his guide?" She took in the timbered ceiling, the ancient desk and chair, and the overflowing bookcases. She'd never seen so much wood, or been so uncomfortable. Even with the blanket and the fireplace, she was shivering with cold. Everything smelled like wet. But this conversation was proving to be enlightening. The little one, the girl, was obviously lying about something. She squirmed in her seat and looked everywhere at once.

"I met him as he came through. We talked many times. I think he liked it here, especially after he met Lelet. He was crazy about her."

Aelle forced herself to ignore the girl's words and watched the reaction of the boy. The look on his face told her the child spoke without thinking. Perhaps she was simple.

"He'd still be here with her, except some nasty little man—oh, I guess that's your father—so the Voice is your father! He came through the Door and tricked Moth—he did not want to go. I don't think there was one thing on Eriis he ever wanted to see again."

"Scilla..." Olly began.

"And that awful little man! He was—"

"Scilla!" Olly took her by the sleeve. "Our guest looks like she could use a glass of water or something."

Scilla looked at him blankly. "So, go ahead and get it."

He pulled her out of the chair and marched her to the door. "Can't you see she's upset? You're talking about her da! Maybe she doesn't think he's awful. And don't say 'little' all the time; it's just rude."

"My father is rather awful," said Aelle. "And I would like a glass of water."

"Perhaps something to warm you up?" asked Olly. "Try this," he poured her a cup of something steaming and fragrant. "It's cider with a splash of rum. It's my master's favorite."

She took a tiny sip and her eyes widened. "Did Rhuun drink this?" she asked. "Did he sit here like this and talk with you?" She waved a hand around the room, which was full of shadows cast by the candles. "Does it all look like this, here on Mistra?" Olly and Scilla were mentally shouting at each other, and unless the humans had the imaginary gift of the silent voice, failing. "You will tell me what happened here," she said. "How did your sister steal Rhuun's heart away from me? How did you happen to meet him at The Door? Why did he not tell you his real name, if he wasn't concerned about you using it against him?" Scilla opened her mouth and then shut it. "Why do you call my father 'awful'? And what did you call him? Voice? This is all just so curious." She drained her cup and held it out. Olly refilled it.

"You should show her your notebook," said Olly. Scilla gave him a glare that could melt sand. "Let her know what happened, this is about her, too." He turned to Aelle. "Why were you in that room instead of Lelet? And am I wrong or did you not look exactly like her?"

Aelle decided to answer him. "She was in danger and I was helping her. I manifest towards face shifting and I was wearing her face so she could leave the palace wearing mine." She leaned towards Scilla. "You made her eat sand? Whatever gave you that idea?"

Scilla looked uncomfortable but said, "It was in a book. A really old book, along with the *klystrons*. She wanted to go to Eriis and find Moth, and the only way to do that was to change her face. And I did it. It worked. Did you know she wasn't really a demon?"

"No one knew." She frowned at the child. "You are gifted with the word. You would have made a fine Mage, I think. Tell me, how did you really come to meet Rhuun?"

There was a long pause. "Show her your book. The Voice is her da. She should know."

Scilla finally nodded at Olly and said, "I have to go up to my room. Will you be okay until I get back?"

Olly nodded, looking not at all sure that he would be anything like okay, and they watched her leave. He bolted the door.

"What about the white giant over there?" she asked.

"That's my master, Brother Blue. He's old, as you can see, and he worked hard magic today. He won't wake up."

"What is your name?" She held out her cup for another refill, and he gave her a small splash.

"I'm called Olly, Lady."

"Ah-lee." She smiled. "Only family matriarchs are called Lady. Since my mother presently enjoys that honor, you may call me Aelle."

"It's not all dark and cold here on Mistra, Miss Aelle. It can be very nice." He paused. "I'm sorry about Scilla. She's young and sometimes her mouth runs away with her. She didn't know Moth, um, Rhuun was your man."

"He's not my man, Ahlee. He was, but we were children. Like Scilla. I think despite Maaya being a human person, he could have done worse." And she realized, here in this cold, dark place, that she meant it. That strange feeling, the feeling in her heart since the day Rhuun had walked through The Door was gone, and only in its absence did she realize it had a name. *How funny*, she thought. *I could feel pain all along.*

* * *

Scilla raced up the winding stair and down the long corridors towards her cell. She passed a gang of novices; they called out to her, asking why she hadn't been to classes, if she was ill. She shouted over her shoulder she'd tell them later and someone please take notes, and finally threw the door to her room open. She closed it and leaned against it, her heart hammering from the run and from the realization that she'd just caught *another* demon. A demon who was daughter to the Voice. A demon she might be able to use. There was no binding spell this time, but once the girl read her father's words, there might not need to be one. Scilla forced herself to concentrate and break it down.

The spell she'd thrown over herself worked only fairly well; there were time gaps and blurry places and she usually couldn't see anything at all outside of the city walls. She was able to watch the spark she recognized as her sister in her comings and goings, and quickly picked out Moth. She knew which one was Ilaan, and which was the Voice—the Counselor. The others were a drifting, shifting mass of dots and lines. She and Blue worked out where Moth was, and since he never moved they gathered he was being imprisoned. Then Lelet started going there. Then he was gone and she was still there. That was when they decided to act, open The Door and bring her home. After all, Moth was gone—either dead or free, she didn't know. Lelet would be furious for leaving him behind (if he was even alive), but they'd deal with that later. The important thing was depriving the Counselor of his prisoner and his prize. And now she held his daughter.

Yes, she could read the notebook. She'd said something about Lelet taking Moth's heart away from her; she'd be very interested to hear what her father said about her ex-boyfriend. Not for the first time, she made a solemn vow that no man would ever make her act like the pack of idiots her sister and this demon girl had become.

Chapter 47

Eriis

"A BINDING SPELL." Ilaan shook his head. "Did not see that coming."

He and Rhuun were propped against cushions with a low table between them in a large, airy room near the center of the tents, with four gently rippling walls and no ceiling. If they looked up, they would see the woven rugs high above them, and the imprints of many feet dimpling them as people walked about. Occasionally, someone would step off the edge of one of these floating rooms and fly to another level, or swoop to the ground. Ilaan turned the plate of fruit and cheese so that the choice pieces faced his friend. He tried to conceal his shock at Rhuun's thin, haggard appearance. He didn't bother hiding his anger. "Just one more gift from my father. He had that little girl's head turned sideways."

Rhuun picked at the fruit and turned the plate back the way it had been. He reached for a cup of soup instead. "She did get me out of the Veil. I could still be there. I guess our translation at the beginning wouldn't have sent me all the way through. Those must have been the missing words we talked about. Your father was working with the Mages, so he had all the words. But how did he get The Door open to begin with? It doesn't make sense."

Each time Rhuun said 'we' or 'our', Ilaan felt it like a punch, or what he imagined a punch must be like. It was kindness and nothing more. He held the blame for the failure of the spell, the mistranslation, even the warning he'd sent had arrived too late.

"Let me start at the beginning." He paused. Rhuun's attention seemed to be drifting, at odds with the conversation. "You're awake, now? You understand me and where we are?"

"Quit asking me that. I'm fine." He'd said that several times, but repetition didn't make it sound any truer. Rhuun confessed no memory of anything to do with the transform farm and only a vague recollection of escaping his room in the palace. Ilaan watched his performance of sitting up straighter, trying to cover his lie and comfort his friend. "Start after I left. I'm sorry I ruined your party, by the way. I've kind of quit drinking *sarave*. Most of the time."

Ilaan shrugged. "Sometimes the mouth gets dry. You didn't ruin my party. I did. You remember my ceremony of the object? Well, that's what started it. There was a scrap of paper from your book in with it. It wasn't supposed to be there, obviously. But the Zaal knew it belonged to someone with human blood right off. And I was all, oh, no, that belongs to the prince, not a human. You know, my *best friend* the prince." Ilaan couldn't meet Rhuun's eyes. "So this is all because of me, talking when I shouldn't. Being so clever." Rhuun said nothing, so he continued. "They got their robes bunched up and came up to the party after you left. It was the first time they'd left the Raasth since the Weapon. Everyone is still talking about it. They demanded your mother turn you over. She told them to eat sand, of course. And I...sent you away." He picked at the fibers of the rug where it had worn thin under the table. "I'm so sorry."

"We will decide who gets sent to the Crosswinds when I hear the rest. I may call for beheadings." He began to laugh, and Ilaan, startled, looked up and laughed with him. Rhuun's laughter turned into a cough and Ilaan refilled his water.

"Tell me about it. About the human world. Did you see horses?" Maaya had told him some of this already, about what they had seen and done together, but Ilaan wanted to keep Rhuun talking.

"Loads of them. They were a little nervous around me at first, but I think I was making some real progress. And there was so much...there was music and harps and cats and whisky and pears, and everything was blue and green. And the rain. And the river. It went on forever."

Ilaan didn't understand most of it, but he knew in time it would become clear. In the days to come when Rhuun was installed on the High Seat and the human girl was gone, they'd have time to examine each memory. "And Maaya?" He leaned forward and whispered, "I think she likes you." Rhuun laughed. "Seriously, she took on the Mages and my father, and she marched through the Door and across the Vastness to get back to you. What did you do to that girl?"

"Well, I kidnapped her."

Now Ilaan laughed. Maaya had been reluctant to talk about the specifics of her relationship with Moth, (to her, he would only ever be called Moth) saying it was private, and Ilaan would have to ask Rhuun himself.

"No wonder she wouldn't tell me. What did you do, tie her up and throw her over your shoulder?"

Rhuun looked decidedly uncomfortable. "I didn't tie her up. And it wasn't my idea. It was the binding spell. Scilla made me do all sorts of stupid things, the sort of things you wish on people when you're a child. I think about what could have happened if an adult with some real power caught me instead of that poor, confused girl, and I have to stop."

"Sounds like it was mainly embarrassing instead of catastrophic."

Rhuun shrugged. "Scilla made me go to her house and torment her family. They thought I was a ghost—a *daeeva*."

"You mean to tell me a human had you in a binding spell and all she could come up with was to rearrange the furniture?" Ilaan asked.

"That's what I'm saying." He shuddered. "Think of the harm I could have done, and me with no way to stop it."

"But you did stop it." Rhuun said nothing. "You did stop the spell, you must have. I mean, you aren't under it now, are you? Did the Mages remove it?"

"No."

After a moment it became clear Rhuun was not going to elaborate, so Ilaan returned to a topic he knew hadn't been exhausted.

"So Maaya. Kidnapping is not usually how we meet our partners; it's a pity you didn't try it sooner. All this dating and dinner and 'getting to know you' nonsense. And instead of screaming her head off and having you locked up..?" Ilaan left it hanging.

"She showed me what being a human person was like. And we became friends. Not at first, I think she didn't much care for me."

"I wonder why!" said Ilaan.

"She decided it wasn't a real kidnapping, that her brother put me up to it, so she didn't have to be afraid of me and agreed to travel with me. She had it all worked out that it was some sort of prank, if you can imagine. I met her brother and he's kind of crazy, like her little sister. A strange sort of family. I can see where she got the idea. And then, while we were on the road," he paused. "A lot of things happened." Rhuun frowned and Ilaan wondered where his mind was.

"You know we spent some time together, Niico and I helped her with her disguise. She's as brave as anyone I've ever met, even if she looks like a meek little jumpmouse."

"You should see her in her real skin, in Mistra," said Rhuun. "You wouldn't say that, about her looking meek."

"Of course, she must look completely different. What does she actually look like?" asked Ilaan.

"Well, a little bit like me, I suppose. They all do, with the wrong shaped eyes. Only a girl."

"Like you? Well, she must be very...tall." They laughed and then were quiet for a while. Ilaan watched Rhuun examine but not eat bread and cheese.

Finally Rhuun said, "Ilaan, I killed three men. Three human men." As always, the pain on his face was there for anyone to see.

Ilaan kept his own face still. He said, "I expect you had your reasons?"

"They killed me first."

Now Ilaan was again afraid Rhuun's mind was wandering. "You mean they almost killed you? Or tried to?"

"No, I mean they succeeded. For just a minute, or a few seconds. But they must have, because it broke the binding spell. Nothing else could have done that. And they had her. And they would have killed her too, after they were...done with her."

Ilaan tried to imagine his sweet, shy, homely friend with blood on his hands and came up short. "You were protecting someone under your charge. No one would expect otherwise." Rhuun shrugged again and looked at the floor. "Do you want to tell me about it?"

"No," Rhuun answered, but Ilaan thought otherwise.

"If you change your mind—"

"It was my fault she needed protecting. I knew they meant us harm and I thought I could handle it." Rhuun moved to rake back his hair, but stopped with his hand over his eyes. "Three human men, they came upon us as we traveled. They were armed. I knew what to do and I hesitated."

"I'm not sure I follow," said Ilaan. "You said you did handle it."

"I should have shown them my True Face and ended them at once. But I didn't want her to see me like that. I was too ashamed. It was my own fault they killed me, and my fault they took her. When I woke up, I found them, found her, and then I finished it." He paused. "She knows, of course. But I don't even think she blames me. She should."

"She loves you. There is no blame, remember?" Rhuun shook his head. "If we start handing out blame, there'll be no one left after the beheadings." This earned him a weak smile.

"Let's leave it for now," said Rhuun. He looked grey with fatigue, and Ilaan wondered if he ought to escort him back to the room Jaa had given him. But Rhuun wasn't ready to finish their conversation. "I wish I was still there. I wish we were there together. So much to show you. And I would be there, but your father, he opened The Door. How? I can't figure that part out."

Ilaan was glad to fill in the blanks and this seemed like a safe subject.

"Well, after the party, your mother enlisted Diia and her people to stand guard outside your door. She thought you'd return right away. The Mages wanted to search your room, they made formal requests and she denied them. My father decried her on the floor of the high chamber every day. Finally, he sued for her removal from the High Seat as a conspirator with the humans and for fraud in not claiming your parentage. I had already been kicked down to the Quarter, I was no use at all. And Aelle was not exactly your best advocate at the time. But your mother—she vanished, just as surely as you did. I still don't know where she went."

"Good old Mother," Rhuun said wryly. "She so does love to pop in and out."

"Diia's folk left with her, and the Mages got into your room. You were gone, but you left a little bit of yourself behind. They found a pair of leggings, big enough for a bizarrely tall, Beast sized child."

"A pair of black leggings with a big tear in one knee. I remember. I shoved them all the way in the back, so I wouldn't get in trouble. They must have gotten caught behind the drawers. They'd have been there for years."

"There was blood on them."

"I fell," said Rhuun. "The older ones were chasing me, and I fell and bloodied my knees." He rubbed his face. "That's how your father opened The Door."

"He couldn't keep it open because the blood was so old and there was so little of it. But it was long enough." Ilaan twisted his hands. "I wanted to try and make it safe for you to come home. I don't know how I could have done that, after telling the world about you. This is all my fault." He was prepared for anger, had been preparing for it since the day he'd started working for the queen. He felt he deserved it. Rhuun wore the blank, composed face Ilaan recognized, also from the queen. Then, unexpectedly, Rhuun smiled.

"There's plenty of trouble and plenty of people to blame, myself included. As I believe we just established. '*All* your fault?' I know you're the smartest, but you do need to learn how to share with others, Ilaan. If none of this had ever happened, where would we be? I'd be in the bottle and fighting with Aelle, and you'd be wearing one of those stupid robes and poking around in the dark. I would never have met Lelet or gone to Mistra. Apologies start and stop at this table. Are we agreed?"

Ilaan sat silently for a moment. "Your mother gave me the book. I put it in the library, in that bookcase. She wanted you to find it." He waited for Rhuun to finish choking on his water. "There's more."

"Of course there is." Rhuun cleared his throat. "I suppose you'd better tell me."

"That was how it started, when she gave me the book. I was just a child."

"I remember. So that's how it got into the library. I always wondered."

Ilaan continued. "I've been working for your mother since then. As her..."

"Spy? Listening mouse? Problem solver?" He laughed wearily. "And here I thought she just liked you better all these years."

"At first it seemed like a great honor, and it was always something to help you." Even as he said it, Ilaan knew how it must sound.

"Yes, I've been helped a great deal, it appears. Just look at me, with all this help. Who knows about this?"

Ilaan thought for a moment. "Diia, probably. The queen never made a move without Diia at her side. And Mother Jaa, she seems to know everything else."

Rhuun gave a strange smile. "So, no one. No one knows about this. Your father, by the way, you were working for him, too, although you may not have known it. He told me he 'put you in my path,' I think were his exact words. You and Aelle both. So much work, so much scurrying around, and for what? A drunk and a cripple." Ilaan, horrified, started to speak, but Rhuun held up his hand. "We never had this conversation. You never told me. You will continue to 'work' for her. She is still contacting you, I assume? From wherever she is?" Ilaan nodded. "And when she does, you'll mention it to me, of course."

Despite his wasted appearance, Ilaan thought for the first time that Rhuun looked like someone who might sit easily on the High Seat. One more thing Hellne got right. He wasn't sure he liked it. He decided there was one more thing to tell, to upend the whole bag of sand once and for all, and let the wind blow it where it may.

"The author of the book, this Capehart person?" Ilaan said. "He's your father, Rhuun." There was no reply. "I only found out after you left. Your mother wanted you to go to Mistra and bring him back because he broke her heart and left her with...with you. She had some...bad things planned for him. He...I'm sorry. He had something to do with the Weapon."

"Please stop apologizing," Rhuun said. "How lucky we are she confides in you. Or else how would I be sure? I always knew she was wrapped up in this somehow. She picked my path and set me on it. I was never anything other than her weapon." He sighed. "I almost met Capehart. He thought I was the enemy. Lelet—I mean Maaya—told me about him. He's an old man, now. My father. Huh."

"Wait," Ilaan frowned. "Maaya knows him? How?"

"He is her sister's teacher at her school. The Guardhouse school. She may have called him Brother Blue. He helped to transform her into one of us, and helped to bring her here. She doesn't know we are related, Blue and I. Nor does Blue either, as far as I know."

"They're the same person?" Ilaan shook his head. "Humans have a lot of names. Moth."

Rhuun smiled drowsily. He no longer looked like royalty, only a tired, pale young man. "I like that name. I liked being Moth. Except for the binding spell part." He yawned. "And even that wasn't so bad. I got to watch her. Every night."

"Watch who? What are you talking about?" Ilaan asked.

Rhuun's eyes snapped back open. "Nothing. Not important. But Brother Blue—he and Scilla are watching us right now. My human family." He laughed softly. "They watch over us, some sort of charm they cast. I don't really understand it. But Lelet told me that when I am ready to travel, they will open The Door and call us back to Mistra."

"Yes," said Ilaan. "About that." He paused. Rhuun's eyes were nearly closed and he'd sunk back against the cushions. "You don't seem very upset. Are you sure you're well?"

He opened his eyes with obvious effort. "Honestly, I'm too tired to worry about all this, my mother, your father. My father. My father. I've never said that before." He shook his head. "Right now I just want to rest, and then go back and look at the river again. That's what I want to do."

"You absolutely must rest, and when you are well we'll talk about the High Seat, and how there's no one in it. Your mother tells me I must convince you to hold it. She says it belongs to you."

Rhuun laughed again, this time more weakly. "That's new. Well, I can barely walk across the room, much less rule from the Seat. But tell my mother I seem open to the idea."

Ilaan hesitated. "Are you and I..."

Without opening his eyes, Rhuun said, "You may be a spy and a traitor, but you're still my best friend. You may have noticed I have them in rather short supply. Let's say we've entered a new phase in our relationship."

One of the silk walls shook and moved, and they watched the ripple travel towards the curtained door. Maaya lifted it aside, her eyes never straying from Rhuun's face. She thanked Leef without turning and met them at the table. "Are you overdoing it?" she asked Rhuun. And then to Ilaan: "Is he overdoing it?"

"I'm afraid I've worn him down with too much talk. I'll leave you. We should meet again at first moonrise for dinner, I believe Mother Jaa will want to talk with all of us."

As Ilaan dropped the curtained doorway, the last thing he saw was Rhuun reaching out with his torn arms for Maaya as she sank to her knees on the cushions by his side.

The friend I sent through The Door is not the same one who returned, thought Ilaan. What is he now?

Chapter 48

Mistra

"LIKE A CAT," olly thought, "*or more like a little doll. But a woman, not something terrible.*" He remembered playing as a small child with his next oldest sister Sesille and her vast army of dolls; they would go to war (the brunettes always riding on the backs of the lowly blondes) and when he was older, tormenting her by switching out their heads. Aelle reminded him distinctly of one of his sister's dolls— tiny and perfect. She would have ridden at the head of any doll army, though, he was sure of that. And if he hadn't had four older sisters, he might not have recognized Aelle's proud manner and sharp tongue as a way to hide what was plainly evident— she was alone and far from home. He thought of the gift he'd found for her, and tried to imagine a smile. Then he tried imagine what Aelle's breasts might look like—perfect, of that he was certain, when he realized Brother Blue was talking to him and had been for some time. "Olly, I assume it's pleasant where you are?"

Olly blushed crimson and said, "Sorry, Brother. I was just thinking."

"Hmm, about starting more foolishness with Scilla, no doubt." Olly thought Blue was still annoyed that they'd not only found the *klystrons*, but understood how to use them. Despite everything they had all seen in the last few months: the big demon, the sister who loved him enough to risk her life, and Scilla's obviously enormous gifts, for starters, Olly thought Blue would prefer to pretend nothing had changed. He was only an assistant—for the moment—but even he could tell. Everything had changed. "Olly, I'd like you to watch over this Aelle woman, if you would. Scilla and I have much to do to keep the binding spell undamaged, and I won't have the girl wandering about making trouble. If she must leave her room, see to it she wears a cloak with a deep hood. Everyone will think she's a novice." This wasn't entirely true, as Scilla was more than meeting the challenge of maintaining her charm. This very morning, she'd seen the speck of light she said was Moth—it had reappeared and was moving fast away from the city. Once beyond the city wall, the landscape started to fill in as she watched. He met up with the light she called 'Ilaan,' and then they'd vanished again. This could only mean they'd gotten him free, and Scilla said she would be on the ready to bring them all home. So far, the disaster Blue predicted had not come to pass; no one on Eriis seemed to have noticed they were being watched.

Olly said, "She's complaining, Brother. She says she wants to see Mistra, the room is too cold, the food is too strange, and she's bored."

Blue shrugged. "We are not operating an inn for demonic travelers."

"She wants to go home, Brother."

Blue scowled. "When she tells me where she wants to go, then we will send her there." The girl reluctantly admitted she didn't know where her brother or their friends had gone, and that the city was no longer safe, not even her own home. In fact, most particularly her own home. "I avidly await the day of her departure, but I'm not a villain. If she is afraid to go, I won't force her into peril. She's only a girl." Then he snorted a laugh. "If she's bored, tell her to read a book." He held out his hand, and Olly helped him to his feet. "I have a class to teach."

"About that," said Olly. "We've met two of them, now. Demons, I mean. Miss Lelet swears by the tall one, and he's their prince. And now this lady, well, she has better manners than my aunties back in the city. Do we...should we...that is..."

"Change the curricula? Toss my books out the window? Two does not make a whole race." Olly handed him his stacks of notes, the same lectures he'd been giving for half a hundred years. "See to the girl."

"Yes, Brother. I'll see to Miss Aelle."

* * *

Olly made a stop at his own room for the bundled gift, and then to Aelle's room, locked from the outside. He found her pacing like a *lyonne*, and as soon as she saw him, she flung a candle at his head. He ducked, grateful she hadn't thrown the whole candelabra.

"What am I supposed to do with a candle?" she asked as he placed it back in the sconce, "when there's nothing to see, nothing to do and I'm frozen to the floor? Are you planning to kill me by freezing or with boredom?"

"Miss Aelle, I brought you something to help with the cold."

She warily set down another candle. "Let me see." He shook it out and she gave a gasp of delight and turned her back. He put the heavy fox fur coat over her shoulders and she moaned—actually moaned—as she rubbed the fur against her cheek. She turned back to him with a brilliant smile. "Tell me what this is, Ahlee."

"It's made from an animal called a fox, it has this pretty red fur. It's warm, and I thought with your coloring it might look nice on you."

She took a step closer to him. "And does it?"

"It, yes, you look pretty. And happier, and warmer." He knew it must be his imagination, but the whole room seemed to be getting warmer.

"Thank you," she said, and took his hand. She looked at him expectantly, and he gave it a brisk shake, feeling like he'd missed something. The look on her face confirmed it. She narrowed her brows at him, but then shrugged and sat on the edge of her bed and examined the sleeves, which were several inches too long. She turned out the pockets and found an ancient linen handkerchief. She waved it at him. "Now I may go out and see the rest of this place."

He didn't want to tell her she'd have to give up her coat for a thin, ugly novice's cape. And part of him wanted to keep her for himself, if he was honest. "Um, no, Brother Blue is afraid you'll startle the students, still. So I have to ask you to stay here. But look, I also brought you some books!" He barely made it out the door before the second onslaught of candles.

She stuck her head out after him. "Ahlee! Bring me some of that chocolate. Not too hot. I won't throw anything." She shut the door.

* * *

The door was open. Olly came to a halt, the cup of chocolate in his hand forgotten. The door was open, he'd neglected to lock it. He toed the door aside and looked in, feeling a bit sick. Sure enough, she was gone. So was her new coat, and one of the books. The handkerchief lay abandoned on the floor. Blue was going to have his head. He decided to look for her first, and maybe there'd be nothing to confess. The corridor led, in one direction, to a stairwell which connected the living quarters to the lecture halls. The other way was more rooms and another stairwell, this one went to the dining hall and to the roof. The door to the lecture hall stair was open. *Which way would do the most damage?* he asked himself. A room full of novices, of course. So that's the way he went.

* * *

"Are you absolutely certain you're a demon, Miss?" piped a young boy's voice.

Olly clutched his head. He'd been past a long series of rooms full of students where everything was as it ought to be, and was just about ready to hope she'd gone to the roof after all, when he stopped short in front of a class where the door was open and the teacher—the human teacher—was absent. The boy continued, “Because we didn’t think demons were really real.” She must have done something dramatic because the class gave a great gasping ‘oooooh’. And then, to his amazement, they all began to giggle. He took a deep breath and went in.

“Ahlee! Light and Wind, I am glad to see you! What are you teaching these poor humans?” She held up the book he’d given her. “Have you seen this? I mean, really looked at it?”

“Um, yes, Miss Aelle, I have.” He looked at the students, who were mesmerized by the petite woman. “Where is your regular teacher?” he asked the boy in the front who had been speaking.

“Brother Maron had a headache and left us to our studies,” the boy said. “We were reading and then *she* came in and asked us if we’d ever seen a demon.” He leaned towards Olly and whispered, “I think she’s a real one. But how?”

“I came here by accident,” she told the boy, “and you may call me Miss Aelle. It is improper to refer to an adult as ‘she’.” She smiled at Olly. “You’ve brought my chocolate! How kind.” She held out her hand and he passed it over. “But this...I can’t even bring myself to call such a stack of lies a schoolbook. And this is what these poor human creatures have learned about us? Really, Ahlee, I am terribly disappointed.” She waved a hand at the bookshelf against the wall. “These will all have to go, I’m afraid, if they are like this one.” She regarded the old book she held with a scornful glance.

“Or,” said Olly, “You could go back up to your room and I could bring you a pen and paper and you could write your own and these children can forget you were here and definitely not tell anyone.” He gave the children a hard look. “Are we clear?”

“We want Miss Aelle to stay,” said the boy in the front row. The other children agreed.

A small girl with long blonde braids said, “I want to go see Eriis!” Another called, “Make fire again!”

Olly groaned. This was getting out of hand. “No one is going to Eriis, and Miss Aelle was just leaving.” But Aelle had settled into the cracked leather chair behind the teacher's desk and folded her hands on the blotter.

"Really, Ahlee, it's no trouble. I'd be happy to stay here and educate these humans properly."

He leaned close to her ear. "Brother Blue will literally kill me. You aren't supposed to be here at all; the other teachers don't know what we've been doing. This is a bad idea."

"Well." She smiled. "Why not let me talk to these other teachers? They might like to see how I'm not dangerous or imposing at all. And then it will be fine, and you won't be in a grain of trouble." He looked pained and she added, "Please, Ahlee, don't lock me up again! I promise, I'll behave."

He was certain that no matter what happened, this was most likely not going to be true.

* * *

"This is my fault entirely," Olly told Blue. "I forgot to lock her in and she ran off."

Blue stared into his mug of spiced cider, unblinking, for a long moment. "Then children have seen her? And she's spoken to them?" The old man rubbed his forehead as if it ached him. "Tell me now, Olly, what have we learned?"

"She's insulted by our textbooks." He didn't add the worst offenders were written by Blue himself, nor did Olly feel the time was right to ask Blue how he'd gotten so many things so wrong. "And she wants to tell the students about her people and her home. I wonder if that's not a bad idea? I mean, we don't have to tell the others everything—about the prince or Scilla's binding spell. Um, either of her binding spells. We could just say Miss Aelle got here by accident and...and..."

"And we are fortunate that she is now able to correct our misconceptions? That generations of history are wrong? That our efforts to guard The Door were wasted? Every family who ever sent a Fifth will be out for our blood."

Olly began to see the implications of Aelle's presence. If there was no need for a Guardhouse, why not open The Door and allow demons and humans to go freely back and forth? If there was never a need for a Guardhouse, why had the elders of the Order sealed The Door in the first place? "Maybe they'll be glad, if there isn't a need any more. Maybe they'll thank us."

"Thank us! Hardly. And the need is just as great as it ever was," Blue insisted. "They were dangerous. Are dangerous. One pretty girl has turned your head, but they lie and call it love. She never told me, never."

"Never told you what?" asked Scilla, who must have heard about the interesting new teacher and come to investigate. She shut the door behind her, and tripped over the rucked up edge of the rug near Blue's desk. "Olly, fix that, would you please? Brother, I'd really like to know what 'she' never told you."

Blue waved his hand wearily in front of his face. "Too long. It's been too long." He closed his eyes. "Everyone, please leave me."

"Not this time, Brother." Scilla folded her arms. "What did 'she' never tell you? And why are we trusting the Voice's daughter?" Scilla had made it clear where she stood on the subject of Aelle: lock her in her room and let Lelet and Moth decide what to do with her when they came back home.

"Scilla," said Olly, "show respect. He is tired. This is a difficult time—"

"It's always difficult," she said. "I imagine seeing Aelle brings it all back, Brother." She circled behind his chair. "Who is she? Who is Ellna? What didn't she tell you?" He reached for his mug and she plucked it off the desk. "Tell me who Ellna is, and you can have it back."

"Scilla, please," Olly said. "He's just an old man."

"Shut it, Olly. Who is Ellna? And then you can rest. Is she a demon? Is she one of them?" Blue's forehead drooped onto his folded hands, and they heard a loud, rumbling snore. "Shit!" Scilla snapped. "This is your fault, Olly. You let him do whatever he wants." She paced in front of the fire. "Well, we've got one of them here, let's ask Aelle if she knows someone named Ellna."

"I hardly see how that matters at this point," said Olly, who was getting tired of being at fault. "The issue now is Miss Aelle and the fact that people have seen her."

Scilla shrugged. "Minimize damage. Let me think...ah, I know. How about this: The demon girl was lucky that she showed up here after getting lost outside of her own city walls instead of getting sucked into the Crosswinds or lost in the Veil. We saved her life and she is in our debt. She can shed a new light on life on Eriis today, with a special focus on the harsh conditions, attacks by firewhirls, political unrest, and danger to humans. One day, it may be hoped, we may open negotiations with our neighbors the demons, but certainly right now it's too dangerous to consider opening The Door. It is only thanks to the diligence of the Order that demons like this Counselor haven't marched through The Door and attacked Mistra already."

Olly gaped at her. "Did you just make that up now?"

Scilla smiled. "The Order first, family second, human third, Mistra fourth. We'll take Aelle to the Masters and she'll tell them the story we want her to tell them. They'll love her."

Aelle turned out to be a fine actress, and with her pretty tears and cries for mercy, the Masters had to admit she seemed quite without harm. Of course, one lovely young lady does not make a whole race. But, as they say in town, exceptions prove the rule. Let her stay with the expectation of protection by the Order and the assumption she'd make no trouble.

Olly thought that if they were looking to avoid trouble, it was perhaps already too late.

Chapter 49

Eriis

IT SEEMED MAAYA had no sooner closed her eyes than she was awake again, and it was a long, disorienting moment before she remembered where she was. The curtained room was still light, she hadn't slept the day away at least. The sand shaded silk walls breathed around her and the soft rugs covering the sandy ground made a surprisingly comfortable bed. She was alone.

Here in Mother's enclave, she felt sure wherever Moth had gone he was most likely safe; that old woman had been ready—eager—to set her ablaze, or make her vanish, or whatever she did with people whom she felt threatened her 'lovely boy.' He was in better hands here than anyplace else on Eriis. But with Yuenne, the Zaal, and what remained of the Peermage after both of them, there was no place on this world that was truly safe. Worse, as long as they were here, Mother Jaa's people were in danger as well. And yet she couldn't be sorry she'd spared the lives of those frightened, croak-throated men. She hoped she wouldn't come to regret her soft heartedness.

She drank some water and ate the rest of the bread and cheese—noting with some amusement that in her mind they really were bread and cheese now—and did her best at finger combing and repining her tangled hair. Without Niico to help her, she was hopeless at creating the perfect back of the head coil the women of Eriis did as a matter of course, and missing a finger didn't make it any easier. Finally she gave up and braided it; at least it wasn't flying all over the place. This was why she kept it cropped short at home, what a nuisance. People were welcome to stare; she'd call herself a trend setter. She wondered if it was safe to change to her True Face to clean off the dust—she hadn't worked out which fabrics were safe and which were flammable. Generally, like back on Mistra, the more delicate a thing was, the more valuable. Best not to take a chance, the idea of being trapped in a giant burning tent like a frightened bird made her feel light headed, even if she knew it couldn't permanently harm her. She'd walked out of the ruins of the Raasth, after all. Anyway, burning down your host's home was frowned on in most places.

Leef was waiting outside the curtained door for her. "Mother says I am to show you to the dry rooms." Problem solved. She was just glad she'd elected not to change, she didn't think Mother was completely on her side yet and an error like that would have hardly endeared her. She laughed to herself as she followed the boy. *If Mother Jaa is such a hard sell, what's his actual mother going to be like? Those'll be some mighty big hoops. Queen sized.*

"Could the tents themselves catch fire?" she asked Leef. "If there was an accident?"

"The tents cannot catch fire," the boy replied. "Mother has seen to that." He turned, wide eyed. "She told me the charms took a year to finish. A year! Once you're outside, though." He gave the shrug she'd come to recognize as the Eriisai version of '*tant pis.*'

The dry rooms stretched along a cliff face twenty paces from the long, shuddering back of the tent village, neat little cubicles cut into the stone. It reminded her greatly of striped, curtained changing rooms set up along a holiday beachfront, minus the ocean. A shoulder height stone wall served for modesty and a bench and hook held her leggings and tunic.

Unlike the last time she'd changed her face, this was a relaxing and refreshing experience, like a hot bath and a massage all at once. She was a little dismayed by the size of the pile of ash at her feet when she changed back, but gave her own Eriisai shrug. You couldn't march through the desert for a week—or two days, or two weeks, or however long she'd been out there—without getting a little dust on your wings.

She was adjusting her robe when Leef came back for her. "I like your hair like that," he said, looking at his feet. She smiled and smoothed her braids, clean now and pinned up milkmaid style.

"Can you find your way back?" he asked.

She thought she could, and joined the other demons on their errands through the great silk city. She wanted to try flying up to see what was happening on the levels and platforms over her head, but worried her unschooled wings would give her away. So she wandered through the dim corridors, peeking into rooms where she found the curtains drawn back. In a large central room, where there was no curtain, she saw a circle of women gathered around a glowing stone bowl. They were weaving threads made of light, passing it from hand to hand in a huge, circular cat's cradle. Something was moving in the light above the bowl, but it was indistinct. The women hummed while they worked and Maaya wondered if it was to pass the time or part of the job, if indeed it was a job they performed. Those walking past gave the room a glance, but she alone stopped to watch. She stood there for a long moment, feeling the peace of the scene surrounding her, until one of the women lifted her hands away from her work and turned to look at her. Fearing the worst, Maaya pulled back, but the women merely gave her a slight smile, lifted a finger to her lips, and bade her enter.

The woman gathered her long tan robe aside so Maaya could kneel on the worn cushions next to her. The woman plunged her hands back into the streams of light and went back to her weaving.

In the light of the bowl a tiny, perfect image of Counselor Yuenne, his smug little smile now a bit forced, sat upon the High Seat—now the Council Seat—and tried to placate the crowd who demanded justice for the Mages. She paled, seeing him there, and noted the crowd was entirely white and grey clad. She saw stripes of green on a hem here and there and wondered if it was to honor the Mages. But the Zaal lived, as far as she knew. She doubted anyone would honor the memory of Eiith, and then felt ashamed for such a dishonorable thought. He was someone's family, once. She would have to tell them all she'd taken the life of the old Mage. While it was true she had been defending her own life, she couldn't swear absolutely she had no choice but to kill him.

Turning back to the circle, she craned her neck forward. It was difficult to hear Yuenne, as if he were speaking from a great distance (which she supposed he was), but the gist was clear. The prince had somehow destroyed the Raasth, committed cruel murder, and escaped. The eye of blame was being cast upon those in the Quarter who had never been loyal to the Counsel. Several were in custody and the Crosswinds would feel their flesh. He knew where the prince (whom he referred to as 'that crippled boy, his mother's shame, a tool of the humans') and the harlot he somehow seduced had fled to, and the queen herself was complicit in their escape.

Maaya shook her head. She doubted he knew where they were, but he'd wasted no time turning this to his own advantage. Ilaan was safely with them, but what about Aelle? And Thayree and her mother? Maaya touched the shoulder of the woman who had called her in and mouthed the words 'thank you.' The woman smiled and nodded, and went back to the image, which had melted away from the Council Seat and now showed a street in the Quarter. It appeared a normal day, if unusually quiet at the moment, so she rose and quietly left the room.

After several wrong turns, Maaya found her way back to Rhuun. He was finally awake, she was happy to see, and Ilaan was with him, looking as if he'd just returned from the tailor with a side trip to the barber.

"Good, I was about to go looking for you," Ilaan said. "Are you planning on getting ready to see Mother Jaa?" He had an eye on her travel-worn brown robe. "And your hairstyle, does it have a name?"

"I did not get the chance to pack a suitcase full of formalwear or a personal maid during my extremely brave rescue and subsequent escape." She helped Rhuun to his feet. "I know he's your best friend, but why?"

"I like this girl," said Ilaan. "She's got—" he stopped.

"What have I got?" Maaya said. "Is it style and grace?" Ilaan didn't reply. He was looking at Rhuun's midsection.

"What are you two staring at?" Rhuun said. "I'm fine." To prove it, he shook off Maaya's hand and straightened his own faded black tunic. "See? Totally back on my feet."

Maaya looked to see if Ilaan saw what she did, and his look of alarm confirmed it.

"What?" Now Rhuun sounded annoyed. "I said I'm fine. I just needed some sleep."

"Moth," said Maaya, "do you not see that?" He shook his head, confused. "Sweetheart, we can see through you. Right from here—" she laid a hand on his collarbone, "to here." She touched his stomach. "You've gone see-through."

"We should have Mother Jaa take a look at him," said Ilaan. "And I know, the blind looking at the invisible, very clever. But," he added, turning to Maaya, "if you have a better idea I'd like to hear it."

"What, you think I'm going to argue?" asked Maaya. "Of course we should take him to see her. She's expecting us anyway."

"I am standing right here, despite appearances," said Rhuun. "And I'm not going to parade up and down the hallway for all to see with half of me missing. I'm not going anywhere."

Maaya folded her arms. "Are you going to make that poor old *genuinely* crippled woman drag herself all over the tents? You just said you felt better."

"Ilaan, she's implying I am malingering. Please mention her hair again."

Ilaan was poking through a pile of drapes and worn carpets stacked and heaped in the corner. "If you think I'm about to intervene you are still missing a chunk of your wits.

Here." He tossed Rhuun a black drapery with an embroidered geometric pattern of circles inside squares. The design had once been scarlet, and now it was almost tan. "This is long enough to make a decent cloak."

Rhuun arranged it over his shoulders. "And now I'm a window." It smelled of dust and age, but covered him to the ankle and hid his missing anatomy. "I suppose this will have to do. Light and Wind forbid a chance is wasted to make me the center of attention."

"Well," said Ilaan, "he's got his charm and good-natured disposition back."

Rhuun glared at them and stalked out into the hall. Maaya laid a hand on Ilaan's arm to stop him from following. "What is this? Ilaan, what's wrong with him?"

"I don't know what this means," he said. "I've never seen its like. But Mother will know. She has...resources."

"Yes," Maaya agreed. "I saw some of them at work today and we should talk about it. But first let's go find Moth."

"No need," said Ilaan. "He likes a dramatic exit, but he'll be back in a minute." At her puzzled look, he said, "He doesn't know where he's going."

And in fact Rhuun pulled the curtained door back a moment later and said, "Is it just me and Jaa for dinner, then?"

Chapter 50

Mistra

“WELL, THIS COAT is nice enough.” Aelle threw the lovely fur like a coverlet over the narrow cot and curled up under it. The room she’d been locked in wasn’t much, but it did have something magical: a window. She’d been imprisoned on a high floor, and she could lie under the fur and look out over the trees (trees!) towards what Olly had told her was called the ocean.

The stupid book had been right on that score; it was exactly as advertised. Huge, blue, and cold. At least she assumed it was cold, everything else was. She didn’t like to touch the glass of the window, it often had ice crawling on it. The stone floor was dreadful to walk on; when she manage to get the window open and stick her head out, thinking to fly away, the air made itself visible in the puffs of her breath.

She took one look at the stomach-turning drop to the trees far below, and left the windows shut. But with the fire in the grate, and now this lovely orange coat, it was pleasant enough to lie on the bed and look at the trees and the ocean and the forever seeming blue sky. Clouds and sun and moons. She wondered where Rhuun and the human girl were, if their plan had worked, if Ilaan and Niico were safe. She tried not to think of her parents.

She knew she needed an ally in this strange place, and Olly would do nicely. He was young and tall and despite the ugly yellow hair, he looked enough like Rhuun to make it almost feel familiar. His halting speech struck her as charming, even if she suspected he was hiding something. One did not rise to the position of assistant to an elder like Blue by being witless. Blue, now, there was a problem. If she was going to get home, she needed to stay close to the old man, and he clearly was agitated in her presence. At their first meeting that strange day, he'd thought she was Hellne, which she found funny at first—imagine the look on the real Hellne's face! But the more she thought about it, the more uncomfortable she became. Whatever passed between the old man and Hellne had not ended well. Olly had kept her away from Blue since then, saying it upset him, and at first she agreed. If left to Blue's mercy she feared for her future; he might put her out on the frozen doorstep, or drop her in the sea. No, she needed someone else, someone human, and Olly would keep her near the old man while protecting her from his increasing confusion. But now Olly himself was turning out to be something of a mystery. She thought she understood the way he looked at her, brought her this lovely gift, complimented her, it all seemed appropriate. But when she'd taken his hand, what was that shaking thing? A rejection she had not anticipated. Maybe he was shy? Or preferred the company of other men? She'd try again, of course, but only after more study.

Ilaan wouldn't be in this mess, she thought. Even poor, crippled Rhuun had managed to make his way. She felt ashamed and swore that when she got home, she would start training with Niico. Her fear, carefully groomed, brought along and cossetted, had failed to keep her safe. Maybe it was time for something new.

So she kept warm under the fur coat, and looked out to sea, and waited for the decision of the old men. They could send her back through The Door at once, although she had begged them not to. It would open into the prison she'd been plucked out of, and to her father. They could lock her in this room until the moons fell into the sand, and that, too, she had begged them to reconsider. Or they could let her teach the students about what her life on Eriis was like: dangerous and unpredictable.

Olly arrived with a bottle of the sweet wine she liked to deliver the decision, with Scilla scowling at his elbow. Aelle greeted them both politely. She smiled to herself at how Scilla carefully positioned herself between them. The child was almost no longer a child, and even if she wasn't sure why, she didn't trust Aelle around Olly. Aelle tried to recall being that young, and the struggle between heart and sense. Although it was clear the young girl distrusted her, she felt a strange kinship.

The day that Scilla had shown Aelle her notebook she'd been more curious than angry about the binding spell, and she'd simply shrugged off the things Scilla had forced Rhuun to do.

"He wanted to be here, he was here. He might thank you for putting Lelet in his path." She'd turned a page. "All this creeping about and stealing? She's certainly more forgiving than I would have been. Or he's perfected his apologies." But when reading her father's words, Aelle had sighed. "I was as big a fool as you, Scilla," she'd said. "My father may have phrased things a bit differently, but this I think is what he thought to be true. Rhuun, to him, was a criminal and worse. He was the product of fraud, and the thief of my father's plans and his children's affection. I'm sorry my father tricked you, but he is very clever. He saw weakness and struck without hesitation. You are lucky to be alive, and so is your sister. And so is Rhuun."

That had been several weeks ago. She wondered if the sister and Rhuun were still lucky enough to be alive, and if the decision of the Masters granting her permission stay here in this cold world made her lucky as well.

"By the way," Scilla said as she took a tiny sip (Aelle thought she drank to be polite, since her sip was always followed by a wince.) "Have you ever heard of a demon named Ellna?"

"Scil, are you still on that? I thought we agreed to let it rest." It was endearing, the way Olly leapt to defend the old man. "It was from a long time ago and it troubles his mind to discuss it."

"Ellna." Aelle frowned and took a somewhat larger sip of her drink. "Sounds like Hellne, I suppose. Why? Who is Ellna to him?"

"Brother Blue keeps muttering her name," Scilla said.

"He does not mutter," said Olly. "Miss Aelle, Scilla here has little regard for an elderly man, but I do. I'm certain it's not important, but a name from someone he knew a long time ago."

"Ellna," Aelle repeated. "What does he say about her?"

Scilla said, "He says 'Ellna, why didn't you ever tell me? Ellna, he's mine.' What name did you just say? Who's Hellne?"

"He called me Hellne when I arrived here, when he wasn't sure who I was," said Aelle. "He mistook me for Hellne, our Queen of Eriis, and Rhuun's mother."

"Lelet's Rhuun? Rhuun, whose father was a human man, the same Rhuun?" asked Scilla. They stared back and forth, the three of them.

"Well, well," said Aelle. "Hellne and Blue. That does some clearing up, doesn't it? I don't suppose your Brother Blue ever used another name? Or wrote a truly dreadful book?"

Scilla looked confused, but Olly nodded. "Malloy dos Capehart was his born name. The Order gave him the shorter one because no one could remember the long one. But the book, yes. I've seen it on his shelf. Never read it, don't much go for fiction. Does Moth, um, Rhuun know?" He directed his question to Aelle.

"I would have said no, but recall we haven't seen much of each other lately. I haven't spoken to him, but once in months, and then the circumstances were...not conducive to conversation."

"Well, he's moving, so maybe you can ask him yourself. They're moving. The lights, I mean," Scilla said. "I saw it this morning. I don't know where they are, though. They all started moving in the same direction, but then, nothing. The map hasn't filled in." She paused and gave Aelle a sweet smile. “Maybe they’re all dead,” she said. Aelle went pale despite herself. She knew Scilla said such things out of a jealousy she might be too young to recognize, but that didn’t necessarily mean it wasn’t true. But if they were lost, so was she.

“Scilla!” Olly said, “You don’t mean that!”

“Oh,” said Scilla, patting Aelle on the shoulder, “I didn’t mean to frighten you. It’s probably not true.”

Aelle took a breath and gave Scilla a long look. “It’s kind of you to be so brave—for all of us. What a heavy load for such a little girl. You do look awfully tired. Perhaps you ought to go lie down? Get some rest.” She smiled. “Ahlee and I have some things to discuss.”

“We do?” asked Olly, but Aelle just gazed out her window. “Um, Miss Aelle is right, you should get some rest.”

Aelle waited until she heard the door close before turning. “Ahlee,” she said, “I haven’t thanked you properly.” She once again took his hand, and before he could react incorrectly, she pulled him close. “For the coat. And help with the Masters. And the, um, candles.”

“It was what anyone would do,” he replied. He sat stiffly on the edge of her bed, still clasping her hand. “And I’m sure Scilla was mistaken, about the prince and them. Being dead, I mean.”

“Can we for just a few minutes not talk about the prince? Or the rest of them? Just for a few minutes?” She let go of his hand long enough to refill their glasses. “Tell me about your home. You are from the city?”

“Yes, Miss Aelle,” he answered. She looked at him wide-eyed and nodded. “Well, I’m from a big family, I have four older sisters, my family is in import-export—”

“How interesting, imparting things, please continue.” She took a big sip of wine.

“Um, well, I’ve wanted to serve the Order since I was a child, and since I’m a Fifth it worked out really well. All the Fifths here are dedicated to the Order. Here, I mean to say Mistra.” He watched her closely, that was good. He was at least paying attention. “I know you’ve been unhappy, Miss Aelle, but it’s really a very nice place, the Guardhouse. And

Mistra, sometimes it's a lot warmer, and we have forests and farms and dogs—"

She sighed gustily and looked at the ceiling. "Ahlee, haven't you ever wanted to do something—"

"Bad?" he asked.

Bad? What did these strange creatures consider 'bad?' She put on a surprised face and stroked the back of his hand with one finger. "I wouldn't say bad, exactly. Secret, perhaps. Something secret. That we keep to ourselves and don't tell any of your brothers or sisters—"

"My sisters back home? Or here? Because that's what we call—"

She crossed her arms. "Ahlee, do you find me desirable or not?"

He laughed and refilled her wine glass. "Ah, that's what all that hand holding business was about. I suspected so. Still, with you being a guest on our world, one would hate to jump to the wrong conclusions and draw offense." At her shocked look, he laughed and said, "Aelle, maybe I just wanted to hear you ask."

She gave him a slow smile. "You are more clever than you want people to think, my new and interesting friend."

"And you are more scared and far less ferocious than you act." He took up her hands again. "I can trust you with my secret?"

"Why do you want people to think you're a short-witted boy?" she wondered.

"If they don't think much of you, they'll talk in front of you," he told her. "You'd be amazed at what I've heard, just hanging back and pouring wine. The decision to let you stay and talk to the novices, by the way? Not even close. You had them seduced thoroughly." She smiled and he added, "On the subject. I know you want me to protect you, and I will. You don't have to do anything...you don't want to do." He stood. "I'll make sure the Masters treat you with respect, and I'll keep Scilla out of your hair, if I can. And don't concern yourself about Blue. When it's time, I'll see to it you go safely home." He gave a short and very elegant bow. "And now I'll leave you. Perhaps if you wish I will escort you later to dinner?"

She leaned back on the bed and held out her hand. "Why not come back here and tell me more about this imparting thing? And later we can go to dinner together."

"Only if you wear your new coat." He paused. "Now that I mention it, it's gotten rather warm in here. Allow me to help you take it off. Are those tattoos? How lovely! How far up do they go?"

She showed him.

Chapter 51

Eriis

MOTHER JAA SPENT some time walking back and forth around Rhuun, poking him in the stomach and muttering to Leef, who followed her with a little notebook, jotting down her comments. Ilaan and Maaya sat at her low table, Ilaan as usual looking as if he'd spent his life lounging among the cushions, while Maaya remained bolt upright. He leaned over and took a *serviette* out of her hands when she'd shredded it into a half dozen pieces. He leaned closer to her and whispered, "Calm down, he can tell that you're upset."

"I can hear you," said Rhuun. "I am not a horse."

"Well, you should calm down, too. I bet being nervous makes it worse," Ilaan said. And to Maaya, "Why does he think he's a horse?"

She began to answer, stopped, and said, "It's a long story. But he doesn't really think he's a horse, I'm pretty sure."

Rhuun threw out a hand, nearly knocking Leef over. "I didn't say—never mind. Mother Jaa, may I sit? These two need reassurance my, um, that this is temporary."

"No," she finally said when they were all seated, "I cannot do that. I have no reason to think it is. I saw the shadow on you when you arrived at my tents, my boy. In fact, I fear quite the opposite."

Maaya turned pale and Rhuun took her hand under the table. “We will figure this out. It’ll be fine,” he told her. She smiled for him.

Ilaan leaned forward and took a platter of neat pink squares of meat and stacks of greens from Leef, and placed the tray so it was the closest to Rhuun.

He sighed and rolled his eyes at Ilaan. “Please stop doing that. I may be vanishing but I can still put my own plate together.” Ilaan, Maaya, and Leef watched as he demonstrated. “And stop staring at me, I’m fine.” He realized with some surprise that disappearing didn’t seem so bad a fate. But looking at the faces of his companions, he felt ashamed. “I apologize. I am not quite myself. Or perhaps a little less of myself.” Maaya looked at him with despair. “That was a joke. See, jokes?”

Maaya sighed and turned to Mother Jaa. “How do we get rid of the shadow?” she asked. “There’s a way. Please, there’s a way.”

“Light and Wind,” said Jaa. “It is Light and Wind we turn to for the answer. Light may drive out the shadows, and Wind blow them away.” She picked up her cracked old porcelain mug and sipped her water. “Light and Wind will show us the way.”

“Oh, that’s great.” Maaya put her chin in her hand. “So we, what? Pray to the elements? Has that ever worked?” She turned to Ilaan. “What about in your old books? The ones you had at your place in the city?”

Ilaan looked at her with wide-eyed amazement. “Maaya, consider your words. Mother Jaa speaks.”

Jaa laughed, somehow a tinkling cackle. “This one comes from a place where words fly straight from your head out of your face. She doesn’t understand. She has the look of an Eriisai, but her heart and mind are human. Humans no longer know how to turn to Light and Wind. But we do. Don’t we?”

Ilaan nodded. “Some of us spend our lives trying to reach them. I think many of the people—of the women you’ve seen here have reached them already.”

"Wait. Are you talking about real people that you can talk to?" Maaya shook her head. "Light and Wind, that's just an expression you all use....isn't it?"

Jaa turned her milky eyes on Maaya. "They are most interested in you. They would like to speak with you."

"What? Why? No," Maaya said. "They should talk to Moth, he's the one with the shadow."

Jaa leaned forward. "You are afraid, *now?* After all you've seen and done? After burning the Raasth to its stones?"

Ilaan said, "Ah, exactly what does Mother Jaa mean by that, Maaya?"

"I talked to Aelle," Maaya replied. Rhuun dropped his head into his hands with a groan. *Perfect,* he thought. *The icing on the fish.* "It was most enlightening. She did exactly as we planned. I hope I get the chance to thank her. She told me all about the Raasth. And I went to see them, Moth, after you were safely away. I went down and down. I went and had a talk with the Mages."

"And how did your little talk go?" Ilaan was clearly working hard to keep his face composed.

"We talked about *La Naa.* We talked about knives. We talked about the prince. And I told them to take what they could carry and leave. And then I burned it down."

Rhuun thought Ilaan might lose the battle with his composure, and was glad no one could see he already had. He could see the white at Ilaan's knuckles as he gripped the edge of the table. "The Raasth," Ilaan said, "The Mages. They let you burn it down. They didn't try and stop you?"

"They tried. Yes." Jaa nodded at Maaya's hands. They were burning, clear and white. "Oh yes, they tried to stop me." She slowly raised her arms, her eyes blank red stones.

"Maaya?" Ilaan got no response. "Maaya, what if I did this?" Her head slowly swiveled in his direction. He sent a sheet of flame at Rhuun's head. Before he could react, Maaya jerked her hands up and it vanished, absorbed into her own fire.

"No," he whispered, "oh no..." Rhuun was finding it difficult to breathe. How had she walked out of this alive?

"One of them did that to me," she said. "Or he tried to. His name was Eiith. Rest him now."

"Rest him indeed. Well, thank you for not incinerating me," Ilaan said. "This changes the order of things, doesn't it?"

Jaa said, "See to the prince."

Rhuun had fallen back, slumped, half off the cushions. Maaya, now extinguished, stumbled over her cushion and knelt at his side. "I'm sorry," she said, "I'm so sorry, but I had to do it. Please, the whole place was nothing but blood, do you understand?"

He opened his eyes and touched her face gently. "Of course I'm not angry. I could have told them what happens when you don't get your way." They shared a smile. As she helped him back up the drape slipped off his shoulder. The look on her face told him there was nothing to reveal. "Can we start doing a thing where no one stares at where I used to be?"

"It's spreading," said Ilaan. "I feel time is against us, as well as whoever is left of the Mages."

"Did you really talk to Aelle about me?" Rhuun asked. "Ilaan, did that strike you as a good idea?"

They glanced at him and then continued their conversation. "Maybe I was only able to burn it because the Zaal wasn't there," she said, "and the rest—other than Eiith—didn't try to stop me. I let them take all their books. It's difficult to describe how it was for me. I was so angry—it felt like I had no choice. I hope I didn't make a mistake."

"We of Eriis are raised to control our impulses, perhaps for this very reason." Mother Jaa sipped her water thoughtfully. "We are never at the mercy of the winds of emotion. You gained a great deal of power without the lifetime of control to master it. And then there are the *klystrons* adding purpose to your power." She nodded. "A fine champion, my boy. A warrior. But a sharp knife. Use her with great care lest she turn in your hand."

"She is not mine to use," said Rhuun. "And I don't much care for the implication."

Maaya touched the back of his hand—the one, he supposed, that she could still see. "I am yours, to use or not. All I intended was to keep them from harming you again. I know you would do no less."

"My father is going to swallow sand when he hears about this," Ilaan said with undisguised satisfaction.

"He's done more than that," Maaya said. "Moth, he's telling the court—I guess the Counsel—that you destroyed the Raasth. I'm afraid I've gotten you into worse trouble. And we have to make sure Aelle is safe."

"Leave that to me," said Ilaan. "I think he would never harm her, and I'll make sure of it. But he and the Zaal, they won't stop until both of you are back in their fists. Mother Jaa, Maaya will consult with Light and Wind. And then, Beast, it's time to pack your bags. Again."

Chapter 52

Eriis

IF YOU'D ASKED Lelet a year ago, she'd have told you that to meet the gods, you'd need some sort of potion to be drunk or smoked; not that she'd ever had visions from drink or smoking before, only a good time followed by a headache. A month ago, Maaya might have wondered if they'd want her to eat more sand. It turned out to be neither; Mother Jaa told her to fly until she couldn't see the shivering spires of silk, and then wait. That was it, not even in any particular direction. Fly, and wait.

Jaa had made it clear her opinion was only favorable in terms of what she could accomplish for 'her boy.' There even remained the possibility that this was an elaborate ruse to separate her from Moth again and return him to the city and to Yuenne. The fire that consumed the Raasth still crawled in her blood. She rather hoped she'd run into the Counselor, despite her promise to Aelle.

She folded her wings and landed—gently, she was improving—and pulled her grey traveling cloak around her shoulders. The scarf kept most of the grit out of her eyes, but here so far from the tents, the wind turned every grain of sand into a needle. At least she could get out of the wind, she supposed. A tan finger of rock thrust itself out of the yellow sand (tan, yellow, grey, ash; when she got home she was going to go through her closet and toss everything in those shades out the window) and she climbed over some half-buried chunks of stone so she could get to the scant shelter. As she rounded the lip of stone, the wind stopped as neatly as if it had been cut by a knife.

"You see, Wind? I told you she'd find us. No need to be shouting out, alerting hither and yon where we are."

"Correct, Light, as you generally are."

Maaya slowly unwound her scarf and tried to understand what she was seeing.

"Please, my dear," said Light. "Do come and have a seat. Tea?"

Maaya sat as instructed on a little three legged wooden stool before a small, round table set upon the rock. It had a lovely white linen tablecloth free from even a speck of dust (at the hem, Maaya noted the monogram *L&W* in fine blue embroidery), and was set with a blue and white china tea service painted with pastoral scenes of sheep and girls and little meadows in Mistra. It was nearly transparent and Althee herself would have coveted it. There was also a silver platter of what appeared to be lemon iced sugar cookies, and another of crust-less sandwiches, cut into neat little triangles. Maaya thought they were watercress and cucumber. The two women, demon women to be sure, looked to be contemporaries of Mother Jaa, with thin, close cropped grey hair, finely wrinkled hands and faces, and perfect little teeth. Light wore a gown of black lace over heavy white satin that would have been devastating a hundred years ago, on Mistra. The delicate lacework rose to her throat and covered her to the wrist. The hem was embroidered with tiny jet beads in a repeating floral pattern. She wore a single rope of grape sized pearls that reached nearly to her waist and threated to dip into her teacup, another pearl the size of a blueberry was on the first finger of her right hand, and she had two smaller but still exquisite specimen in her ears. Wind wore a vintage silk chiffon that scandalously showed her ankles and a bit of the soft, creased flesh above her collarbone. Her feet were bare and she had gold rings on three toes of each foot. The dress was, without question, Ever Blue. She'd paired it with more diamonds than Maaya had ever seen in one place. It was something of a miracle she could hold up her hands for the variety and number of stones.

"Would you prefer cream or lemon?" asked Wind.

Maaya simply pointed at the lemon slices, and a cup of tea appeared in front of her without either woman lifting a finger. Maaya sipped. It was water.

"I imagine you are wondering about our appearance, dear." Maaya nodded. "We didn't want to alarm you so we pulled some images from your mind. Things that are nice. How did we do?"

Maaya sipped her water. "Wonderfully well. I feel as if I am back on Mistra among my grannies. Thank you for the tea." She turned to Wind. "Your dress is beautiful," and to Light, "and yours is exceedingly elegant."

"Please, help yourself. We made more than we could possible eat." Light laughed. "If we ate, of course."

Maaya thanked her hosts again and took a lemon cookie. It tasted like sand, or nothing at all. She smiled and took another and set it on her plate.

"Really, it's such a shame what's happened between our worlds," said Wind. "You're the first human we've seen in ages. So exciting, it used to be. All that coming and going."

"The humans are vulgar, of course," added Light. "Always have been. Noisy. Dramatic. As my sister well knows, excitement isn't everything."

"And then the War," agreed Wind. "Excitement we could have done without. Well, you would know about that, human girl."

"No, Madam," Maaya said. "I knew nothing at all about the War until I met Mo—until I was privileged to meet the prince. Most humans don't even know Eriis is a real place."

"But you know it now," said Light. "What will you do, now that you know? Will you help us all, or are you only concerned with your lover?"

She took a breath. "I am here at your request because Mother Jaa asked for your help in restoring him. If that helps Eriis I am happy to oblige."

Light and Wind tilted their heads towards each other. Expressions flitted across their faces, pieces of smiles, slivers of doubt, a slice of a frown, nothing that Maaya could truly recognize.

Finally Light said, "We will help you." Maaya began to thank them, but the old woman lifted her hand. "Before you fly off the cliff, look down, my dear. Now. Our prince, Jaa's dear boy, his troubles stem from the time he spent in that room of his. It's only because of the human blood—"

"I know," snapped Maaya. "The human blood that makes him weak, and vulgar, and crippled. Well it's my blood too, and I made it here."

The two old women looked at her with mild disdain. Light sipped her tea. "One might let one's elders, and perhaps betters, finish a sentence," said Wind. "The human blood in his body is the only reason he's alive. A proper demon would have perished under the weight of all those charms. We just aren't as...sturdy as you humans."

Maaya flushed scarlet. "Please accept my apology. I spoke without reason. My only excuse is my fear for him."

"Yes, well." Light waved her hand dismissively. "Of course. But it's the door, that's his current problem."

"The Door? The Door between our worlds?" asked Maaya.

"Not in this case, although he made that his problem in the past, didn't he? The boy has a recurring issue with doors, can't decide if he's coming or going." The two ladies shared a laugh and tapped their teacups in a mock toast. "No, in this case, the door that held him captive. It didn't much care for the Mages, and it liked being used as a prison even less. Doors are generally simple things—open and shut, one might say. This one became confused, too many conflicting orders. It began to make decisions for itself—most unusual. Finally it got to the point where it decided to uncomplicate its lot and throw its loyalty to the one with the strongest will."

Maaya smiled. "The prince."

"Indeed." Light nodded. "The prince. And he has that pesky human blood to thank again. So the door gave him a gift. A great gift. His heart's desire."

Maaya's hand covered her mouth. "His heart's desire." *Stop looking at me, I don't care for the way you are all looking at me.* "The door gave him a shadow so he can disappear. Oh, Moth."

"And then you tricked it into locking again. It didn't form a very high opinion of you, either," said Wind.

"Can I go back and somehow make it up to the door?" Maaya thought grimly, if I have to get on my knees in that hallway and apologize to a slab of wood, I will do it.

"A bit late for that," said Wind. "Although it would have been a nice gesture. I'm afraid that Counselor fellow has had it dismantled. In a rather permanent fashion."

"What do your people call it?" said Light. "Toothpicks?"

"I am sorry. I wish I'd known it wanted to help. What can I do for the prince, though? Because his wish is coming true. He's starting to vanish and Mother Jaa says even she can't help him."

"Yes, he is in a shadow, and one day soon it will fall across his heart, and that will be that." Light helped herself to a sandwich. "Do try the cucumber. I think we got it just right."

Maaya did as she was told, trying desperately to figure out how to get them to come to the point. "Delightful," she told them. "I would be pleased to serve these in my own home. When you say, 'that will be that', you mean he'll be permanently invisible?"

"Well, being dead is a form of invisibility, so I suppose that's the case," said Wind. She toyed with her massive diamond and sapphire bracelet. It looked to be the right size for a human wrist, it reached halfway to her elbow. "No living being can support going unseen by the eyes of their fellows forever, no matter what the prince may or may not have wished for. If you go without for too long, you forget how to be seen at all. You're standing right there, but you're only a shadow of a memory. And then no one remembers you. And then you're dead."

"Please, please help me. Help us," she breathed. She realized she'd dropped the fragile teacup, and bits and shards of white and blue china glittered around her feet. "Please, help me bring him back."

Wind snorted and said, "Oh, very well. I just hate to see all this lovely food go to waste, but if you insist. Light, we might as well get on with it." Light raised her hand and the table, the tea and broken cup, the service, their elegant human dresses and jewels were gone. The wind returned instantly. Light was a column of glittering dust, and Wind could only be seen by the sand thrown against her rippling form. "You wish to restore the prince? Are you sure?"

"I am sure," she said.

"And if there is a price?" asked Light.

"Well, isn't there always? A price?" asked Wind. "That's how these things work. That's how magic gets made. Or unmade."

"It was a rhetorical question," said Light. "She knows there's a price. She can always say no and walk away and go back to the human world. It may be another generation before we find our champion. But we will, sooner or later."

"Whatever your price is, I will pay it," said Maaya.

"So quick to answer! A price, certainly. Of course there is," said Light. "It won't be paid in more fingers, you'll be pleased to know. Here it is: the prince will ask you to accept his spark. Not soon, but soon enough. You will deny him."

"The blood of Eriis is dilute enough. No child of yours will sit on the High Seat," said Wind. "It would be practically human."

"This will break his heart," said Maaya.

"His body today, or his heart tomorrow. Your choice. Oh, and it would be highly disadvantageous to tell him why you must refuse him," said Wind.

"Why are you helping me at all?" asked Maaya. "Why not let him fade away?"

"We considered that. While we cannot hold his pedigree against him, we find his choice of companionship most...distasteful. You may understand it's nothing personal, my dear. We just don't care for humans, even if they are rather exciting."

"But, he is still the rightful prince of Eriis. And he has a destiny. One we would very much like to see unfold. With your help he can fulfill it. But that doesn't mean we wish to make it easy on you, human girl. Are you ready? It isn't complicated, but it does involve some..."

"Travel?" said Light.

"I was going to say deduction. But travel, yes. Luckily for you, to restore your prince to his former, ah, anatomical completion, you must take him back to Mistra. It cannot be undone here. But you haven't sworn to do as we say, human girl. To pay our price. Do you wish to deny him the future to restore the present?"

"He is my future. I swear it." As soon as the words left her mouth, Maaya began to think about loopholes. She'd have to sit down with Ilaan. The wind gusted and she felt a sharp yank on her hair, as if some unseen hand pulled her closer. And then voices in her ear.

Bitter races to the sky
Unease is ever present
Tears fall through the air
Shadows may fall at the fall of shadows

The wind died and the dust settled, and Maaya found herself sitting alone on a knob of rock just out of sight of the tents.

She sighed. "Terrific. A fucking riddle."

Chapter 53

Eriis

"SIIA. PLEASE OPEN this door." Yuenne stood and waited. "You're going to have to come out of there and talk to me eventually." No answer, nor had there been one for going on a week, since the day after Aelle had vanished. Yu had no idea where his cloud-headed daughter had gone off to, but Siia looked around her home, found it empty of her children, and accused Yuenne of driving her children away. The High Seat, she'd accused, sat unoccupied, for all Yuenne's talk of a new council, and why had the queen left her beloved palace? The prince gone as well, and even though she held no great love for him, Siia saw her husband's hand at work.

"Fine, it's my fault," he finally said to the locked door. "Every bad thing that happens here in Eriis is because of me. Every time someone wanders off, I'm to blame. Sit in there and talk to your stones, and see if they hold this city together." He was bitterly disappointed, Siia of all people, his rock, his princess, how could she find fault when everything he did was for their family?

He had to find Aelle and bring that silly girl home. That would pour water on Siia's heart. She, after all, was the sensitive one.

He knew just who to ask, and as it happened the man was right upstairs.

* * *

It wasn't as if he'd had much of a choice, when the Zaal and four of his Mages showed up on Yu's doorstep.

The Zaal had spent the night on the sand with Yuenne, searching for his quarry, only to return and find his Raasth a smoldering wreck of slagged glass, and a few of his Mages milling about the statue garden. They were blinking in the unaccustomed light of day, and muttering accusations at each other and at the human/demon/*daaeva* girl—for no one born under the moons of Eriis should have been able to do what she did. Their long unused voices sounded like stones rubbing against each other, but the Zaal got the meat of the story quickly enough, and related it to Yuenne. The Mages who survived the human girl's wrath had fled, back to their families or if finding a cool welcome, on to the Edge, some of them. Others had put on new faces and started over in the Old City. A few had consigned their fates to the Crosswinds. The loyal few he saw before him had fled with their lives, for which he would later make them repent (for what were their lives against a hundred generations of Mages who protected the Raasth successfully?) and more importantly, they had managed to save some critical books and items. 'And the blood?' he had asked —quietly of course, because there were dozens of curious eyes on them now. 'Yes', answered a sour faced old Mage. He himself had saved the blood while the rest thought only of their own skins. The other three had glared at the old man, who had just elevated himself to the Zaal's second.

"Well," said the Zaal, "as the others are dead or fled, we will not say their names again. Now that it appears we are all speaking." The Mages had the sense to look contrite. "Now let us find a new Raasth, where we may continue our work. This attack may not rise to the level of invasion, but the humans surely will come again. We must prepare." It was certainly a setback, he'd thought, but if they had the blood, they had everything.

That was what he'd told Yuenne, standing in the street, and Yu could hardly argue. In addition, the Zaal pinned the blame on Yu for this unprecedented disaster, and come looking for sanctuary as his right, not as a gift or a favor.

“I may have miscalculated,” Yuenne admitted, once he had ushered his guests safely inside, away from prying eyes, “in keeping the prince above ground. But that would not have prevented this human woman from taking him out of your hands, would it?” The Zaal grudgingly agreed. From all reports, the girl’s power was corrupted and beyond the scope of the Mages to withstand. “And I can’t help but ask why, even as you looked inside her—you remember that?—how you missed it. I mean, a good forgery, to be sure, but still.” To this, the Zaal had no answer. But talk of blame ended there, and the remaining Mages began their work of setting up glasses and bowls, assembling their books and charms, and carefully storing the silver bowls of blood. They had a weapon to build, after all.

* * *

They were at least quiet houseguests, although when one of them showed their face in the great room or the kitchen, Siia fled as if she were under attack. The maid was also frightened of them. Had it come to this: he himself would have to fetch their meals and necessities? He hoped not. “I trust you are finding these accommodations to your liking?”

The Zaal glanced dismissively around what had once been Ilaan’s tower room. “We have what we need for now,” he sniffed. “More room of course would be preferable. A larger work surface. And it’s far too bright. But you know it isn’t our way to complain.”

“Hmm, of course. Well. I am pleased you are settling in so nicely.” He paused. “I wonder if I might ask...”

“As we discussed, the prince is temporarily hidden from us. When we locate him, and we will—”

“I don’t recall asking where he’s gone.” Yu took a breath. It was already starting to smell like dust and blood up here; the first thing the Mages had done was close and cover the tall windows. “I wish to discuss something else.”

The Zaal cocked his head. "The human girl is gone as well. If we were still in our home, in the Raasth, with everything at hand's reach—"

"Zaal, I come to inquire after my daughter. Aelle is missing. I wish to ask if you might be able to find her. I fear the human girl might be involved." He made a pleasant face and waited.

"You seem to have a habit of misplacing people, Counselor." The Zaal smiled. "And your own daughter, why, you must be terribly worried. To come all the way up here." He pursed his lips and picked up his pen, making marks on the paper on the desk in front of him. Yuenne couldn't read what he was writing, if in fact it was writing at all. "I'll assume you have already exhausted your usual channels?"

"You would be correct." His usual informants had come up dry as an old creek bed. He'd learned some interesting things about his son and their friends, but whether Aelle left on her own or had been snatched up, no one seemed to know.

"Well, we are quite busy tracking down the prince. And the human girl, *and* the queen—you asked after her as well, didn't you?"

"Your display of grace in handling this burden is an inspiration to us all. But I have a gift for you, Zaal. Something I think you'll find most interesting. Something quite new." The Zaal's look brightened. "No, you'll have to wait and see. This must be handled delicately. But perhaps after your gift is delivered you'll be more inclined to spare a moment for my poor daughter."

The Zaal turned his attention back to his page. "Aelle is not in the city." Yuenne began to thank him, but the Zaal lifted a hand. "Gifts, as I understand, do not usually require a down payment, but you have piqued my interest, Counselor. Bring me something nice, and we'll see about finding your daughter."

Yu shimmered back down from the tower to his own office, a comfortable, light filled space which opened, as most of the private rooms in his home did, onto a large courtyard. The outdoor space was ideal for parties, but he hadn't had an event since the night the prince had fled Eriis, the Mages had left the Raasth, and Ilaan had broken his heart and his plans. It seemed a long time ago. His house was quiet and empty, save for his wife, locked away with her stones and her chants, and his guest, who sat and fidgeted in her seat, waiting for her appointment.

"Rhoosa. How kind of you to come and see me."

* * *

"I'm sorry, Counselor. Sir. I don't know where Aelle is." Rhoosa sipped her water, the cup clattering a bit as she set it down. She folded her hands in her lap.

"You are one of her fondest friends. Surely she confided in you." He leaned forward a bit. "Now that her brother is...no longer at home, I know she must have turned to others." He watched her try to figure out what he wanted her to say. Her large, dark ruby eyes shone. Was she afraid? He didn't think so, not yet. "Well," he continued. "If she didn't say anything, perhaps she spoke to someone else, someone you also know? Niico, perhaps?"

Ah, there it was.

Hollen, that slow-witted lump, had the most interesting things to say about his daughter's dear friend Niico. All Yuenne had to do was imply how grateful she would be and how she would need a steady minded companion in the days to come. And how delighted she'd be to see him flying in a proper match—not to worry, those things could easily be arranged. Of course if Hollen knew anything that might endanger the Council, it was his responsibility to let Yuenne know. And if there was one thing Aelle loved above all others, it was a friend she could trust to be honest. Niico, he was clearly not that friend. Hollen just might be. Hollen had poured out what he knew like sand through a screen and wandered off, dreaming of conquests in the air and on the ground.

"I...she and Niico are good friends," Rhoosa stammered. "If she told him where she was going, they didn't say anything to me."

Time, Yuenne thought. *Time to let the girl know her extra-curricular activities had not gone unnoticed.* "Not even at your little evening get-togethers? What were you children calling them? Ah, of course. The Night Cafe. That did sound like fun." He waited and watched her fear bloom.

"It was...just an idea I had...we didn't mean anything by it...."

"Tell me, Rhoosa. Does one go about the street or appear at the Council in any color they choose?" She shook her head, no. "And is it even written into our law? Colors that are proper and those that are not?" A yes. "And do you think laws are for other people?"

"No, Sir, I'm sorry." Tears stood in her eyes. "We've stopped. We won't do it again."

"Well, that's a given. You held these events in secret, so you knew they were wrong. When someone does something wrong, they are generally punished. How do you think I ought to deal with you now?"

"I...what? I don't...." Her lips formed a thin line. "I've said I was sorry. No one came to harm." He caught a faint blurring in the air around her, and was rewarded by her look of surprise. No one would be shimmering in and out of this room without his approval, his friends upstairs had long since seen to that. Now she looked terrified.

"Daala, now, she wasn't contrite at all. Not like you. No 'sorrys' from Daala. Do you know, she actually accused my Aelle of conspiring with that human girl and with the prince? She had the nerve to sit there, in the very seat where you are now, and tell me my own daughter was working against the Counsel, against Eriis, and against me. Do you know what happened to Daala? No, of course you wouldn't. Tell me, dear, do you know what The Crosswinds are?"

"A...story to frighten children. They were real after the Weapon, but now..."

"Oh, they are still real. And children should be frightened."

They were real, but a damned inconvenient method of disposal. After all, no one marked for punishment would voluntarily offer themselves up. He'd had to have the Zaal still Daala so she couldn't run or shimmer off, and sent Bremm, his favorite household guard, on a long march through the Vastness to leave her there. The man had drunk half a bottle of *sarave* at a gulp upon his return and swore to his friends that Yuenne could slice his wings off and leave him to die in the sand before he'd go there again. He said there was something in the wind that knew the girl was there, and whatever it was, it came for her. "It left her hair and her teeth," he'd said, beginning to weep. "Her hair and teeth, just spat them back out," but by then he was so drunk no one could understand him. Yuenne paid handsomely for his comfortable retirement to a little farm on the Edge.

"Well," continued Yuenne, "let's just say her position at the Counsel is vacant. Her husband is finally free to drink in peace." He'd been planning on disposing of her loutish husband the same way, but abandoned it as too much trouble. But now, with this new people-moving tool, perhaps he might look into it again. Yes, there were quite a few that would improve the Councillary by their absence. He looked up with a smile. "Did Aelle do those things? The terrible things Daala accused her of?"

"No," Rhoosa managed to whisper. "Never. She never said anything to me about Rhuun, but that she wished he never came back." She wiped her face with the back of her hand. "Please, Sir. I don't know anything about where Aelle's gone. And I'm sorry about the colors..." she trailed off in sobs.

"Now, now, no need for tears. I think we can work something out." She looked up. "I understand you have a special gift, Rhoosa. I've heard all about it. This way you have of moving people about. That's quite unusual. One might say our law also demands that you should have presented yourself for service at the Counsel as soon as you manifested, but let us leave the past in the dust. I might have uses for you. Yes, I think I have things I'd like you to take care of for me. I already know you can be discrete."

"I am happy to serve," she gasped. "What...what sorts of things?"

"Don't worry about that now. I do have some friends I'd like you to meet. They'll tell you more. It'll be an instructive experience for you, I'm sure, and what a perfect opportunity to pay off your debt and right your wrongs. Now, you recall Ilaan's old tower room? Why not start by heading up there right now. Let's see how this gift of yours works."

Chapter 54

Eriis

BITTER RACES TO the sky
Unease is ever present
Tears fall through the air
Shadows may fall at the fall of shadows

"Say it again," said Ilaan. He was carving greens and meat into squares and passing them to Rhuun, who indulged his friend by eating. Ilaan said he found it particularly interesting because Rhuun was increasingly invisible. One moment the bite of food was suspended in midair, the next, gone. Ilaan's cavalier attitude towards the whole thing, as if it were some sort of experiment, was starting to wear on Maaya's nerves.

She stopped pacing around Mother Jaa's low table and threw herself onto a pile of rugs which served as a seat. "I've already said it a million times, it won't make any more sense if I keep saying it."

Rhuun watched Ilaan and Maaya bicker. "It sounds dreadful anyway," he said. "But if it's back on Mistra maybe it won't be so bad."

Maaya held her hand out and he took it. In the two days since she'd returned from the desert and Light and Wind, he'd rapidly faded. Now she could only see his face in profile if she turned towards him quickly, and then only for a moment. He said he could see himself as well as ever, and she shouldn't worry because he looked fine.

"In comparison to what?" asked Ilaan. She knew he was trying to lighten the mood, which was decidedly tense, but she wished he would stop teasing Moth.

"Bitter. Unease. Tears," she said. "What do they have to do with each other? Is it a place?" She tried to get the conversation back on track. Even Mother Jaa didn't know how long it would be before the shadow erased Rhuun completely.

"When I hear those words, I think of childhood. A school?" Rhuun asked. "Is it about the Guardhouse? That's a school, isn't it?"

"I'm thinking we would be best served by going back to Mistra and decoding this thing with Scilla. We're wasting time." Maaya and Ilaan both looked towards where Rhuun sat. A cup of *sarave* moved across the table and floated through the air. It was understood he would be the one to finally decide whether to go, or let himself fade away.

"I agree," he said. "At least I won't have to hide under a stupid hat. That was a joke." The cup rose and fell again. "And I've done nothing but eat and sleep since we arrived, I'm not going to get any better. Look, my clothing fits. Um, I suppose you'll have to trust me. But really, there's no point in waiting. This is it."

"I must say, this is perhaps the best you've ever looked," Ilaan smiled. He immediately jerked his head to the right, barely missed a blast of flame. "Maaya, nothing will be gained by scorching me. We've been doing this since we were children." He paused. "I think perhaps it is time to set our jokes aside, though. We're both upsetting her, which seems a little hazardous right now."

She was pale with horror. "I am so sorry. I didn't even realize until after." She looked at her simmering hands. "It's really, really time to leave. I'm going to kill someone. Someone else."

"Well, let's get started," Ilaan said. He set the knife she would need on his cushion, and they sent Leef, who as always hovered just outside their room, to fetch Mother Jaa.

Then the two of them cleared the plates and cups off the table. Rhuun tried to assist, but they told him to sit down after Ilaan crashed into him a third time. He said nothing, but they all knew a sulk when he was having one. Ilaan said, "Anyone else would have wished for a beautiful palace and a lovely partner—oh, but you already had that; two of them, in fact. You brought this on yourself. So don't get that face."

"I do not have a face," Rhuun replied. "And that was not a joke."

"I am going back to Mistra by myself if you don't stop this," Maaya told them. "Ilaan, that was beneath you. Apologize."

Ilaan folded his arms. "You are of course correct. You do not have a face."

"Do you see how he is?" Rhuun said.

Maaya stabbed the table. "We are trying to help you," she said through her teeth. "So for now you'll do as I say. And you," she stuck her finger in Ilaan's face, "Come with me."

She marched out into the shimmering hallway. It was barely dusk and the stones were starting to glow. Those who passed could not help but notice the young lady who had lost her composure. They did their best to look elsewhere.

"What is wrong with you? Are you not his friend? Why do you provoke him?"

Ilaan looked down the corridor, away from her. A demon flew down and landed lightly a few steps away from them. He looked the pair over, nodded politely and immediately flew off the way he'd come. "You're scaring the locals, Maaya."

"I don't care about them. I only care about him." She stopped and frowned. "To a really strange degree."

Ilaan looked at her, a little more kindly. "You don't know us, Beast and me. This is how we are to each other. If I was to act upon what was in my heart, I would weep from fear. Your poem is incomprehensible, and you said yourself Light and Wind seemed only slightly inclined to help us. If he fades away, they will wait for their next champion, if it takes a thousand years. Should I go sit by his side and wring my hands? Will that put him at ease? Or you?"

She put her hands over her eyes. "I swear to you, I am normally not this...insane. This compulsion to protect him, it's not me. I mean, of course I want to take care of him, but this is coming from somewhere else." She felt her composure slipping away and struggled not to cry. "You don't know how I am—I go to parties. I drink too much. I embarrass my sister and fight with my brother. I don't burn down buildings and kill people. When I think of my family now, I miss them, but I don't really care. What's happened to me?"

"The *klystrons* would be a good place to start, I suspect." She looked at him curiously. "Don't you understand what they're for? Even now? They don't just help a child manifest. They give, but they take, just like every elemental thing. Just like Light and Wind, I suspect. They gave you the riddle. I wonder what they took."

"I can't talk about that," she answered instantly.

"No, I didn't imagine you'd want to. But the *klystrons*, they don't give a gift, because what they give has a price. Now, if you're a child of Eriis, the price is an easy one to pay—you are tied to this world. They come, and our abilities and gifts, they all come from the rock and bone of Eriis. He *is* Eriis. If I had any doubt he would one day claim the Seat, you burned it away, with the help of those little bags of sand. You see? It calls to protect its own. Jaa was right, he couldn't have a finer champion. You're one of us, now. But you will kill someone, and it'll probably be me, unless you get him back to Mistra."

Maaya took a calming breath and looked at her hands. "We had no idea what we were doing." She looked up. "Maybe the *klystrons* put themselves in our path?" She shook her head. "There was a time not long ago I would have laughed in the face of someone who rattled off mystical garbage like that. 'In our path.' But look at us—he needed protecting and I had the means. I just need to make sure I'm protecting him from the right things. And that obviously does not include you."

"So, do we understand each other?" Ilaan asked.

"I promise. No more fireblasts. But what happens when I go home? Will I still be like this? At least I won't be able to set anyone on fire." She held her hands out again. "Will I?"

"I admit to being curious about that myself. As I said, you are tied to this place. If you were here longer I would teach you how to maintain yourself. You are...what are those things called? You are an unsecured artillery."

They pushed the curtain aside and walked back in together. In the middle of the room, just past the table and a foot off the floor, The Door stood open. Maaya could see her sister on the other side, and several others in the dim firelight behind her. On the table was the knife and a smear of blood, and next to it, scratched in a beautiful, flowing hand:

Please get me out of here

"You're not the only one who's been paying attention," said Rhuun.

* * *

In the end it was as simple as that, simplc as a short walk across the room. But only simple if you have the right tools and a decent map.

Maaya wanted to leave at once but they agreed to wait for Mother Jaa, who met them with Leef near her elbow as always.

"Some of us will be making a return trip," said Ilaan. They all looked at the table, where the fingernail-thin bloodstain was already drying. It wouldn't be enough. "Beast, we need—"

"No," Maaya said at once. She felt her hands start to steam. "He is not to be touched."

"It is not up to you, Warrior girl," said Jaa. "We don't have a thief to snatch a pen this day, do we, Ilaan? That pen was made of the bone of Eriis." She swiped her finger through the sticky mess on the table. "And this blood is the ink."

"But we can open The Door from the other side, Scilla already did it," said Maaya. She wasn't convinced of the necessity. "And, and, what do you mean to do with it? With the blood? You don't need it."

Mother Jaa smiled. "This one doubts my sincerity and my intentions. Tell me, what if our good queen reappears and must see to her son at once? Or what if trouble befalls the people at the Edge who helped to save their beloved prince? Shall we shout into the Veil and hope for the best?"

Maaya felt her face burn, but said nothing. It wasn't up to her, no matter what the *klystrons* whispered into her ear.

"Please," said Rhuun, who had made his own decision. "Would you all wait in the hallway? Ilaan, stay." Maaya felt his hand at the back of her neck. "It's fine. I don't mind." His cool lips brushed her ear. "Don't be afraid."

She was, though.

* * *

When they were called back in, Ilaan was putting the knife away. He looked sick. Rhuun's draped form hunched against the table, and Jaa put a gentle hand on his head. The porcelain cup was full of blood.

Leef broke the silence by dragging in the great sack of boots and shoes and tunics and traveling gear that had been collected for them, and gave Maaya an enormously oversized robe. Her tunic, once passed through The Door would not fit her, if Scilla's charm worked. She would carry her boots, in case it did not.

Maaya turned to Ilaan, who still could not meet her eye. But if Moth didn't hold it against his friend, neither would she. "There will be more color than you've ever seen," she warned, trying to make Mistra sound both exciting and dangerous. "You might get dizzy. Moth told me at first he couldn't figure out what to look at. So if you get confused, just ask. And it will be really cold. I don't know if it'll bother you or not, though." She looked through The Door, where Scilla was pacing impatiently. She hesitated to step through because once she was back in her human body, she didn't think it would be safe for her to return for the others. Eriis may have gotten a bit cooler, but it was still too hot for humans. She recalled how Yuenne had simply stood in the doorway and chatted with Moth, but Scilla pointed at her ears and shrugged. Perhaps if they had a full complement of Mages at their back it would have been possible, she didn't know. So she tried to prepare Ilaan, who had laughed off the idea of staying behind, saying they wouldn't last an hour without him. "I don't know how my sister and the others at the Guardhouse will react when they see you, but I promise, you're under my protection."

He raised an eyebrow, drawn in. "Your protection, well. Just don't set anything on fire. I am looking forward to seeing what all the fuss is about, over there. Hey, Beast, will you take me to see horses?"

When Rhuun's favorite subject got no reply, Ilaan and Maaya exchanged worried looks. "Moth," she said, "Can you hear us? Are you still with us?"

Mother Jaa, who had found Rhuun with no effort, sat by his side, her tiny, bent hand hovering in the air just above the table. "He is here. Aren't you, my boy?" As she held his hand, he faded into view, but instead of flesh, he was an outline, a red and gold aura shot with black. "This is how I see him. Beautiful, no?" she asked. She took a deep breath, this was costing her. "It is dark, where you are?"

There was a pause before he spoke, as if the sound had to travel a great distance. The dark drape, which was still visible, shifted and pulled. "It's not so bad. More dim than dark. I can still see you. But did the Mages do this? With my blood? I hadn't expected it to turn so cold here."

Maaya frowned at Ilaan; it was slightly less hot, that was all. Wherever he was, Rhuun was no longer in the same place as the rest of them. Jaa patted his hand and said, "Listen to me, my boy. You look for the light. Find it. Follow it, but don't lose your way. Remember us, because we will remember you. And then come home." She let go of his hand and the aura winked out.

They went one by one, Maaya holding Rhuun's hand, and Ilaan last, through The Door.

Chapter 55

Mistra

SCILLA WAS THE first to greet them, her face bright with joy through her obvious exhaustion. Olly held a clean white towel to her arm.

"You've gotten tall!" Lelet cried, pushing Olly aside to embrace her. She looked down at her sister, though not as much as she had. "Scilla, how long?"

"Just over a year. Welcome home."

"And May? And Rane and Pol? And how is Father? Is everyone well?" She realized with relief the indifference she'd felt over those back on Mistra had evaporated. Her desire to protect Moth, she held that in her heart, side by side with everyone else she loved.

"May and Stelle were here in the summer," said Scilla. "But they'll know you're home. I wrote them a note; I did it as soon as I got Moth's message yesterday. Rane, Pol and Father are still up at the farms. Rane's giving Father white hair. They, ah, they don't know what you've been doing. Or where. They think you're staying with Althee's family in the South."

Brother Blue's study was much the same as when she'd left (A year ago? And more?), with piles of books and pens and plates and cups scattered across the huge, dark oak desk. But she hadn't noticed the aching cold, the damp, the smell of mold until now. She moved closer to the fire and looked through the leather bag she'd left behind, still sitting on the floor shoved against the wall behind the firedogs. Her thick stockings and sturdy leather shoes, she put those on right away, and using the robe as a sort of tent, she put on her own dark blue dress and undergarments as well. The knife. The leather belt. And the stub of a candle, and even the stupid hat. It was all waiting for her. She set it aside. "But what happened to your arm?" Scilla held it out. Scratches, the kind an enthusiastic kitten might leave, in the same elegant hand that had written on the table:

Please get me out of here

Along with evidence of past communication, long healed into barely visible white lines. Lelet saw: Door, and Prince, and Help, along with the faint shadows of LIES DON'T GO.

Scilla took the towel from Olly and blotted the marks. "It's nothing, but you know with this, less is more. *Now* would have done it. Which one are you?" she asked Ilaan. "Where's Moth? There were supposed to be three of you. Do we need to go back and get him?"

"I'm Ilaan, Scilla. I've heard a great deal about you." She held out her hand. Ilaan looked down at it for a second and then laughed and said to Lelet, "She does it too! Light and Wind, Maaya—I mean Lelet—but you're tall."

Lelet shrugged. "Told you." She ran her hands through her white hair, now showing a great deal of darker roots. "Where is he? Moth?"

"I'm here." Even the heavy drape, which he'd brought with him, was now invisible. He laid his hand on her shoulder and she flinched. He hadn't felt so cold, back on Eriis. He withdrew his hand and she thought, *Watch yourself. It's just cold. It's still him.*

"Well, put your skin back on," said Scilla. "No need to hide, here."

"He can't," said Ilaan. "He's not hiding. That's why we called you. You're good at riddles, right?"

"I'm good at everything," she replied. "Lel, what's going on?"

Olly had already started pulling chairs closer to the fireplace, and passing out cups of spiked cider. Lelet, who was keeping a close watch on Ilaan, noted the genuine smile of appreciation he turned to Olly on tasting the warm drink. To her surprise, Olly colored and looked at the floor. Ilaan was charming, she thought, but he wasn't *that* charming.

"One more chair, please," said Lelet. "Olly, never mind. I'll get it."

"Sorry, I forgot he was here."

They watched the chair move closer to the warmth and could see the cushions shift and move. Olly held a cup of cider out, and it slowly floated through the air as Moth took it. "I'm sorry," Olly repeated more slowly and loudly, "I forgot you were here. With the being invisible. Sorry."

"He can hear you," said Lelet, "Can't you?"

A pause. "I can." They waited for him to say more.

Lelet cleared her throat. "Um, okay, so, this is Ilaan, our good friend," she said, "and this is Olly, who is—are you still Brother Blue's assistant?"

"More Scilla's, now. Brother has had some setbacks, health wise. Hasn't taught a class in some weeks, now." Olly was snatching glances at Ilaan when he thought no one was watching. *What is that all about?* Lelet wondered.

"But he's here?" said Moth. The cup moved forward and the chair slid in a bit. "I can meet him?"

"I think we should get your...situation resolved before you meet him," said Ilaan. "Does everyone know...?"

"Know what?" asked Scilla. "That he's Moth's father?"

"Scilla!" hissed Lelet, "What's wrong with you? That's absurd!" No one spoke. "Seriously? Who knew about this?" Ilaan held up his hand, and then Scilla and Olly followed. Lelet sighed and rolled her eyes. "Of course."

"It wasn't hard to figure out," said Scilla. "He talks to Hellne all the time and asks about the boy, and we know Hellne is his mother. Someone should tell Moth, though." She frowned. "Oh. Does he...did you know?"

"Yes, Scilla," he said. "I knew. Never mind." He leaned back. "I've waited this long. Wait until he is well." The chair moved closer to the hearth. "Was it always so cold, here? I don't recall..."

Scilla and Olly were having a quiet conversation, their heads together. Scilla said to Ilaan, "There's something you should see. Olly, please take him up, if you don't mind." Lelet began to speak, but Scilla smiled. "No one will bother them. Ilaan, take one of the capes hanging by the door. The ones on a lower hook should be just about right for you."

Once they had gone, Scilla said, "Lel, I need to tell Moth something."

Lelet looked surprised, and said, "You don't need my permission, he's right here."

"Something private. Go stand in the corner."

Lelet laughed. "Nice to see you haven't changed much." But did as she asked and pointedly looked away as Scilla knelt next to Moth's chair. She looked out the round window at the world—her world. When she'd left Mistra, the leaves had been changing. Now it appeared to be deep winter. There wasn't snow, but the branches were bare. When she touched the glass, she could feel the cold in the bones of her hand. She stared at her fingers, all nine of them, they looked huge and clumsy. She had a memory of fire, and it felt like a memory of a dream. She smoothed her dress over her thighs, and thought her legs had never felt so outsized. She didn't want to think about her giant feet. Her skin twitched and shivered, overloading on sensations which came rushing back as she settled into her sensitive human skin.

"Thank you, Scilla," she heard Moth say. "But there's really no need, now. And you can. You will, I think."

"You can come back, now." Scilla sat back down at Blue's desk. She looked right at home despite its grand dimension. She took her little red and gilt notebook, now quite battered and nearly filled up, out of the desk and opened to the first page. As Lelet peered over her shoulder, she leaned over the book and wrote:

1. Turn my sister into a demon.
2. Tell Moth I am sorry.
3. Turn the demon back into my sister.

She closed the book and tucked it back into the desk drawer. "Now, what's this about a riddle?"

* * *

Ilaan followed Olly down long, dimly lit corridors, and as he trailed his hand along damp stone he wondered if the whole of Mistra was cold and wet. There was a lot of wood, though, which warmed things up a bit. The torches which lit their way gave off an acrid stink that reminded him of home. And the drink was nice, nicer than *sarave*. Not that he'd turn down a glass of that, right now. The humans that passed them, a parade of giants, looked at him without even pretending not to stare, but they were merely curious. He wondered if a human walking down the street in the Old City would be left to their own errands.

The boy, Olly (another giant, though not as big as Rhuun, and with bizarre sand colored hair) led him up flights of steps and past a series of doors (real wooden doors, not even ashboard) that stood open. They appeared to be classrooms, but most of them were empty. Some had been cleared of chairs, others looked to be storerooms. They all had windows, and he was desperate to look out at this new place. But Olly had stopped at the door to a room that was occupied. Ilaan thought he must be dreaming or wandering in his wits, because the voice he heard sounded awfully familiar.

"Now this, this is all wrong." He peeked around the corner and was glad he had the doorframe to lean on. It was Aelle, lounging in a huge chair at the head of a class full of wide-eyed human children. She was wrapped in a red fur coat that was bigger than she was, and had her bare feet propped on a small charcoal brazier. She held a large book on her lap. "Obviously we don't all look alike. You humans, on the other hand, how you can tell each other apart is a mystery to me."

A novice's hand crept up. "But don't you all have red eyes? And black hair?"

She gave the boy a look that clearly made him wish he'd stayed in his cot that morning, or perhaps under it. "Is there more than one shade of red? Hmm? I thought so, even here on this...ice cube." She turned the book so the students could see the page. It was a full page plate on expensive glossy paper, an extremely detailed pen and ink drawing of a monster with bulging, blazing eyes, claws like a wild beast, a lolling obscenity of a tongue, sexless, unclothed, and on fire. The creature was wreathed in flame, it took up the whole page. He strained to see the caption. It read:

The Demon of Eriis in its Natural Habitat

"I mean, honestly. Do I appear anything like this...whatever it is? To any of you?" she demanded.

"Oh, I've seen you before breakfast, Aelle. I think that's a pretty fair likeness."

She looked up and screamed and leapt to her feet, tossing the old book aside. The boy who'd questioned her caught it before it hit the ground. The class knew their rather volatile teacher had a habit of throwing things.

"Ilaan, Light and Wind! Finally! I thought I was going to be stuck here forever." She turned to her class. "This is my brother. He's very clever, even if he is extremely rude. Enough for today." As the children filed out, doing their best not to stare she called to them, "Read the next chapter, and tomorrow we'll go over why it's all incorrect." When they had all gone, she said, "You've come to bring me home? It's all over and everyone is safe?" Ilaan shook his head. "If you're not here to rescue me, why have you come? Who else is here? Has something gone wrong?"

"Maaya is here, she led us. But we must call her Lelet, now." Aelle gave a short laugh. Ilaan shrugged. "I know, but it's her name. She'd be offended otherwise." He paused. "And Rhuun."

"It worked, then? Our plan?" She kept her face still. "He's well?"

Ilaan sighed. "It goes poorly with him. You should see him, though." He shook his head again. "Poor choice of words."

"What are you talking about? What do you mean, poorly? Where is he?" she asked.

Olly had hung back to let the siblings talk, but now he offered her his arm. "Miss Aelle? Your friends are in Blue's study. I'll have some chocolate warmed and brought up for you."

"Thank you, Ahlee." She gathered the soft fur around her throat and ran across the cold stone floor to slide into her heavy tan suede slippers

Aelle sailed through the school as if she were its queen. Ilaan smiled to himself. She'd won over these people in a way she hadn't ever done back home. He was glad she appeared to have made a place for herself and even found some pleasure in this cold world, because when she saw how it went with Rhuun, he feared her happiness would turn to ash.

* * *

Aelle followed Ilaan and Olly into Blue's study with a deep breath and her most careful smile. A tall, ugly human woman with black and white hair sat near the fire—in Aelle's own seat—and wrung her hands most strangely in the air. That would be the miraculous Lelet, she supposed. The girl, Scilla, sat at Blue's desk with her feet tucked under her, as she so often did these days. Olly moved to build up the fire.

"Well? Where is he?" She stood in the center of the room and looked from face to face. Both human women looked worried. And was Rhuun playing some game, being invisible? Surely he didn't think he could hide from her. The white-haired girl held out her hands in a pushing motion, and a moment later, she knew where Rhuun was. She could hear his breathing. Cold radiated off his body.

"That was you, wasn't it?" he asked her. His voice was so quiet, as if far away. "As Daala. It was you. But why did you help me?"

"Well," she replied, "someone had to get you out of that awful place, and I was the only one who could do it. As usual." He laughed, very softly, and then she felt his arms around her. "You smell like an attic," she said, and then burst into tears.

She felt the touch of the old, dusty fabric on her face, his hand. "Are you angry with me?" he asked, close to her ear.

"No, I'm too cold to be angry. It's so good to see you. Ah, sorry. I mean—" she struggled to find the words. "I'm glad you're here. I mean, I'm glad we're here. I...don't know what I mean."

"I know."

It felt rude to speak through him, so she stepped to his side and said, "Maaya, who is now Lelet. I see we all survived. So why did you wait so long to come, and why are we all here? And Rhuun," she turned to him, or where she thought he was, "what is the meaning of this?"

Lelet and Ilaan looked at each other, and Ilaan gave a little shrug. "There's much to tell. How long have you been here?"

"Longer than I intended, which was not at all!" she replied. She noticed Ilaan eyeing her fur. "It's called fix. Do you want one?"

Olly handed her a cup of hot chocolate and whispered in her ear. "It's called fox. I have several." Apparently, when Fifths from the city came to study, they were often relieved of possessions that might cause envy in their less well-to-do brothers and sisters. The fur coat had been in storage for many years until Olly dug it out for her.

"I've been here long enough to have my own room, my own clothes, and my own classroom. My room looks out over the ocean. Ilaan, you must see the ocean. It's delightful. It goes on simply forever."

"Wait," said Lelet. "Did you say your own classroom?"

"Someone had to inform these humans about us. They don't know a single thing! And their manners, atrocious. All along I thought it might be Rhuun, to teach them, but I suppose until he arrives..." she looked puzzled. "But. He's..." she looked around. "Wasn't he just here?"

He had returned to sit close to Lelet's side. "I'm here," he said. "I also thought it would be me."

Ilaan and Lelet told her the story of the trip to the tents, and how Yuenne had made his move. "It is well enough you've been here instead of there," said Ilaan, "because if he spoke to Daala he probably knows what you were up to."

"You and I," said Aelle, "we will have to have a nice long talk with Father, don't you think?"

"After our friends are proved safe, we'll see about him," replied Ilaan.

"And Niico?" Aelle said.

Ilaan looked at the floor. "He's fine."

She gave him a curious smile. "He is? He's out of father's reach? He's safe and gladly let you leave? You know how he feels about Rhuun; I can't imagine he wouldn't have something to say." She gave a short laugh. "And when he hears that I'm here, also? Ha! I'd hate to be flying against him that night! But what did you tell him?"

Ilaan looked up at her. "He doesn't know I'm here. He thought I went with Beast as far as the tents to ensure his safety, but no further. We agreed no further. But how could I leave Rhuun to go on alone through The Door? Look what a hash he made of it the first time. You know how he is."

Lelet cleared her throat. "I believe he can still hear you, Ilaan."

"Who can? What are you talking about?" asked Aelle.

Ilaan had gone red faced. "I didn't mean it that way, Beast, I know you can make your own way. Let us say I wanted to see this place for myself. Aelle, I will make Niico understand. And I mean to go home soon and tell him in person, but we have some things to do, first."

"What is everyone talking about? What do you mean, things to do here?" Aelle frowned, it was right on the edge of her mind, what was it?

"We have to fix Moth, of course," said Scilla. Aelle whispered an apology. But if he was offended by what he'd heard, he made no mention. He was motionless and silent. He might as well not be there at all.

Scilla had written the riddle on a slate, and propped it up on the desk so they all could see it. "Does this mean anything to anyone? Because the answer is here. We just have to figure it out."

Chapter 56

Mistra

THEY SPENT THE next hour throwing ideas at each other.

"It's a place. I still think it's a school," said Ilaan. He had started to inventory the bookcases and was making a pile of things he wanted to take home with him. A wooden carving of an animal with great horns branching from its head. A brass orb for burning incense. A thing made of different colored metals that had tines which moved in a circular pattern around a sun and two moons, painted with a clever design on its face. A hand sized (a human hand, that is) wooden box inlaid in colored, melted glass with a design of horses, gold, black, and red. "If we ever get home and I see Beast again, this would be a nice gift."

Everyone nodded in agreement, and Aelle said, "Yes, I think he'd like that. It has those animal things he used to talk about all the time."

Lelet watched Ilaan and Aelle with their heads together, and understood Olly's strange reaction to Ilaan—they really did look startlingly similar. She watched Aelle examine the horse box and remembered with a start who it was for. "Sorry. Moth, is that something you might like? The horse box?"

"I might like..." He sounded like he hadn't been paying attention, either.

"You think it's a school," said Lelet, trying to focus. "We're in a school, and I still can't see him." She realized she was out of ideas, and wanted out of the room. She stood and stretched. "I need some air."

"You should go to the roof," said Aelle. "It's pretty. You can see to the edge of the world."

"Would you like to come with me?" Lelet asked. As the words were leaving her lips, she looked from Aelle to Ilaan and couldn't recall who she asked. A cold spot on her arm—a hand, his hand—reminded her.

Olly led her up the stairs, up past the empty dormitories and abandoned classrooms, with Moth's cold presence at her back. They reached a door which led to the last set of stairs, narrow and rather dark despite being just below the roof line. Thin slits cut into the exterior stone let the light in, they were too high to be windows, and the cold wind made the place uncomfortable. Olly swung open the big wooden door to the roof itself. It was slatted with iron braces but had no lock. He told Lelet he would stay inside and wait.

"You be all right out here by yourself?" he asked.

"I'm not—never mind. I'm fine." He pulled the door shut. "Stay close to me," she advised Moth, partly because she didn't want to go back inside and accidentally leave him up there.

Once outside, Lelet had a sudden rush of vertigo. The part of the roof you could walk on wasn't all that large, and it was unfenced and unwalled on three sides. Marked onto the stone walls and slab floor was evidence of generations of novices and students using this place for a bit of privacy: incantations scratched in stone, trash fires long gone cold, broken glass and bits of paper, initials and hearts and crude genitalia. The marks that humans make in their passage. She felt like she might step off the edge and float away. After months of nothing but desert and clouds and heat, the intense blue sky of winter and the swath of forest, made her dizzy. The cold made her nose sting. She went to the western edge, where there was a waist high stone retaining wall, so she could look out over the trees and see, less than a mile away, the ocean.

"A blue desert?" Moth's breath was icy on her already cold neck. "Is that what that is?"

"It's water. That's the ocean. You know what that is." She wished he'd move away from her, just a little bit.

"Oh. It's beautiful." He sounded flat and distant. "At least your people will never want for water."

"No, you can't drink it," she said. "It's not like the river, it has a bad taste. You can swim in it, though. Not right now, it's far too cold. You'd like that, I think." Either he hadn't been so cold when they'd been in the tents, or she hadn't minded it, with all the heat. No, she realized, it wasn't that at all. Just as when Ilaan had sent the beam of fire through her hand, she knew it was hot, but she didn't really feel it. She'd known he was cold, but in her demon body, it hadn't mattered. She had welcomed it, and gladly gone to his embrace. But here, in the grip of winter, and with the freezing wind coming off the ocean, it was almost unbearable. *He is afraid and in the dark; don't make this worse for him*, she thought. She forced herself to hold still as he leaned against her, forgetting for a second why there was a cold weight against her back. And in that second her body betrayed her, a shudder, pulling away. And the weight lifted; he felt it. He knew. And she knew he would never touch her again unless she did something fast.

At the moment he drew back, as she began to turn towards him, something splashed her cheek and ran across her lips. Surely not rain, not on such a perfectly clear day. Sea spray, then? No, not sea spray, not so far from the shore. Tears?

Tears.

She spun around and blindly reached out, finding him standing an arm's length away, and she pulled him to her and kissed his cold mouth. As she did, he slowly reappeared. His beard had begun to grow in since she'd last clearly seen his face, and as it had before, it gave his features a slightly rougher edge. She still thought he needed a haircut. He wiped his eyes with his sleeve and stared at her without comprehension.

She kissed him again and he said, "I'm sorry, I can't see the ocean. It's gotten too dark."

"Can you see me?"

"Yes," he said. "I can still see you." But she couldn't see him anymore. He'd vanished again.

"Then follow me and don't get lost. I love you. It's going to be fine." She took his hand and hauled him back across the roof to find Olly opening the door to the tower. "We have to go back to the study, right now," Lelet said. "Can you gather everyone?"

Scilla was already there, drinking coffee and making lists of words. Lelet paced and fretted as Olly fetched Ilaan and Aelle, who had gone to see her room.

"Tears," she said, when they had all gotten settled. "What are tears?"

"An indulgence," said Aelle. She had changed to a floor length black mink (Apparently, Olly had hacked off the bottom eight inches with a pair of scissors) and given the fox to Ilaan, who looked quite striking. She folded her arms with some difficulty through the bulk of the sleeves. "An embarrassment."

"Maybe. No." Lelet flapped her hands. "What else?"

"Pain," said Ilaan, looking at his sister. At Lelet's exasperated sigh, he added, "If you think you know something, you'd better come out with it."

"Salt," said Scilla. "Tears are water and salt." And she smiled.

"And where," asked Lelet, "might one find the air heavy with water and salt?" And she watched with relief as it dawned on all of them, all except Ilaan, who after all before that very hour had never seen or even heard of the ocean.

Chapter 57

Mistra

"BUT THE OCEAN isn't bitter," said Olly. "It's salty." He passed Aelle another cup of her chocolate and went to poke at the fire.

"I think it's a liberal interpretation of the text," said Ilaan. "But may we assume Light and Wind know as little about this ocean thing of yours as I do? Maybe they just know it tastes bad."

"I've heard it described as bitter. Anyway," said Lelet, "the rest of it fits. Aelle, you said it yourself— the ocean goes on forever. Right up to the sky. And unease means the same thing, almost, as restless, and the tides never stop moving."

"It makes me uneasy, that one's dead on," Olly said over his shoulder.

"What does?" asked Scilla. "Heights? The ocean? Spiders?"

"I think Ahlee is wise to be cautious," said Aelle, coming to his rescue. "The ocean is too big to trust. Unease, yes, that's it exactly."

Ilaan settled back to watch the performance between Scilla and Aelle play out. Scilla glared at Aelle, who ignored her as was proper, smiled politely, and sipped her drink.

The air next to Aelle's head said, "Do you mind if I try— " Aelle shrieked and the cup spun out of her hand. She'd forgotten, as he himself had, that Moth was sitting next to her.

"Sorry, I'm sorry!" Olly and Lelet hurried to mop up the mess and picked up the china fragments. Aelle turned to the empty chair. "What did you want?"

"Nothing," Moth said. "Sorry I startled you." She'd already looked away.

"And we already have the next part," Lelet said, sitting back down. "Tears in the air must mean the salt spray. If you go to the beach, the air tastes salty."

"Not bitter," said Olly.

"Moving on," Lelet continued. "What about this last bit? Shadows?"

Scilla hopped down from her seat at the desk and went to look out the window. "Shadows may fall. Where do they fall?"

"Well, in this case they'll be falling on the sand thing next to the ocean, isn't that the idea?" Ilaan realized he was rather enjoying this. It was nice to see his sister so engaged again, after all the sadness she'd endured. And the humans were entertaining, with their little flirtations and interactions. Ugly, of course. They reminded him of Beast, in a way. He wondered how his old friend was doing. Who was sitting right there. *"Rushta,"* he muttered.

"You mean the beach, I think," said Scilla. "So shadows fall on the beach. When?" She finished her thought. "Sundown. And it had to be here, you had to bring Moth here because on Eriis there is no sundown."

Ilaan nodded. "And there's no ocean, for that matter. We have plenty of sand, but no ocean. So his shadows will fall away when the sun sets—" Scilla joined him in finishing the sentence, "—in the ocean."

Lelet rose to her feet. "Moth, get ready to leave, sweetheart. We're going swimming." To Olly she asked, "What time is it? How long do we have?"

"If you leave now, you'll make it with a few minutes to spare," he replied.

"Little late in the day for a swim, Lel, isn't it?" asked Scilla.

"Cold, too, I'm thinking," agreed Olly. "But if you're set on sticking your feet in, there's a clear path through the trees right to the beach; we use it often during the warm weather. I'll take you down to the head of the trail. Getting close to sunset, though. You should leave now."

* * *

"Well," said Ilaan to his sister as soon as they were alone, "care to tell me what's going on with you and that yellow-haired human?"

She smiled and shrugged. "I appear to have a type." He rolled his eyes. "Oh, don't tell me you're upset. You need me as your best ally if you don't want Niico to incinerate you. So be nice."

"Fine, Madam. Join with impunity." He looked at the piece of paper in his hand. He'd written, 'Rhuun is right here, you just can't see him.' "We have deeper problems than who is *scorping* whom. What if this doesn't work?" He passed her another card with the same note on it.

"Could have used this a bit sooner," she said. "If it doesn't work we won't need these, because I don't think he'll be coming back. So we'll go home and deal with Father ourselves. Father won't expect open rebellion from his children, so we'll have the advantage of surprise. But I think she'll save him, and we still won't need these. I think our human friend would drag Rhuun back from the Crosswinds if she had to. I mean, Light and Wind didn't care to consult with me. Or you."

Ilaan shook his head. "This place has uncorked your mouth, sister. Father would either combust or promote you to best prospect if he heard you now."

"Late for that. The question is, if we move against Father, we may have enough power among us to remove him from the High Seat. But, then what?"

"It's easy enough to say that we make him pay." Ilaan had thought long and hard about taking revenge against Yuenne, but placing himself at the scene, he was unable to say how he would fall. "And what about the Seat? Would you take it?"

Aelle sighed. "Who would follow me? The devoted daughter of the one just thrown down? If it comes to it, you are the oldest friend of the fallen prince, everyone from the arch to the Quarter knows Father broke you from the family. But I think we ought to wait until morning at least to continue plans." He could hear heavy feet—human feet—outside the study door, and Olly and Scilla came back in and warmed themselves at once in front of the fire.

"Bitter out there," said Olly. "Not sure why your sister wanted to go for a walk....oh." He read the notecard Ilaan handed him. "Good idea."

Scilla squinted at her card and said, "I should have thought of this." She folded the card and put it in the pocket of her dress and went to the round window. "It's sunset. It's already dark. If it worked, it worked by now."

Ilaan looked over her shoulder. "There's still light on the tops of the trees." Then, seeing Scilla's agitation, he added, "Your sister is a warrior. And Beast would rather do anything than disappoint her. He'll come back in one piece, ugly as ever, just to make her smile." That made Scilla smile, and the mood in the room eased.

"What we ought to do," said Olly, "is light their way. The forest, I mean. It'll be full on dark, and clouds moving in. And what if they're delayed?"

"It's better than sitting here and waiting," agreed Aelle. "Ilaan, you and I can light some fires, can't we?" Olly led them through the school, past groups of three or four or five students. Ilaan noticed that they were seeing the same faces, over and over, and he felt proud of his ability to tell these odd looking creatures apart, and apprehensive that such a big place should be so sparsely attended. *We have brought as much change to this place as they brought to us,* he thought. *It's just taking longer. This little visit of ours, it won't end when we leave.* He laughed to himself, although it was hardly funny. *We did this, Beast and I, we changed everything. All thanks to that stupid book. He wanted to see horses, and look at where it's led us.*

They gathered at the great front door of the Guardhouse, a slab of oak and iron much taller than even Rhuun, but balanced so that a human as small as Scilla could swing it shut with one hand. They started with the lanterns on either side of the entrance.

"These are gas, so they'll burn until we turn them off," Olly said. They were big enough to serve as birdcages and cast a creamy, warm light. "But I think we can do better." He led them to a shed two dozen paces from the entrance and set into a neat hedge border. "These are torches," he said, passing them back over his shoulder. He showed them how to set them (sticky, black end up) into the cast iron holders already in place in a row around the drive. But then he collected them back because neither the two demons nor Scilla were tall enough to fit them into the braces. "We burn them on holidays and when we hold events out here on the green." The torches formed a ring around what during the warm months must be green, but was now a large, circular brown lawn. A road came out of the darkness and ran around the green, then back into the forest. Aelle and Ilaan went from one torch to the next, and Olly and Scilla watched as the fire leapt from their hands to the tar. When they were done, the front lawn was lit up like it was time for the Quarter Moons party. "The ocean is back the other way, on the other side of the Guardhouse, but the path leads around front, and it should be bright enough for them to find their way back."

"What do we do now?" asked Scilla, staring at the smoky torchlight.

"We wait," said Olly. "Perhaps inside?" Aelle smiled at him gratefully.

Chapter 58

Mistra

"I WISH YOU'D say something." Lelet whipped her head around, hoping to catch a glimpse of Moth. Nothing. The dark drape he'd brought with him through The Door had, like the rest of his clothing, become as invisible as he was. But she felt an icy feather-light brush against her cheek and knew he was beside her.

"It's hard," he said, "because it's so dark."

It was late afternoon, the blue sky of midday deepening to cobalt, with a few clouds on the western horizon starting to blaze with the gold and melon colors of sunset. Sunset, when the shadows fell.

"We're nearly there," she said, hoping she sounded reassuring. She wound her way between frost-blanched sea grape trees and bare-branched beach roses, their crimson hips giving the landscape its only color. As the ground turned from gravel to sand the path between the dunes started to slope upward. Just beyond the crest of the dunes, the sea boomed and called. "Do you hear that? That's where we're going." She stood at the top of the rise and inhaled deeply. "Olly had a point. It doesn't smell like bitterness to me, but I still wouldn't drink it." The surf churned, unsettled. "Are you ready?" She got no reply.

She led Moth down the weathered wooden stair set between a pair of bent over pine trees, onto the beach itself. The wind off the water made her eyes tear and it was cold, much colder than the other, sheltered side of the line of dunes. In the summer season, even this late in the day there would be people everywhere, swimming and sunning and setting out picnics. Today, with the afternoon fading fast, they had the beach to themselves. She looked behind and saw his footprints appearing in the damp sand, that much of him was left to see. The sun was nearly at the edge of the dune line, and the little ripples in the sand at the shore, the chunks of rock and driftwood buried half in the surf, the bits and trails of seaweed, were all thrown into sharp relief. Shadows were falling.

"It's time," she said. She held out her hand and moved it until it landed on his arm. He was very still. "You need to go in."

There was a long silence. "I would. I want to. But it's so dark," he said again.

"Can you see me?" she asked.

There was another long pause, as if he was trying to decide. "Yes," he said finally. He sounded far away, but maybe it was just the wind.

"Then follow me." Lelet hung her cloak on a barren pine branch, took off her dress and hung it on another, and tucked her shoes and stockings where the high tide wouldn't reach. The wind, heavy with salt spray, puckered her skin with gooseflesh instantly. She clamped her jaws shut to keep her teeth from knocking together. "They promised. Light and Wind promised. So it'll be fine." And before she could change her mind, she turned and walked across the beach and into the sea.

At first the water was too cold to even feel it, and it churned against her ankles as she quickly sank into the soft sand. She struggled forward, giving little screams through chattering teeth as it slapped her thighs. She couldn't feel her feet and knew she couldn't stay in the water much longer. "You have to follow me, Moth, we're running out of light." She couldn't hear her own voice, the wind tore it out of her mouth.

But he had followed her, and she could see him now, wading past her and moving fast. The waves created a living statue, he appeared made of glass. He bent and dipped his head and flung his hair back and the last sun caught it; a warm spot, a shower of sparks. He paused to look in her direction and then turned back towards the horizon. Something was under the water, shining like a submerged star, bright and deep, and he was moving towards it, swimming towards it, and when had he learned to swim? He dove for it, was pulled down towards it, and then the bright place was gone and so was he.

The suck and heave of the tide pulled at her and a wave hit her in the face and she choked and lost her footing. How had it gotten so deep? She thrashed against the waves, it was as dark in the water as above and she was disoriented, which way was up? She got her head out of the churning water and screamed, knowing there was no one to hear her.

"Send him back, you promised." She slapped at the waves, the water was in her nose and she coughed, but it was calming fast. In a moment, she was simply standing in hip deep water, gently but restlessly moving in and out with the tide. How long could he stay underwater? And how long before she froze? Her fingernails were blue, although it might have only been the increasing shadows.

"You promised," she repeated. Her teeth had stopped chattering, and she had a dim memory of that being a very bad sign. She spat a mouthful of gritty saltwater and pushed her wet hair out of her face. There was nothing to see except slivers of light on the edges of the waves. "Please," she whispered, "you promised." But the water was stirring again, something was moving fast towards the surface, and again she was knocked off her feet by the now violent waves. The sun had sunk behind the dunes, it was almost dark and hard to see, hard to keep her head up, but she saw something perhaps twenty yards away explode up out of the boiling ocean. Something big. Not a bird. It created a shock wave that sent her tumbling in the dark surf. As she struggled, something grabbed her by the wrists and pulled her up—the air was colder than the water—and skimmed her along the tops of the waves, dropping her on the sand.

She was shaking with the cold again, she couldn't speak for her teeth clattering, so she couldn't say anything when she looked up and saw Moth, his hands on his thighs as he bent to catch his breath. She couldn't say anything, but only stare in wonder at the wings that rose from his back. Unlike the delicate leathery bat wings Maaya had sported, like every other demon on Eriis, his wings were made of feathers, the longest as long as her arm, and each one as black as a drop of fresh ink. They slanted sharply out and down and brushed the sand behind his feet. He looked down at her, realizing she was there, and fell to his knees in the sand, opening his arms for her. She threw herself against him and he was warm, he was hot.

"You came back," she said, when she could speak.

He held her as her shivering slowed. "I will never leave you."

* * *

He reached past her and yanked the drape off the branch where he'd hung it and wrapped her inside, and then found some rocks that would serve for a quick lighting. When he was done he found her calmed and watching him. Her not being Maaya, not having the slanting red eyes of everyone he knew, it gave him a start. He realized what she was staring at and gave a sort of shrug and the wings folded themselves away.

"Are you really all the way back?" she asked. "Are you entirely yourself?"

He realized she was a little afraid. "You said to me, 'we won't be apart, but just in different places.' I remember, you said that before we did your awful plan. You were right, we've been apart and then together but always in different places. And now we are in the same place, finally." He knelt on the cold sand next to her. "There is no part of my life that is not in your debt."

She said, "In love there is no debt," and put her arms around his neck. He placed his own hands over hers.

"*Rushta*, Lelet, what happened to your *hand*?"

She laughed. “Got in a fight with a door. It happened ages ago, its fine.”

He flushed. “Ages ago? And I just noticed. And you did this for me, no doubt.”

She shrugged. “It was part of my awful plan. I still can't believe I got you to go along with it.” She looked out at the dark sea. “This one wasn't much better. Walk into the ocean and hope for the best.”

“And you nearly drowned. For me.”

“It's not a contest, sweetheart. But maybe we can ease off saving each other's lives for a while? And I need to get dressed, I'm freezing.”

He pulled the drape off her shoulders. “I can make you warmer than your dress, I'm pretty sure.” He rubbed her hands, taking particular care with the damaged left one, and kissed her, licking the salt off her lips. “I am entirely myself,” he said, “and so are you.” He bent to make sure her body was warm, and it took some time, but he was quite thorough. A few of the larger rocks blazed up spectacularly—one of them cracked in half—but nothing else caught fire.

Afterwards, she laughed with exhausted relief and slid her hands along the new raised ridge of muscle on either side of his spine. “You prefer me this way? White hair, no wings? Big feet?”

“I would love you if you were demon, human, cat, horse—but yes, I like you this way very much.” He cupped her foot and rubbed the sole hard with his thumb, making her sigh with pleasure. He didn't think they were particularly large, her feet.

“I do, too,” she said. “Prefer my human self, I mean. It's different. It's hard to explain. I feel things more easily. I feel you more easily.” She paused. “If we stayed there on Eriis, if I remained as Maaya and we were together, I think I would have asked you to do things you wouldn't want to do. To me. Do you understand?”

He only had to think of Aelle's wrist. “I do. I could tell it wasn't the same for you. I'm sorry.”

She laughed again. “I didn't go to Eriis for a sex vacation, don't apologize. And you were hardly in the best state. But,” she stretched and kissed him again, "now you seem to be back to normal."

"Normal? That was a lot of noise for 'normal'." He knew she'd ask about it soon, the light and his wings and the water, and was happy for this brief respite with nothing to explain or recount. He thought when she pushed him away, when they'd stood on the roof, it was over. His path had led him from *La Naa* to something less painful but just as final, and that was fine. He'd been ready to let go, at that moment. But when she'd turned and kissed him even though she didn't want to, he was reminded of what he'd been missing. Her pleasure, and her heat.

She poked his shoulder. "Like you were silent. You have to teach me some of what you were saying. Aya Naya or whatever it was."

"Ah," he smiled, "I said that? I suppose I did. *Aea Nea A.* It's old, a very old expression that gives thanks to being returned to one's beloved garden."

"A garden! That's sweet."

"It is implied that the speaker has been separated from the garden for some time, and is most grateful to find it again in fruit and flower. It is a thing that a man might say."

"I don't think I've ever heard you say it before."

"I don't believe I've ever been so grateful before," he told her.

"All that, in one little phrase?"

"High Eriisai is a dense language. That's why we don't speak it much anymore."

She curled against him. They watched the twin moons rise and ripple on the calm sea. "Should we talk about this? What just happened, what happened in the water, Moth, your wings..."

"I didn't think this could be real. The ocean. The way you described it, it's too much."

"What did you see down there?" she asked. "What was that light?"

He tried to find the words; a light drawing him in and away from the dark and cold place that closed around him. He could hear Lelet calling him, but she felt far behind. He had to find the light, it was calling him too, and it was down, under all that water, far more water than he'd ever seen, much more than even his river. Could he drown? He'd be the first in his family to do that. He found his breath unimportant, just as the crushing weight of the water and the bitter chill of it were unimportant. He had to reach the light. He was unable to describe the face of the woman he saw there, but it was a kind face, if an alien one. He settled on the sandy ocean floor beneath her, feeling like a child in her presence, and came as close as he could to her, the only source of light in this dark deep place.

"Welcome, Prince," she said. "I've been expecting you."

"I want to stay here," he said. "It's too dark back there. May I stay?" The thought of leaving the light was unimaginable.

Her image shivered and spun, reformed and unformed. "Stay with me, oh yes, stay. Oh, that would please me, yes. But you are so quick to ask. Might you not miss the world above? I would suggest you do not ask me again unless you mean it, though, as I am in a mood to give a gift. So tell me, is that your true wish? To stay here with me?"

The world above, that was important, wasn't it? There was light here, but it was a cold kind of radiance. The world above was warm. He remembered that. He shook his head, remembering warmth, and why he had come. "No, Madam. I spoke too quickly. Forgive my change of heart. I do wish to return to the world above, but that is not the wish I would have you grant."

"Well you want something, all your kind do, always filled with desire. What is your desire?"

Her eyes were the bluest things he'd ever seen, and for a moment his only desire was to stay and look into them forever. Then he realized he could feel something, and it was cold. "I wish to have this shadow lifted. I don't want to be invisible anymore."

"You want your people to look at you? To see you as you are?" She sounded amused. "The desire of your heart has shifted rather completely. The shadow was cast on you at your own request."

"It may have been my request, but it was unexpressed by me. Unspoken."

"Is that so?" she smiled, somehow, with her lipless mouth.

He could hear his own voice, then, "Stop looking at me, I don't care for the way you're all looking at me," and the angry, broken voice of a child, "If I were invisible, no one would bother me ever again."

He sighed, thinking of that child, and watched a tiny trail of bubbles rise from his nose and mouth. "Then spoken out of foolish frustration." He cocked his head, his long hair drifted in front of his eyes. "Do you change, here in the world below? Can you change?"

"Ahh, beautiful one. Are you truly asking?" She felt close, smooth and cool, and she flickered in blue and silver. "Do you ask for me, or for yourself?"

He watched her ripple and undulate, and couldn't look away. "I have never seen an ocean before. I only know deserts, and light and wind. And they never change. But I do. I have."

"The ocean changes every day, at every turn of the tide. We are constant, yet never the same." He could feel her streaming over and around him, cold comfort. He'd read that phrase in his book and never knew what it meant, until now. "Are you the same?" she asked.

"No. I'm not the same as anyone. I never understood why I was different from my brothers and sisters of Eriis. I think it's the human part of me that hungers for change, because my own people are so slow to accept it." He wondered briefly why he was admitting what he'd only realized himself to this marvelous creature, but there was something about her presence that invited confession. "It is no longer what I wish, to be unseen. I have nothing to hide. Let them look." If he could withstand the gaze of the Ocean, what were the eyes of the court, of the world to him?

She nodded and then smiled, raising her hands. They were finned and fronded with slowly drifting brown-gold weeds. "I have a gift for you," she said. "Something you'll like. Something you'll need."

"The shadow—"

"Is gone. It was given in error, but without malice. And since I've taken your shadow away, I must gift you something to take its place."

He nodded. That was the law, one for one. The woman's eyes came closer, they were huge, perfectly round and lidless. Her skin was the same endless shade as the water. He felt her chilly fingers on his throat, stroking his face, skimming the taut flesh of his stomach, toying with his sex. It was cold. He didn't move. "I wanted to give you fins and scales and keep you here for myself, beautiful one, I am tempted. Are you tempted as well? I think you are." He was. She gave a little, bubbling sigh. "But you are needed elsewhere. I shall have to console myself with your shadow." And he watched as a darkness rippled out of the darkness behind her and slid across her silvery body. He realized with a shudder it was his own size and shape. She kissed his cheek and her hands pressed against his shoulders, searing him with cold and pushing him up and away from her, towards the world above. "Enjoy your gift. Send Light and Wind my regards."

The light went out.

"...And then I realized I had to breathe and it was really cold, and I...opened them. My gift. And I saw you in the water and I grabbed your hands. That's all."

She considered this. "So it's not the ocean, it's the Ocean, and she's a friend of Light and Wind."

"So it would appear." He smiled. "She said I was..."

"What?" Lelet pinched his arm. "Tall? Darling? Good at jokes?"

"She said I was beautiful." He blushed and couldn't meet her eye. "Of course, she was a fish lady, so..."

"You got molested by a sea goddess," she snickered. "I just got water and cookies."

He looked at the moons' cold light on the waves. "Perhaps she got what she wanted."

Her smile faded. She said, "You were desired by a goddess, and you came back to me." She dropped the drape onto the sand and went into his arms. "They took your blood; they tried to take your life; they tried to make you fade away; they can't take you from me. Even the Ocean herself can't take you away from me. *Aya naya, shani.*" This time she was thorough, filling him with enough light and heat to make him forget the strange, cool caress of the Ocean.

The water churned and roared, but the tide was low and it couldn't reach them.

Chapter 59

Mistra

WINGS, I'VE GOT *wings, and I've got fire*...Rhuun watched the waves hurry in and out and the ripple of the moons as they crossed the sky. They were past peak and heading for the dune line, and low clouds were following them in from out at sea. He knew it was late and he knew there were places they needed to go, people to see and talk to and reassure, but right now it was unthinkable that he should move. He just watched the water and held Lelet and listened to her tiny snores. Here they were again, under the stars, and both of them lifelong city dwellers. It had never occurred to him to sleep outside before, and with the constant blowing dust and grit of Eriis, if you wound up making your bed on the sand it was usually because something had gone terribly wrong. But here in this gentle place, as far as he could tell there was no place that wasn't safe enough for sleep. Not that he wanted to make a habit of it, though, for her sake. He thought about what she was used to, and what she deserved, and made up his mind then and there. They would go back to the city. He wanted to see Mistra through her eyes, he wanted to see her room from the inside, sleep with her in her bed among the piles of silk pillows and blankets he'd only glimpsed through the glass. He wanted to go home with her and begin again. Of course, she didn't know that, and maybe now it wouldn't matter.

Wings...There was an upwelling of something strange in his chest, something he barely recognized. He wondered if this was how everyone else felt all the time. How could they stand to chat and argue and gossip and eat and fight when there was so much joy? He barely knew where to put it.

I can't stay here forever. Not on this beach, not in this world. A little longer. Even thinking about home and ash and desert, that didn't make the feeling evaporate. He tried it out—I'll have to go home, I'll be too big, with no power, and eyes on me, wherever I go. She may not even be with me. The new feeling flickered but he held it between his hands and kept it alive. Did normal people push it down, or did they just get used to it?

* * *

Lelet yawned and blinked and rubbed her face.

"You were asleep," he told her. "I didn't want to wake you."

She had been tucked under his arm, and reached across him for the now rather sandy drape to keep off the fine spray in the air. She wasn't cold, he of course saw to that, but she was getting damp. The tide was coming in. "We should go back," she said. "I imagine they're frantic." She squinted at the moons, trying to figure out how late it was. "And it'll be a dark walk, even with the moons."

"Walk?" He helped her to her feet and handed over her dress from the high branch.

"Well," she said, giving a little sigh as he pulled his trousers back on, "I know you've got...um...wings. And they're very nice. But don't you want to practice?" It was only too easy to imagine falling through the frigid air into the trees. She rubbed her arms.

"I think I can do it. It wasn't that far. And you're light. We should try." He held up his shirt and examined the back. "But I suppose I'll need to make some adjustments."

"Ah." She snapped her fingers and poked around on their little patch of beach until she found a stone which had cracked in half. "Save your shirt until we can get you some scissors and a proper needle and thread. Put this drapey thing on, over your shoulders, like normal." When he'd wrapped it around himself, she took the sharp edge and sawed through the old fabric where it covered his shoulder blades. "Now you have wing room, and you don't have to walk back into the Guardhouse half dressed. And you can use it to hold me up. I'll hold your shirt."

He agreed that wasn't a terrible idea. "Come here, and put your arms around my neck." He lifted her. "Now your legs." She locked her ankles around his waist and he twisted the drape to help hold her. "Now let's see what happens." She felt his body tense and then relax, and as he did, she looked over his shoulder at the beach behind them. The bright moonlight, now streaming over the dunes, showed her a man-sized shadow with wings easily twice as wide as he was tall. He flexed his shoulder and brought one forward so they could both look at it. She stroked a long, black feather and found it warm. He concentrated for a moment and then moved it so it brushed her cheek.

"But why feathers?" he asked. "My father wasn't a bird."

"Maybe someone back at the Guardhouse will know."

"Hmm, yes. I'll ask Scilla."

This surprised her. She imagined he'd want to hide these beautiful treasures away. "You're going to show them?"

He smiled. "Lelet, I'm going to show everyone." He bent his knees and leapt straight up, imitating the way they did it back home, and the huge wings bore them up and out over the water. At first he struggled to find a rhythm and she couldn't help but scream and bury her face in his neck. He was saying something.

"What?" she asked. The wind was loud in her ears, and the wings, when they swept past, made a deep whoom she could feel as well as hear.

"You're choking me," he said.

"Oh. Sorry." She loosened her grip. "We're going the wrong way," she told him. All she could see was water, and she craned her neck to look for lights in the deep. If Ocean called out to him again, would he be able to refuse? To her relief, there was nothing but black water and the silver shimmer of reflected moonlight.

"I'm practicing," he said. "It would be easier to fish you out of the water than out of the trees."

"This is not comforting news," she said, but in fact she felt as safe as if she were doll sized, carried in a giant's hand. She looked past his shoulder at the icy glitter of the stars, and the moons, now closer to sinking behind the dunes, and the clouds that seemed to be following them. She suddenly missed her own wings. What would that have been like, to fly at his side with the ocean falling away behind them? She imagined she'd have a hard time keeping up, her wings had been dainty little things, and she remembered tiring easily, even though it had been great fun. Feathers, and black ones—different and special, again. If Ilaan had something clever to say she'd make him regret it.

They were over the trees now and moving fast. She listened as the great wings whooshed past her head, she could feel their passing in the bones of her face. The way he flew reminded her of an owl or a hawk—long glides, and when he got too low, a few beats to regain height. Through the trees, she could see the lights of the Guardhouse coming up. She felt him shift her weight from one arm to the other, and pressed her lips against his ear. "Is it hard?"

"No," he replied, "but kiss me and check again."

"Ugh...that's not what I—"

"I know what you meant." He laughed. "That was a joke! See, when you said—"

She groaned again. "Please drop me."

"Oh, come on, that was a good one!" He landed with a stumble, but righted himself before he could fall on top of her. "That part, I have to practice," he said, half to himself. Setting her carefully on her feet, he said, "There. I didn't drop you into the trees even once."

They had landed in a blaze of torchlight on the winter blighted lawn at the Guardhouse's main entrance, at the head of the circular gravel driveway. Ilaan, Aelle, Scilla, and Olly stood in the doorway, identically openmouthed.

"Hello," said Moth. "It's good to see you. And it's really very nice to be seen. Look what I got!" Lelet glanced at him. He was positively beaming.

Ilaan moved first, circling him, much as Mother Jaa had so recently done. "These are nice," he said cautiously. "So I take it the ocean thing was a success?"

"Oh, very much so," Moth said, "Ocean was expecting me, can you imagine? She gave these to me." He looked at them again, at their suspicious faces. "Oh, stop. The riddle, the one from Light and Wind, sent me to their acquaintance, I guess you'd say, Ocean. And she took the shadow and gave me these wings instead. So, thank you. It worked." He swished his wings back and forth happily.

Olly said, "If you can put those....them away, you can fit through the door. It's freezing out here." He was looking towards Aelle, who stood half in the entrance and simply stared.

Lelet shivered in the night air and moved to stand inside the arc of his wings. She thought sourly that now the tables were turned and she was so cold, he didn't mind her clinging close. He didn't pull away. Heat poured off of him and she knew it was partly for her. She felt ashamed and made a promise to laugh at his next 'joke.' But he had turned and taken her hands in his and looked at her, now serious.

"I have to ask you something, and it's quite important."

He was so beautiful and looked so happy she could feel her heart twist in her chest. *No, not yet*, she thought, near panic. *I thought we'd have more time.*

"Lelet, your face!" He was smiling at her, curious. "Are you all right?"

"Yes," she whispered, dry throated. "What do you want to ask me?" She noticed Ilaan and Aelle were watching them closely.

"They have it here," he said, oblivious to the stares, the cold. "They have chocolate. Can I try some? Like, now?"

Her laughter sounded something like a sob. "Oh. Oh, yes. Oh, Moth, of course. Let's go inside, Aelle, you look positively blue."

As she followed them in, he leaned down and said, "You should have seen the look on your face. What did you think I was going to ask you?"

She shook her head and smiled, her best and blandest Eriisai smile. "I don't know what got into me. It's nothing. It was nothing at all."

* * *

They gathered in Blue's study and everyone watched as Olly presented Rhuun with the cup of hot chocolate. If he'd looked happy before, he was positively transported now.

"Better than baby lamb chops," he decided, "but not as good as pears." And held his cup out for a refill.

"What's wrong with your face?" blurted Aelle. It was the first time she'd spoken since they'd landed at the Guardhouse door.

"Hm, well it's very nice to see you, too," Rhuun replied. "This, I assume you are referring to, is called a beard." He held his chin up for everyone to admire.

"More like a couple days of stubble," muttered Olly.

"Are you going to fix it?" Aelle asked. Her brows were drawn together and she was visibly distressed.

"I like it," Lelet said. "It makes you look sort of...dangerous."

"He should keep it," said Scilla. "Makes him look less like a girl."

"One day soon," said Lelet, "you and I will have a conversation about not saying every single thing that comes into your head."

Scilla smirked. "Can I have a feather?" she asked. Everyone turned to look at her. "What? He's got something no one else has, and I want a sample. For experiments."

Rhuun cleared his throat. "I honestly don't know if I can fly without all of them, I only just got them." At her crestfallen expression, he added, "But I promise. If one falls out on its own, I will absolutely save it for you." He leaned towards her. "I was hoping we could figure out why I got feathers, when no one else has them."

She looked confused. "What do you mean? What else would they be made of?"

Ilaan stood up and setting down his heavy coat, gave a sort of shrugging shoulder roll. His own wings, delicate pink-tan membranes, unfolded. They rose slightly above his head and were about as long as his outstretched arms. "Aelle, care to join me?" She pulled her fur around her shoulders and shook her head. "Well, doesn't matter. Hers look the same as mine. The same as everyone on Eriis, in fact." He stood still and let Scilla gently touch an outstretched flange. Held up to the lamp light, one could see the thin, fingerlike bones. "Beast, I don't know that they'll let you compete in the arena with those things."

Rhuun merely laughed. "Another lifelong dream denied."

"If these were from the ocean, I mean Ocean, she would give you something she's seen," said Scilla. "She wanted to give you wings, what kinds of things that fly does she know about? When you landed, I thought they look kind of like a seagull."

Olly shifted forward. "Could be a heron, they're big. Or a petrel."

"Or an albatross," said Scilla. "Maybe a, a cormorant."

Lelet leaned closer to Rhuun and whispered, "That's what you are, my Heron Prince." He turned to ask her what a heron was, but catching her gaze, found he couldn't speak.

Scilla rolled her eyes at them. "Could be an aardvark. Or a flying pig."

Olly grinned at her. "A badger with wings."

"I find I am quite tired," said Aelle suddenly. Olly nearly knocked his chair over getting to her side. She allowed him to escort her away with a barely audible goodnight. The others followed behind, agreeing the hour was more than late. Ilaan didn't seem to be suffering from lack of sleep and he and Rhuun lingered in the cold stone hallway outside the little room he'd share with Lelet.

"We'll talk in the morning," Ilaan said. "We have a lot to figure out. We have to start making plans."

Rhuun nodded, the inevitable argument could wait for light. He'd already made his plans, and they didn't involve a return trip through The Door, at least not right away. "Plans, of course." He paused. "And I'll tell you how I got my fire while we're at it."

Ilaan raised a brow. "Fire? You? You suddenly manifested fire. Just now."

Rhuun nodded. "Recently. I was as surprised as anyone."

"You are an unfolding mystery, Beast." Ilaan folded his arms and cocked his head. "Can I see it?"

"No. No, I'm fairly certain not." He lowered his voice and explained the situation in which his fire manifested.

Ilaan laughed delightedly. "Seriously? Feather wings and *scorpfire*. I can't wait to see what you come up with next. Niico is going to love this."

"Go on to bed, Ilaan. We'll talk more in the morning. Plus, there'll be coffee and eggs."

"You don't want me to go to bed at all, you just want to show off. So, eggs, huh? That's some kind of food?"

Rhuun nodded again, looking slightly smug. "There's all kinds of food. I'll let you know which ones are good. Toast is nice, especially with butter and sugar. Oh, you should try sugar. I can't recommend ham, though. Had a bad experience. But you'll see."

"Sugar." Ilaan nodded. "Ham. Eggs. Got it."

Lelet stuck her head out the door. "Kiss him goodnight, already. This place isn't going to warm itself up."

Ilaan rolled his eyes and under his breath sang, "Someone's got a new binding spell." He turned with a wave and headed towards his own room. "Eggs," he said as he rounded the corner out of sight. "Don't set anything on fire."

Rhuun pulled the door shut behind him. "You know, I once swore I would never close a door on myself again." He opened and closed it a few more times, just to make sure he could. "This is nice," he said, looking at the low beamed ceiling (any lower and he'd have to walk hunched over) and dark oaken floor. The fireplace was tiny, and he was reminded of Scilla's little room, the one he'd fallen into.

Lelet had gotten a fire going, but it didn't do much to heat the room. He'd figured out long since that just as great stone blocks on Eriis held the heat of the day, here on Mistra those same stones gathered cold and seemed to exhale it at night. The only furniture was a writing desk with no drawers, a wooden chair he knew he'd never fit into, and a bureau, a doll sized version of his own back home, only the drawers didn't quite fit and the top was scarred by generations of pens and knives. *No wonder all these rooms are empty,* he thought. *I'd never send a child of my own to live in such mean conditions.* He seemed to recall Scilla's room being slightly more comfortable and told himself they would see to it before they left. Lelet was already in the narrow bed (his feet would certainly stick out) with the covers over her head. Still feeling uneasy in a small room with a closed door, he went to the window and pulled the curtain to the side.

"Lelet, get up."

She poked her nose out from under the blanket. "Why? What's wrong?"

He had the yellowed lace bunched in one hand and pointed out with the other. "Something's burning. Something big."

She pulled the coverlet off the bed and joined him at the glass. Looking out, she smiled.

"It must be far away," he said, "because I don't smell anything. But look at all the ash; it must be huge. Is the city on fire? Should we tell anyone? What should we do?"

She took his hand. "I promise you, nothing is burning."

"But—"

"I swear on my life. On my wings." She twisted the little iron lever and pushed the widow open. A gust of cold air carried a drift of snow inside.

Chapter 60

Mistra

EARLY THE NEXT morning, Rhuun left Lelet and Scilla to their coffee in Blue's study. It was time and past time to have a conversation, one he was not much looking forward to, but there was no reason or excuse to put it off. He thought a gift might help, so he asked the boy preparing breakfast if he might have an extra cup of chocolate. The boy handed him a hot, fragrant mug, and Rhuun nodded thanks as the boy gaped at him. He looked around the room and saw all the other novices, waiting for their eggs and doing the same. They were reduced in number, but not in their keen interest in those from the other side of The Door.

"Sorry sir," the boy stammered. "I know she—you all—it isn't polite to stare. Sorry."

"When you see a new thing, you want to know what it is. But as you see, I am nearly like yourself. No need to apologize."

The boy leaned across the ancient wooden table. "Can I ask you something?" he said in a low voice. "Are you all like you? Or are you more like her? I mean, on your side."

Rhuun laughed. "Well, we definitely all look like Aelle. And you saw Ilaan, didn't you?"

"The other one," said the boy, then looked confused. "The other, other one."

"Yes, the other one. Her brother. Yes, everyone back home looks like they do. You might imagine I stuck out a bit." He smiled at the boy. "In fact I would say I am the other, other one."

"She says you're special," said the boy. "That no one else could do what you did."

"She said that? About me?" Rhuun wondered what Aelle meant by 'special', exactly. "Do you know where I might find her?"

The boy lowered his eyes. "She's on the roof. She's up there a lot. And you should hurry, she won't like it if the chocolate gets cold." He looked back up with a shy smile. "Miss Aelle is quite particular."

* * *

When Rhuun opened the heavy door leading to the roof, he had to stop and close it again—the whiteness was blinding. He was certainly used to things being one color, but that color had never been so white, and the sun had never thrown such a blast of light back in his eyes before. In a moment he was able to try again to step back out and look around with cautious squints. He found he had no word for the beauty of the scene, or even if it was beautiful at all—it was simply too alien. The snow that had fallen overnight hadn't left more than two or three inches on the flat part of the roof, collecting into deeper drifts against the walls, but where yesterday there had been a dark green and deep brown forest, it was dusted with white. Like ash, but clean and glittering, and it left your fingers wet, not sooty. Lelet had sworn to him that it was likely to snow again, and he was determined to fly through it. For now, the sky was a soft blue and the sun was still low. He would have to come back up here every few hours to check on the changing light and colors. He noted a neat line of holes punched in the new snow leading to the roofline that faced the ocean. Aelle had cleaned a spot on the wall and sat there now, looking off to the sea. The wind teased strands of her long hair out of its coil and blew it around her head.

"I heard you might be up here. One of your students, I believe. He says you come here a lot." He handed her the mug, which she accepted with a guarded smile.

She looked pointedly behind him. "Where's the Princess Consort?"

"Aelle, please. I hoped we could talk." He stomped his feet to get the snow off the tops of his boots. They were made for sand and heat, and he could feel the icy water seeping through already.

"Because she doesn't like to let you out of her sight. Particularly now that she can see you." She smiled thinly at her own joke. He looked at his wet boots.

"She's with her sister. They have some catching up to do. As do we. May I join you?" She shrugged, tucked a wind-plucked loose strand of hair back into her neat coil and looked at him expectantly. He brushed a layer of snow off the stone wall and sat next to her. "I wanted to apologize."

"Did you?" She fiddled with the mug, licking foam off the rim. "How nice."

He sighed. He knew she didn't have a reason to make this easy, but had hoped he'd find her in a forgiving mood. He shivered. This was the coldest he'd ever been in his life—even Ocean's touch hadn't been so cold. The drape he'd worn through The Door was falling apart, and when he'd reached for it upon rising, Lelet had snatched it away and told him he was forbidden from wearing it again. "*You're the prince, you can't go walking around looking like you slept in a doorway,*" she said, and he had to admit she was correct. He needed something heavier than his faded old black silk tunic and woven leggings, though, and Olly had shown him where to find a coat or cloak. It turned out there was a whole series of rooms, a warren of coats and hats and shirts and gowns that had once belonged to novices and teachers, brothers and sisters, now long dead. This was where Aelle's collection had come from. He was pleased to notice many of the items were the correct size, and his eye had gone to a hooded cloak of some sort of plush grey fur, lined in silk. The lining, crimson on crimson, had a repeating pattern of an animal that had wings and claws and blew a stream of flame from its nostrils; the whole creature was no bigger than his palm. He marveled at the intricacy of the design, hidden away where it would be only seen by its wearer. But his hand had fallen on a coat of plain black wool. The wind went right through it. "Aren't you cold up here?" he asked.

"I find it clears the mind. And this coat helps." She eyed his coat. "You might retire your dedication to your house color and your insistence on austerity and find something warmer inside. I'll wait."

"No, I'm fine," he said, pulling the thin wool closer. "I want to apologize, as I said. About last night. I know you must have been terribly worried."

"Last night. *That's* what you want to apologize for?" A flurry of expressions went across her face.

"Well, yes. It was thoughtless of us to make you wait nearly the whole night. I'm sorry if you were worried." He sat back. She opened her mouth and then shut it, then set the cup on the wall and rose and walked back and forth in front of him until her long fur coat had dragged a path in the fresh snow.

"Worried. I suppose I should thank you for letting me know when I am supposed to be worried." She kept walking, four paces towards the door at the top of the stair, four paces towards the open edge of the roof and the forest beyond. Her cold hands were clasped behind her back.

"I didn't mean to imply—"

"Oh, no." She came to a halt in front of him, again pushing the hair out of her face. "I am grateful. You see, all those other times, I only *thought* I was worried. Like when you drank yourself blind every night because you couldn't bear to look me in the eye. Like when you vanished through the *scorping* Door without a word —nothing for months— like I never even crossed your mind! And you were supposed to love me! I thought I was worried when Father dragged you back home, and inside the Arch they called you a traitor and a criminal, and outside you were a hero who would save us all and make it rain. And that scene I walked into—you slowly bleeding to death in your own room. I imagine it was my own foolish imagination and not worth an apology at all." She waited but he said nothing. "Last night? I gathered you and the magnificent Princess Lelet were joining under the stars and would wander home in your own good time. Or hers. But thank you for the apology." Her hair blew in her face again, and she pushed it away. "*Rushta*!" She roughly yanked the pins out and pulled her hair free of the coil, and faced away from him so the wind would blow it back.

"Aelle. I did love you, I swear it. Just..."

Without turning, she said, "If you say 'like a sister', I will tear off those pretty new wings and shove them—"

"Don't be ridiculous! I'd never say that." He had been about to say exactly that. "I loved you, but not as much as you deserved. Or the right way." He had loved her, though. He loved her, he thought, like you love the last minute of light at the end of the day. Like you love the last inch of *sarave* in the bottle. Like you love the flame when it doesn't come. What you cling to, what might save you. At the time, it felt like love to him.

"But you love her," said Aelle. "And the right way. You know, your mother will have something to say about that." She sat back down next to him. "I doubt a human girl meshes with her plans for you."

"My mother. Well. I don't think she gets much of a say in anything that happens next, do you? I mean, Ilaan, did he tell you?"

"About her giving him that stupid book? Yes. We did some catching up of our own last night, while you were...occupied." She picked up the cup and sighed. "You're almost ready, aren't you?"

"I'm not sure what you mean." He took the cup out of her hands and held it and warmed it back up. She took it back and sipped, and now finding it too hot, set back down.

"You're almost ready to go back. You'll take on my father and the Zaal—and Hellne, if it comes to it, and take what you are owed." She began to repin her hair, but gave up and let it fly around her face.

"I can't leave things as they are. I'm sorry; he's your father—"

She laughed. “Might we put your mother and my father on a little boat and watch it sail away?”

“I think it’s pronounced bo-hat,” he said.

She looked at him curiously. “It most certainly is not. Who told you that?”

“You know, I don’t remember.” He tried it out. “Boat. I’ve gotten such a lot of things wrong, that’ll be just one more.”

She punched his arm. “Stop that at once.”

“What?” He rubbed the spot. She had a strong arm for such a petite woman.

“I have known you since you were a small child—well, a huge, funny looking child, and there is much in you to admire. But your predilection for self-pity is not on that list.”

He smiled. “This world has had an interesting effect on you. Isn’t it strange, you can show people on your face what’s in your heart, and you aren’t whisked off to the Crosswinds.”

“They don’t have Crosswinds here. The nearest thing, I can tell, is called ‘going home for the holidays.’ Did you know they celebrate the War of the Door here? They do some dreadful thing called singing songs. What a racket! And they don’t even know what it was. I had to explain it to them.”

“Yes, you’ll have to tell me how you became a teacher. And what that means for the future of this place. I couldn’t help but notice it’s practically deserted.” He pulled the coat closer around his shoulders and thought longingly of the warmth of Lelet and their borrowed bed. “Does it have to do with you and me coming here?”

She nodded. “Once they let me out of a locked room, apparently some of the parents pulled their children as soon as they heard there was an actual demon amongst their little flowers. Others don’t think it’s a reasonable expense to keep the Guardhouse open at all, since we represent no threat.”

“I’m not so sure we don’t.” He wondered if Ilaan had told her about the Mages plan for his blood, and where those plans now stood. “But that left enough students for you to teach. What do you tell them? Who is left?”

“Those parents are practical. They see a future in commerce, where once was theology. Those are the ones I try and teach. They mostly aren't terribly clever, but they do pay attention when I talk."

He thought about the boy who'd given him the chocolate. "I am not surprised. They're lucky to have you." He looked at the horizon, where the sea and the sky gave up being two different shades. "Did you ever think we'd be here like this? You and I? Look at the colors. You have to admit, I was right to want to come here." He gently bumped her with his shoulder. "I think you like it here."

She smiled and looked at the sky. "This place is not without its diversions."

"So, you and Olly?"

Now she grinned. He couldn't recall ever seeing so many of her perfect little teeth at once. "Please don't tell Scilla. She'll be running this place one day and I don't want her to be even more cross with him. She doesn't appreciate anyone coming between her and the object of her attention. I think that was what got Lelet in trouble in the first place. Scilla is a clever girl, but I can't recommend you go against her. Well, you know that." She paused. "She let me read her notebook. A binding spell? Really, Rhuun—that's just careless. I'm surprised you seem so comfortable in her presence."

He thought of Scilla's brown braid swinging against his cheek, her whispered apology. "She seems contrite."

"She has adopted you. She sees me as a threat, even if she's still too young to understand why. Ilaan is just as clever as she is, and nearly the same size, so he's her new brother. You're her pet."

He laughed. "I think I'm insulted."

"It could be worse. Olly is her slave, devotee, sand bearer, and Light and Wind preserve him, probably her future husband. And it's a good match, really. He may play at being a peasant, but he comes from a great deal of wealth from an old family in the city. If his people lived inside the Arch they'd sit in the Counsel Seat, telling us what to do. And," she said, looking him in the eye, "he's clever enough to say things like, 'I don't enjoy a flame, it hurts me when you do that.' Can you imagine, having that audacity? Having a preference, and stating it? Of course, the humans are always quick to say what they think. But you never, never did."

He paused, and waited for the pain in his chest, the panic, the desire to vanish. To his surprise, he found he only felt a little sad. "Did Ilaan tell you?"

"We talked about it after you left. We talked about a lot of things. Things I didn't want to believe, until I thought about them. Why did you never tell me yourself?"

"I didn't want to hurt your feelings."

She gave a short laugh. "I think it was your own feelings you were trying to spare. You just tried so hard, all the time, to act like you were normal."

"Was I now? Anything else? Please don't hold back."

She laughed again, this time more gently. "You're such an idiot. You were never anything like normal, and that made me feel special, too. If I wanted normal, believe me, I could have gotten it. *Shani*, you should have told me."

He touched the back of her hand. "Can you forgive this idiot for a lengthy list of crimes against his betters?"

"It's already done. And a good thing. You and the princess will need all the friends you can get once you're back home." He frowned and looked away. "Won't you?" He didn't reply. "What, then?"

"I don't intend to go home. Not yet. I'm...you said I was almost ready." He huddled in his mean coat. "I don't know if that's true."

She hopped off the wall and stood in front of him, so they were nearly eye to eye. "What's wrong?"

"Well, nothing. I'm fine," he said at once. He found something to look at behind her head.

"Fine? Rhuun. Even now? Look at me. I know you're not 'fine'. Tell me."

He looked up at her then, and let her see the despair in his eyes. "Do you know what my life has been, these months? I wake up and sometimes I don't know where I am." He pulled up the sleeve of his coat and she paled. His forearm was more scar than skin. "I look at my arms and I don't know who they belong to..." He swallowed hard. "I thought I was going to die."

"You were poorly used," she said softly, pulling his sleeve back down. She took his freezing hands in her own.

"That was not the worst. That was just fear. The worst was when I was afraid I *wouldn't* die. I wanted to. I longed for it; I ran towards it. And even when Lelet was there, finally I didn't care. She stood between me and death, and I wanted her to get out of the way. That was the worst. That is what they took from me. I couldn't fight them. I had nothing. I was nothing."

She lifted his chin with two fingertips. "That has never been true." She leaned forward and kissed him. He hesitated, and she put her hand on the back of his neck. He sighed and his mouth opened beneath hers. For a moment the life they might have shared, side by side on the High Seat, flickered before him. It would not have been without its pleasures, but it would never happen.

She pulled away from him and smiled. "You will be fine, *shani*. Give yourself some time."

He rubbed his eyes. "I'm sorry, we shouldn't have done that. I shouldn't have said those things."

"I disagree." She sat back on the wall and sipped her chocolate, cool enough for her now to drink. "You should perhaps have said them sooner." She peered at him. "How do you feel?"

"Fine." She threw her hands up. "No, I mean it this time. I'm fine. Better. Maybe a little tired. And like I want a drink."

"Hmm, well, that's a conversation for another day. Listen to me. Take the princess back to her city. Rest. Trust yourself, and trust her. And don't think about going back to Eriis without her. If you leave her behind, Ilaan tells me you will have abandoned your finest weapon." He stood and turned his back. "Rhuun? Don't tell me you haven't considered this."

"Of course I have. But how?" He turned again to face her, the wind off the sea making his eyes water. "She would have to be transformed again, by the *klystrons*. And she would have to leave her home again, and go to an uncertain fate. And for how long? To what end? How could I even ask her such a thing?"

Aelle shook her head. "You really are an idiot." She stood and brushed the snow off her soft fur. "Tell her you're leaving her behind, then. See what happens." She chuckled. "Just promise you'll wait and tell her when we're all there to watch. That, I want to see." He realized he had folded himself nearly in half against the cold. His shoulders hunched up to his ears, not that he could feel his ears. "Is there something wrong?" she asked with a polite smile.

He gave a sigh and straightened up. "Aelle," he announced, "I am not enjoying this. I am extremely uncomfortable and would like to go inside."

She laughed and clapped. "The humans are right about confession!"

"And," he continued, "I'm going back to the cloakroom and getting the heaviest, most ostentatious coat I can find. It may have as many as two colors."

"We have unleashed a monster," she noted.

"I may even find my mother and raise my voice."

"One thing at a time, Prince Rhuun."

He held out his arm and they walked back through the snow to the warmth of the Guardhouse.

Chapter 61

Eriis

ONLY EVER CAUGHT once...

It was good to be quick, and better to be clever. If you were one or the other you might make it through your day without a fight, but if you were both, you only got in fights you knew you'd win. And when it came the Ugly Prince, Niico knew the moons would fall into the sand before that misshapen Beast would ever fight back. So when Niico, giddy with his freshly fledged wings, first hit the Ugly Prince with a fireblast, and no one from the Palace came a-knocking on his father's door, he knew why he was made quick and clever. He would make the Ugly Prince pay. The boy was nearly his age, and bigger, taller, and probably stronger, but he acted weak and ashamed, and that made Niico sick with rage. Rage at the Ugly Prince, who wanted for nothing; and for his friend, the radiant Ilaan, a feeling just as violent, but one he could not name.

For a long time, what he did to the Ugly Prince couldn't really be called a fight, and although he never dirtied his tunic or walked away with a fresh burn, it never felt like a victory. But then came the day in the play yard when the Ugly Prince had nearly torn his wing off, had laid hands on him. It was the radiant Ilaan who put him back together. It turned out it was never hate he felt for Ilaan at all.

But he only got caught stealing once, and he swore it would never happen again.

Niico was in a foul mood.

Ilaan and Aelle had both done exactly what he knew they would do, and while he was usually delighted to be correct, here he was, right and alone. He didn't know where Aelle had run off to, but he had no doubt it had something to do with the Ugly Prince. And Ilaan. Even thinking about it made his skin steam. *"I'll go as far as the tents, and then come home to you. I can't leave him alone, he's ill, he needs me."* One way or another, for this or that reason, Rhuun once again called out, and Ilaan ran behind. Had he actually gone through The Door? If the Beast beckoned, he had no doubt of it. Well, he was looking forward to flying tonight. He'd have the skin and wings of whatever sorry fledge went up against him.

He was already in his singlet, and he could hear the crowd inside the aeronasium, he could smell the packed dirt of the floor. His hands tingled, he was ready.

"Ah, Niico. I was hoping to run into you this afternoon." Yuenne, with the scowling Zaal just behind him. They blocked his passage to the floor.

Niico swore under his breath and forced a polite smile. No doubt the Counselor wanted to ask after Aelle again. They'd been through this over dinner, during a meeting at the Councillary, in the privacy of Yuenne's office, and now again, here. "Counselor. Zaal. It's nearly time for my bout, you should take your seats."

"Oh," said Yuenne cheerfully, "I think we have a moment." The two of them crowded Niico away from the entry to the main floor, where a match was still underway, and into a dimly lit side corridor. It had collapsed entirely during the Weapon, and was still full of rubble, pushed to the sides.

"Have you heard from Aelle?" Niico asked, figuring he might as well jump to the meat of it. "I'm becoming concerned."

"Are you? Concerned?" There was a tone to Yuenne's voice, Niico did not care for it.

"Of course. There aren't that many places she could go. Perhaps she just wishes for a period of peace and quiet." He didn't think this was true, but he had to say something.

"You don't think she and her brother are enjoying a period of peace and quiet together? Someplace they ought not to be?"

The Zaal was fiddling with something hung around his neck, a great vulgar glass charm. "Let's get on with this," he said.

"Have you enjoyed your many evenings at my table?" Yuenne asked, not waiting for an answer. "And such a comfort to my daughter in this difficult time, we—Siia and myself—were pleased to make you feel at ease in our home."

"Of...of course." Niico swallowed with some difficulty. "And I am grateful. But as I've told you, Aelle did not share her plans with me, and I am as concerned as—"

"And if you wanted something from my home, did I make you feel as if I would refuse?"

"I don't follow." Niico wondered if it would be possible to fly out of the narrow space, or if he ought to shimmer, and how long before he ought to do one or the other. He could hear the crowd just around the corner and inside the arena. "I will be missed. I am to—"

"You have already been replaced," said Yuenne. "Hollen is flying his first bout tonight, in fact, it's about to begin."

"Hollen? Is flying in my place?" Niico's bad feeling continued to get worse.

Yuenne nodded. "So no need to worry. He hasn't your skill, but at least he knows who his master is. You see, Hollen benefits from his relationship with my family. He gave me something, and I did the same in turn."

"What did Hollen give you?" The crowd let out a roar, the match must be over.

Yuenne's smile showed his teeth. "He told me a story about my table. I set a fine table, don't you think?" Niico nodded slowly. "And I hope you'll agree I ask for little in return. But it appears you find my table insufficient, because when you rise from it and leave my house, you go straight to the house and the table of Ilaan."

Well, there it was. No point in denying it. "I did. I couldn't set him aside. I haven't your strength of will, sir."

The Zaal snorted a laugh. "Just tell him," he said to Yuenne. "She'll be here in a moment."

"Yes, you are lacking in will, I never doubted that. You can move a man inside the Arch, but the truth always rises, doesn't it? But it wasn't simply spying on my family. That, I might have overlooked. It is Ilaan, after all. But even spying wasn't sufficient. So tell me, have I not been a generous host? Have I not provided you a seat at my table, made you feel welcome in my home?" Yuenne no longer had the little smile. He had gone red and his cool voice was ragged with new rage. "In my home," he repeated. "You took something from my home."

That was enough. Niico made to shimmer out, and was shocked to find he couldn't. In fact, he couldn't move at all.

"You have been caught," said Yuenne. "Did you think I wouldn't know? I let you in my home, the son of a *sdhaach*, and you repay with theft and lies." He took a breath and gave himself a little shake. "You and Ilaan and that human girl, what wouldn't you do for your prince? Well, no matter. Our project continues. We have enough of him left to move forward. And we have some wonderful new tools."

"Ah, here she is." The Zaal held up his charm so that he was looking through it. It was an eye, a dark red eye, darting frantically inside a little glass globe. The Zaal could see whatever the eye was looking at. "And about time."

Rhoosa appeared at the dark end of the corridor, picking her way through the rubble. Niico gasped. "What have you done to her?"

She looked at him with her remaining eye, not appearing to recognize him at first. Her hair was dirty, but her face was clean. The missing eye was a dark blot, as if an angry child had scribbled over it. She wore a white silk robe which was also spotlessly clean. Then she focused on him. "Niico. I was hoping it would be someone else." She raised her hand as if to wipe away tears, but stopped before touching her ruined face. Two fingers were missing at the first joint. "Maybe next time it will be you," she said to Yuenne, who gave a little laugh at her foolishness.

"I am well protected by my good friend, here," he replied, indicating the Zaal. "And I think we both know where harsh words lead."

"You will pay for this," Niico gritted. It was barely possibly to speak. "When people see what you've done to her—"

"But no one will, and you certainly won't be in a position to say anything. Anyway, she's fine. She has a good occupation now, don't you?"

"I am happy to serve the Councillary," she said. The eye in the globe was fixed on Niico, as was the one in her head.

"The prince will come and kill you both," said Niico. "The prince and the human woman. They'll burn you to the ground."

"Rhoosa, be a dear and deposit this thief at the Crosswinds. Then come on home, and perhaps we'll think about cleaning up? Be a good girl now."

"Where are your children?" Niico said to Yuenne. "You have nothing." The packed dirt floor of the arena, he could smell it; all he had to do was open his wings, and he could fly away. *"Fly away," said Ilaan. "Fly to me."*

Rhoosa reached out her hand to Niico. "I'm sorry," she said, and they were both gone.

EPILOGUE

Eriis

"I'M AFRAID THIS might be nearly the end," said Hellne. Diia was too tired to respond; she just handed the cup of water she'd transformed to her mistress. Hellne drank it all without a word. Niceties and rituals had long since been left behind.

The two women rolled out the map, now nearly unreadable for stains and rips, and a great tear along the side when a storm had blown it into jagged rocks.

"We should be there," Hellne said not for the first time that day. "It says so. Why would the Zaal have bothered to send me all this way for nothing? He could have stilled me and sent me to the Crosswinds, or locked me in a charmed room if he just wanted me out of the way."

"It worked on your boy, for a while. A charmed room, I mean. Wonder if he's still there?" Diia's tongue had loosened gradually over the weeks they'd been traveling, and Hellne doubted she'd take off her hiking boots and slide back into the slippers of a servant when this was over—assuming they didn't both die in the desert. Neither were greatly skilled at transforming sand into food, although Diia was passable with water, and the provisions Mother Jaa had packed for them at the tents were nearly gone.

Jaa had not been surprised to see them the day they showed up at the tents, and though they were wrapped in the drabbest of robes and hidden by cheap veils, she recognized them at once. *If she's really blind, I'm Queen Loquacia of the Fairy people,* thought Hellne sourly.

"If you know who we are then you know why we are here," said Hellne, who felt caught a bit flat footed. She tried to hide her astonishment at what the little *dacha* in the hills had turned out to be—not a little villa or even a big one. The tents were nothing short of a small city of sand colored silk. Had Jaa done this, along with the small army of demons who came and went? Or had she found it like this, all those years ago? If Jaa knew what Hellne was after, she made no sign of it.

After Jaa and her young assistant Leef led them through the shimmering corridors that shifted and moved like live things, they entered what Hellne assumed was the old woman's chamber. It was as simple and sparse as her place in the Quarter had been. But after all, what did a blind woman need with frippery?

Jaa settled on her cushion, her porcelain cup as ever in her hands, and waited until both women had eaten and drunk their fill before addressing any questions. "Tell me about your boy," she said, "and set an old woman's mind at rest."

Hellne shifted, and sipped her water to hide her unease. "He's in a place where I can't help him. He's alive and will remain so. Plans are underway to assist him."

"Plans to assist him? Are we talking about a wheel fallen off a cart?" Hellne didn't reply. "What is more important than—"

"I would recommend you do not lecture me on my responsibilities," said Hellne. "Rhuun is not the only one in need of help. And I remind you he wouldn't take my hand to pull him out of a firewhirl. You know that. He's got his friends and that girl—well, you ask questions I think you know the answers to."

"Then you may enlighten me on this; why have you strayed from your High Seat and your home? Why have you left your son's fate to children and humans? I know you seek something, but even I can't see the end of your path."

Hellne took a sip of water to buy a moment while she made a decision. "Diia, show her the map. Let's see what she thinks it looks like." If Jaa had some special insight, she might be willing to help them on their way. If not, there was nothing lost. Diia pulled out the map and Leef placed small stones at the corners to keep it flat. "Do you know what this is?"

"A lie, more than likely. Smells like Mages. We'll have to air the place out." Jaa traced a finger along the route they'd been following. "You have hard days on dead sand ahead of you. But no, I can't see what you seek. Thanks to the Mages, I gather?"

"Thanks to one of them. It was the Mages or Yuenne, and the Zaal offered me this map. Yuenne had something more like the Crosswinds in mind."

"He'll see his life turn to sand, that one," said Jaa. At Hellne's look, she added, "You don't have to have visions to know he'll come to a bad end. I just don't know the details. Not that the Zaal is any better. I look at the path they walk and see dust. Just dust." She frowned and fingered the edge of the map. "Does this lead you to dust as well? Or something he didn't foresee either?" She sighed. "It is hidden from me. Perhaps it would be better for you to tell me. Perhaps not."

At Hellne's nod, Diia rolled the map and tucked it away. Nothing lost, and perhaps something to gain. "Can you tell me what's going on back home?" She hoped that unlike the Zaal, Jaa wouldn't make her pay for information. She had nearly nothing left to give, and did not intend to reveal what she really was after—her family. Her brother Araan and her real family. She preferred to live without Mother Jaa's reminder that her real family was currently imprisoned and in great need. As she said, he wasn't the only one.

"You gave me this place, Madam," Jaa said. "It is my duty to put it to use on your behalf. You will not be surprised to hear that Yuenne's children work against his wishes. You already know the human girl has arrived through The Door. She's an interesting one, that girl."

"Well, she won't be staying long. I'll tell Ilaan he must think of a way to get rid of her."

"Send her away and you may send the prince along with her," Jaa said. "Or he may turn his attention to the High Seat, should he live to claim it."

"He has to live," Diia blurted. Hellne gave her a sharp look. Diia lifted her chin, daring her mistress to disagree.

"In that, my friend, we are in agreement." Jaa instructed Leef to resupply the two for the rest of their journey. "The charm you use to talk to Ilaan," she said, "it uses you up. Are you finding it more difficult to transform your meals? Yes? Use it sparingly, or better yet, use it once more to direct him here. And then let that boy alone."

"Then you'll help them?"

"Someone must," Jaa sneered. "You gave me this place and so you are always welcome here. It would be best if you were to be on your way, so that you may be welcome here another time."

* * *

Hellne looked around at the dead sand, jags of rock, weathered stone, and the dust, the dust that even the finest scarves from inside the Arch couldn't keep out. If they had such things, which they didn't. By now the memory of Jaa's judgmental tongue felt like a small price to pay for cool water and a clean pillow. Their short time at the tents seemed an eternity ago, and those rations had run out, as had her hope. *Yes, this is probably nearly over*. She hated the thought of giving up almost as much as she hated the idea of Yuenne on her seat, but, as Jaa had accurately predicted, the last time she'd contacted Ilaan she'd been unable to rise off the sand for the better part of a day. *Well,* she thought, *at least the children should be safely with Jaa by now.*

Where had Diia gotten off to? She had become increasingly quiet as their food and water dwindled. Hellne had come to rely on her for transformation, and she supposed the woman was saving her strength. But now she had wandered off and was examining a cluster of rocks, not much different from every other lump of rock that joined hands and made up Eriis.

"Madam, come and look at this."

Hellne slowly rose and brushed the dust off her hands, a gesture, she knew, that would do nothing. On reaching Diia the first thing she noticed was the smell, so bitter and rank that she looked back over her shoulder to see if the Zaal had crept up behind. But of course no one was there, only dust. She knelt on the stones and with Diia's help began to move them aside.

"*Rushta*!" Hellne shook her hand, she'd nicked her finger on a sharp sliver of rock. The blood stopped almost immediately, but the rank odor grew suddenly stronger.

"The smell, Madam—something is wrong here. We should move on."

"I think not," said Hellne, who saw a shadow where only rock and sand should be. "Help me. Move these." They found the energy to lay hands upon some of the larger rocks and shimmer a few feet to one side or the other, it was far easier than lifting them. And finally, a thin shaft of darkness, the source of the bitter scent. Hellne crouched in the dirt and laid her eye as close to the opening as she could. Then she sat back up, and found the sharp rock she'd cut her hand on, and used it to slice open her palm. For the brief time the wound remained open, she held it over the chasm. Not enough. She held out the sharp stone, and after a long moment Diia added the blood of her hand to the damp stain on the rocks. When Diia was finished, Hellne took back the stone and reopened the wound on her palm. Then she added the gore-slick rock to a handful of pebbles, and made them glow. She tossed them into the darkness, and peered down after them.

It seemed to go on forever, a dim and grey tunnel which gained size as it receded out of sight. Most of the stones rattled and bounced until they were gone, but one or two landed near the entrance. It was light enough to barely see.

Something moved. A face looked up out of the gloom at her.

She gasped and put her hand to her heart. “Araan? Brother?”

Rhuun and Lelet will continue their adventures in Mistra and Eriis in THE GLASS GIRL, coming Fall 2016.

"EVEN THOUGH I'M a stash?"

He cocked his head curiously. "A what?"

She frowned and tried to make her mouth form the odd sounding combination of letters. "A suh-dash? Or sh-dash?"

His look darkened and she was afraid she'd made a mistake. "Was it *sdhaach*?" She nodded. She realized she rarely saw him angry, and this was definitely one of those times. "Where did you hear that?"

She shrugged uneasily. "I just heard it. She—they said I was a stash, all human women were, and I ought to be in a shed. What did they mean? What's a stash?"

He stood and went to the window. "I'm sorry you heard that. A *sdhaach* is...well, it has several meanings. The original meaning was sort of like a tool. Like, 'get me the *sdhaach* that levels the sand'."

"A tool. And what else?" She had a pretty good idea.

"Well, it came to mean a person who was...who made themselves available for joining. For payment."

"Oh, so a whore."

He turned to faced her. "Yes, I believe that's the word I was looking for."

She laughed. "I've been called a whore, believe me. Nearly every human girl hears it at some time or another, whether they're virgins or, uh, actually a stash. It's usually some boy's idea of the worst thing you can call a woman; as if that had anything to do with it. My wonderful brother Rane called me that before I knew what it even meant. Honestly, I don't think he did, either. I went and told May and she locked him in his room with no dinner." She paused. "What's the shed bit mean?"

He looked away. "The thing is, it is not a well-respected profession. It is an insult here as well. One does not seek out the services of a *sdhaach* for affection. It is said that because of their work, they no longer feel anything at all. They are considered something to be used, and then set aside."

"Locked in a shed with the other tools. Your language is really pretty." She sat on the edge of the bed. "So they think you're using me, and it's time to put me away." *If I was from here*, she thought, *I would know all this, and I would know the proper response, and I would defuse it and we would laugh*. "I've never even heard you use the word before."

"I was raised not to say such things." His mouth formed a hard line. "Please tell me where you heard it."

She frowned, not wanting to get the girl in trouble. She was just being honest, whoever she was. "I didn't see her face. It was in the hallway. I don't know who said it. Let it go." He didn't reply. They were quiet for a moment. She watched him frowning over some papers at his desk. "Have you ever been to one?"

He laughed, clearly surprised at her boldness. "No, of course not." He shook his head. "You have the funniest ideas." He turned back to his work. "No, I've never seen a *sdhaach*."

Acknowledgements:

Before we go any further, let me correctly thank the Roberts clan for the couch space at Lake Rosemound!

A bouquet and a pony go to Crime Dog Carly Bornstein, my editor, who understands what I'm talking about even when I clearly do not.

My fellow Fabulous Fictionistas: Daphne, Sami-Jo, Genevieve and Kenya, and especially our ringleader, my long-distance sister Cait.

My close-distance sister Antigone. (You know what it's been.)

The gang in Adams Morgan: Matthew, Michael, Mike, Tony, Kitten, Vanda.

My first alert readers: Laura Eilers, Jerry Rubinow, and future state senator, Eryc Courmac.

Far-flung family: Jaysen, Jasper, Mira, Barbara, and Dennis.

Four-legged household members: Leeloo and Onion.

And as ever my husband Dyon, who continues to believe.

48662582R00244

Made in the USA
Middletown, DE
24 September 2017